No Other Tale to Tell

Other Books by Richard Perry

Changes
Montgomery's Children

Richard Perry

NO OTHER
TALE TO
TELL

A Novel

William Morrow and Company, Inc.

New York

Grateful acknowledgment is made to the National Endowment for the Arts and to the New Jersey State Council on the Arts, whose grants supported the writing of this novel.

It is the policy of William Morrow and Company, Inc., and its imprints and affiliates, recognizing the importance of preserving what has been written, to print the books we publish on acid-free paper, and we exert our best efforts to that end.

Library of Congress Cataloging-in-Publication Data

Perry, Richard.
    No other tale to tell : a novel / by Richard Perry.
       p. cm.
    ISBN 0-688-11595-0
       1. Afro-American families—New York (State)—Kingston—Fiction.
    2. Afro-Americans—New York (State)—Kingston—Fiction.
    3. Family—New York (State)—Kingston—Fiction.   4. Kingston (N.Y.)—Fiction.
    I. Title.
    PS3566.E714N6   1994
    813'.54—dc20   93-42950
                                                                            CIP

Printed in the United States of America

First Edition

1 2 3 4 5 6 7 8 9 10

BOOK DESIGN BY DOROTHY BAKER

For my children

Malcolm David Perry and Alison Wright Perry

For, while the tale of how we suffer, and how we are delighted, and how we may triumph is never new, it always must be heard. There isn't any other tale to tell, it's the only light we've got in all this darkness.

JAMES BALDWIN, "Sonny's Blues"

No Other Tale to Tell

*   a note before the telling   *

———————————

For the longest time in Kingston, New York, schools taught the basics of hometown history: that the city was settled by the Dutch, for a while it was capital of the state, and once, during a snowstorm that paralyzed the region, George Washington had slept there. Acknowledgment that a black community existed, or that Negroes had called the city home from its beginning, didn't make its way to textbooks until 1985. Then, when it staggered into print, exhausted by two centuries of waiting, it wasn't really a story, just a recitation of dates, some names, and a brisk dismissal of a prophecy.

If you want the good stuff about Kingston, like details of the city's nineteenth-century spiritual crisis, or how much rain fell that spring when all the dead were women, you have to ask historians or black folks. Historians know because they've done the research and published it in journals no one reads but them. Blacks know because they were there to see what happened, and because they tell stories to keep their past alive. If you're blessed to listen in, you'll marvel at the ease of their remembering. You'll think remembering is central and sustaining, that blacks have always collected to do so. And you'd be right, except for those years when they didn't.

That quarter century's silence started in 1941, and it's why, since schools didn't teach them, more than a generation of Kingston's kids grew up knowing so little about their history. Before 1967, none could have repeated the prophecy's sweet promise, or said who'd hung the deaf mute from a tree. None knew who Max was or why he'd been exalted. And if they didn't know this, then of course they didn't know about Carla, and what she'd lost, and why she lived the way she did.

The kids didn't know, but the old folks were there when all the losing started. Ten years after, had you approached them under the right conditions (say on an evening whose blue fall triggered memories of disappointment), maybe they'd have broken their silence and told you just a little. "Max," they might have said. "He disappeared, didn't he? Whatever became of the Marches?"

Well, the original Marches, all except Carla and the youngest boy, are dead. Max had indeed disappeared, vanished in a burst of flame, in his wake a yard littered with roof beams and a family's destruction. What nobody at first paid much attention to is how, out of the ashes of that fire, a new family was born. In 1980, all eight members lived in a green, two-family house. One could have been a dancer. One's an idiot, another white; the man with bad feet spent serious time in prison. Not all are related by blood or marriage. Still, they're a family, one whose coming together ought to inspire something, a TV special or an epic blues. If Homer and Leadbelly were alive, they'd hook up to sing this tale, tour America in the back seat of a red 1979 Mercedes strewn with sheet music and fast-food wrappers, some lucky black boy from Ohio their chauffeur. Then people all over the country (stunned by the marriage of minor chord to couplet) would know what Kingston's Negroes quit telling in 1941.

I

Carla March turned 44 in 1966. In the first seven months of that year, three people came to her door, all in the last week of January. One was a doily salesman on his way home to Albany, his quota for the month unmet. Three days later, two sisters from Christ the Savior Church brought the semi-annual invitation to spend eternity in heaven.

Carla closed the door in the sisters' faces. But the salesman she'd invited into her kitchen, gave him tea laced with cinnamon, examined his doilies, which were too frilly for her tastes. Then she went to put in her diaphragm, and to lock Phoenix's door, so that if he awoke he couldn't disturb her. She steered the salesman across her living room, swept books and magazines from the couch. As she shrugged from her dress, her eyes never left his face, eyes so flat they'd have led him to pause had he not been so dazed by his fortune.

But it wasn't her eyes that drew him; it was the arc of nut-brown shoulder, that and the perfect breasts, the luxurious growth beneath her belly. When she turned to drape her dress across a chair, he winced at the scars from shoulder blades to thigh backs. She said it had happened in Korea, a hand grenade, and when he wouldn't believe that lie, she clutched him in a way that made his eyes close. Then she pushed him onto his back, mounted him, searched for a rhythm to build her pleasure by. When she couldn't find one, she shut her eyes, imagined evenings slicked with rain, gnats wheeling frantically in sunlight. She reproduced the moan of a one-time lover, another's sweet butt curve. Finally she called on the memory of the afternoon twenty-seven years ago when she'd burst into the bathroom to find Max wide-legged in the dark. Exhilarated by her discovery of power, she'd closed the door, turned on the light, and touched him. His eyes went dark.

"Don't," he whispered.

But even that memory couldn't charge this less than thrilling moment. Beating back frustration, Carla drained what joy she could from the salesman's meager thighs. When he left, he stuttered, promised to call, write, send flowers, return before the week was out. Resolutely, she pushed him down porch steps into winter, backed inside, stared at the feeling in her hands. It was green, gelatinous. It said not even her surface had been satisfied. Woodenly, she fell onto the sofa. Despair sat down beside her, but she couldn't take time to listen. Her son was at his room's locked door, hammering to be set free.

In August 1966, the man on her porch made her heart trip with attraction and the sense that her life was threatened. He came early in the afternoon, a Sunday, both he and her response so unexpected they sent a quick hand to her neck. The danger loomed, arresting, like a neon sign in a meadow—this man would, if she let him, take her life.

Her eyes narrowed, probing the threat. She was calmed a little by his size: slender, half a head taller than she. White shirt open at his throat, a hollow made for licking. He said his name was Oliver Henry Jackson, but people called him Miles. Melvina Turner's second cousin on his daddy's side, he'd stopped by Kingston on his way to the Grand Canyon. Having grown up in Florida, he'd always wanted to know what dry air felt like, and to see if he could stand on the edge of the biggest hole in the universe and look down without getting dizzy. At dinner last night, Carla's name had come up, and he was interested, so he was here to see for himself.

His voice was measured, one-half beat faster than too slow. Still, Carla hadn't spoken. Miles glanced past her. A small library's worth of books and magazines littered the smallish room.

"Read a lot, eh?"

She ignored his question. "What charitable, Christian things your cousin tell you?"

His eyes were steady, an ordinary brown. "That you live by yourself in this two-family house. Your first house burned down, put you in the hospital, killed two babies. My cousin said Max did it. Your son's an idiot. You're not quite right in the head yourself, but you're still one of the finest things to walk these Kingston streets."

She blinked. Green plants would flourish in his smile. "She didn't tell you that."

"The *fine* part? No, I figured that out myself."

"What else?"

He hesitated. "The rest ain't so flattering. She said you use the Lord's name in vain and sleep with white men."

"She left out the devil?"

He nodded ruefully. "Yeah, she said that, too."

"Well?"

"Well, what?"

"Aren't you offended?"

"No," he said. "I don't believe in the devil. I got no choice but to believe in white men, they all over the place. But you ain't my woman, and you *sho* nuff ain't my child."

"You figure that out by yourself, too?"

He grinned. "All by my lonesome. But just to be on the safe side, I asked around before I came over."

"Oh. *Did* you?"

He held his hands out. "Well? Can I come in?"

She stared, began, with the same reflex that ensured her breathing, to make ready for his leaving. "Please," she said, moved books from the sofa, invited him to sit. Herself she placed in a chair across from him, glanced at the angle where his thighs met. He had small feet. She imagined he was a dancer: balance, muscle, grace.

"Where's Phenus?"

"Phoenix," she said. "His name is Phoenix."

"Oh. The bird keeps getting born. Out of the ashes."

When he saw her surprise, he said, "Used to cook on a boat called *Phoenix*. Owner rebuilt it after a fire."

"Most people think he's named after a city in Arizona. Anyway, he's sleeping."

"Uh-huh."

She'd pulled the window shades against the sun, couldn't see his eyes, but she could hear the silence. It was funny about silence; she'd have said she was used to it. Outside of her child's grunts and whines, the occasional man she pulled into the empty of her need, she'd lived in this house with silence since her brother Willis had left in 1959. But this silence was awkward, and she lurched to break it.

"So how come they call you Miles? You like to travel?"

"'Cause I look like the trumpet player. Miles Davis?"

She nodded. "How long you plan to stay in Kingston?"

"Till I'm ready to leave, I guess. Grand Canyon ain't going no place soon."

"That's so."

She looked at hands folded in her lap, discovered what she was wearing: a pair of her father's overalls, her brother's football shirt. Bare feet, the toes wore peeling polish. If she'd known he was coming . . .

"So why?" Miles said.

"Why what?"

"Why you live the way you do?"

"How do you think I live?"

"Well . . . all alone for one thing."

"I'm not alone. I live with my son. Who do you live with?"

His face said he'd walked into a trap of his making, but he had grace enough to smile. "I guess I just got double jumped."

"Then king me."

When his laughter stopped, sound that filled the room like light, she said, "So? Who you live with?"

"No one."

"All by yourself? Why you *live* the way you do?"

"I'm working," he said, "on my checkers game."

He was smiling again, but it wasn't dazzling. This smile asked to be let off the hook, to be allowed to redirect the conversation. She waited, wondered what it would taste like to lick his throat.

"Well . . . " He crossed his legs. "The life I lead . . . it's hard to ask someone to share it. Moving from place to place . . . " Discomfort tightened his face; he shrugged. "Last five years I've lived in Pittsburgh, the Bronx, Brooklyn. . . .

"The truth is . . . " he said, and looked above him, as if he were surprised to be speaking of truth, as if he'd found it in her ceiling. "The truth is I'm getting over something. It's taking longer than I thought."

"A woman?"

"A wife."

"Passed?"

"No. She's alive." He paused. "I don't tell anybody, usually. It makes me feel I'm being weak to talk about it. It's not like it was yesterday. It's been three years."

"Ain't nothing weak about grieving someone you love."

"I ain't mentioned nothing about no grieving."

"What do you call it?"

He was still, then leaned back against the chair. "This conversation is weird."

"Weird?"

"Here I'm speaking on what I only talk to myself about, and I don't even know you."

What was weird, she thought, was how easy it was, how right it felt, when only minutes before she'd been threatened. "Want to see him?"

"Pardon me?"

"Phoenix. You want to see him?"

His eyebrows arched, but he said okay.

Phoenix slept on his back, the gray sheet up to his navel. He was tall, at least six feet, Miles guessed, with blond hair, skin a cautious yellow. Perspiration beaded on his lip. He was one of the prettiest people Miles had ever seen, what his ex-wife would have called drop-dead pretty, and it was hard to imagine anything wrong with him, that he wouldn't, while they stood, wake to stretch, discuss his favorite baseball team, the weather. Across the darkened room a fan droned in a window. Miles rubbed his chin, thinking it was time to whisper something appropriate. He had all kinds of generous expressions for people's babies, but what did you say about one who was easily six feet tall? He started to speak, but Carla put a finger to her lips, and he held his comment until they'd gone into the hall.

"He's a good-looking boy."

She blinked. There was a tenderness in his voice she didn't associate with men. As she descended the stairs, she wondered if he *was* weak. She felt his eyes, imagined what it would be like if at the bottom he pulled her to her knees. How sad if he were weak. As though sunlight might clarify, she went to the windows, raised the shades. Miles sat; light fell across his feet. Why had she offered to show him her son? Why did it feel like allowing a glimpse inside her, a look at the unhealed place?

She said, "So you lost your wife, and now you're on your way to Arizona."

He paused; it wasn't exactly what he'd meant. "Sort of."

Some people lost things and stayed to tend the soul's grave site; some took off into the world.

He said, "Do you play?"

"Play?"

He pointed to the piano.

"No. What's Pittsburgh like?"

"Pittsburgh?"

"Yes. Would you like some tea?"

"No thanks," he said. "I got to be going. Got a few errands to run."

She looked into the moment she'd been waiting for; she wasn't ready. Was it the offering of tea, or was it Pittsburgh?

Miles said, "But I'm going fishing in the morning. Want to come?"

"Fishing?"

"That's when you throw a line with a hook. . . . "

"I know what fishing is."

"Well?"

She was again, inexplicably, afraid. "I can't."

"Why?"

"Phoenix. I got no one to sit for him."

"Take him with us. You make lunch. I'll drive."

"He's never been fishing."

"So?"

Jesus. Take Phoenix? "I don't know. . . . What time?"

"Six o'clock."

"In the *morning?*"

He said, "You ever eat grapefruit?"

"*Grape*-fruit?" She leaned away from him, baffled, as if he'd asked to stay forever, and he laughed, part seduction, part delight, confident now that he was back on familiar, bantering ground.

"I'm sorry," he said. "You just sound so surprised at the ordinary. Fishing, the fact there's a six o'clock in the morning, grapefruit . . ."

That wasn't, she thought, exactly fair. He'd come barging into her living room, revealed a part of himself she didn't expect from men, made her feel all those crazy things, including fear, and expected her to be . . . what? Normal? And then he'd just up and announced he was leaving. It was the way men said good-bye when their plans didn't include returning, and before she could properly resent that, he'd asked her to go fishing. Not dinner or a movie. *Fishing.* And she was attracted to him. A quick attraction she didn't know what to do with except acknowledge the novelty and the threat. But she wouldn't let him know that. If she knew how to do anything, it was how to take care of herself.

"Six o'clock," she said. "Don't be late."

"If I am, what happens? You put me over your knee?"

He was smiling again, that wry, confident male smile, and his fingers danced as they built a pyramid beneath his chin. Annoyed, confused, she almost blurted: *That's not where I'd like to put you.* It would have been interesting to see what happened to his face. Because she wouldn't say what she thought, she had to make up something. She couldn't. There was too much going on: threat like a neon glitter, annoyance, the preparation for his leaving, wonder, all of it crowding the interval that held the door closing at his back, her finger lifting the shade an eye's width from the casement, his blue Buick crouching before it leapt.

Now she examined this feeling that her life was threatened. The truth was it didn't make sense. Of all the details left by his visit— his feet, his openness, that throat crying out for licking—not one suggested that this man who could have been a dancer could also be a threat.

She carried the feeling into the kitchen, offered it to sun that poured through the window above the sink. She put on the kettle for tea, sat drumming fingers against the table, remembering, for no reason she could make sense of, the night when she'd first dreamed of counting spaces left by those she loved. That was twenty-four years ago in 1942; earlier that afternoon they'd bur- ied her father. She hadn't thought she'd sleep, but she had, and then her dream voice pulled her wide-eyed into waking.

What an accumulation of leaving! In less than two years her brothers Alton and David burned up in that fire, Max disap- peared, Lucinda, her friend, was shipped to North Carolina. That last was just after Carla and a neighbor's son had moved her father's sickbed to the attic. Not yet fifty, her father was willing himself to die. He said he needed space and privacy in which to do this, that the unused rooms were thick with furniture, and the cellar was too damp. They'd humored him because that's what you do for a loved one who wills himself to die; you move his sickbed where he would.

And all that time her father insisting he wasn't afraid, saying he'd welcome death, but when it came, he'd screamed, flailed, and smashed the lamp, so that death, when it snatched him, had to do it in the dark. By the time Carla had raced from the kitchen, he was gone, face a howling mask that made the undertaker pause when he bent to rearrange it.

She'd been shattered by her father's dying, hadn't begun to put the pieces back when her mother went seven months later, eyes batting, breasts spurting cream-colored leaking, as if death were not the grown man her father battled, but a sucking infant, much like the one her mother left behind. And Carla piggybacked her grief, tried to use it to inspire tears she hadn't shed for Alton and David. She couldn't.

Despite what she'd done, she hadn't deserved to be that singularly cursed. No one did. Despondent, she obsessed about her own death, looked for it beneath the bed, in the basement, spun to catch it in the space that yawned behind her while she ironed. In this obsession she discovered fear. What if death were not not-being, but existence marked by bright lights and alone? Or worse, what if death were a country into which people she loved came to satisfy her longing, stayed the night, then vanished before dawn? Those were two reasons she stopped thinking of dying; a third was two children to care for—Phoenix, her son, and Willis, her infant brother—and she found distraction in this task.

So there she was, alone in a two-family house except for the children—one an idiot, the other a lover of boats. The boat lover was Willis, who'd grown up to join the navy. Phoenix she'd only to watch over, but Willis she'd raised, gotten him off to school, labored over homework, agonized through Little League. She'd weathered measles and chicken pox, croup and fever. And how swiftly childhood passed; she'd turned a moment, and when she looked again, Willis reared above her, armpits thicketed with hair. His voice fell overnight to bass; distance stepped between them— girls in his life, a whole house full of secrets. All of it was proof; Willis was almost grown, and he'd be leaving.

Of course she'd always known he'd leave. As early as toilet training she'd been consumed with his departure. As she cleaned shit from his underwear and washed between his tiny ass cheeks, as she perched on the edge of the tub, soothing the fear that head-locked his bowels, she'd think not of the ancient, thankless duty, but how one day he'd be gone. Each small rite of passage—his first haircut, his discovery of boats—tacked another reminder on her heart: Willis is going to leave you.

And he did, and she told herself that this was just the way life was, that everyone you loved left before time's fullness, some by death, some by disappearance, some because they loved boats and went off to join the navy.

Carla pushed back from the table, turned off the kettle. After her father's funeral, she and her mother had gone to see the lawyer her father, Rufus, had retained. The investment plan had already been established, the money from Max's ministry put into annuities and bonds. Nearly half the twenty thousand dollars insurance went into passbook accounts, Rufus figuring that the banks wouldn't fail again in his wife's lifetime. The house was paid for, and when her mother died there was enough money for Carla to live on, although once Willis was in school, she chose to work.

The combination of a single woman and a decent inheritance brought the suitors out in schools. Carla slept with nearly all of them, but when none succeeded in bringing her to orgasm, she realized she didn't want to marry, and although it was a long time before she acknowledged it, she settled in to wait for Max. She didn't give up sex; sex brought pleasure: respite from aloneness, the newness of strange flesh, the lover's secret weakness and her power. Her decision not to wed caused a rumbling in Christ the Savior Church, prevailing wisdom being that a woman needed a man's protection, and that it was better to marry than to burn. Well, Carla told the pastor, for protection she had her father's shotgun. As for burning, she'd already survived a fire, and if he meant another kind, she knew how to put that out. When she began to experience a desire to go to church, this exchange made it too awkward to show her face, and she began to feel, even though she'd done the leaving, that the church had abandoned her.

So she lived a life defined by keeping to herself, raised her brother, watched her son, and made a ritual of waiting. Still, beyond that ritual burned her desire to be connected to the world, to let it know of her existence. She knew the key lay in a two- or three- or four-ness with other people. But she also knew isolation was essential, for though it deepened loneliness, it kept from public scrutiny her private, shameful self. It was a self so tender the gentlest touch would bruise it (yet she longed for touch), so drawn to others in its need for love that giving in to it meant giving up, being swallowed, as if the self's extinction lurked on needing's other side.

There were times when she wept at the unrelenting burden of an idiot child, a life less than a life, and everybody leaving. Still, during all the years, with a rhythm no drummer had discovered, no lean fingers plucked from steel guitar, came the flashes, the fleeting episodes that said her life wouldn't always be this way; a change would come. Hope drove her to focus on the children, and she'd talk to them incessantly, one who understood her, one who didn't. She'd explain wind and stars, why living things grew toward the sun. Or she'd read to them, and when she grew tired of the sameness of children's books, she'd tell about the winter it didn't snow until January and that spring when all the dead were women. At first she told these stories straight; then she embroidered, shaped them to her will. Invention was instructive, taught her patience; she learned that if she waited, it would come. And when it came, the pleasure was in telling; in this act she'd forget her wounded self. This is why she told compulsively; over and over she related to Phoenix the story of his father, Max, who'd vanished, but promised to return. That's why she was alone; she'd vowed to wait. For all these years she'd kept that vow. Sometimes she'd forget she'd made it; then, when she attempted to understand her life, she'd remember, and everything made sense. She was alone because she chose; she'd kept her promise.

And now here was this man who'd lived in Pittsburgh, to whom she was drawn, by whom she was threatened. The threat was simple; it came from considering betrayal. What would she say if in the evening Max came knocking at her door? After all the years of waiting, how could she explain that she'd given it up, lured by a throat and small feet? She told herself to put it away for a while. She didn't have to make any long-term decisions. Why not try to enjoy the shock of having met a man who could have been a dancer, one who spoke openly of loss and would come to take her fishing in the morning?

That night she packed a lunch—cold meat loaf sandwiches, orange juice, and apples, then went to bed, endured dreams in which Miles didn't return, others in which he came to find a darkened house, his knock unanswered. Each time she woke telling herself to get some rest or she'd be thick-headed in the morning.

When gray light edged the drapes, she went to awaken Phoenix. He slept on his stomach, and when she'd gathered his clothes, she roused him with a back rub. Then she led him to the bathroom, washed him, first the beautiful face, then his neck and shoulders. She sat on the tub's edge, hand sure between his muscled thighs, efficiently cleaning his genitals, the dark valley bisecting his butt. His penis thickened, but she paid no mind, no longer flustered by length the color of frozen butter, the dark veins lining it with blood.

Once she'd mourned that her son would never know a woman. This seemed so unfair that she'd half considered soliciting one for him—a bored wife, perhaps, or one of those fast young girls up at the high school. But the truth was that Phoenix had never demonstrated interest in sex. He'd grow hard when she washed him, but the same reaction would result from a sudden change in temperature or his biting into beef. In the years before she'd gotten used to it, she'd looked up to watch him on the floor, eyes closed, gorgeously aroused. She'd wondered what flickered through his brain, whether the aroma of green beans or the car that hummed in the darkening street were agents of tumescence.

And just like that, his swelling would subside. Nothing she could point to with any certainty had changed, except her breathing.

Now she shuttled him down the hall, pointed to his underwear. When she was satisfied he was dressing, she went to her room, stepped over books and clothing, stood at her closet. Outside, a car pulled up. She flew to the window, pushed aside the drape. Miles wore a shirt greener than a traffic light, jeans too blue to have ever been washed. When he knocked, she went to the head of the staircase, yelled, "It's open," heard him enter. Her heart got silly on her. She dashed back to the closet.

"Girl, fish ain't got all day to wait for us," Miles called, and she was smiling, holding a dress to her throat with all the expectation of a young girl going nighttime dancing for the first time, although it was morning of a day so new it was still wet, although she'd witnessed forty-four birthdays, enough to know normal folks didn't wear Sunday dresses to go fishing. She dropped the dress, grabbed a pair of jeans from the corner of the closet, snatched one of her father's shirts, pawed through the laundry basket for clean underwear and bra. Dressed, a brush railroaded through her short-cropped hair, she raced down the hall to fetch Phoenix.

When she saw him, she groaned. He'd taken off all his clothes except his undershorts, which he wore on his head like a chef's hat. Crouched, his penis hanging like a pump spout, he was fastidiously inspecting his toes.

It was just past six in the morning, and she was exhausted. She'd gotten Phoenix dressed again, strapped him in the harness, nearly dragged him downstairs, said to Miles, "Good morning," "How you feel this morning?," "I'll be ready in a minute." She touched Miles's arm; he smelled of lime. In the kitchen she checked the lunch basket, nagged by a feeling that she'd forgotten something. She turned the apples to make certain for the fifth time none had a brown spot. She'd remembered napkins, and paper cups. . . .

"Miles," she cried, and slumped into a kitchen chair. He was in the doorway—"What it be?"—and she—"I ain't got pole the first. There may be a bucket around here someplace, but I ain't got line or hook. I gave 'em away when my father died."

And he laughed. "I got all that, Carla. Enough for you, enough for Phoenix if he want to fish. Now come on, let's get moving."

That wasn't it. Yes, she hadn't remembered the equipment, but that wasn't what was nagging. Had not Miles been so aflame with impatience, she'd have stopped, devoted the time to recollect. Instead, she half-stepped from the moment, consoled herself with one of the most treacherous lies ever invented: If you didn't remember something, it must not be important.

Finally they were in the car, pulling away from the house. Miles glanced in the rearview mirror. He'd said good morning to Phoenix; Phoenix hadn't looked at him. Maybe he didn't like anybody messing with his mama, or maybe that was just the way he was, unmoved and unresponsive.

"Can he follow what I say?"

"No."

"Why you put a harness on him?"

"Keep him from wandering off. He doesn't understand danger. Fire he knows. I guess he ought to. He almost burned up."

"How old is he?"

"Twenty-six."

"He was born that way?"

"Most the doctors could say was probably. I didn't notice anything until my father died. Then it hit me how he never cried. A little whimper if he was wet or hungry, but not a real lung-clearing cry. He'd lie for hours wherever you put him. I thought he was just a good baby. I started worrying when he wouldn't crawl. . . . "

Her voice trailed as she recalled her efforts to reclaim her son from idiocy. If determination could do it, she'd reasoned, it was done. But determination couldn't do it.

*   *   *

Miles slowed the car, made the right turn onto Route 28. Indolent in the brand-new sunshine, cornfields spread away on one side of the highway; fir trees lined the other. The sky had left its clouds home, wore a seamless gown of first-class blue. It was a good-looking morning, and Miles said so.

She agreed. "Where we going?"

"Shokan. Heard that's the best place for fishing around here."

"I used to go there with my father."

"You did?"

Then, with a shift so abrupt she at first thought he still spoke of fishing, "Want to go to church with me next Sunday?"

She looked away. She hadn't set foot in that church for more than twenty years. Then she was thinking: *So he'll be here at least till next Sunday.*

"We'll see," she said. "We haven't been fishing yet."

"Am I moving too fast?"

"No, just changing lanes without a signal."

He checked the rearview mirror. "Ain't no other traffic on this road, is there?"

"Not at the moment. But you never know where the trooper might be hiding."

"Then I got to be more careful," he said. "Too nice a day to get a moving violation."

She laughed, he laughed, and it was there again; in the middle of an easy time stalked the disapproving silence and the danger. With nothing to say except what she was thinking, she settled into her seat, watched the road, imagined the car swallowing it, gulping sky, trees, and farmland, storing it rolled in the trunk, so that behind them if she chose to look stretched space absent of detail. She turned to find Phoenix sleeping, snuck a glance at Miles; she thought he was talking to himself, but he was singing.

The last time she'd gone to the Shokan, it hadn't been to fish, but to walk, and sit beside the water. She'd been eight, was with Max and her father. Originally, she'd not been included in the outing;

she'd cried, her father grudgingly relented. Between her and Miles was a space like the one where Max had sat, and Max's head had leaned against her father's side. At the Shokan, she'd made sure to hold her father's hand, but it was Max he'd talked to. Time had dimmed the memory of what he'd said, something about Max's ministry, but she recalled the cadences of her father's voice, and how she didn't once that day find her reflection in his eyes. She took what comfort she could from knowing that on the ride home it would be her turn to sit next to him. That was her right; it was only fair.

But she didn't trust fair, and as they walked from the water she was plotting how to maneuver so that when they got back in the car, she'd be the one in the middle. Of course, Max had tricked her, had one of his holy seizures; he'd stiffened, went moaning to his knees, looked imploringly at his father, and slammed backward to the ground. There, eyes rolled to bone white in their rapture, he convulsed and cried out in a language her father proudly said was Greek. It was an experience that left the blond boy limp with bliss, and she remembered how carefully her father carried him, sat him in the middle, soothed him. "It's all right, baby, all right."

That wasn't all she remembered. She remembered how she, outside the circle they made, sat watching, and how astonishing it was that her heart could keep falling and never reach a bottom. And she remembered how Max's smell had changed, became the one you got when you struck two stones together to make a spark strong enough to set a fire.

That was thirty-six years ago, and she'd not returned to the Shokan since. Back then, she'd been blinded by her rage, diverted by her heart's failed try to reach a bottom. This morning, she witnessed the beauty. From the top of the hill the Buick had just now crested, the road snaked down to the black-topped parking lot, beyond which lay the water. Boats nested on the glinting surface, bits of white and gray. And the lake, enormous jewel, pine trees soaring at its edge, image duplicating in the water; it was lovely.

Miles parked the car; they got out, Carla drinking the day. She gathered Phoenix from the back seat; he rubbed his eyes against the brilliance. Miles was groaning his stretch felt so good, *he* felt so good, thinking all this water *had* to be full of fish looking for a store-bought breakfast. He could feel the weight in his arm when one struck.

As Carla retrieved the picnic basket, it occurred to her that they looked so normal, like a family: a red-and-white-checked cloth, cold meat loaf sandwiches, orange juice, apples without blemish. Even her son's harness just seemed . . . ordinary.

They walked toward the lake, she holding Phoenix's leash and the basket, Miles carrying the tackle, the swinging pail of minnows they'd use for bait. The trees were so close together that at this level all she could see of water was its shining between dark trunks like filaments of silver. She'd begun to count the filaments when the birds sensed Phoenix's presence. Finch and wren and sparrow, robin, thrush, a hundred birds, two hundred, enough, as they rose collectively, to darken sky, birdcalls like screaming. On the lake men surged to their feet, mouths circles of panic, of prayer and disbelief; the boats rocked.

Phoenix bolted, the jolt as he reached the leash's end dumping the picnic basket. Carla remembered. Her son was bent, mewling, hands protecting his head. Miles had dropped the rods and tackle box. On the pavement minnows gasped, thrashing green and silver. Miles was in a boxer's crouch, on the balls of his feet, chin tucked, as if a left hook, perfectly thrown, would return them all to normal. A whole sky of birds like a storm cloud heading east, their calls growing faint. The light came back. Phoenix began to shit.

Carla said, "Take me home."

Miles looked at her, his left arm cocked, his face dumbfounded. "Jesus, Carla. What's going on?"

"Nothing," she said. "Just take me home."

Later, she told Miles how the birds had first appeared, as if threats, or plague, or someone's twisted idea of a gift. They were everywhere: dark handfuls in the yard's far corner, clumps, blue-black, stiffening on her porch. Sometimes the necks were broken, but mostly just the bristling feathers hinted at foul play. It was their eyes that got to her; they were open, stunned, like victims forced to witness their own slaughter. As she buried them, wrapped in tissue paper, she thought it was a stray cat desperate for food, but when she left milk on the porch it was untouched in the morning. The answer didn't come until Phoenix, all golden with pride, brought the sparrow to her kitchen, a nail through the head fixing the creature to a shingle, the tongue stuck to its beak. It had taken time to do this; the bird was stinking. She didn't bury that one. She walked it at arm's length to the back-yard, stuffed it in the bottom of her garbage.

That was June 1949. Phoenix, once he'd begun to walk, had become so quick, as if compensation for idiocy was in lithe mus-cles, in hands so fast they snatched birds out of air. She'd put a bell around his neck to warn the birds, had barely tied the knot, but already he was changing. His shoulders slumped, his feet dragged; that period of quickness ended. Deprived of something he didn't have a voice to tell her, Phoenix retreated, locked the door to the small room where his mind lived, stored in the closet the boy flesh that should have climbed and swung for nothing but the joy.

Still, the damage had been done, the result of which was that birds refused to gather anywhere around them. Struck by the absence of birdsong, so vividly remembering that sometimes she hurried to the window, certain the melodies in her head came from a tree, Carla invented a story, one that gave pleasure while making sense of loss. Birds refused to stay in her son's presence because Phoenix was Max's child. Max had set a fire that destroyed their homes, and there hadn't been a warning. Birds accepted this violence as part of sharing life with humans; it was the ritualizing that incensed them—killing become art form—and after Phoenix's experiment with sculpture, they moved to retaliate. They'd do this until restitution had been made.

In their choice of punishment, the birds showed compassion. They could have killed Phoenix, formed bird hordes to perforate his eyes, driven beaks into his spinal cord, devoured his liver while he lay shocked and paralyzed. Instead, they deprived him of their songs.

The birds would have done the same thing to Max, Phoenix's father, but they didn't know where he was.

They'd planned to go fishing. They'd look like normal people anywhere; even though her son had blond hair and wore a harness, still they'd look okay, just another family on an outing. Phoenix had shit all over himself. The bathrooms were on the water's other side. Phoenix cowered in the back seat, smelling to heaven; she mortified and sick to her stomach. She wanted to scream, to drive her head through the windshield where sunlight foolishly glinted. She wanted to choke her child until his blank eyes understood.

So much for being normal. She couldn't tell what Miles was thinking. They were driving in silence, his hands at a quarter to one on the wheel, she trying to think of nothing, afraid even to acknowledge that sunlight had gotten past the windshield and curled up in her lap. She'd wanted to tell Miles not to bother, to just drop her off with her soiled and idiot child. She'd wanted to sit in the space between them, hide her head in his side.

*   *   *

Now, in the dimness of her living room, Phoenix cleaned and locked in his room, the birds explained, she sensed it in the way animals sensed a coming storm—Miles was gathering to leave. Space swelled inside her. She wouldn't give in to it. If only he'd slipped off while she was cleaning Phoenix; if he'd just go, quickly, now. She opened her mouth to say it was easier if he left without excuses, made no promise to return.

"Don't go," she said.

He was sitting in the chair she'd cleared for him the day before, legs crossed. He touched a hand to his forehead. She was furious with embarrassment and need, furious that she'd said it.

"I'm not going anywhere, Carla. At least not yet. What is it? Why you hurt so bad?"

She was comforted a little; she was frightened.

"I'll be all right," she said. "It's just been trying."

What a word—*trying*. She tried to smile, but smiling wouldn't come.

"What is it?"

"I'll be all right," she said.

He moved to her across a room cluttered with books and magazines.

"Tell me," he said.

He pulled, she let him; she was in his arms, her face in a curve of throat and shoulder, breathing fish bait, lime aftershave. She took the risk of looking into his eyes. They were brown and curious and kind. They made her want to weep. She'd find a way to explain it. It was only for this little while; she wouldn't give her heart.

"Oh, Lord," she said. "Help me."

"Tell me. How can I help?"

"Hold me." Maybe that would be enough.

He held her. Behind her eyes a humming made her quiver. She was wet, open. Had he been another man, she'd have pulled him to the couch.

"Come to bed with me."

He leaned back, careful. "Is that what you want?"

"Yes."

"You sure?"

"Yes. But only if you want to."

"Is it too quick?"

"I don't know. Not if you want to."

"Okay," Miles said. "I do."

She took his hand, led him upstairs to the room no man had entered, stood while he undressed her. He paused, eyes narrowed, touched her scars.

"The fire," she said. "I . . ."

He pressed a palm to her mouth, kissed her back. His lips were cool. She shivered, lay across the bed, admiring his body as he undressed, the flat, graceful planes, the thickening between his thighs. He was standing the way he'd stood yesterday on her porch, allowing her to look.

She said, "I've got to go to the bathroom."

"Okay."

In the bathroom, leg raised, one foot resting on the tub's edge, she put in her diaphragm. Then she turned to the mirror, holding her shoulders, arms across her breasts. She looked haunted. "He's black," she said. "He's in my bedroom."

She opened the medicine chest, took out cologne, dabbed behind her ears, beneath her breasts, stood wide-legged, left rose scent on her thighs.

When she returned, he was standing naked at the window. She closed the door.

"Miles?"

He turned, held out his hand. She crossed the room, drew him to the bed. Her left breast slipped beneath her arm as he stretched beside her; their knees collided. He touched her face, and when she moved again, they were on their sides, thighs and bellies flush. He had ripples in his stomach, like a washboard. Shifting, she raised her top leg, slung it across his waist; the fit was perfect. She was trying to feel everything at once, but that was impossible, and she focused on the hands stroking her back, thinking how gentle he was, how he touched, the way he moved. The stroking was peeling away the outer layers, the gauzelike protection she was wrapped in. She was warm and almost safe and she tried to give up all the way, to let him touch the core, the wounded infant heart, but it was too frightening, too much like falling into a hole whose only map was depth and darkness. She stiffened, and he held tight until she found a place she could allow him to touch without panic. It was like slipping into a healing sleep, except that here was his smell, here the hard/soft body planes, his hands, and the rigid tube against her belly.

She wasn't sure when it changed, if he moved, or she, but where she'd been warm, now she was burning; he was on top, inside her with a thrust that took her last breath, the one she only now realized that she'd been saving. She wrapped her legs around his waist, squeezed, and found, to her astonishment, that she was coming. Eyes wide, breath whistling in short, hard bursts, she rode out the convulsions, then lay collecting her scattered self.

He waited. When the whistle left her breath, he kissed her, long and hard, and before she could register marvel at what was happening to her lips, he stared into her eyes and moved again.

In her head, words assembled like a song, repeated: *He looked at me, he looked at me.*

Later, without speaking, he massaged her feet. In a little while she went downstairs, made tea, brought it back to bed, where she sat with knees drawn to her chest, watching him through mist the steaming liquid made. She was trying to do two things at once: to hold to the feeling of being connected and yet prepare for his leaving. Things bubbled on her skin, struggled to get inside; she wouldn't let them. Miles set his cup on the night table, touched her thigh, and smiled. She wanted to say: "What's going to become of us, will you stay forever? Move in with me, we'll plant a garden." But if she did, he'd remind her that he couldn't stay, he was on his way to Arizona. Or he'd artfully evade her, or, "Yes, I'll stay," and then Max would come back and she'd have to admit she'd given up the waiting.

Now, in the confusion caused by that thought, she longed to be alone. She looked at him and saw that his eyes were closed.

"Are you sleeping?"

"No," he said. "How you feel?"

"Okay."

"You sure?"

"Uh-huh."

"That story you told me about the birds," he asked lazily. "Was that true?"

"True?"

"I mean," he said, turning, resting his knee against her waist, "did it really happen?"

"Why's that important?"

"I don't know. Truth matters. Don't it?"

"It's true," she said, "if you think so."

He laughed. "You mean anything's true if you think it?"

"It's a story. Either you believe it or you don't. That's all. There's a shovel in the basement. You need proof, go dig up in the yard. There still might be some bones left."

There was an edge to her voice. Maybe, he thought, you didn't fuck with a storyteller's tale. Maybe you just listened and took from it what you would.

"Well, it's a good story," he said. "You ought to write it down."

"What for?"

"So you won't forget it."

She grunted, moved so they didn't touch. "I won't forget it."

It was a wonder, he thought, that her grunt didn't have an echo. She was lying next to him, but she might have been on the other side of the Grand Canyon. It could, of course, have nothing to do with the story; it could be how she was after sex. He'd known women who were like that. Once their need was met, a shade got pulled across a window, a high wall built. He let his disappointment sweep him. Still, maybe this worked out for the best. He'd already felt too much too soon, and that for a woman who had her share of problems. He didn't know what they were, just that they were more than he could handle. And he wasn't going to try. He didn't do that anymore.

He lay for what felt like a decent time. Then: "Listen, I gotta be going."

She said, indifferently, "I know."

He rose, began to dress. She watched him, male person in her bedroom. He moved to bedside, bent to kiss her. Their foreheads bumped.

"Sorry," he said.

"You'll forgive me if I don't see you to the door."

"I forgive you."

"It's just . . . "

"It's okay," he said. "I'll talk to you."

She nodded and he was leaving, first his back receding, then everything was gone. She listened to his movement along the hall, counted the seventeen steps he descended, winced when the front door closed. She lay, trying to think of nothing. If she didn't think, she'd be fine.

But she couldn't stop thinking. She'd allowed a man into her bedroom, he was black, she'd allowed herself to feel, it left her weak. He didn't believe her story. Here came the edge of a familiar rage; pain hit so hard she moaned. Knowing that to be active was to hold the pain at bay, she slid from bed, careened to the center of the room, turned in a circle. She stumbled into the hallway, clutched the banister all the way downstairs; in the kitchen turned the faucet on and shut it. She touched the stove, opened the refrigerator, saw the milk bottle, a leftover lamb chop, the last two apples. She unlocked the door to the basement, went down the narrow steps.

It was cooler here, darker than her bedroom, but light enough to see the shapes of things. The concrete floor was cold. She went past the workbench with her father's tools: the hammer, the awl, the plane, all in their proper, labeled places. Her father was dead. There was the washing machine, past that the water pump and furnace; the humpbacked shadow was the oil tank. She turned back to the workbench, reached for the hammer, feeling its smooth hardness, its weight, the handle inexplicably warm. How stupid to let him in her bedroom, to tell that story, how dumb to feel. Weak light flowed through the grimy window above the washer. She imagined crushing its gleaming dials, its solid, white perfection. Rage swelled again, and she sank, naked, to her knees.

"Damn you!" She slammed the hammer against the floor. It bounced in her hand. Again she smashed it.

"Damn you! Damn you!" Damn her life, damn Miles, damn her father for not loving, damn her mother, and Max, damn Lucinda for going away.

When she stopped, she was kneeling before a field of impressions, each the size of a quarter. She got to her feet, returned the hammer to its setting, went upstairs to draw a bath. Lying in the steaming water, only her head and knees exposed, she wondered if she'd seen the last of Miles. Probably. It was better this way; it would be messy if he were here when Max arrived. And Max *would* come back; she couldn't stop holding on to that, and when he did he'd put an end to all the leaving.

In his car, Miles turned on the radio. Somewhere in Texas a man with a rifle had opened up on a crowd in a shopping mall. Before he'd absorbed the fact that ten people were dead, an announcer tried to sell him over-the-counter sleeping pills. He switched off the annoying voice, heard his engine idle. Houses had their shades drawn. Cars hugged the curbs like patient, staring beasts. The street was hushed, expectant, as if, despite the sun's position, it waited stupidly for dawn.

He drove away from the curb. Birds had leapt and darkened the sky. Boats rocked on the water. Phoenix had shit all over himself.

He thought of Carla, her taut body, her breasts like those of a woman who'd never suckled, how she'd clung to him with what smacked of an emptiness a man could spend a lifetime laboring to fill. His fantasy of being the one to do this was his weakness. He could see himself, sleeves rolled, the yawning cavity, a moist, dark mound of caring into which he stubbornly plunged a shovel. Then what? Settle in, be the one she'd turn to, or split, resume his quest to look into the Grand Canyon without getting dizzy? It was, no matter how you spliced it, a third-rate movie. "Quest-man," they'd call him. Black man perpetually journeying toward the largest hole in the universe, pausing to plug lesser varieties along the way. At film's end a flaming sunset backlit the woman's good-bye wave; her life restored, she wept with gratitude. Sappy music blossomed; credits rolled. Not a dry eye in the house.

He told himself he was okay, no longer did that. He wasn't on earth to solve other people's problems. Neither did he have to keep everything he came across; sometimes remembering was enough. Instead of figuring out what he could do to fix her life, he'd think about the perfect fit, and how she'd whistled when her love came down.

It had been, if he did say so himself, some outstanding pussy, world class by anybody's standard, which meant, not at all merely, that it inspired you to lie. He smiled, remembering the early evening he and the guys had been sitting around the caddy yard in Jacksonville, Florida. The next day was going to be a bitch; the sun hung behind the sixth green like a blood clot, palm trees leaned wistfully above a shriveled pond. As usual, the conversation got around to women, and the current exercise in imagination was in response to the question: "What's the best pussy you ever had?"

The stories were rich. There was a Japanese geisha girl in World War II, a white schoolteacher outside Lancaster, Pennsylvania, a sister in Memphis whose legs put Harlow's to shame. Somebody invented a Creole woman who was two hundred fifty pounds of butter fat, but had magic hands and a love canal that did the Charleston. The story about Josephine Baker in the silk-sheeted bed of a Paris penthouse was hooted down: "Nigger, you lying. You ain't fucked no Josephine Baker."

It was Eddie Robinson who told that tale, "Little Pro," they called him, who, in spite of his size, could drive a golf ball three hundred yards. "If I'm lying, I'm flying," Little Pro said, and began to describe the birthmark on the inside of Josephine's left thigh.

Yes, there were some stories told that afternoon, and so much laughing that Miles had to keep wiping tears from his eyes. If he were there now, he'd have a tale to match them. He'd say the best pussy he ever had was in a place called Kingston where he'd met a scarred-backed woman with sad eyes and perfect breasts. They'd done it in a cluttered room of a green two-family house, down the hall from the locked door of an idiot. When her love poured down, she whistled in two part harmony.

That was the essence of it. That was all that needed to be kept.

He wondered how the guys were doing. It would be nice to get together, to stick it in the ground, know the joy of fierce, friendly competition. It seemed a long time ago, in another country.

He was headed downtown, toward the river and the heart of the black community, past a small grocery, a cleaner's, the gaping door to an empty pool hall's dark. Most of the storefronts were deserted; some housed churches or poverty programs. One, huddled on a slanted corner, sold candy and soft drinks, dream cards, the *Daily News*. Old people thinner than Saturday's edition leaned from windows, sat on stoops in an indifferent morning sun. Children exploded from doorways, played tag and catch. There weren't a lot of young men. He wondered where they were, what they were doing. Maybe Vietnam, a war he was happy to be missing.

On the sidewalk, young girls jumped Double Dutch. Straight ahead, below him, the river brooded, broad, like smoked glass, the bridge bright orange above it, and at the bottom of the hill a railing. To his left, brick and lawnless, squatted the low-rise housing project where his cousin lived. He watched the bridge all ugly in the sunlight. The mood left by the memory of his pals was fading, replaced by restlessness. He made a U-turn, went back up Kingston's hill toward the golf course. Not sure how long he'd be staying with his cousin, he'd gone two days earlier to sign on as a caddy at the country club. That would provide him with extra pocket money, and the chance to play golf on a decent track. Today was Monday; the course was closed to members. It was the one day that the caddies, most of whom were black, could play.

Golf courses are, for the most part, beautiful places, and this one was exceptionally lovely. The fairways, lush and manicured, spoke of the soothing patterns one found flying over farmland in America's fertile heart. The difference was that the farms were plain, like the name of the region they lived in; golf courses were dressed for Saturday night.

Here, owning one of the hills, was the clubhouse, a sprawling, squinting-white Victorian; fairways fell away from its flower-banked front door. The flowers were white and red and yellow, the grass an emerald, cut and polished by hand. Pools of water glistened next to sand traps that winked with pleasing shapes: amoebas, cat paws, a sleeping white man's palm. Trees lined the fairways: birch, oak and maple, a profusion of dogwood at the fifth hole, rows of lovely evergreens, some planted for division, while others marked the edge of woods the course was carved from.

Already, Miles felt better. He parked the car, got his golf clubs from the trunk, changed into his spiked shoes. Two black men stood like rare cranes on the practice putting green, repeating pendulum strokes that rolled white balls toward purple, knee-high flags. One looked up, and Miles waved and asked by pointing if he wanted to play, but the man shook his head. That was no problem. Golf was one of the few games you could play by yourself.

He dropped his bag on the first tee box, did a couple of knee bends, stretched, then pulled his driver from the bag, teed up a Titleist, took a practice swing. Then he set up above the ball.

At that moment, the world had fallen away, or more accurately, been reduced to the white ball on the thin red tee. At impact he felt the shock in his wrist and hands, the almost erotic feeling of a solid hit. He stayed down through the swing, came up and under to see the ball arcing away, soaring toward blue sky and sunshine. One of the men on the practice green shouted something complimentary, and Miles waved, picked up his bag, and started walking, feeling glad to be alive.

He played two holes alone; then, as he approached the third tee box, a man halfway down the fairway beckoned him. As Miles got closer, he saw that the man was tall, maybe fifty, skin the color of ripe plums. Perhaps he'd some Indian in him; his long hair, streaked with gray, was pulled into a ponytail.

"Mind if I join you?" Miles asked.

"Please do," the man said. "You new around here?"

He held his head in a way that made Miles think he was trying to smell him. He dismissed the unsettling notion, said, "Rolled in a few days ago. Staying with my cousin, Melvina Turner. You know her?"

"Sure do. And her husband, Jesse."

Miles looked at the man's golf shoes. They were black-and-white, top-of-the-line Footjoys, at least a hundred dollars in the stores. He'd cut holes where his little toes were. White socks showed through. Miles understood about bad feet. Bad feet could change your outlook on life; bad feet were nothing to play with. Still, it seemed a shame to cut up a pair of Footjoys that way.

"Where you from?" the man asked.

"Miami, originally. New York City of late."

"Staying with us long?"

"Haven't made up my mind yet. What you recommend?"

"It's a nice place," the man said, "if you don't need much excitement."

"What folks do in the winter?"

"Some of the fellas go down your way, to Florida. Others stay here. You can always get some kind of work if you want it. By the way, my name's Bradley Douglas. But everybody calls me Junkman." He reached a hand out.

"Miles Jackson."

The hand was large; the shake strong, but not meant to intimidate. Miles liked that. A handshake could tell you a lot about a man. "What do you do in the winter?"

"I run a junkyard."

"How come I should have known that?"

Junkman smiled. "Your putt."

Miles rimmed out the twelve-footer, tapped in. They headed for the next hole.

"So you've lived around here all your life?"

"All except for twenty-five years," Junkman said.

"Where were you for those? Military?"

"Prison."

"Prison?"

"Just got out." Junkman nodded. "It's where I learned to play golf."

"In prison?"

"They put me to work in the gym. Guard was a golf nut. At night he hung exercise mats on the wall and hit balls at 'em off a piece of artificial turf. Asked me if I wanted to try, showed me how to set up, and before long that's how I was passing the time, just as hooked as he was. This game'll do it to you. Wish I had a dollar for every ball I hit. Buy me a new pair of feet."

"I hear that," Miles said. "What you do all that time for? If," he apologized, "you don't mind saying."

"They claimed I raped a girl. And resisted arrest. And killed a policeman."

" . . . They claimed . . . But you didn't?"

"The cops came in on me in the bathroom while I was taking a shower. They didn't say nothing, just started beating me. I struggled and one of them slipped and hit his head on the toilet. He was white. Both of them were. It was an accident. And I didn't do the rape."

"The girl said you did?"

"Her mama. Girl didn't say nothing. Got sent away before I went to trial. When I got out I went to see her daddy. He said he didn't know where she was, hadn't heard from her since she got out the crazy house. I think he did know, but wouldn't tell me."

"She went crazy?"

"That's what he said. So I told him if by some chance he did hear from her, give her a message. Tell her I loved her."

"You *loved* her?"

"That's right. Still do."

Not concentrating, Miles hooked his ball into the pond that protected the front of the green.

"Too much right hand," Junkman noted. "Not hardly enough shoulder turn. The drop area is over there."

Miles played his shot, walked with Junkman to his ball. "How'd you keep from getting bitter? All that time for something you didn't do, for an accident. I'd be bitter."

"Oh, I tried to be," Junkman said. "But every time I did I kept figuring things work out for the best. So I stopped."

"Hm . . . You know Carla March?"

Junkman nodded. "I used to love her, too."

"Damn," Miles laughed. "You fall in love with all the girls in Kingston?"

"No. Just her, when I was a kid. Then Lucinda, the one they said I raped. Ain't never loved no woman but them."

"Well, I just had a weird experience," and Miles told about the birds.

Junkman's eyebrows rose in interest, but he didn't seem surprised. "Didn't have to be what she thought. I seen birds do that lots of times. Something spooks 'em and they take off, look like more of 'em than there are."

"It was weird, though."

"I can imagine."

They crossed the bridge to the next hole; a black frog slept in the swirling water. The hole was a gentle dogleg left that rolled serenely to an elevated green four hundred yards away. Trees guarded the left side of the fairway; a huge, forbidding sandtrap glinted on the right.

Miles said, "So you were around for Max, and the house burning down, and all of that?"

"I was here."

"What do you make of it?"

Junkman seemed to think about it. "It was unfortunate."

"What's wrong with her? Did something happen?"

"Carla? She's sad. Been sad most of her life."

They'd reached Miles's drive; he took out a five iron, sent the ball flag high, twenty feet to the right of the flag.

"Good shot," Junkman said.

"Thanks. You know why she's sad?"

"Can't rightly say. Some people born like that. Or something happens early on what shapes 'em."

Junkman, who'd hit his drive fifteen yards past Miles's, stood absolutely still above the ball and drilled a seven iron.

"That's right at it," Miles said, and Junkman grunted, bent to retrieve his bag. They headed for the green.

"Which one was it for her?"

"Pardon me?"

"Carla," Miles said. "She born that way or something happen?"

"Don't know. First time I seen her she was sad. Eleven years old. But I don't know how she was before that."

On the green, Miles lined up his birdie putt, left the twenty-footer fourteen inches short. Disgust on his face, he said, "Don't you hate not to get a birdie putt to the cup?"

"Makes me want to bite rock," Junkman said. Easily, he stroked his putt into the heart of the hole.

"Good three," Miles said. "So you never got a chance to ask Carla what made her sad?"

"No," Junkman said, "I didn't. Where'd you learn to play golf?"

Miles paused. Was the conversation being changed?

"In Miami. Palmetto Country Club."

"You got a good swing."

"Thanks."

"Well, I got to cut you loose now, give these feet a rest. If you plan to work here steady, we'll meet again. I'm always here caddying on the weekends."

Miles said he hoped so, and shook his hand. Junkman cut across the eighth fairway toward the clubhouse on the hill. When he turned to wave, Miles was still standing near the green-side bunker, watching.

"You know a man named Junkman Douglas?" Miles asked.

"Junkman?" Melvina said. "How you know about him?"

They were in the kitchen, Miles at the table while his cousin cooked.

"I met him on the golf course."

"I heard he was out of prison," Melvina said. "Is it true he's talking?"

"He talked to me."

"You know he used to didn't," Melvina said. "He'd sing, but he wouldn't talk."

"Really?"

"Not a mumbling word. Had these business cards made up on what was wrote he wasn't talking out of respect for his daddy. His daddy was a mute got lynched back in . . . Let's see, I'd just come out the high school, so it must have been nineteen twenty-four, around the time me and Jesse commenced to going together. Junkman wasn't no more than nine or ten. Carried on something awful at the funeral, screaming he'd murder every white man he laid his hands on. That was just talk. Menfolks round here took matters in they own hands and made whites pay for what they done, but if Junkman's daddy looking to Junkman to revenge him, he in the right place for long time waiting."

"Black folks avenged his father? How?"

"Set fire to an apple orchard. Burned *it*, barn, wagons, whatever in the way of fire went *that* night. County placed Junkman with a family over in Tillson. When he got grown he moved back to Kingston, and it was right after that he clammed up. Next time anybody paid mind to him he was dancing at the fire what burned the March house up, carrying on like he African or something. For a while folks thought he set the fire, though nobody could figure out for what."

"His dancing wasn't no stranger than Rufus singing," Jesse called from the living room. "Singing ain't what most folks do when their house burns up."

"I thought you was reading the paper."

"I am."

Melvina rolled her eyes. "Anyway," she said to Miles, "no sooner had Junkman done all that dancing than he commenced to prancing up and down Broadway, singing and wearing fancy shoes. Lord, he had some *splenderifous* shoes. Nobody ever did find out what all that parading was about, or, for that matter, what he was singing. Next thing you know he done killed a policeman and raped that gal. Lucinda was her name. Not all that pretty, but smart as a whip."

"Junkman says he didn't kill that cop. And that he didn't rape that girl."

Melvina grunted.

"He said he loved her."

"*Loved* her?"

"He used to love Carla, but then he loved Lucinda."

"Well, if that don't beat the band," Melvina said. "He loved that crazy woman?"

"He said she was in an asylum."

"I wasn't talking 'bout Lucinda. I meant that March gal."

"Carla? She don't seem crazy. High-strung. And maybe hurting. But she don't seem crazy."

Melvina thrust toward him like a threat. "You went round there?"

Miles nodded.

"What's it like inside?"

"A house," he said.

"Did it smell funny? Did you feel the devil? Would have been cool, like a breeze up around your knees."

"Mel— It was a house."

"You look in her eye?"

He hesitated. "As a matter of fact, I did."

"And you didn't see nothing?"

"What do you mean?" Miles asked.

As if the memory were in pieces she had to rearrange, Melvina shook her head, two short, violent movements. "The day they buried her daddy," she said, "Rufus was his name, fine-looking man till he decided to die, then he just wasted away. . . . Anyway, Helen Moncrief, who was a personal friend of mine, went up to Meridian—that was Rufus's wife—in the back of the church. She went to say if there was anything Meridian needed, it was hers. Even though all the years Max was making them that money she never got invited to their house, never got a card at Christmas, Helen swallowed that. She wasn't going to let a little stumbling block keep her out of heaven."

Melvina swiveled to stir a pot, lifted the wooden spoon to her lips, added black pepper to the chicken. Then she stood absolutely still, head held as if she searched for the source of some faint and distant sound.

"You all right?" Miles asked.

"Yeah. Just a quick dizzy. It's gone now."

"Why don't you sit a minute?"

"I'm fine now. You know," she said, "it's been a long time since I told this story. I used to tell it all the time." She sighed. "Anyway, I'm in the line, too, waiting to pay my respects, about three or four people back. Helen's standing there talking to Meridian, and she looks at that March gal's face. . . . "

There'd been a shield around Carla; Helen could feel its electric pulsing. Startled by all that energy, she'd reflexively placed a hand over her belly before making the mistake of looking into Carla's eyes. What she saw was a rage so deep it shook her, a look thick with the inexplicable wish that the woman before her would die.

What did I do to her? Helen thought.

She never forgot that look, would take its memory to her grave, for she was convinced its venom had infected her ovaries and fused the horror in her womb. Hers was the only recorded birth of Siamese twins in Ulster County. The babies, both girls (whose feeble movements Helen insisted were efforts to break apart), lived four days, long enough to leave their mother haunted by dreams of shit-colored infants joined at the head. The experience had permanently scarred Helen, and although she was only thirty-five and had years of childbearing to look forward to, she'd leaped at the doctor's suggestion to tie her tubes.

"Three years after that, hair started growing on her face, and she moved to California. She wrote a couple of times, then I didn't hear from her no more. That March gal had put it to her."

"That's nonsense," Jesse called. "Them twins wasn't nothing but bad luck reminding folks it's still around. That's twenty-some years ago. Folks done even stopped talking about it."

"I'm a woman," Melvina said to Miles, "and I'm telling you what I know."

"It was probably all that starch she ate." A small man with laughing eyes, brown as a berry, Jesse came into the kitchen. "Me and that woman's husband used to hunt together. Talk about somebody who could shoot straight. I saw him nip half a worm out a bird's mouth from twenty-five paces. Didn't even aim. Just pointed that twenty-two and *bam*, half a worm laying on the ground, bird quick up and ate the other, lest he lose it too."

"Sure," Melvina said. "And tomorrow's Thursday," and Jesse looked at her and grinned, and turned to Miles.

"Well, her husband told me Helen got to eating starch when she was pregnant, went through a case of Argo like it was Chattanooga cherry wine. At the time he didn't think it done nothing but make her mouth turn white. But when them babies was born he figured it was starch made 'em stick together."

"Starch ain't had nothing to do with it," Melvina said. "She didn't eat none the first five times she got pregnant. Them babies was all right."

"Don't pay him no mind," Melvina said. "Come eat your supper."

"Now that's something you can do," Jesse said. "You's a first-rate pot shaker, a world-class grit maker. But you can't tell a tale from a tick."

"You eating, Mr. Gentlemans, or you going to stand there insulting me?"

"No sir," Jesse said, pulling a chair from the table. "Don't know a fact from a factory." He sat down, grinning. "But good God, you sho can cook. Now hurry up and feed me. I'm dizzy."

After dinner, Miles stood in his room at the window. Outside in the early evening, a group of black boys played a full-court game of basketball. As he watched the ebb and flow on the asphalt, he wondered what, by the age of eleven, had happened to make Carla sad, and where the rage came from that Helen swore by. He didn't believe the story that her look caused Siamese twins, but something in him accepted rage in the young girl's eyes.

He turned away from the window, noting the sharp edge of his restlessness. Usually golf and dinner combined for a feeling of peace and a good night's sleep. But not today. He roamed the room for something to read. There was only a Bible, a pocket-sized edition of the New Testament. Sighing, he lay on the bed, hands laced behind his head, studying the ceiling. When he understood that he was annoyed with himself, he admitted the source of it: Carla—he wanted to see her. Despite his resolve, he'd apparently exposed enough of himself for her to get a hook in. He thought of her response in bed, imagined that as he remembered, she, halfway across town, at the top of the hill she lived on, was thinking of him, sending signals pitched to his ears only.

Yes, it was stupid, but so was so much of everything, so was the ease with which hearts were smashed, lives broken, snipers mangling a Texas afternoon, a quarter of a century spent for crimes you didn't commit. If you didn't take what you wanted for as long as you were able, you were, simply, a fool. Everybody else did.

He stopped creating his defense. What did he want? Why did he want it? Why so hot to know what had happened, assuming something had, to make Carla live the way she did? So what if a bearded woman who'd moved to California had once found rage in her eyes. So what if she was sad. The world was full of sad people, probably most for reasons that didn't deserve exploring. What did it matter?

"Nothing," he said. "It don't matter nothing."

He got up, looked at the telephone on the table near the window. Then he walked into the living room where his cousins watched TV.

"You got a telephone book, Mel?"

"In the kitchen. On the shelf next to the door."

When the phone rang Carla was deep in a fantasy of feeling safe in the arms of a man who could have been a dancer. They were lying on a beach in Cuba; the sun was setting above a turquoise sea, lengthening a palm tree's shadow across the sand. The sand was snow white, the sun was fire.

The ringing startled her. The phone seldom rang; Willis, her brother, had called a month ago from Okinawa, and if it were he, it meant, God forbid, bad news. Anxiously, she picked up the receiver. When Miles said "Hello," she found herself unable to react.

"How you feeling?" he asked.

She didn't know. It was her dimly grasped conviction that it took her longer than other people to know what she felt. "Fine."

"What you do the rest of the day?"

"Took a bath, read. Me and Phoenix just ate. You?"

"Went over to the golf course. Played a few holes."

Inexplicably, she looked behind her. "Nice day for it."

"I ran into somebody who knows you."

"On a golf course?"

"Yeah, a man named Junkman Douglas."

"Oh. I heard he was out of prison."

"Yup."

Carla didn't say anything.

"Did you know him?"

"I knew *of* him. He was around."

"So you know what he went to prison for."

She said, flatly, "Nothing too serious. Just rape and killing a policeman."

"He told me the policeman was an accident, and that he didn't do the rape."

"Well, neither the policeman nor Lucinda is around to tell the story."

"You think he's guilty?" Miles asked.

"The jury did. To tell the truth, I don't much care. Whatever happened got Lucinda sent away."

"You were close to her?"

"Lucinda was . . . my friend. Something happened. . . . She went away."

"Something might have happened," Miles said, "but Junkman said it wasn't rape."

"What would you expect him to say?"

"I don't know. But there's no reason to lie. He's already paid for it. They can't put him in jail again."

"If you'd raped somebody, would you come out of jail and admit it?"

Miles thought about it. "No, I guess not."

"Well, then."

"He said he loved Lucinda."

"He had a strange way of showing it."

"He said he used to love you, too."

"Yeah," Carla said drily, "I know. He wrote me once to tell me."

"He said he used to love you, but then he loved Lucinda, and he's never loved anyone else. That don't sound like a man who's a rapist."

"Neither does it sound like one with good sense. Everybody knew Junkman wasn't all there. His daddy wasn't all there."

"I had a nice day with you," Miles said.

He had that way of changing course in midstream. Did he do it deliberately? Was he trying to keep her off balance?

"Really? Have you forgotten what happened?"

"I haven't forgotten a thing. I just remember some more than others. What are you doing? I want to see you."

"Oh? Why?"

"The truth?"

"That would be preferable."

"*Preferable?*"

"Yes, preferable. Do you need me to tell you what it means?"

"No. I need you to see me."

"Why?"

"How about, I'm not so sure?"

"Not good."

He laughed. "How about, I like you?"

"You still haven't told me why."

"It's the way you whistle."

"The way I *what?*"

"The way," Miles said, as if he were talking of the shades in her living room, "the way you whistle when your love comes down."

Mouth open, she reached for a wall; it wasn't there. "I don't *believe* you."

"Why not?"

"You're little, but Lord, you got a lot of nerve."

"Little?"

"You know what I mean."

"I know I want to see you. Can I?"

"Tomorrow."

"I want to see you now."

Part of her tasted the pleasure of his confession, part wondered why he couldn't be like everybody else and just leave. Part was happy that he wasn't. She sensed there were too many parts to it. She'd go slow, be in control.

"Tomorrow," she said.

He hid his disappointment. "Can you get someone to sit for Phoenix?"

"Yes."

"Okay. I'll pick you up at ten."

"Make it eleven."

"Okay."

She'd turned the tables on him, heard it in his voice. "What'll we do?" she asked.

"What would you like to do?"

"I don't know. Go for a ride?"

"Then we'll do that."

"A ride," Carla said brightly. "The man's going to take me for a ride."

She waited expectantly for his reply, wanting to prolong the pleasure, but apparently, he'd lost his mood for joking, for he let her comment slide. She'd blown it. She should have said, "Okay, come on over," and she'd have made tea and they'd have sat and talked and the evening wouldn't have been so empty. She could still say it, but she didn't want him to know she needed so much time to figure what she felt.

She said, "I'll see you at eleven."

Carla got Mrs. Sharp, who lived across the street, to stay with Phoenix. Mrs. Sharp had sat for Willis and Phoenix when they were small, and when Carla went to work in the library, and she'd kept them for the week in 1952 when the infection Carla picked up from a man whose face she couldn't remember had sent her to the hospital. The hospital staff treated her with a barely concealed scorn, and one nurse said that if she continued to be promiscuous she'd find herself unable to have more babies. Carla told her to go fuck herself, and refused to blink or cry out when the nurse, changing the intravenous needle, deliberately missed the vein.

It was the day after he'd come to take her fishing, little more than twenty-four hours since birds leaped into the sky. She'd come home, her infant heart in full bloom. She'd gone to bed with him a day after he'd appeared at her doorstep wearing a white shirt that bared his coal-black throat. He'd brought the feeling that her life was threatened.

Here, in the car with him, there was nothing threatening. He asked what she watched on television; she said she didn't own one. She used to, but there wasn't anything but foolishness on it, and she'd rather read. As they crossed the city's limits, the road wound past shade trees and neat frame houses. The houses were blue or brown or yellow, and he wanted to know how she'd gotten into reading. She said while she worked at the library. All those books were around, and she figured she'd find out what was in them.

"It was in books I discovered I wasn't alone, that others feel what I do."

"Really? What do you feel?"

She looked away. "It's complicated."

"Okay, what *do* you want to talk about?"

"Tell me about Pittsburgh."

He laughed. "You asked me that before. Why do you want to know about Pittsburgh?"

"You lived there."

"That's fair enough." He said parts were colored with smoke from the steel mills that had made the city famous, part was slum, but there were areas of beauty. He'd lived in a sixteenth-floor apartment, a bedroom that overlooked the Monongahela; there were mountains to the east. In summer the river looked clean from the window. There were lots of boats.

"What did you do there?"

"Work? I was a cook in a hotel."

"How'd you learn to be a cook?"

"In Florida. Guy I caddied for was retired, a big-time banker, lived on a yacht half as long as your block. *The Phoenix*. I was his handyman, a gofer, till I started hanging around his chef, little Italian guy must have been a hundred years old. He saw I was interested and taught me what he knew. When he died, I took over. Stayed for ten years, till I met my wife. We cruised to Bermuda in . . . let's see, September nineteen fifty . . . nine. I saw her on the beach with a group of girlfriends. She liked foreign films."

"Foreign films?"

"Private joke. We were different. I liked sports, she liked French and Italian films. I tried to be what she wanted, more of a gentleman, you know? Cultured. But it wasn't who I was. I loved her and I tried, but it didn't work. She wasn't happy. And she couldn't tell me. Not that I didn't know. You can't be with someone and not know if they're happy."

"So what happened?"

"I came home when I wasn't supposed to and found a man in my bed."

He waved away her murmur of concern. "It's not even a good

story. Been told too many times. Lord knows I ain't the first it's happened to."

"Maybe not. But you don't feel that when it's happening."

"No, you don't. What I felt— I ain't never been violent, didn't think it was in me. But I wanted to kill them both. Instead, I packed and left. We did the divorce thing through the mail."

They were passing through a small town that disappeared in two blinkings of an eye: a hardware store, a church topped by its penetrating steeple. Then the road opened into farmland strewn with grazing cattle, a red barn, a white house set far back from the road. Above this, cirrus clouds like smiles in a giant's flat, blue face.

"Look at the cows," Miles said. "Mooo."

"And you're still not over it."

"My ex? I'm beginning to think it's something you never get over. The best you can do is find a place to put it." He grinned. "Maybe that's why I'm so hot to see the Grand Canyon. Maybe I know that's a hole big enough to put it in."

"What was her name?"

"Victoria."

"What attracted you to her?"

"She was fine. That was the first thing. Skin like a Hershey bar. Smooth, the same color. Everything where it should be, just enough. And her hands! You should have seen her hands. She could have modeled if—"

"I get the picture."

"And she was self-sufficient. I was looking for a woman who knew how to take care of herself. Then, when I found one, I went through all these changes trying to make her need me."

He slowed for the curve, the small covered bridge over a stream of twisting water. In the brush that lined the bank Carla caught a glimpse of refuse, a dark abandoned article of clothing, a coat, perhaps; something that glinted like a bottle.

"You still love her?"

"Love her?" He seemed genuinely surprised. "Hell, no."

"You sound like you do."

"I thought I was answering your question."

"I asked you about Pittsburgh."

"She was part of Pittsburgh. And you did ask me about her."

"I asked what attracted you. Not for a dissertation."

"A disser-what?"

She said, "You're very young, aren't you?"

"What's that supposed to mean?"

"Exactly what it says."

"It sounds like an accusation."

"No. *Ob*-servation."

"I get it." He nodded. "I'm talking too much about myself. Enough about me. Tell me about you."

She shook her head. "What you see is what you get."

"Seriously, why aren't you married? Why you live all by yourself? With your son," he added, smiling. "Tell me about your friend, Lucinda."

"Some other time," she said, and turned to the window at her right.

Farmland flowed past; in the middle of a fallow field a man hunched on a dark green tractor. Miles hummed a fragment of a blues song. She didn't know the song's name, but she understood its meaning. He'd lost his wife, his family, and he longed to have it back. He still loved the woman he'd lived with above the Monongahela. She stared at the green fields swollen in the sunlight; a truck chock full of migrant workers spewed dust through head-high corn. There were books in the library that no one ever borrowed, and in them she'd read that slaves once worked this land. Nobody thought of the North when they thought of slavery. They thought of Mississippi and Georgia, fields of cotton, dark heads bowed above the soil. But there'd been slaves here, too. She'd spent weeks trying to discover if they, like those in the South, had suffered the smashing of their families, and if being sold down the river had a northeastern equivalent. Now she tried to imagine this stretch of earth thick with toiling bodies, head rags of red and blue and yellow, but the image wouldn't come. When she was little, her mother's grandmother had come to visit. Her name was Penelope, and she'd been born a slave. Her mother said that when Penelope was younger, she could tell the future, but age had stolen her gift. Now she lived in a confused, shadow-infested space, huddled between past and present, death the only thing of interest in her future. In her own lifetime Carla had sat on the lap of a woman who'd been a slave. She felt a personal connection. It wasn't all that long ago.

They went through New Paltz, a town sprawled lazily at the feet of towering mountains. To her right was the college Lucinda had attended, low-slung sandstone buildings, lawns like green chests crisscrossed by ribbons of pavement. Lucinda, hair falling gloriously down her back, Lucinda pulling Carla into her arms. "*Grief is like that sometimes,*" Lucinda said, "*so big you can't even cry it. Your father won't die. Max will come back for you. Our kids will grow up together.*"

They'd reached the border of the town. Past a lumberyard, untamed tree and rock and brush reclaimed the land. She was about to break the silence with a question about golf when Miles said, "You haven't said a word for five miles. Did I do something to make this happen?"

"Silence makes you uncomfortable?"

"*This* one does."

"No," she said, "nothing's happened."

" 'You can't be with someone and not know—' "

"Okay. It's the way you carry on about your ex."

"I made you jealous?"

"As a matter of fact, you did. Are you satisfied now?"

He said gravely, "I humbly beg your pardon."

"Don't make fun of me."

"I'm not." He rolled down his window, held his hand out, palm up. "See? In my hand? Ex-wife. Watch. You watching? Woosh." And he threw her out the window.

Carla smiled. He was silly, but a nice silly. "Thank you."

"You're welcome. And thank you."

"For what?"

"For telling me what you feel."

Then, in that way he had of changing conversations, "Hey, let's have lunch in New York City."

"New York?"

"Yeah."

"I've never been to New York."

"So?"

"I told Mrs. Sharp I'd be back this afternoon."

"We're talking about another few hours. We're only ninety minutes away. Call her. Come on, let's do it."

"I'm not dressed right." Blue jeans, sneakers, a sweatshirt cut off at the shoulders.

"Dressed? You look good enough to eat."

He might have been asking her to go to the moon. All those miles between her and Phoenix, and what would happen to him if she didn't return? Miles had a boyish expression on his face, a kind of six-year-old pleading that she remembered from Willis when he was dying for something she didn't plan to give. She took a deep breath and discovered she was tired of being frightened. It wasn't forever.

"I'll have to call," she said, and Miles whooped and did a wild U-turn that had her holding to the seat. They found a public phone; Mrs. Sharp said everything was fine, and they took off down the Thruway to New Jersey, the blue Buick humming through the sunlight, Miles buoyant, she infected by his mood. He was off on a nonstop talking jag, saying how fine it was to do things on the spur of the moment, just like rich white folks. She laughed and shook her head, looked out the window. To her right a prison marred the countryside with barbed-wire fences; a guard stood motionless atop a tower. He said she looked good enough to eat. Was he being coy; was he into double meanings? The few black men she'd been with had frowned when she'd asked for that, as if she'd invited them to stick their faces into a toilet. She looked at the speedometer, saw the red needle hovering at seventy. "Slow down," she said to him, and to herself, "You'll be all right."

As they approached the New York skyline from the Palisades Parkway, she remembered what Max had said about the city: that it had so much energy and was filled with sin. Rolling across the

George Washington Bridge into Manhattan, she sensed only the energy. She was amazed at the heights of buildings; four of the larger ones, from whose tops one might see forever, marched from the bridge like white giants toward an eastern rendezvous. Each of these stood majestically by itself, but the surrounding ones were so close together she imagined one sprawling structure. The spaces buildings left were fought for by cars and people. Black and brown and white people congested sidewalks, leaned from windows; groups of men dotted the space at curbsides, played checkers, dominoes.

If what she'd read was true, you could discover most of the world in this city. Immigrants had come from all over, persevered and prospered. You could turn a corner in New York and hear nothing but Chinese spoken, turn another and encounter Greek. She looked for a Chinese person, but didn't see one.

"Is this Harlem?"

He'd made a right turn onto a street whose sign said Amsterdam Avenue.

"Washington Heights. We're headed toward Harlem."

"It's huge. So many people."

"People be doing some serious you know what," he said. "You hungry?"

"I could eat."

To her left was a park, length of defiant grass and trees behind a head-high iron gate, benches whose slatted seats peeled green. The park was jammed: children, dogs, mothers at the helms of strollers. She rolled the window down and sounds surged in: cars, horns, trucks, voices, all of it set to music. Did everybody have a radio in New York, and was the custom to play yours as loud as you could? On a corner, a blind man tapped a white cane as he waited to be told the light had changed. Next to him, oblivious to passersby, a middle-aged couple, the woman wearing a red scarf at her throat, necked flagrantly in the sun.

They drove until nearly everyone was black. Miles said, "This is Harlem, 125th Street. Capital of the Afro-American world."

It wasn't what she'd expected a capital to look like. There were no gardens, no monuments, just the dark buildings, the bright colors, greens and yellows at the fronts of stores, fruit stands, men hawking wares on sidewalks. Pedestrians, rushing as if they were late for things important, drove wedges through multitudes of children. On a corner a tall black man gestured angrily from a stage of milk crates. The crowd that gathered was curiously still, even though the man, who wore horn-rimmed glasses, had worked himself into a frenzy. Three policeman stood away from the group, not looking at the speaker.

Miles parked the car in front of a restaurant named Mabel's. Inside, the room was sparsely populated, the smells familiar: chicken, something green, sweet apples, corn bread. They ate, or at least he did. She was too busy taking it all in—a man in a white suit, a gold mine on his fingers, sat across from a woman whose beauty ought to have driven him to his knees. A lean young man with a goatee read at a table in the back, legs crossed, blue-sneakered foot a pendulum. A woman with a shopping cart of laundry, a minister whose white collar seemed painted on his throat. Outside, she heard the blaring of a siren, and when she turned, she saw beyond the window an old man turn inquiringly in the street. He was tall, with hair so white it made his skin seem blue.

She twisted back to Miles. Where did everybody work? How many schools did it take to educate the children? Why was the man on the milk crate so angry? And Miles answered what he could, shrugged at what he couldn't.

They went to the car, she not remembering what kind of food she'd picked at. The angry man was still on the corner; the crowd had thinned. They drove beneath a train thundering on a trestle. Instinctively, she ducked until the structure was behind her.

"This is the West Side Highway," Miles said. "Further up, it's called the Henry Hudson."

The road was tree-lined; on their right sprawled the Hudson River. It was strange to think that this was the same river that passed by Kingston. Scattered across the shining water, white boats blinked. Above them, like a backdrop, cliffs glowed purple in the sun; at their top was an amusement park.

Miles pointed to the city. That was the Empire State Building,

67

he said, the tallest in the world, and there the Pan Am building,
looking close enough to jump to from its neighbors.

He drove to the end of the island so she could see the Statue
of Liberty, which was green. They circled the tip of Manhattan
and went up the East side of the island a little distance. Tires sang
as they crossed the Brooklyn Bridge, and then they were spilling
into a borough whose sign announced it was a nice place to visit
and a better place to live. Beyond the traffic light, the avenue grew
wide, like the pictures she'd seen of Paris boulevards. There were
lots of people, but still it wasn't as crowded as Manhattan.

Miles went up some streets, down others, and suddenly she
was surprised again. The huge buildings and bustle seemed mag-
ically replaced by a quiet neighborhood thick with trees and well-
kept rows of brownstones. Miles stopped the car before a
building.

"I used to live here."

"You did?"

"On the top floor."

She looked at the building; the door was red. Sun filtered
through the trees and beat against it. Black iron gates defended
the windows, and she could see into a room that had bookshelves,
a white ceiling so high she'd have to use a broom to touch it. She
said it was pretty. "Couldn't you always hear your neighbors?"

"Not unless they wanted you to." He gestured to his left. "A
few blocks over that way is Pratt Institute. Leading art school in
the world."

"Where's Coney Island?"

He pointed. "Over there."

"Can we go?"

He laughed. "You want to go to an amusement park?"

"Is all of it an amusement park? Isn't there some beach you
can just sit on?"

"Yes."

"That's what I want to see."

"Can I ask you why?"

She said, "I've never seen the ocean."

"Really? Are you familiar with the custom?"

"What custom?"

"An old black one. Whoever shows you the ocean for the first time can't be refused. You have to give him what he asks for."

"You made that up."

"No," he said. "I didn't. And you've been warned."

Now they rolled through streets whose buildings were smaller, and for blocks at a time stood houses unconnected to one another. These had small back yards with awnings, hammocks, gardens defined by care. Then another stretch of buildings, less imposing, and they went up a hill and burst onto a highway, on the other side of which lay water.

No, Miles said, that wasn't the ocean. This wasn't nothing compared to the ocean.

Still, it was pretty, a small ribbon of grass and concrete between the water and the highway, a contingent of bicycle riders, a couple holding hands.

They went around a curve and Miles pointed to the muscular silver structure that spanned the water, joined the land on either side. "That's the Verrazano Narrows Bridge. Over there is Staten Island. New Jersey's on the other side of that."

She said, "Oh," wondering how it was possible to build a bridge that high, that long. There was so much she didn't know, despite the reading, a whole world that ran efficiently without her knowledge or participation, without its knowing her. This thought preoccupied her for a while, and when she let it go, they were leaving the highway. Miles twisted down some streets, around corners, and suddenly, the ocean was before her.

It was vast. Photographs hadn't prepared her for its size. Miles retrieved a blanket from the trunk, and she stood on tiptoes, staring. She'd read that water covered three quarters of the earth. Now she believed it.

They held hands through a park whose ground was smooth stone blocks between which tufts of grass grew; old white men leaned above a chessboard beneath a sheltering tree. She imagined the floor of the park a chessboard, trees the giant pieces. When they reached the sand's edge, Miles stopped. "Take off your shoes."

The sand was warm, soft. They wound around sprawled bodies, black and white lying so close you'd have thought they were related or had overcome their history. To her right, she could see the ferris wheel, the roller coaster, guarding the beach like beasts risen from the water's depths to find land and humans to their liking. The water reached in a smooth thrust toward the pale blue, cloud-streaked sky. She looked behind her and found a city.

Now they were away from the crowds; here the beach was rocky. They walked to the water's edge. She stood, staring at the vastness.

"We'll go to New York on the weekends," Lucinda had said, *"sail to Paris."*

"We're facing east, now, right?"

"That's right. Turn a little to your left."

She pointed. "So France is out there?"

"A quarter turn to your right." He said, gently, "It's a long way, Carla."

"I know."

"You're not into French movies, are you?"

"No." She smiled. "Just food. And, once in a while, some fashion."

"You want to sit down?"

"Okay."

He spread the blanket. She drew her gaze back from the ocean to the shore, the sweep of gunmetal gulls, their pink claws arcing, the stiff walk of a bird whose name she didn't know. If Phoenix were here, the birds would leave. Out on the water, a black length against the sky, a fishing boat at anchor. The boat looked motionless, but the water moved at the land's edge like a tongue. She lay on her side, facing the water, Miles behind her; she reached and pulled his arm around her waist. If the sun were going down, it would almost be her fantasy; she'd only to plant palm trees and bleach the sand. She closed her eyes, listening to the sounds, bird cries whose absence she'd grown accustomed to, water lapping, what seemed a faint rumbling from the bowels of the earth. In a little while she moved, and they sat back to back, supporting each other while she gazed out at the water.

I did it, she thought, *came all the way to New York, and I'm fine.*

They spent an hour on the beach, then headed back to the car, went silently along the Belt Parkway, cut back through the city and up the West Side Highway. Soon the George Washington Bridge leaped into view. She liked the Verrazano better.

They curved off the bridge, sped along a jewel of a road, trees in the green flush of summer, grass trimmed as neatly as a lawn. Below, through the trees, she caught glimpses of the river, like diamonds in the light. The world, she decided, was a beautiful place.

Miles asked, "You all right?"

"I'm fine. Is this the way we came?"

"Yes."

"It looks different."

On the other side of the road, from the top of the hill they were at the foot of, a red sports car wove in and out of traffic.

She said, "This has been a good day."

Miles smiled. "It has."

Carla dozed, and when she opened her eyes, Miles was saying, "Well, here we are. Right back where we started."

"You coming in?"

"No, I don't think so. I'll go see what my cousin got in her pots."

"You can eat with me."

"Thanks, but she gets funny if she can't feed me. It's been a good day," he said. "I'll see you tomorrow."

"Okay."

She leaned to kiss him. "'Bye."

" 'Parting,' " he said, " 'is such sweet sorrow, that I shall say good night till it be morrow.' "

"*Romeo and Juliet.* How'd you know that?"

"If I told you, you'd get mad."

"Oh, *her.*"

"See?"

"Get out of here," she said.

"I'm gone."

When he'd pulled away from the curb, she'd stood waving, fingering the promise that they'd meet tomorrow, watching his taillights until they disappeared. In the almost dark above her yard, fireflies blinked, and she felt a faint stir of misgiving. Was she doing the right thing getting involved with him? What would happen when he left? What if he wouldn't leave and she had to make him? Something cool touched the back of her neck. She shook it off, savored the edge of defiance. She'd had a taste of the world; it was wide and beautiful. She'd gone into it and survived. All of that felt good. She'd hold to the feeling a little longer.

For the next three weeks they were together; even on the days Miles caddied at the golf course they'd spend evenings in each other's company. They went for a picnic in Van Saun Park. They'd taken Phoenix that time. Before they entered the park, Miles had cleared the area of birds. He'd told her what Junkman said, that it didn't have to be what she thought. She'd insisted in a tight, still voice, and he, feeling foolish, walked forward waving a white towel, shouting, "Yaah! Go away!"

After they ate, he listened to a ball game on his transistor radio. Phoenix slept. Carla read a little, but mostly she just lay and daydreamed and looked at her lover, his hands and feet, the body she'd so quickly grown accustomed to.

Twice Miles took her bowling, a sport for which she had no talent, establishing, he said, the North American record for gutter balls. The one time she'd rolled a strike, she'd screamed, raised arms in exultation, then ducked when surrounding bowlers cheered.

They went to dinner, got dressed up and dined in Kingston's best restaurant, The President's Room, at the Governor Clinton Hotel. They were the only black people there. She felt everyone was staring at them, but Miles said she was mistaken. It felt good to dress up; she liked the way she looked. She'd let her hair grow enough to pull it severely from her face, a small knot at the back, a style Miles said did great things for her cheekbones. She went shopping for three-inch heels. Her dress was black, fitted, 4 inches above the knee; he wanted to make love while she wore it. She said she'd let him, but he'd have to ask real nice.

They talked. He told her about golf, said it was the closest to life a game could come, how in order to play it well you needed patience, balance, a steady head. So much of it was mental; you had to be able to accept the inevitable mistakes and recover. You had to learn to wait. He took her to the driving range where she watched the effortlessness of his swing, how the red-striped ball soared when he struck it, something beautiful about its flight. She took a turn on the mat, found it was almost impossible to hit the ball, much less send it soaring. Laughing, they decided all her athletic talent was for bowling.

They talked about the war in Vietnam, the news coming out of Mississippi. When Kennedy was shot, Miles was on the fifth hole of a county golf course; she'd been at the library shelving books. Miles had been in Malcolm's presence, heard him speak, mourned when assassins cut him down. He'd gone to hear Martin Luther King at the March on Washington, shared the dream. Carla listened. She envied his experience of the world.

They made love everywhere, on the couch, in the kitchen, in the shower; she wore her diaphragm constantly, washed it daily. Once, on their way upstairs, he'd grabbed her waist as she reached the second step, lifted her skirt, growled at the discovery of no underwear beneath it. She stood giggling while he licked the backs of her thighs until her knees buckled, until she leaned forward, all the laughing gone now, and let him take her from behind.

Another time he warmed baby oil and rubbed her body down. When he'd washed away the oil with a warm, wet cloth, he spread her legs, spent the afternoon like a man who was starving. She couldn't walk when she stood up. He'd had to help her to the bathroom.

And through it all, the wondering. He was the only man she'd ever let into her bed, the only black man who'd made her come. When would he leave, and if he didn't, could she really make him go? She imagined Max returning, appearing at her door with a smile and a fistful of roses, and her saying, "Sorry, baby, I waited long as I could." She imagined neither Max nor Miles here, and herself grown old in a room of books her weakened eyes had difficulty reading, not even the small, fleeting comfort of random couplings now that her flesh was dry. Who'd be there except Phoenix, who'd fumble in the evening for her hand? Who would she kiss good morning when the first light came?

And Miles, sensing some struggle in her, was patient, playing it like the game he had such reverence for, treating it like the shot at hand, the lob over threatening water to a green flanked by yawning sand, making himself stay within the moment. He could see she was blossoming, a new light in her eyes, but she wouldn't talk about herself. Her self stayed in a room he wasn't allowed to enter. When he pointed this out, she said the door was open, and if he stood outside and listened, he'd find what he needed to know.

"I don't want the made-up version, I want the real deal."

"You're getting it."

"Why do I have to solve a puzzle?"

Her eyebrows raised as if the notion of a puzzle would never have occurred to her; then, magnificently, she shrugged. "It has nothing to do with puzzles."

"I'll ask Mrs. Sharp," he threatened. "She'll tell me. She likes me, you know."

"She might like you, but she won't tell you a thing. Being a man, you wouldn't understand it, but she's loyal."

"You're half-stepping. You're pulling that woman thing, making a mystery out of something ordinary just to try and keep me interested."

"Nice try." She smiled. "But you can't provoke me into nothing."

He stuck his tongue out. "Bet I can," he said.

He delighted in her strength, her stubbornness, a sometimes lightning wit, and he'd wonder if he had to fear the neediness he'd first encountered, or if here was a woman with whom he could take the risk of promising to spend his life. He'd tell himself to slow down, but things would be so sweet he'd think he didn't have to. Then her strangeness would surface; she'd get tired and anxious, distance herself with silence. Or she'd cling to him, or interrupt while he listened to a game or read the paper. "Do this for me," she'd say, or that, or "give me a hug." "Let me sit on your lap." And then he'd remember whom he'd promised the rest of his life to—himself—and that his journey called for a minimum of baggage. Weight was the key; he didn't have to keep everything he came across.

"Tell me about your family," she said. "Tell me about your growing up."

He didn't like to tell that story. But if he opened up to her about his past, maybe she'd tell him hers.

Both parents were dead. His father had been a waiter on the Silver Meteor, which ran the thousand miles from Miami to New York, and when his father died in the middle of a moonlit night, whistle moaning as the train knifed across the Georgia landscape, it marked the ending of family life as the fourteen-year-old Miles had known it. His mother spent half the insurance money on the funeral, an affair highlighted by six white horses pulling a silk-lined casket through Miami's streets at dawn. The horses were sleek, the ebony carriage gleaming, and when it turned a corner in the early morning gloom, the sun came out and lit the procession like a movie. Traffic stopped. Wings beating in the glistening air, birds hung, too mesmerized for flight; dogs stood at quivering attention. Residents who'd gotten up to witness the event gathered in bathrobes and slippers, holding mugs of coffee they were too open-mouthed to drink. When the carriage passed, they went inside to dress for the service, which was scheduled to begin at seven. The minister, who'd been to college, recited John Donne's "Death Be Not Proud," and the choir, dressed in burgundy robes, made everybody cry.

Later, folks agreed that if you couldn't have a funeral like Matt Jackson, there wasn't any sense in dying. When their own loved ones passed, they moved to imitate it, until they found how much it cost.

After Miles's mother watched them cover her husband in the ground, she went home to accept the consolation of her neighbors, undressed, and went to bed. Frightened, the children hovered at her side. Absentmindedly, she stroked her youngest's head.

"I did right by your father, didn't I?"

A week later, when she hadn't risen except to go to the bathroom and to eat what little she did, Miles knocked on her door. When her substanceless voice bade him enter, he stepped inside the drape-drawn, tomblike room.

"Mama?"

"Miles? That you?"

"Yes, Mama."

"How's my big boy?"

"I'm all right."

"You know you all I got now. I know I can depend on you."

"You can depend on me, Mama."

"Good." Her head turned on the pillow, throwing her face into profile.

"I'm tired," she said. "I need to rest a while."

"Mama, we don't have no food."

"I don't have no money, Miles."

"What we going to do for food, Mama?"

"I'm tired, sweetie. You figure it out for me."

In the morning he prepared his brothers and sisters for school as he had all during the previous week, but this time he didn't go with them. He went to the golf course, caddied for thirty-six holes, brought dinner home. Then he went to the all-night diner, washed dishes until four in the morning, came home to sleep a couple of hours, got up to prepare the others for school, then headed back to the golf course. The first rainy day panicked him; he couldn't caddy when it rained, and he went from door to door, explaining his situation, begging odd jobs whose completion demanded no immediacy and could wait until it rained.

He kept this up for six months. Despite his effort, and the collection taken up by the church, there still wasn't enough money, the balance of the insurance having gone to pay off the house. Neglect hollowed the faces of his brothers and sisters, shaped behavior. Teachers sent notes that were neither seen nor answered; store owners complained that the children stole.

Then Miles came down with a fever that put him in the hospital for five weeks. When he recovered it was to find his brothers and sisters placed in foster homes, and the decision made that he was to live in another. He was ashamed and angry, the former at the separation of his family, the latter at his mother, who still refused to rise. He made the effort again, worked harder, stopped by to care for his mother, visited the four homes that housed his brothers and sisters until something broke in him again. This time it was not his body, but his will that snapped, and he knew that if he would survive he had to get away. As wide as the world was there seemed only two choices: California or New York City. Since he'd been around heat and palm trees all his life, he packed what little he had and hitchhiked north. But he was only fifteen and afraid of going too far from home, and he got off the sixteen-wheeler in Jacksonville, where he went looking for a golf course.

"You mean you've got brothers and sisters in the world that you don't see?"

"I don't even know where they are," Miles said. "None of them showed up for my mother's funeral. I don't know if they're dead or alive."

To his astonishment, she began to weep.

He held her. "It's okay," he said.

"No," she said. "It's not."

He'd thought that by opening up about his past, he'd encourage the telling of her own, but she wouldn't talk about a thing except her brother. She'd seen Willis last a little more than a year ago when he'd stopped by with his brand-new wife on his way to Okinawa. Elizabeth was white, barely out of high school, pregnant. Phoenix was in the hospital with appendicitis. When they'd gone to visit him, he'd still been running a fever. He'd hissed weakly at Elizabeth, tried to sit up, fell back against the pillow.

Elizabeth had talked about what was going on in Mississippi, said she felt she ought to be there. Carla had liked her, even though at first sight she'd felt a pang of disapproval, a sense that

Willis, in choosing a white woman, had rejected her. The feeling was so fleeting she had to identify it in its absence. When she had the time she tried to figure it out and was relieved to find the disapproval had been some kind of reflex that preceded thought. Maybe it was in the blood, instinctive, or maybe it was history.

Her reaction to Elizabeth caused Carla once again to consider her own condition, how the word on the street was that she wasn't to be honored because she slept with white men. What would they say if they knew she'd spent more than half her life waiting for one? Then it struck her that she never thought of Max as white unless she was angry. The rest of the time he was Max.

She'd decided that what mattered was her brother's happiness.

Now Willis had a child, Cassandra. They called her Cassie. Here was her picture.

"She's pretty," Miles said. "Look at those dimples." He held the photograph at an angle. "You know what? She looks like Phoenix."

"Let me see that," Carla said. "You know? She does."

Why had that made her feel so strange? They were, after all, related.

"What about your father?" Miles said. "What was your mother like?"

"Like anybody's parents."

"You ducking?"

"Isn't ducking when you bend real quick?"

"Your father's name was Rufus."

She nodded.

"What did he do for a living?"

"Worked in a lumberyard. Until Max came."

"And then?"

"He didn't."

"My cousin said he willed himself to die."

"Did she now?"

"Well? Did he?"

"He died. That's all anybody knows for sure."

* * *

Patient still, Miles taught Carla to play blackjack and poker, cooncan and pitty-pat. She was lucky at cards, played for keeps, refused to return the pennies she gleefully piled before her. He leafed through some of the books littering the house, most of which were novels.

"Why do you love them so?"

"They tell the truth."

There it was again, the notion that truth lived in what everyone knew was invented. "What truth?"

"What people feel on the inside. What they're afraid of. What they want."

"What are they afraid of?"

"The dark, being successful, loving, life."

"What do they want?"

"The same things."

"That doesn't make any sense."

"It does if you think about it."

They went to the movies; she leaned against his arm. There, in a darkened room, breathed into life by a column of light above her, people overcame extraordinary odds, found love before the credits rolled, vowed to stay forever. She watched, gave in to the seduction. Maybe he wouldn't leave, maybe she loved him. If he promised to stay forever, could she take the risk?

Maybe she could, but first she had to have the promise. She dropped hints; he heard them, but like some wily fish declined to rise to the flashing of her bait. She could tell she was making him nervous. Perhaps it had to do with the differences in their ages. Maybe he was looking for someone younger.

"Am I too old for you?"

"Age ain't nothing but a number."

"I know that," she said. "But some numbers are bigger than others."

"What makes you think you're older than me anyway?"

"I can look at you."

"How you know I ain't as pretty as I am from clean living?

You do know people live a clean life look younger than they are?"

"Okay, how old are you?"

"Seventy-five."

"Miles, I'm serious."

"I can *see* that. I just can't figure out for what. I'm thirty-six, okay?"

"Most men *want* younger women."

"Then I guess I ain't most men."

"You saying you *prefer* older women?"

"I ain't said nothing yet. Except that I like women."

"And age doesn't make any difference?"

"Not as long as they got one thing."

"What?"

"Tight pussy."

In spite of herself, she giggled. "You are im*poss*ible."

"I know," he said. "Now come here and give me some."

When she thought about it, she realized he'd avoided the issue, and that meant it was important, that some day when she least expected, it would blow up in her face. It was left to her; she had to be the one to talk about it.

Later, when she reconstructed the events, she couldn't recall what had made her choose that moment. She wasn't even feeling particularly anxious. They were in the kitchen. Miles had offered to go for Chinese food, but she said she'd cook. She was sifting flour, cornmeal, and baking powder. He bent above the Pittsburgh box score, lamenting Roberto Clemente's slump.

"He's got no protection in the batting order. He doesn't get anything to hit."

Carefully, she broke an egg into a cup. As she watched the smooth way egg white slid from shell, it just came out of her mouth.

"Miles? What's going to become of us?"

Clemente bolted from the room. "Oh, we'll live a while," Miles said, "and then we'll probably die." He smiled, but didn't look up. His shoulders hunched, as if the room's temperature had plunged in the wake of Roberto's departure.

She said, "Do you think you'll ever love again?" She added milk to the mixture.

"Do you?"

She began, furiously, to beat her bread.

For a week she refused to sleep with him, dreamed of her father, her friend Lucinda, a sunswept morning lined with birdsong, and Max returning, surprised at how she wept. "I told you I'd come back," he said.

Miles let the freeze-out ride, treated it like a slump that time and patience held the key to. When he thought about it later, he considered what might have happened if he'd confronted her. But she wasn't a child. He wasn't playing any silly games.

"What about the Grand Canyon?" she said. "Aren't you still wanting to see it?"

It had been a week of trivial conversation and the kind of silence that looms between people who avoid what needs to be said. They'd exhausted the possibilities in weather, ground current events to pulp. One evening she read in her room while downstairs he practiced putting across the living room rug into the mouth of a green-bean can. When he tired of that, he sat plunking chords on the untuned piano.

"You trying to get rid of me?"

She took a deep breath. "I need to know, Miles."

"Know what?"

For a moment she wondered if she hated him. "What you're going to do. What *we're* going to do."

"I don't know myself."

They were in the kitchen; he'd cooked this time, simple: broiled chicken and baked potatoes, broccoli, supermarket rolls. They sat over empty plates, half-filled cups of tea. He smiled at her. It was a beautiful smile; it would be nice to keep it around.

"When you came by that first time," she said, "you asked me why I lived the way I do."

"And you asked me the same."

"But you told me. I never answered."

"I figured when you were ready."

"Well, I'll tell you."

"Okay."

She said, "Remember the first time we made love?"

"Yeah."

"I upset you that morning. Afterwards. When I got distant."

"I wasn't upset. I just knew something had changed."

"Part of what I felt was frightened."

"Of me?"

She nodded.

"I do something to make you frightened?"

The salt was low in the shaker. She had to fill it. "I don't know. I felt there was something about you, that if I gave in to it, my life would change, it wouldn't be mine anymore."

"I don't understand."

She forced herself to look at him. "Some of it has to do with Max."

"Phoenix's father?"

"Yes. I've been waiting for him . . . I've been waiting for him to come back."

"After twenty-some years?"

She nodded.

He was frowning, as if, all of a sudden, waiting was foreign or unsportsmanlike. "You ever hear from him?"

"No."

"You know where he is?"

"No. Just that he's alive."

"How do you know?"

"If I knew how I knew I'd tell you. But I don't. I just do."

"You're kidding me. You had a baby when you were a kid and the guy splits on you, and you're going to spend the rest of your life waiting for him? That's—" He stopped, decided not to say it.

"What?"

"Wasting your life."

"Maybe," she said. "But it's mine."

"Okay."

"There are ties that time can't break," she said. "I've learned that. Some things seem like one thing, but really are another."

"Such as?"

"I thought I hated Max. But I loved him. I learned it after Lucinda left and my parents died. It was inside me. Sometimes it hurt."

Miles said, "I ain't exactly no authority. But that doesn't sound like love to me."

"Oh? What *does* love sound like?"

He looked at her, the tight jaw, the eyes flat, challenging.

"I don't know."

She said, "Then don't make it sound like you do."

"Okay, Carla, you're smarter than me."

"Not at all. Just more honest."

"You lost me."

She left him lost, said, "That's what kept me going. Whenever I couldn't go on anymore, the waiting kept me going. After the kids, it was the most important thing in my life." She took a deep breath. "Until now. You changed all that in . . . what? Three weeks? Four? I can't believe it's not longer, it feels longer." She shook her head. "You're the first man I really wanted to be with, not just to fuck. The first one I've let in my bed. The first black man I've come with. Sometimes I don't come with white men, but I never did with black men. Until you."

"I don't know, Carla. Having an orgasm isn't. . . ." He searched for words.

"What?"

"Maybe it's not as much as you make it."

"Maybe not. But it's the first time I'm willing to take a chance that it's all right to stop waiting."

"Nothing ever happened to anyone because they stopped waiting. You got a right to go on with your life. If you think not, you're in trouble."

You couldn't explain your life to people. They begged you, *Tell me, tell me,* but when you did, they never understood. She said, "Everybody's in trouble."

"But the point is—"

"You've made a difference in me, Miles. You make me want to take a chance, make me think about taking care of you, being with you for life. What do you think of that?"

She knew what he thought. She could see the squirming, the rubbing at his face as if her words were a net that trapped him.

"I think I'm flattered," he said. "I think it's too quick."

"Quick?"

"You wait for somebody all these years, and in three weeks you talking about permanently hooking up? We don't even *know* each other. All I know is I'm attracted to you."

"*Four* weeks," she said. "What else is there to know?"

He looked at her; he had no answer.

"I thought it was you who thought the waiting ought to stop."

"It ought to. But why can't we . . . ?"

"What?"

"Take our time. Be. . . . "

"Friends?"

"That too. But I mean why can't we go about this like two normal people? Spend some time together. Get a feel for things."

"You mean spend more time waiting."

"I'm not talking about taking twenty-some *years*."

"You're shouting," she said. "How long are you talking about?"

"I don't know. A couple of months. I can't answer that."

"And what happens in a couple of months? If you need more time? Take another couple?"

"Maybe."

"And after that?"

"I ain't got no crystal ball," he said.

"So the answer's no?"

He bristled. "Come on, Carla. Give me a break. You're dealing with your stuff, I'm dealing with mine. I came through here on my way to the Grand Canyon. You know what I mean?"

"Sure. I understand the need to know what dry air feels like."

"You *don't* know what I mean."

"No," she said, "I don't. But I know a *no* when I hear one."

"Why are you trying to start a fight?"

"Go on," she said. "Get mad. It'll make it easier for you to leave. Don't want that hole to fill up while you wait."

"Why you doing this?"

"Yesterday," she said calmly, as if she were discussing the price of grapefruit, "I fucked somebody while you were at the golf course. He works at the bank. A white man, a vice-president. He'd been after me for a while, and yesterday I let him."

He grew still, rigid. "Why are you telling *me*?"

"Who else do I tell?"

He shook his head.

She said, "What are you going to do about it?"

"*Do* about it? It's been done. Ain't *nothing* to do about it."

She laughed a short laugh, but there was nothing funny in it. "I can see why your wife found another man."

"What's my wife got to do with this?"

"Your *ex*-wife."

"Carla, this is me you're talking to. What's the deal?"

"You've got no backbone. You can't make up your mind."

"Why are you doing this?"

"Did you stand there and watch?"

He stared at her.

"Did he make her moan? When you walked in, did she have her legs up in the air?"

He said, "Why, Carla?"

"Because I'm tired. And scared. And you can't make up your mind."

"Why didn't you ask me?"

"I did. You said you didn't know."

"So you're making it up for me."

"No. I'm making *mine* up for *me*."

He seemed to consider that, seriously, and then he sighed. "I'm sorry, Carla. Really."

"The man is sorry. Does he want to fuck me?"

"What?"

She stood, a smile on her face.

"I asked if you want to fuck me. Before you go. For old time's sake. You better do it now. I'm getting older by the minute."

"You win, Carla," he said. "But you didn't have to do it. You could have just asked me to leave."

She hadn't asked him to leave; she'd asked him to stay. How hopeless it was if he couldn't tell the difference. "Sure you don't want to fuck me before you go?"

"I'm sure," he said, and stood, fighting despair, fighting anger. "What kind of a woman are you, anyway? How can you be waiting on somebody who burned your house down and killed your brothers? And how's fucking white men gonna make it better?"

She smiled, taunting, seductive, and he felt his fists ball without commanding, his body coil, and at the same time the rising in his flesh. How could he want so much to take her, and still be furious? Make love to her and smash her, bend her to his will, wipe the smirk off a face he'd from the first considered lovely? If he didn't go now, he'd do something he'd regret. Either that or cry. And he'd promised that never again in life would a woman make him cry. He took a deep breath, relaxed his hands, spun away from her. It felt like flesh ripping.

She stayed on her feet until the door closed. Then she slouched at the table, blinked at the wilderness of empty plates. A fire siren curled above the city. Something or somebody was on fire. So what? There was always fire. He'd have left anyway, one day. There was always leaving.

She stood, began to clear the table. This was the cup he'd drunk from, the plate with an abandoned broccoli stalk.

She opened her hands. China smashed against the floor.

Outside in the idling car, Miles leaned his head against the steering wheel. *Why? Why'd she do it?*

Fuck it, he thought, and took a deep, lung-clearing breath. He'd promised himself he'd never let another woman turn him upside down, and Carla wasn't nothing but another woman. He threw the car into drive, squealed away from the curb. *Why'd she do it?*

The fire siren was bleating. The sound was on top of him, and as he steered recklessly around the corner, he slammed on his brakes, swerved up onto the sidewalk as trucks shot from the station, veered wildly down the street. He waited until all of them had gone, four blood-red thunderbolts, white men in black-and-yellow slickers. He closed his eyes, remembering as if it were yesterday. Victoria's legs *were* in the air. The blond head turned, the blue eyes widened. A beard shades darker than the hair. Stupidly, he'd thought: *A white man?*

He sat, car pulled to the curb, beneath a tree whose leaves had just begun to change, wondering why, now that help was on the way, the siren didn't stop. She'd done it deliberately. Violently, he turned on the radio, twirled the dial, a harsh medley of static and voice and music until he came to the throbbing of a steel guitar.

Go on and cry, the guitar said, but Miles cursed and gritted his teeth and wouldn't.

II

There was a time when blacks didn't talk about that fire of 1940. Now, when they tell the story, they don't start with its destruction, but with how it drove one man to singing, and lit another's dance. Of course they know two children perished in that blaze, and that a third (from whose arms white men pried a golden infant) was burned from shoulder blades to thigh backs. But children's deaths are painful to remember, and so they build the story slowly, speaking of song and dance, and how astonishing it was in moonlight. Only then do they mention flame, note how complete its looting: curtains, radio and skylight, photographs and children. The whole house, not a wall left standing, swallowed in less time than telling took.

That's when (nothing but foundation left) firemen were told that the preaching boy was missing. The men clawed at cinder block and roof beam, drove sticks through mounds of rubble. They were good men, soot-streaked and thorough, but they found no trace of Max. They did find the rabbits stuck together in their cage. They did find the father's secret stash of whiskey. But as for Max, nothing.

All during her stay in the hospital, all during the healing of her burns, Carla waited for someone to come and say he knew, to ask her why she'd soiled the Lord's anointed. When that happened, she'd resolved to tell. Because the person would insist on proof, she'd compiled a list of episodes, her motivation. But none of it provided what she looked for: the weight of reason, clear-cut and indisputable. She must have overlooked something. And if she couldn't remember, not only had she set into motion events that destroyed her family, but she wouldn't be able to explain. The hatred in her father's face would never leave; people would say for as long as she breathed that she'd soiled the Lord's anointed and caused the death of her brothers. And she'd done this for nothing worth the name of reason. She hadn't even had the grace to grieve.

Lord knows she'd tried to grieve. She'd stood in dark places, unmercifully pinched her flesh, dug fingernails into her thighs while she called out the names of her brothers. "Alton," she'd say. "David." But there was nothing. The place where sorrow should have been was there below her heart; she could feel its outline with her fingers. But there wasn't any pain.

Already frightened, now she was terrified, and then the emptiness returned, this time without the colors. As she looked at its gray, unsightly presence, she knew that until she discovered the reason that would explain to others why she'd done it, she'd never be forgiven. She'd never know grief's consolation, never win her father's love.

When she awakened that first time, Carla was on her stomach, legs spread and kept apart by bandages. The dream lay heavy on her back; her mouth was dry. She opened her eyes, then squeezed them shut, assaulted by the dazzling white of curtains, across which flew the image of her child, all gold and beautiful. She called for him.

"He's all right," her mother said. "Carla? Can you hear me?"

A nurse hovered in the doorway.

The second time she awoke she asked about her brothers. Her mother's face drove her into sleep again. In the evening the room smelled of disinfectant; her father wasn't there. She asked for Max. Meridian said he'd vanished.

All during her recovery, Carla persisted: "How could he disappear; where'd he go to?" but no one would pursue the matter. Not her mother, not the missionaries who daily circled her bed, not the policemen with their questions.

The evasions deepened her curiosity. Maybe the ether had done it; suddenly she wanted to know everything: where Max had gone, what it looked like to be on fire, why it was impossible to grieve. And since she had only her mother to talk to, that was why, on that December day in 1940, four months after the fire, Meridian was patiently telling her daughter what Carla already knew, that she'd fled the burning house with the child she hadn't named yet, that the house was reduced to ashes when her father began to sing.

"You came out running," Meridian said, "flame like a wing down your back. A fireman grabbed you. It took two men to pull the baby from your arms. The first one threw you down and rolled you. His hat fell off."

Meridian blinked. How neat the repeated telling of a thing could make it. She'd relived the night so often she didn't have to remember, simply open her mouth and the tale streamed forth, complete except for inflection. She'd stood back from the house, on the road, watching. To say she was rocked was to be feebly accurate, like saying midnight and the ravaged heart were both made up of darkness. Her daughter was on fire, there were mounds beneath streaked sheets, the child who hadn't been named was screaming. Beyond the density of smoke, the shocked heads of assembled neighbors, the evergreens were lovely, strung with glitter, and in the sky, the moon pulled mystically. But she must not think how beautiful the trees were, mustn't note how mystical the moon.

"What else?"

"It was noisy. Men shouting. Fire hissing when the water hit. The fireman picked up his hat. He didn't put it on straight. The one with the baby laid him on the front seat of a truck."

"A banging woke you?"

"I don't know if it was real or I was dreaming. Like pots banging on a stove."

"What about the orderly?"

To Meridian's left the curses of a man in agony. She turned and saw the white-clad figure sink to his knees, huge hands fluttering to peel the dress from Carla's back.

"He was cussing," Meridian said, "and crying."

"What did he say?"

"He took the Lord's name in vain. Your back was smoking."

"And that's when Daddy began to sing?"

Oh, Jesus, the orderly wept, *Oh, goddamn Jesus.*

The night had stilled, the curses carried, a hiss at the end of Jesus. Meridian was about to consider (finally!) what lay beneath streaked sheets when song erupted, familiar, and yet so unexpected she had to concentrate to name it. It was Rufus, rigid in the searchlight, voice deep-throated blue above the ruin. One moment he was there, alone and singing; then there were two of him, then one again. And when Meridian had blinked, Junkman had shuffled to her husband's side. The mute crouched and twirled a shovel. He took two steps and threw his hands up, two more steps, and brought them down. He danced in a wide, slow circle, arms like airplane wings; he leaped and sneezed ("God bless you," someone called).

Meridian batted her eyes, trying to clear her vision, and on the road, the lines of watchers shifted in the moonlight, and a man commenced to hum a replica of her grieving husband's song. Women joined in, voices high; some sang in harmony. All of it was so arresting that the firemen paused to stare at this evidence of human spirit. It made Meridian proud to see her man that way, battered but defiant, and she tucked a wayward wisp of hair behind an ear and looked above her. The moon was swimming. Across the yard, something white was moving in the trees. Her heart froze just before she fainted.

Carla said, "Was it Max?"

"I couldn't tell. For a minute I didn't think it was human. But something told me it was. It could have been that Van Etten boy, the one who stole his father's money. It could have been anybody."

"It was Max."

"I got no way of knowing."

"Do you remember the song?"

"Song?"

"Daddy's."

"I'll never forget it. It was made up. Ballast to hold to when the storm came. A door for any hard knock circumstance might offer. That whoever had done this would never be forgiven."

"What was Junkman doing there?"

"I don't know. I guess like everybody else he'd come to see the fire."

"The police question him?"

"You know Junkman doesn't talk."

Carla said, "I know he doesn't talk. But he can write. And why was he dancing?"

"I don't know."

On the morning of September 18, 1924, black people set fire to an apple orchard just outside Kingston's city limits. The destruction was in response to the lynching of a Negro, a man "not quite right," black folks said, which meant there were unfortunate boundaries to his ability to reason. He'd been accused by the orchard owner of stealing a horse. At first the man didn't understand the charge, since he could neither hear nor read, the former the result of a long-ago throat infection, the latter because no one had taught him.

One afternoon in his childhood, he'd stood at the edge of a summer road, wide-eyed as white men thundered by, angled above the backs of horses. The great beasts threw dust; the cloud enveloped the boy, filled his mouth and made his eyes close. But before that happened, he'd permanently consigned to memory what he'd seen: horse flesh heaving beneath taut skin, nostrils cavernous with flaring. Because he was small and already aware of his limits, the vision of blinding dust and power could easily have frightened; instead, the moment fell over him like light. For the rest of his life, though he never had a horse to call his own, he preserved an open space inside him, a nut-brown plain across which he galloped toward a mute horizon.

His explanation, once he understood the charge, was simple. He'd admired the mare from the road, had climbed the fence, inhaled and caressed the object of his dreaming. When he'd satisfied his desire, aware all the time that he was violating boundaries, he turned toward the relative safety of the road.

The horse followed. Smiling, the deaf man shooed her, slapped her flank; she rolled her eyes, snorted, and refused to leave him. His delight fading with the onset of anxiety, he stood scanning the red barn, the rows of dark trees stubbornly on their way to distant endings. It was out of those trees that the white men came.

Black people argued eloquently on the accused's behalf. How would he get the horse beyond the fence: dig beneath it with his hands, carry the animal over? Where would he hide it? Through it all, in a wordless, grating whine, the deaf man disputed his guilt. Anyway, he'd been hung, without benefit of trial, in a rolling field, the tallest hill of which held one oak tree. It was early evening, a Tuesday; the sky was high, a pale blue rinsed with light that could have come from roses. From the bottom of the hill where the Negroes gathered, the body had no thickness, only length and width pasted on the air in stark, dense silhouette.

Rufus March, Carla's father, who stood there with the rest, lowered his eyes and tried, unsuccessfully, to pray. When he raised his head, it was to lock his vision on the figure of a white man who stood apart from his fellows, as if he couldn't determine his connection to the event. The man wore a gray hat, a red sweater deeper than crimson. It was the sweater that did it; the deep, rich warning of a red that lit the rage in Rufus. *Bastards. Ungodly bastards.* He longed for a shotgun, a pocket of shells to empty in their faces, the thrill of a white man's throat beneath his knife. It was Rufus who organized the arsonists, swore them to secrecy, he who sent them to steal kerosene from white homes and the ferry slip in Highland, he who set the hour for revenge.

And when they had enough of the precious fluid, the Negroes gathered in the mist of not yet dawn, some bold, some quaking; these asked for a moment of prayer. When they were finished, the man raised their buckets, anointed the squat, misshapen trees, struck a match and scrambled toward safety. The flames leaped at the sky, hissed, beat back the darkness. Rufus watched it. How extraordinarily lovely the fire of revenge.

Junkman was the mute who danced at the fire that burned the March house down. The lynched man was his father.

"Did you know Junkman used to hang around the house? Before the fire?"

"No," Meridian said. "I never saw him."

"Well, he did."

"What was he doing?"

"Nothing. Just being there."

"Junkman's strange, but everybody knows he's harmless. He didn't frighten you?"

"No."

They were in the two-family house they'd moved to after the fire. Here, in the east kitchen, the appliances were yellow. Sunlight drenched the window above the sink, bathed the table. Outside a bewildered earth noted that it was December, and the season's first snow had yet to fall.

Meridian's hands weighed her swollen belly. On the floor, on a blanket on his back, Phoenix seemed to contemplate the mystery of ceilings. He hadn't moved in an hour. Carla bent to wipe drool from his mouth. As she straightened, she looked through the window of the kitchen door. On the other side was a foyer barely large enough to turn in, then another door; beyond its window lay the second kitchen. In that room the shades were drawn. The dark made her think of her father. Rufus had gone out, as he did every day, to search for Alton and David and Max. He scoured alleyways, neighbors' yards, the woods that ringed the scorched earth where his house had been. He stopped passersby on the street. "Have you seen my boys? Two are this high, colored. The third got blond hair and mismatched eyes. He'd be carrying a Bible."

"No, Rufus," they said, "we haven't," and when he'd turned, they solemnly shook their heads.

"So they took me to the hospital?"

"I wasn't awake for that," Meridian said. "When I came to, I was in Sister Pauline's house. The bed had four posters, high off the floor. Somebody put a cool cloth to my head. I tried to sit up, they wouldn't let me."

"Where was Daddy?"

"Across the room, looking out the window. When he saw I'd come to, he sent the women out. He held my hand. 'Meridian,' he said."

"The men were looking for Max?"

"A bunch of them sifted the rubble the firemen went through. The next day some of the sheriff's men searched the woods around the house. Those rowboats they keep down by the swimming place? One was missing. The men went out onto the river. Some dove, some checked the shore for miles. Then they stopped and went looking for the mayor's boy."

Suddenly, the sheriff had his hands full with missing children. Ezra Van Etten, a seventeen-year-old distinguished by his passion for idleness and the regularity with which his father whipped him, had disappeared the same day as the March fire, taking with him a quart of bourbon from the parlor and sixteen hundred dollars from a bedroom safe. Since his daddy was the mayor, and serious money was involved, the sheriff's manpower was directed to searching for him.

The most diligent work in the case of the March fire was done by Rufus's neighbors, who, over the next six weeks, combed both sides of the riverbank halfway to Poughkeepsie, searching the places where a boat or drifting body might have washed ashore. Jason Deadstreet, a white man who'd tried to drink himself to death before Max had lifted him, carried to the scene of the fire the shirt he'd worn at his conversion and gave his hound the scent. Immediately the dog flew into the woods, where she stopped, sniffing furiously at a small depression in the earth. She looked beseechingly at Jason, turned in small, bewildered circles, whined. But the confusion was temporary; the beast reclaimed her bearings, laid back her ears, and tracked Max's smell to the river. Pausing, tongue hanging at a silly, glistening angle, she made a sharp left turn and loped down to the rowboats. She sniffed in and out of several, then went back to the spot on the rocky shore where the zigzag trail had led. There, she and Jason gazed out at the water.

"What you think happened, Betsy? What would you tell me if you could?"

The river was flat and broad and silent. On the other side the land mass formed a stunted, deep-gray graph. Jason squatted, picked up a rock.

"Max," he said, "if you set that fire, may the Lord forgive you. If you didn't, come back and tell us why you left."

He stroked the rock, eyes closed. "If you had a problem, Max, you could have come to me. I'd have helped you."

Then he said, "May the Lord bless you. May He keep you and cause His face to shine on you."

Jason stood, hefted the rock, sent it spinning. A soft, thick splash; it disappeared. He stood a moment longer, then went to tell the others what he'd found.

Jason was a white man who'd accepted Christ, finding in religion relief from the erotic dreams he'd suffered ever since an April night in 1937. He'd gone to the club in Tijuana with his heart in his mouth, had slouched in a second-row seat. The room had a half dozen fans suspended from the ceiling; it was thick with smoke and the sweet smell of taut-eyed women who clung to the arms of their men. The house lights dimmed, and through the purple curtains stepped a short fat man, wearing a red sombrero. The man said something gravely in Spanish, after which the room filled with silence so deep, so fraught, that Jason closed his eyes.

Later, he opened them, saw muscles leap in the arms of female attendants, was close enough to see the terror in the bound woman's eyes as the harness raised her to the heaving brute, close enough to see the blunt-tipped donkey cock shining as it entered, distending the hole between her thighs, turning her face deep blue. He heard the murmuring of the taut-eyed women, a gasp, a cry that was either pain or pleasure, and he was illuminated, not by desire, but a deep and deadening revulsion.

When it was over, he stumbled into the Mexican night, lay in the lumpy bed of a cheap hotel with a bottle whose worm turned at the bottom. He drank until the room spun, until the dim light beneath the fly-specked shade shattered into rainbows, transformed the crucifix on the wall, carved in the air the face of the woman from whose Catholic loins he'd sprung. Finally, he tumbled into the first of dreams in which he looked on, horrified, as he lay with dogs, explored pig genitalia, labored mightily above the backs of sad-eyed sheep.

The dreams mortified him, and his solution before he gave his life to Christ was to attempt to drink himself to death. One day he'd staggered into the YMCA, whose neon sign made him think it was a bar, and there, so far above him he seemed to stand on heaven, was Max, in his pure white suit, speaking, as he paced, directly to him. Jason felt the surge of hope, his heart was lifted, and he set off down the aisle. On both sides folks were pleading the blood of Jesus, welcoming him, and when he reached the stage, Max, smelling of innocence and power, leaned forward, laid cool hands on his cheeks, looked lovingly into his eyes.

"Brother," Max said. "Will you pray?"

Carla asked Meridian, "When did you see Max last?"

"When he went outside after dinner. You were upstairs with the baby. Your daddy was reading the paper in the living room."

"Did he seem different?"

"Your daddy?"

"Max."

"No different than he'd been since the baby was born. Jumpy. Dazed . . . There *was* one thing. His appetite. He hadn't had much of one, but that night he had a second helping."

"And everybody went to bed. And that's when he set the fire."

"You know we're not sure Max did it," Meridian said.

"Who else would of?"

"I'm not saying he didn't. I'm just not saying he did."

"What do you feel in your heart, Mama?"

"Not knowing, honey. Not knowing's in my heart."

"You mean sometimes you feel he did?"

Meridian flinched. She was remembering what she'd seen in the instant before fainting, projecting now behind her eyes a blank screen, neat and white as a wall without hangings, onto which flashed the morning Max had come. It was she who'd found him, she who'd left the bed she shared with Rufus, gone down to the kitchen where windows framed September's light. Still half asleep, she wondered if she'd dreamed that Rufus had slipped from bed last night, and returned smelling of kerosene and smoke and apples. She knew she hadn't dreamed of making love, of floating from dream to find herself and the sun relentlessly rising, her throbbing keeping time to a siren's pulse. Smiling, considering going back to bed and waking Rufus with her tongue, she put up a pot of coffee and heard the birds. Mildly curious, she went to the door, opened it. The evergreens were thick with birds; they were black and screaming. She examined the sky for signs of a coming storm, then rolled her vision over the yard, across the road. Nothing moved, neither cloudless sky nor broad and shining river. It was beautiful. How could men be so cruel; how could they hang another from a tree and live in a world so lovely?

The siren was bleating. Was it another fire or the same one, burning still? Behind her, Rufus sang his way downstairs. As she reminded herself to ask why he smelled of kerosene and apples, she looked at her feet.

"Rufus," she called. "*Jesus*, Rufus."

"Make up your mind who you want," Rufus said. "What's all this fuss so early in the morning?"

"Somebody left a baby on our step."

"A what?"

"A baby."

"Jesus, Mary, and Joseph," Rufus said. He squeezed with her into the doorway. "Well, I'll be damned. This baby's *white*."

Meridian was kneeling. "Look at his eyes."

"My Lord," Rufus said. He scowled out toward the edges of his yard, as if whoever had cluttered his morning with a child might be hiding among the trees, or swimming to an unencumbered life across the river. Then he fell to his knees. The infant stared up at them, the straight blond hair, the narrow forehead, eyes larger than ordinary, one blue, one hazel. He was wrapped in a blue receiving blanket that exposed his feet; Meridian remembered thinking, *He'll be tall.* There was a paper pinned to the blanket. She unfastened it, read the girlish hand.

His name is Maximillian. Please take care of him.

"Ain't white folks a *mess*," Rufus said. "What we supposed to do with a white baby?"

Meridian whispered, "Look at his eyes."

"Go get the mayor," Rufus said. "Get the sheriff. Get whoever you got to get, but get it out of here."

Meridian picked up the infant and smelled the coffee. Thrusting the child into Rufus's arms, she bolted for the kitchen, rescued the boiling pot. Her head lifted; the birds were still. Rufus, furious, trotted into the room holding the child away from him.

"Take this baby," he said. "Find out who belongs to it. Don't let it be here when I get home from work."

The fire siren was bleating.

"That thing's been going through the night," Meridian said.

"So it has."

"Is it one fire, or lots of little ones?"

"You know how time is. It'll tell."

"Somebody's in trouble."

"Ain't nothing new."

"It could've been us."

"But it ain't."

"Still, it makes you thankful."

Carla, twenty-two months old, waddled into the kitchen.

"I *am* thankful," Rufus said. "I'm thankful all the time. I'm thankful for being in a country what hangs us from a tree. I'm thankful white folks got they foot up my ass to the knee. *Good morning, baby.* How could you think I ain't thankful? I know what you thinking, Meridian. Get it out your mind."

Meridian knelt to show the baby to her daughter.

"What his name?" Carla asked.

His name was Max. He came in the wake of a lynching, in the middle of a fire. In a little while he was a legend, saving souls up and down the eastern seaboard, laying hands on the sick, giving back to the lame the gift of walking. Once, they said, on a sun-shocked afternoon in Philadelphia, he made a blind man see.

Rufus didn't want Max, but Meridian did. She was moved to protect a defenseless life, and she was enchanted by eyes that reminded her of rare stones you come across once in a lifetime, like cat eyes, though she'd never seen them in a human. But Rufus was rock hard in his insistence that the baby leave, and it would have happened except for the county making him so mad.

White people, who'd misjudged the seriousness with which Negroes regarded lynching, were deeply offended that not only had their darker brothers set fire to the orchard, they hadn't left enough evidence to be properly accused. Neither would any Negroes lend a hand to put out the blaze. It was while brooding over this breach of neighborliness that the folks at the county became troubled by a white child living with coloreds. Their mouths were polite, but Rufus found distaste in their cheekbones and the set of their shoulders, signals that would have been detected by men far less sensitive than he. The county said the Marches had to turn the baby over. Not only did Rufus refuse, he came perilously close to saying no white man anywhere could tell him what to do, not even give up a baby he didn't want.

Stunned by his behavior, the county temporarily retreated.

There was talk of punishment for Rufus, but the truth was that following the lynching more than one white man bolted upright in the night, haunted by dreams of dangling black men. Others grimly calculated the economics of orchards that bore no fruit, and considered that little they owned was safe from fire. So nobody was exactly eager to threaten Rufus, much less hang him, and they spent a couple of days exploring options.

While they explored, Rufus got himself a dog and a double-barrel shotgun. Three days later the folks from the county pulled up in a blue DeSoto with a bent fender. Two were heavy men in rumpled suits, the third a woman whose black dress sharpened her thinness. They parked on the far edge of the road, keeping their distance from the dog, and called out that they weren't necessarily coming to take the baby, but they had a responsibility and there were things to be discussed. Rufus stood in the doorway, listening with what seemed appropriate civility, and when they were finished, he went inside, got his shotgun, aimed above their heads, and pulled the trigger.

The folks from the county didn't go back to the office. They went to see Reverend Sweeny, who was pastor of Kingston's only black church. Nobody knew what the Reverend said, but the county left Rufus alone.

The strangest thing was how Rufus didn't act like a man who'd gone one on one with white folks and prevailed. Instead of victory's tilt in his shoulders, he wore a soft curve, and a face that made people think of rain. Word was that he blamed Meridian for having another mouth to feed, and ignored the baby except to angrily insist that Maximillian was too much name for a white boy, and from then on they'd call him Max. Word was that he and Meridian now slept in separate beds. That wasn't true. What was true is that their lovemaking changed. No more teasing as a prelude. No more long kisses, no delicate, dancing fingers that left on her flesh faint prints she could trace in the morning.

For the next five years, Rufus lived in the middle of a bleak and distant sullenness, distraught that revenge had served no other purpose than to mock him with a white child in his house. Nothing consoled him, not prayer, or the exact portion of starch in his shirts, not his head scratched or his toenails clipped. There were evenings when he opened a door to find Meridian longing, and he did the kind of about-face men employ when they've wandered into a neighbor's bedroom. Now, when they made love, it was after he'd awakened her with rough hands between her thighs, and hardly had she understood that she was no longer sleeping than he would roll on top without a kiss, slip it in, thrust, and leave her hanging. She didn't talk to anyone about it, didn't wear black or indulge the urge to weep. Instead she dreamed: hard length beyond her reach, tongue licking not her thighs, but space above them. In the mornings she lay and fingered those dreams, resigned that she'd go to her grave deprived of the passion she'd grown used to.

But wasn't she wrong, didn't she have another thought coming? There, at the frayed end of her rope, swung the miracle. Max revealed his calling, and Rufus swam back to the surface of the depths he'd sunk to, shook himself, and flat out fell in love. Everyone was so astounded by his change that no one thought to ask Rufus what he felt like. If they had, he'd have said George Washington Carver, he'd have said Moses around the corner from the Promised Land. His was the song of the soul who'd suffered all that tribulation, the one who'd made it through the storm to find his hands and feet were new. His feet he kept on the ground, but he couldn't keep his hands off Meridian, and the boys came, David and then Alton, one right after the other, and Rufus had a dip in his hip, a glide in his stride, and his face came in from the rain. All over town black folks were smiling, saying what went around had come around; Negroes *hadn't* been forgotten, the prophecy *would* be fulfilled.

And my, *oh my*, how things had changed.

Yes, there was a prophecy; the beginning of the story, really, and it goes back to a time hard on the heels of slavery, half a century before Max arrived. Picture Kingston's square the way it looks in those drawings up at the courthouse: hard ground and hitching posts stuck between hill slope and sullen river. Note the slouched buildings, windows weak with yellow, dirt street abandoned long before perspective has its way.

Above this unhappy scene, a sky skinned from fish belly, ditchwater clouds. These last make a shroud that hides the hilltop.

It was out of that shroud that the Negroes came, unannounced, wraithlike, and silent. Leading the group, a grim rectangle in the gloom, were four men who bore a rag-wrapped body, on top of which lay the miniature flame of a single wild red rose.

The date was June 3, 1869; the Negroes numbered fifty-four. The square into which they straggled was the end of a journey begun in Canada, and the dead man's name was Joseph Drake.

Drake had been this small group's leader. Three days before, weak with the fever that would kill him, he'd had a vision, and had begun to prophesy. All of them were, he'd said, a chosen people, among whom would appear a child of God, in the presence of whose light they'd flourish.

Some of the group began to dance. "This child of God," they called. "How will we know him?"

"What will he look like?"

"How do we prepare?"

No one was surprised when Drake didn't answer. His life had been defined by silence. Some said it marked his strength and spiritual conviction, others that it was contrived to gain unquestioning allegiance. All were mistaken. Drake was silent because of what had happened to him, something so damaging he'd forgotten it and the things that made men human: his name, what he'd done, and where he'd come from, all of it assembled in a feeling that lived two paces from his back. He'd taken another name (a family of ducks crossed his path, a line so straight only love or the military could have drawn it), but the feeling, which he couldn't locate when he spun, refused to hint at who he was.

When the group began to dance, a small smile lit Drake's features. These were his people; they believed him. The next thought unplugged the smile: *Should* they believe? The prophecy had just popped into his head; no language, just a tableau of images in Technicolored hue. What would happen if it didn't come true? Shouldn't he share his uncertainty, say the vision could have come from sickness, or some demon who dangled before black folks yet another empty hope? But it would be a shame to interrupt their dancing; it wasn't often they got to celebrate.

He wavered. Some of the old folks were hugging one another; three women threw a song into the air. A girl child stepped forward, laid roses in his lap.

Drake closed his eyes, moved beyond love, beyond devotion. No, he had to share his reservations. He opened his mouth to speak, but it was like trying to lift his body with his jawbones. Stunned, he felt his chin fall to his chest; his body spasmed. The young girl stepped back, wide-eyed; the singing stopped, the dancers held their breath. A half hour later, Drake was gone.

He'd been a big man, over six feet tall, and he died quietly for his size, left with the same lack of fanfare that marked his arrival in their midst. One day he'd materialized out of the tail end of a blizzard wearing a deerskin coat, a hat of the same hide jammed above his brow. Exhausted, he made it to the first line of cabins that formed the village, then fell face down in the snow. When strong hands turned him over, he looked into a ring of curious black faces.

"Where am I?" he asked.

"You in Deliverance, Canada. You can stop running now. You free."

Most of Deliverance's 173 adults were escaped slaves or their descendants. That's what they thought Drake was, and beyond their welcome lay an unreasonable expectancy that he knew of kin they'd left behind. They waited until he'd eaten and warmed himself, then asked him where he'd come from.

Drake was going to tell them the maddening truth, that he didn't know where he'd come from. But he felt ashamed to say this, so he said, "I come from the swirling snow."

"Did he say snow?"

"What place?"

"Georgia?"

"Mississippi?"

"Did you ever come across a woman by the name of Gaines?"

"Did you go through North Carolina?"

Drake didn't answer.

In the spring they helped Drake build a cabin. By then everyone had accepted that silence was his answer to personal questions, although in conversations about religion or the weather he was as adept as any. As curious as his silence were his refusal to eat meat, and his failure, despite the abundance of single women, to marry. In the winter of his second year, in the grip of religious fervor that made veins leap at his temples, he declared his vow of celibacy. Then he began to shout and speak in tongues, for the duration of which he was wrapped in a bright blue mist.

The announcement was so startling, and the mist so blue, that nobody stopped to realize Drake had volunteered the information.

When they asked why he'd taken the vow, a good-looking man like him, who was not, it appeared, yet forty, they were met, of course, with silence.

All of this—the mystery of where he'd come from, his refusal to eat meat, his chastity, and his size—caused some to think of Drake as a leader, although for seven years after his arrival, he never hinted at ambition. Then, when news found its way to Canada that the Civil War was over, he announced he was going to Kingston. Before anyone could ask why, he said Kingston needed them. He said that once, during a snowstorm whose flakes didn't vary, George Washington had slept there.

"Where is Kingston?" people asked.

"How you know it needs us?"

"Who's George Washington?"

Not everyone in Drake's small group instantly embraced the prophecy. Those who didn't simply chose not to challenge him, not only because they were certain he wouldn't respond, but because he was dying and it wasn't right to spend a man's last thirty minutes on debate. Among themselves, of course, the question was contested. The conventional response was that the Hebrews enjoyed the prestige Drake had promised. The philosophical pointed out that if God could do anything, He was perfectly capable of having *two* chosen people. The weight of this argument ruled for a while, although dissenters raised the troubling question of what, exactly, they'd been chosen for. Faithful readers of the King James version of the Bible, they knew Ham wasn't just another cut of meat. In the end, even believers prudently hedged their bets, declining to keep more than one eye out for the child of God, and when he didn't show up in a timely fashion, they refused to fret themselves into exhaustion. Instead they stored the prophecy on the back shelves of their memories until 1929.

But before that, fifty-three of them followed Drake to Kingston. There, in the gray light of their arrival, a woman writhed and moaned in labor. They laid her on a blanket beside the horse trough in front of the bank, which had closed for the day. The four men relieved themselves of Drake, who was already redolent of death. Deep in the circle of privacy drawn by her fellow travelers, beyond the melancholy gaze of whites and the stink of a dead man's body, the woman gave birth to a nine-pound boy.

After they'd buried Drake, the Negroes scrutinized the infant, wondering if for once they'd get what was theirs without the waiting.

"You think he's the one?"

"He might be."

He might have been. But he wasn't.

No matter what anyone thought about the prophecy, Drake was right about one thing. Kingston needed them.

In 1869 there was already a handful of Negroes in that city (an assistant to the stable owner, several servants to wealthier farmers), but none could remember the last time a black woman had conceived. This was one reason for the small black population; two others were that Kingston wasn't a place that slaves escaped to or where free blacks chose to settle. The former kept going to Canada; the latter stopped in Poughkeepsie, to the south, or in Montgomery, some forty miles due east. Since few came voluntarily to Kingston, and the black women there didn't conceive, it's likely that if Drake's group hadn't showed up, Negroes would have disappeared from Kingston, and the melancholy that gripped the city would never have been relieved.

For a brief period in the eighteenth century, Kingston was capital of New York State. In 1797, the statehouse was moved to Albany, and Kingston, its spirit broken by the slight, slid feet first into depression. For decades, men of sturdy Dutch descent found it difficult to rise in the morning or to plow fields in symmetry. Women who'd slaughtered pigs with clear eyes now wept for the legs of trapped rabbits. Children refused to fly kites, to leap from rooftops, or experiment with sex. Nobody was inspired to make art. Even the few Negroes repeated the same songs, as if the needle of their collective muse was stuck in a not-yet-invented record. But what was most unusual was this: for seventy-two years in Kingston, no one fell in love.

Then, in 1869, Drake's group arrived from Deliverance. On the following morning, whites began to feel better, rediscovered passion, started to invent things, regained their taste for work and sacrifice. At first no one made a connection, but as years passed and Negroes multiplied, so did whites' good spirits. When white people began to understand what had led to their revival, none considered the implications. In time, however, the understanding expressed itself in contradiction: benevolence on the one hand, cruelty on the other. The cruelty came from realizing that inferior people were crucial to their mental health. It was this that led to that baffling behavior, why whites would force black men off the sidewalk, why they paid black boys to fight until only one was standing, why they publicly speculated about the genitalia of black women they trusted their children's lives to. It didn't happen all the time, but because it didn't, Negroes began to move among whites with a caution mistaken for reverence, or indifference, or stupidity. This didn't change until 1924 when, pushed past the legendary boundaries of their patience, black people set fire to that orchard.

Carla said, "Did you ever try to find out who left Max?"

"No. There wasn't any way to. I told you about the woman with the baby. No one got a good look, but it must have been him."

"The one with the nice legs. A green dress and she stared at black women."

"Everybody was upset. They'd hung Junkman's father two days before."

"I wonder why she left him. I wonder why she chose us."

"I've asked myself a hundred times. How could you leave your child? Someone so little, so helpless?"

"What was I like, Mama? When I was little?"

"You were a good baby. I thought your father would bust from pride. He made a song for you."

"A song? How did it go?"

"Let's see," Meridian said. She hummed to herself, then sang:

> Got a new baby girl, as sweet as a ripe cher-ry.
> Got a new baby girl, sweet as a ripe cher-ry.
> Want to know why I'm smiling, now you know what
>   the reason be.
>
> Build me a castle, finest you ever seen.
> Build me a castle, finest you ever seen.
> Don't worry 'bout money, just make it fit for a queen.

"It had another verse, but I can't remember."

Sun was a flame, golden at the window. Her father had loved

her, made up a song. When had he stopped singing it?

"What was I like when Max came?"

"You didn't like him at first. That was normal. Later, you were good with him. On the weekends, you'd let me and Daddy sleep late. You'd go and get something from the icebox, a piece of fruit or something and bring it to his crib. You'd play with him till we got up."

"When did that change?"

"It wasn't all perfect between you. You fought. You were . . . *kids*."

"But things changed."

"Yes. When we discovered Max's calling. It wasn't just you, honey. Everything changed."

The signs that Max was special were there back in the beginning, but no one read them. They just thought it was cute the way he sat in church, clapping his hands, rocking to the music, unusual rhythm for a white boy. And when the preaching started, that's what he loved the most. He'd sit, rapt, eyes shining, while other kids would sleep. Soon he was imitating the sermons, preaching to his kindergarten classmates during recess. This his teacher found amusing until he started holding prayer meetings during naptime. Rufus and Meridian got called to school; it was still the season of Rufus's discontent, and Meridian went alone. Max's teacher said she couldn't allow him to disrupt her classroom, and Meridian came home and talked to him. He promised to behave himself, but you could see, Meridian told a friend, he wasn't happy.

That was April 1929. A month later the Young People's Regional Revival was held over in Montgomery at Pastor McClain's church. It was the custom to have a preach-off on the first Thursday of the event, an occasion when young preachers lined up and got fifteen minutes to strut their stuff. There was a missionary meeting that night over at Evangelina Miller's, so Meridian wasn't there. But Rufus was, and for all the years that he and Max were on the road he'd open the service by relating that beginning.

Rufus had been sitting in the back, mind wandering. He'd

looked up at the line of six or seven would-be preachers whose heads exhausted the possibilities of bowl-shaped haircuts, and there, in the middle of the line, was Max, clutching the white Bible he'd wanted for his birthday. Rufus had chuckled; Max, so much smaller than the others, looked straight ahead, without anxiety. Still smiling, Rufus started to get up and drag Max away when something said to let it be. Unaccustomed to being told what to do, nevertheless, he listened. The rest was history. Max tore up the church. His text was taken from the soul-rending cry of Jesus on the cross, nailed between two sinners. *Their* Jesus about to enter death's uncharted plain with nothing save a loincloth, a crown of thorns, and resurrection's sweet, untested promise. He, who'd healed the sick and raised the dead, *their* Jesus, was calling: "Father. Why hast thou forsaken me?"

It was a cry to break the world's heart; the sky grew black. Even now, two thousand years later, its echoing along time's dim corridor still caused grown men to weep.

But of course His father had done nothing of the kind.

Oh, did that boy preach! Had people jumping into the aisles, blocking passage to the altar, waving hands above their heads in absolute surrender, confessing, for all the church to hear, the depths of their depravity. "I stole," some cried, "I lied. I slept with my sister's husband. I beat my dog." It was amazing, sinners crawling all over one another, and Rufus, although he didn't include this in his telling, sat dreaming of fists full of green.

That's how it started. Rufus pulled Max out of school, got a tutor for him. That same year, they formed the Temple of Love, and went out on the road.

Carla said, "You know what I was thinking?"

"What?"

"When the dog died, and how Max carried on."

"And your daddy buried it in the back yard and had a funeral. You sang a song. What was it?"

" 'Amazing Grace.' Max cried like a baby. The boys were scared. They tried to comfort him."

"Your daddy wanted to get another dog, but Max wouldn't hear it. So he got the rabbits instead."

"All male."

"Remember what your daddy said?"

"Yeah. He didn't want to end up with a rabbit farm. So he just got males."

"Life was good then," Meridian said. "Me and your daddy had started to talk about another baby. Just one more. David and Alton were four and three. . . . "

"I love you, Meridian," Rufus said. "Lord, how I love you."

"Is that so, sugar man?"

"That's so."

"What do you love most?"

"I love this," he said. "And this. And this right here."

"Love it, Rufus. . . . " She raised her head from the pillow. "What's wrong?"

She was swinging from bed, thighs already cooling. "One of the boys."

"I don't hear nothing."

"That's because you're not a mother."

"You come back here. I'll show you what I am."

"Oh, I'll be back," she said. "You be ready."

She went to check on her child. A bad dream, maybe. He just needed to be held. . . .

"You remember anything else?"

Meridian cleared her throat, glanced at Phoenix on the floor. Oh, did she remember. She remembered the fat legs of her boys, how she'd loved to suck the flesh behind their knees. She remembered their first steps, that they'd loved Max above all others, even her, had fallen into his arms, radiant with laughter. . . .

"Mama?"

"I miss my boys, Carla. All of them."

"I know, Mama."

"I loved my babies, I didn't make no favorites between them and Max. I loved you all."

"I know."

Meridian had loved Max, but she was also in awe of him, felt privileged to be charged with his temporal care. She'd struggled with the distance his calling carved between them, but after a while, she gave back to the Lord what He'd given. Of course, she'd no idea of what lay before them, and now that her house was gone and her babies dead, she found herself considering that it was she who'd fought for Max to stay. It wasn't easy to admit that if she'd gone along with Rufus from the start, the boys would be alive right now, pulling at her skirts, asking for milk and cookies, permission to go outside. That they weren't meant she was responsible. Not totally, but how did you determine the portion of disaster for which you were to blame? And even if you computed its weight, its length and thickness, what did you do once its measure was taken?

"Mama."

Meridian's head came up; her eyes veered to the window above the sink, beyond which a cloud moved, swallowing the sun. In the same unexpected way, events had swallowed her life. She was a grandmother before her time; she was pregnant. Her husband had gone looking for his boys. Two slept beneath the cold, December earth; the third had vanished.

"I'm sorry I didn't say something, Carla. I'm sorry you didn't feel you could talk to me. I kept thinking it would go away, that whatever you and Max were going through would pass. I've seen that kind of refusing to face what was happening happen with other folks, and I always told myself I'd never do it. I had a cousin who everyone could see was slow, but no one said it. I've known people who live with pain rather than go to a doctor and find out what was wrong." She sighed. "But I learned you can't meet trouble with silence. Trouble thinks silence is a welcome. That's why I keep working on your daddy. He'll come around."

"You think Daddy will get better?"

"He'll get better. It's just grief."

"Why can't I grieve?"

"Oh, baby, you're grieving. You just don't know it."

"How can you grieve and not know it?"

"I don't know how, just that you can." Meridian reached, touched her daughter's arm. "I'm tired, honey. I'm going to lay down before your daddy gets back."

"You going?"

"To lay down. Wake me when your daddy comes. We'll talk later. We won't stop talking, I promise you."

Now that her mother was gone, the room was empty, stripped of warmth, connection. In the months following the fire, whatever it was inside her that responded to leaving had lost its ability to determine boundaries, found no difference between leaving that was permanent and that which wasn't. If she didn't concentrate, she'd be set off by something as uneventful as sunlight swallowed by a cloud, or the sight of her mother's back as she left a room.

"I'm all right," Carla said to Phoenix.

She moved her chair so she could lean above her child. "The fire went out," she said. "They took me to the hospital. I was asleep. I tried to wake up, but just before I did I started dreaming. . . .

"Phoenix, can you hear me . . . ?"

"Can you hear me?" her mother said. "Carla? Can you hear me?"

She heard, but her mouth was dry. She wanted pineapple juice, wanted to sleep. She struggled to ask for the juice, began to dream, a country road, brown and winding, a white church luminous in sunlight. Somewhere someone was singing, a bell-clear, cathedral-sweep soprano, and she in the audience, and now a line of black girls hip-shaking up the aisle, and Max, in their white, short-skirted wake, palms stained with red dye held above them. . . .

Then, in the way of dreams, she was in another place, blind-bound in the damp fist of a summer's night as Max, wrapped in a snow-white sheet, was flying through a window. And what rejoicing filled the congregation, and what words Max threw above them: fornication and adultery, bestiality and masturbation, and all over the rocking church moist-eyed and gasping women punched fists where smooth thighs met. Across the aisle a blue-gummed sinner whooped and threw his bottle down, another swung a crutch and shouted, walked without limping, danced. Here the hard place in the stomach had dissolved, night sweats distilled to vapor. "I am made whole," they cried, "the hand of the Lord has touched me."

And when they grew quiet it was to beam and bless the Lord's anointed and to drop the fluttering green into the baskets.

Money. So much money. . . .

In the dream she felt nothing, knew that she felt but wouldn't admit it, and she was in her house, racing for the bathroom, hand on the doorknob—it was locked. "No," she said, and woke into a painful white, the smell of disinfectant, her mother's blinking eyes. Beyond that disconcerting movement loomed her father. He was considering his fingernails, the pearls of half-moons where the dark flesh stopped. He was counting to himself from one to five, listing the deformities that flowered in his mind. Two were the bodies of his sons, one the absence of Max, fourth, the disfiguration of his hatred, last his grief, and when he'd done with counting, his eyes found floor and wall and fixture, everything except the bed on which his daughter lay.

Carla thought, *You are my father. Look at me.*

But he hadn't looked, and now she rested her head on the table, echoing the hurt child's universal cry, the one that could startle with perfect pitch even though you were gnarled and gray and the origin of hurt a life's worth of years behind you: *It isn't fair.* No reason anybody would consider, but still, it wasn't fair.

*   *   *

She was twenty-two months old when Max came. Predictably, she hadn't liked him, had pulled the covers off him while he slept, yanked the bottle from his mouth, had to be watched lest she experiment with how far fingernails would go into his eyes. Her mother was vigilant and firm, sending Carla to consider her behavior in her room, or when that punishment didn't accomplish change, delivering a slap or two to her bare bottom.

At some point, as Meridian had said, Carla stopped trying to maim Max, and later there was a stretch during which they'd fought and played like any siblings. This ended with the discovery of Max's calling. Then the house was thrown into a whirlwind, and the dark inside her father changed suddenly to light. Now, in the twinkling of an eye, she felt as if she lived alone. It was all Max and her father, Max and her mother, and there were times when she tried to climb between her father and Max and she'd be pushed away, and times when she'd be banished to another room so he could talk to Max in private. On other occasions she was commanded to be quiet because Max slept or prayed or was doing whatever it was that holy boys did. Sometimes she stood, mouth open, witness to one of her brother's abrupt intersections with the spirit. All the blood rushed from his face, his eyes rolled, body thrashing where he'd fallen. Rufus would make them stand back, lead them in prayer. When it was over, Max would come to them, one by one, lay hands on their cheeks and kiss them. When it was her turn, she could smell his almost fire smell of two stones rubbed together, the sign, her father said, of his anointing.

As she grew older, she was conscripted into service. It was she who kept the boys quiet while Max read his Bible, she who was her mother's company while Max and Rufus were on the road. When they were gone, she missed her father, but enjoyed having her mother to herself. Hardly would she grow accustomed to the pleasure than Max came back, and everybody hovered around him, crowing about what had been, apparently, a great success. Her father made a big deal of counting the money, dumped piles of it on the living room floor. Finally someone would acknowledge her, and she'd be handed the laundry from their trip.

Through it all, Max acted as if what she did for him was right

and ordinary, although sometimes when she came into his room
to collect his dirty underwear, or asked that he move so she could
strip his bed, his sharp, pale face would soften with a look that
said, "Don't blame me. It's not my fault."

Well, maybe it wasn't, but it wasn't hers either. He could, she
fumed, at least stop to talk to her about it, or take the small step
to be the ally that she craved. But he didn't. He treated her as a
sister whose presence he tolerated, a minor servant to the Lord's
anointed.

For a holy boy, he was messy. Shit stains marked his underwear; his socks were stiff, and he had to be reminded that the
sole purpose of water was not baptism. He was fond of eating in
bed. Crusts of jelly sandwiches hid beneath his sheets, apple cores
and peach pits, and once she found the week-old remains of a
pork chop in his pocket.

"You're a slob," she said. "Why can't you pick up after yourself? Why can't you use a garbage can? Mama, why do I have to
do this? Why can't he clean up after himself?"

"That's the way boys are, honey. He's your brother, remember
that. He needs to keep his mind on the Lord. One day you'll
receive a blessing."

"Tell her if she's going to be worth something to a man, she's
got to know how to take *care* of a man."

Her father said that. He was reading the newspaper. She was
standing five feet away, but he spoke to her mother.

Inside of Carla, below her heart, an emptiness was growing. The
feeling wasn't frightening, just there and strange; it had a weight
that sometimes shifted with her movement. Because this space was
all she had to call her own, she began to cultivate it, and as it
grew into wonderful shapes she could see only when she closed
her eyes, as it shimmered in shades of violet and magenta, she
found herself dreaming of its beauty. It accompanied her to
school, where teachers complained that she didn't pay attention.
It affected her relationships with children her own age, who, already wary of her position as Max's sister, began to taunt her

about the separateness she moved in. When she saw the taunting had power to hurt her, she built a wall, and in a little while her classmates couldn't touch her, except to make her wish she could cause them all to vanish.

There were things she had to do—go to school and finish her chores—and she did these, but she resolved that she'd do nothing else. She wouldn't go outside, wouldn't play with other children. She'd just build her wall and live life on the inside, in that empty place with the beautiful shapes and colors, a place that, since no one could enter, no one could ever leave.

As for her new brothers, the ones who'd come one right after the other, she looked and felt nothing. As they grew older, this changed, and she began, against her will, to love them, even though they, too, loved Max more than her. It was Max into whose waiting arms they took first steps, Max they called to when he came into the room, Max they cried for in his absence.

That is how her childhood went. And she might have gone on this way forever, for though she could imagine the morning she would leave this house, go far away and make her own life, she couldn't imagine how the day would get there, or what, when it arrived, one did to make a life. Then, one night in the late spring of her sixteenth year, she woke from a dreamless sleep.

It was the emptiness below her heart that woke her. She lay, measuring the space, preparing so that when she stood and it shifted, she'd be able to maintain her balance. Then she slid from bed, walked barefoot to the door. In the mirror her reflection was ghostly; she couldn't see her face, only the white gown in the darkness. The house was cool, she shivered, reached for her robe. In the hallway she looked both ways, then moved halfway down the staircase. Below, in the living room, flame filled the fireplace. Shadows flickered, hid in Max's hair, slow-danced with her father's eyes. Her feet were cold. Her father was on the couch, Max on the floor, covered with a blanket, his head against her father's thigh.

"You warm enough?"

"Yes," Max said.

They sat, watching the fire, and then her father cleared his throat in that way he had when he was about to say something important.

"Today," he began, "is the day we chose for your birthday. Today you're fourteen, and ready to be a man. Happy birthday, son."

"Thank you, Daddy."

"You're welcome. I want to talk to you this morning about the human condition. You know what I mean by that?"

"No," Max said. "I don't."

"Okay, then listen good. When I say human condition, I mean many things. I mean disease, poverty, random heartbreak and destruction, I mean the appointment unto man to die. But that's not the heart of it, my love. The heart of the human condition is *alone*. Nobody in the universe but you alone. You got to be able to accept that, feel it in your soul, your veins and arteries, the marrow of your bones. Just sit here for a spell. It's three minutes past four o'clock this May morning in nineteen thirty-eight, and I want you to feel how alone you is. Just sit."

The fire snapped, discovered pine cones at its center, burned sweet and green and blue, and she was trying to understand, turning her father's words as if they were jewels that refused, despite their facets, to reflect the light.

"Now because you smart, Max, you probably thinking, how can I be alone if Daddy's with me? Well, I'm with you, but nothing I can *do* for you. If the angel of death was to waltz into this room, though him and me was to tussle till daybreak, he'd win, Max, and leave here with your spirit in his briefcase. Were sickness to swoop in from the air, should some demon take your mind, drive you to the woods to live with beasts, I'm nothing but a spectator. You got to feel that. You got to accept being beyond human aid and redemption. When you do, you'll have taken away alone's power to make you fear. You hear what I'm saying? I want you to consider that. . . .

"Are you considering?"

"I am considering," Max said.

"Do you feel it? Do you *feel* alone?"

"Yes."

"Are you afraid?"

"No," Max said, "I ain't."

"Good." Rufus lowered his head, kissed Max's hair. "A few weeks ago," he said, "I dreamed man had built a space ship what got him to the moon. Before he set foot on it good, man was off again, looking for some other rock to poke a stick at. Well, I keep dreaming this, three nights running, and I know I'm dreaming 'cause I want to understand. Man do and do and do, but the question is: Why *does* he do? I turn it over, Max, but can't come up with nothing. The third night was the kicker. The third night brought a voice, off to the right beyond my vision, speaking from the deep infinity of space, a quiet voice clear as my own in my ears this very minute. And what it said was this: 'We are not alone. Out here in all this non-air, there's something else. They might have frog eyes and blue skin, but they out here.'

"No sooner had the voice finished, Max, than that great big old ship lifts off the face of that disbelieving moon, soaring like some silver bird to stop before me. And I'm considering: Great God! What a specimen of mankind's genius. What a piece of work is man. I'm in awe, Max. And as I gaze at this miracle of man's imagination, I recognize the shape. I start laughing: Ain't *this* a development? You know what the ship's shaped like? A penis. That's right. And in the middle's a window of cream-colored light, like a baseball diamond, except there's too much room from second base to home, and first and third is right on top of each other. And then this light gets a light within the light right smack where the pitcher's mound would be, and the second light starts pulsing like it's sending out a signal. I look behind me, quick, but ain't nothing but a dark so deep and cold it makes my teeth ache, and when I turn again the light's still pulsing. I figure it's Morse Code, but ain't no language I can speak. And then it just comes to me, and I'm laughing to beat the band. Picture, if you will, me, Rufus Alexander March, out by my lonesome in blackest space, hee-heeing so hard tears come to my eyes.

"You know what the light was? A woman's private parts. That's right. A woman's private parts out there winking so whatsoever was there could see it in the dark. And then I understood, Max. I understood what drives man is the need to connect, the need to overcome *alone*. That's why man does. And ain't but three ways to connect, unless you got a space ship, and that's religion, sex, and money."

He paused, gathered himself. "Now I want you to consider sex, Max. The touching, holding, penetration and engulfing, keeping off the ending not for discipline, but 'cause ending starts the journey back into *alone*. Sex is the way man tries to get to where he come from: the warm wet of the womb, the perfect oneness, all hooked to the illusion of safety and the need to connect. If you want a word for what man's looking for, call it comfort, connection, call it consolation.

"But here's the rub, Max. Once you accept *alone*, you realize sex ain't worth a hill of beans compared to money. Money will comfort you, you hear me?"

He paused and looked above him, seemed fixed by the riot of flame shapes on the ceiling. "Now I don't deny it, Max, we've made some money. We've made it in Albany and Ithaca, and Lord knows we went through Liberty like Grant through Richmond. We've taken the gospel to heathens of all colors and persuasions. But to make real money, you got to start preaching about sex. 'Cause money and sex is the main competition for religion. And since most folks never have enough money, that leaves it up to sex. . . .

"Are you following me?"

"I am," Max said.

"Okay, then you ready for the real deal. Quiet as it's kept, most folks are ashamed about sex, as they should be, 'cause it's sinful unless you married and trying to make a baby. That's all it was meant for by the Lord our God, and folks are always trying to put it to some other use. The point is: *You* can take advantage. Take sex away. Preach the pleasure, but stress the sin. Attack it, Max. Declare war. Men on one side, women on the other, don't let 'em touch. Put Jesus in the middle, the only comfort, all that's left. They'll pay you to tell them this. Then take your bag in the back room and start counting all that money, knowing at the same time that you're saving souls.

"You hear what I'm saying? I wish I could explain it better, wish I had some learning. But even so, this ain't in no books. You understand?"

"I think so."

"You sure?"

"Well," Max said, "what about heaven?"

"You got to take care of this life first," Rufus said. "The next will take care of itself." He paused. "That's the first thing. The second is you ain't got to be poor to be holy. The Lord mean for his people to have what they need. Hear what I taught you. Don't get hung up in this 'blessed are the poor' stuff."

"I won't," Max said.

"Good. Any more questions?"

"I don't think so."

"All right. Listen good. Even though you understand, even though you got the money, you need to know alone is a monstrous thing and will sometime get the best of you. I made you up a song for when that happens. Every time you feel you going under, take it out and sing it. I promise it will pull you through. Okay? Here it is."

He began to sing in a room soothed by dancing fire, voice deep and rich and powerful:

> *I'm all alone, and all by myself, too.*
> *I'm all alone, and all by myself, too.*
> *Got my song in my pocket, and I know just what to do.*
>
> *Gonna sing my song till it keeps me company.*
> *Gonna sing my song till it keeps me company.*
> *Gonna sing my song what my daddy give to me.*

"Now you try it, Max," Rufus said, and Max cleared his throat, squared his shoulders, and began to sing, voice rising to embrace the one left in the air by his father. His was a sweet voice, thin, full of feeling and trust and the desire to please. And when it was over, Rufus threw his head back and laughed out loud sitting thirty feet away from where his daughter hid, neither white nor male, nor holy. And Rufus hugged Max and said, "Mon-*ey*," and Max laughed, and Rufus said, "That's my boy. Now tell me this: Who are you?" and Max cried, "I AM THE LORD'S ANOINTED."

"Not so loud now, you'll wake your mother. Who is?"

"*The fulfillment of the prophecy!*"

"Amen! And in whose light?"

"*Black people will flourish!*"

'All right! Now tell me one more thing, who loves you?" and Max turned, smile radiant, mismatched eyes ablaze with devotion.

"You do," he said, and Rufus laughed again, and said, "You got that right, yes, Lord, you got that right."

And what of her? She, girl child stranded in the dark above them on the staircase, keening beyond their circle and the fire's light, the one who hissed (not loud enough to hear): "*I hope you die.*"

She didn't tell this last to Phoenix. Even though he'd fallen asleep, lulled by the rhythms of her voice, still she didn't tell him. She got up to lift him from the floor, then stopped and sat again. Footsteps had thudded on the porch. Rufus, huge, dark, was slumping through the door. He went past his daughter, stepped over Phoenix, managed a grunt of greeting.

"Mama's lying down," she said.

"Yeah. Max back yet? Boys home from school?"

She responded the way her mother had directed, matter of fact, but firm. "Max is gone. The boys is dead."

Rufus didn't answer.

Tired from her telling, weighed by grief, Meridian had climbed the stairs to lay across her marriage bed. Now she studied the profusion of roses in the wallpaper's pattern; they were shimmering as if at the bottom of a pond, but her mind was on how their lives had been broken, and what she could do to heal them. The hardest thing to accept was how her feelings for her husband had changed, and she pushed the thought away, choosing instead to focus on the gulf between Rufus and his daughter. She should have said something from the get-go, should have said: *Rufus, she's a child, she needs you. She didn't do it by herself. And she didn't kill no one, she made a mistake, got pregnant, but that's no crime. Max committed the crime, yet it's Carla you punish. You won't come out and say it, you blame her for what happened, but you won't say it. And I said nothing, and I'm a grandmother before my time, pregnant in the autumn of my life, trying not to hate you for what's happened to my children. I promise this one in my belly I'll protect from you. . . .*

Rufus wandered into the room.

"I know they're out there someplace," he said. "I'll find them."

He sat, still in his overcoat, head turned toward the window. The winter that hadn't known snow had left ash on his face, and Meridian, as if he'd brought the chill inside, pulled covers to her chin. "Take off your coat," she said. "You'll catch a cold."

Silently, he obeyed, then sat again. She watched how he filled the window. She'd wondered when they'd met if she could bear the weight of such a big man, if she had room enough inside for what he'd bring. Later, she'd laughed at her worry. In the middle of it, he'd been weightless, and her room so perfect she'd joked that it was custom-made.

Now, staring at his brooding figure, she was pulled between compassion and the desire to take from this half unlived-in house *all* the children, born and unborn, and vanish. Her decision to stay came from a place thick with memory: the history of illnesses faithfully attended, the joy of birth, laughter, the conversations, muted, while the house slept. She remembered passion sharper than knife blades, all the times she'd bared her thighs to Rufus in all the unexpected places: the kitchen, the bathroom, the cold, damp cellar wall. This, she knew, was what kept her from leaving: history, and the hope that things could again be as they were.

"When you get up," Rufus said, "take my good suit out. We're going to church in the morning."

"To Christ Savior?" They hadn't attended service there in ten years.

"You don't think we're going to worship with the white folks?"

"No, Rufus, I don't think that."

"Well, then."

In a voice that said he hadn't heard his meanness, he asked, "You got something suitable to wear?"

"I do."

"Good."

"Why we going to Christ Savior?"

"You'll see."

He sat a while, then, with the tone of a man who'd been carrying the question in his heart: "Why'd you wait so long to tell me you were pregnant?"

She was in her bed, across the room from her husband; she was frightened. "It was only a month, Rufus. And I've told you a hundred times. I wanted to be sure."

"We could have been unsure together."

"I'm sorry. I was worried and grieving. I didn't know how you'd take it. I didn't know how *I* felt about it. I know you said we had to start all over, but that was right after everything happened, and you might have changed your mind."

He grunted.

"Have you, Rufus?"

"Have I what?"

"Changed your mind?"

"No. Have you?"

"It's not my mind that needs changing. It's how we are. It's what's happened to us as a family."

"You're not saying you don't want the baby?"

"I'm saying I want things to be right between us."

He nodded at the window. "Everything's fine," he said, "and getting better."

"Everything's *not* fine. I stood next to you, saw them shovel dirt on my babies, and you won't accept it. You won't accept that Max ain't coming back, that for whatever reason, he set that fire."

"The boys are out there someplace, and I'll find them."

She closed her eyes.

"Do you believe me?"

"What about your daughter?"

"Do you *believe* me?"

"I believe you, Rufus, but what about your daughter?"

"Thank you." He raised his arms, laced fingers behind his head. "Think we'll get any snow this winter?"

She didn't answer.

"I asked if you—"

"Eventually, Rufus."

"It's strange," he said. "Boys going off like that . . . " He shook his head, then brightened. "But you know, we were blessed, Meridian. We were blessed to live in the same house with the Lord's anointed. It was sin that made him leave, and when we purge that sin, he'll come again. That's our great and glorious promise."

"Rufus. What about your daughter?"

"Where you think he's staying? How's he keeping warm? He didn't take his winter coat. He left his boots."

"Your *daughter*, Rufus."

"Why'd she do it, Meridian? Why'd she drive everyone away?"

"Carla *didn't* drive anyone away."

He shook his head and popped a mint into his mouth.

"Oh yes she did," he said.

On the night that his house burned down and his children perished, Rufus collected what was left of his family and went to bunk with neighbors. On the day before they put his two sons in the ground, reeking of smoke, unable to rinse from his mouth the taste of charcoal, he paced the length of his neighbor's yard, arms folded, his hatless head thrown back. Then he stood massaging his neck, gazing up at the sky where blackbirds spun crazily, then out at the river where, sixty feet away, a dark tangle of debris sat sphinxlike on the water. It looked like junk found near the edge of anybody's river: brush and old clothes, a bottle winking shrewdly in the sunlight, and Rufus wondered why it didn't move. He knew the river at that point; wade ten steps from the shore and the earth gave way like a broken promise, sloped steeply down and out. Where the debris disfigured it the water was thirty feet deep, and it was unlikely that something he could put his arms around had parts that reached the bottom.

He shoved his hands deep in his pockets, rocked on his heels, wondering if this was one of nature's marvels, if it were possible that currents could meet in such a way as to deny their movement. As he wondered, something opened up inside him, and the refuse turned, began to float downstream.

Rufus watched it, aware now that the opening inside of him was dread. Above him, birds screamed in frenzied circles, passed through sun that made him squint, and he looked back to where the refuse left ribbons in its wake. Then he knew. It was the sober movement that told him: The debris was his hatred of his one remaining child.

"Jesus," he whispered, and the refuse stopped, revolved, and floated *up* the river. Rufus slumped. What kind of cruel laws ruled the universe; why was this happening now, here in unrelenting sunlight, when what he needed was a clean, dark place in which to grieve? Besides, he didn't hate his daughter. He recalled his firstborn's birth, the quick disappointment that she wasn't a boy, then joy that from his loins had sprung this wonder. He'd begun, Meridian teased, to handle the infant as if she were an apple whose sole purpose was to shine. He'd made a song for her, and sang it. Meridian was his wife. She'd been there, and she knew.

Debris floating both ways on a river was mistaken.

So intent was Rufus on how easily the episode had ended that the idea of a beginning never crossed his mind. Nor did he realize that relief found in denial had created an addiction only death would kick. As it did to any addict, there were times when truth intruded, and then he'd groan and weep with rich abandon. When the pain was unbearable, he'd lurch toward the temporary solace of forgetting, go to sit at the window of his borrowed room, waiting to sight on the near horizon his three boys coming back from where they'd gone. His daughter limped home from the hospital, weak, expecting the worst; he didn't look when he spoke to her, lest, in that instant, his boys showed up, only to leave because he wasn't watching. When he snuck a glance at Carla, the sight made him shiver with what felt so much like fear that it confused him, and he decided he wouldn't look again until he chose. Yes, she must be punished. But he'd determine when.

Having bought time with this decision, he adjusted the angle of his hat, then whirled back to the window, pulled by what he thought was movement. But there was nothing, just blue sky and horizon.

When the insurance check arrived three months later, Rufus stood, took a last look through his neighbor's window. It was then he realized he'd been staring out onto the back of a sky-blue house whose spirit had been broken. The roof sagged around the sore thumb of its chimney. Nobody had cleaned the gutters. This last evidence of neglect brought tears to his eyes, and he reached for his handkerchief, only to find himself doubled in pain. At first he thought it was gas or appendicitis. But the misery was too low for these; its source was well below his belly, behind the dense growth at his groin. He fingered it, and snatched his hand away. The pain had teeth; it was alive, and humming.

"Who are you?" Rufus said.

"Me? Your hatred."

"What you want with me? Why you here troubling a grieving man?"

"I'm gonna eat your Johnson."

Dangling flesh shriveled up toward the hole it came from. "Why?"

"You're supposed to be so smart. You figure it out."

So Rufus embarked, that very moment, into figuring. His problem was of some proportion, and he examined his position with the intensity of troops fired upon in peacetime, hastily concluding that the enemy was fate. In an attack whose duplicity would be unmatched until Pearl Harbor, fate had come in the night to reclaim what it had given, what he'd worked to build and hold to, what he'd loved, and he'd reacted first by singing, then by staring out a window. Now he saw that if he wished, ever again, to make love, he must revise his tactics and respond like a man. Otherwise, that which made him a man would be devoured.

Hemmed between a rock and hard place, Rufus began to create a plan to relieve the excruciating pressure. Had he not been so vulnerable, had he time, he might have come up with something that rivaled the originality of the song he sang the night his house burned down. Since neither was the case, his plan was ordinary. First, he'd start over, begin a new family. Second, he'd prepare for his boys coming back by buying a house large enough for all of them to live in. Third, he'd divert the hatred at his groin, feed it by striking out, by smashing, by making others hurt as he did. Chief among his targets was the daughter he couldn't bring himself to look at, much less confront. This inability maddened him, and he took to imagining the deed completed, saw himself in black, his eyes on fire. "You're the cause of this heartache," he'd say. "You're why my boys are gone. Hussy. Liar. Ungodly bitch."

Even then he couldn't accuse Carla of the real crime, which wasn't that his house had been reduced to rubble, not that his flesh and blood were gone, but that Max, whom he'd loved without equal, was missing. He told himself that he'd been wounded, needed time to heal, and when that came to be, he'd do the right thing, insist upon his daughter's leaving, preside at the thrown-back door she'd pass through. At his elbow Meridian held the infant they hadn't named. Carla couldn't take him, for he was the child of the Lord's anointed, and couldn't be raised by a harlot. Nature itself expressed displeasure; it was snowing, the dead of a nighttime storm, and it was into this, head bowed, that Carla walked. Committed to the end, he wouldn't be looking when she vanished.

"You got to talk to your daughter," his wife said. "Can't you see she's suffering?"

"We're starting over. My name is Rufus Alexander March, and I will not be defeated."

"I understand," Meridian said. "I understand we need to start again. But what about your daughter? This is our family. All we have left."

Something more than family was on the line. "We're starting over," Rufus said, and he went looking for a house on the white side of Manor Avenue.

Nowadays, black people live all over Kingston, but back before the Great Depression, Manor Avenue had been the line they couldn't cross. With few exceptions, one of whom had been Rufus before the fire, the better off that black people were, the closer they lived to that street. Most were worn out by the time they made it, for getting there marked an emotional climb only a few degrees less than perpendicular.

Manor Avenue is at the crest of the hill that Kingston is built on. The hill moves up from the river in a gentle slope broken by a series of plateaus where folks could, for a year or two, pause to compute those sacrifices necessary to complete the journey. This stop-and-go strategy took time. When the travelers reached their destination they looked around and discovered what everyone knew who'd ever climbed a mountain: Once you'd had your fill of the view, you realized everything of interest was happening below.

Had anyone chosen to share this discovery, it might have redirected energy. Black people might have held on to their riverfront property (now thick with white-owned luxury condos). In fairness to Rufus, had he not been so distracted, he would have made a different decision, built something near the river or refurbished one of the homes already there. But he was hurting, he needed a place to live, and there was the time-honored response to his condition that folks called change. He also felt he had a right to live where he wanted. Now that many of the spacious houses on the white side of Manor were empty due to the Great Depression, he'd exercise his right. If, in the process, he set white people's teeth on edge, that was icing on his cake. Because he had the insurance money in his pocket, plus the money he'd buried in his yard, it wouldn't take a lifetime to do it. He wasn't worried about becoming one of those uppity Negroes who'd been climbing so long he'd forgotten where he'd come from. He had no plans for trading his blues for Mozart, or for taking his afternoons with tea.

The house Rufus settled on was a green two-family affair, sixteen rooms in all. When the real estate agent unlocked the door to the east side, the Marches entered a foyer, beyond which climbed a walnut stair. No one had spoken since they'd left the agent's car. Carla shifted the infant in her arms. Rufus looked grave and businesslike, but he was trying to remember why he was here. He popped a mint into his mouth to counteract the burnt taste.

Only Meridian seemed involved in buying property. Batting her eyes, a habit she'd acquired since the fire, whose heat and brightness had damaged her tear ducts, she examined the windows in the dining room, the appliances in the spacious kitchen.

The real estate agent, a tall, redheaded woman, was trying not to stare at the baby, wondering by what combination of genes the striking child had been produced. Blond and gray-eyed, the infant had skin that slept in the interval between dull gold and jaundice. Both adults, as was the girl in the too-long purple dress, were the deep brown of Colombian coffee. Each was handsome. But their good looks didn't explain the blond hair or the eyes. The agent was dying to ask, but she knew that questions of skin color were upsetting to Negroes, especially when they concerned whites in their family tree.

She smiled at the child, stuck a finger beneath its chin. The fingernail was scarlet. The baby began to scream.

"Oh . . . " The agent reddened.

"It's the fire," Carla said.

Meridian shut off the gas-stove burners, and the infant dropped into silence as wide as the agent's eyes.

Stimulated by the outburst and the sugar in his mint, Rufus remembered why he was standing in the middle of an empty dining room. There was work to be done, decisions to be made, and he turned to stride back through the living room, up the stairs to where a bath and bedrooms claimed the second floor. He knocked thoughtfully on the wall dividing the house, then climbed the tight staircase to the attic, empty except for a stack of black roof shingles tied with baling wire. There, in the room he'd die in, he spun, retraced his steps and led them all down to the cellar. Someone had begun to finish this space; walls were framed with two-by-fours. Rufus considered what he'd looked at and was pleased.

For the past ten minutes, while one part of Meridian's mind efficiently weighed the house's features, the other wondered where Rufus was coming from. Why was he considering such a large house, why a two-family? Did he want the extra rooms in which to grieve? She cleared her throat.

"Isn't this more house than we need?"

For a moment she thought he hadn't heard, but as she started to repeat her question, Rufus answered.

"The house needs *us,*" he said.

He might have been shouting to someone across the street, and the people at his back jumped, then looked away. It was the kind of silence that follows a comment utterly off a public wall. In its presence a man in touch with himself listens and moves to clarify. Rufus said it again, louder.

Meridian stared at him. People were saying the fire had sent her husband off the deep end, but she, because she understood his pain and hadn't yet grown to hate him, hoped he was simply deep. Grief did that to people, made them reflective. Still, she wasn't sure. If she had been, she'd have told him she was pregnant.

"It may need us," she said. "But it's too big."

Rufus turned to her, and she braced for argument. Instead, he smiled, seduction so luminous she blinked.

The smile was deception. Rufus understood her hesitation; he just felt no duty to explain. It was, in every sense, his business. A good businessman was like an artist who let the work spell out his vision. Still smiling, Rufus did a little hop, leaned like a sprinter listening for the starter's gun. Then he sauntered out onto the back porch where he pushed his blue Stetson up from his forehead, put his hands in his pockets, and rocked back on his heels.

Two inches over six feet, lean and wide-shouldered, he was a man whose middle years had barely aged him. A touch of gray lingered at each temple, and he had enough belly to give the impression he wanted: He was successful, but not yet gone to pot. This pose—the hat on the back of his head, the hands just so in his pockets—he'd practiced to perfection, convinced that in addition to its style, it was one of the few positions from which the true worth of things could be measured.

Before him, weeds claimed the yard with the zest of squatters. This and the slatted fence made the plot seem cramped, but Rufus wisely saw room for a garden and a sandbox for the baby. He'd tear down the fence, create the illusion of space. An oak tree wearing a shawl of chattering sparrows dominated a corner; Meridian could string a clothesline to the porch.

Rufus felt good, like rolling up his sleeves and working. But as he imagined attacking the yard with a freshly honed scythe, the blade weight tightening his forearms, his change began to come: dry mouth and tingling cheekbones, space opening inside him. Still rocking, he looked above him at a suddenly lowered sky. Abundant sunshine had given way to thin, indifferent light; November's afternoon seeped through the crack dividing fall and winter. The moment enveloped Rufus, made him lonely, made him well with his recently acquired, unmanly urge to weep. Sighing, he peered into the bordering street and stiffened. Gathered on the sidewalk, spilling off the curb, was a small army of white people. Rufus didn't take time to notice that their faces wore nothing more than disbelief that, having just survived a depression, they, like Job, were being tested once again, and he was too far away to hear some of them whisper that to gather in the street was less than good behavior. The only particular that registered beyond their skin was the red sweater worn by a woman who held a baby. As he gazed at the sweater, wondering why it was so familiar, and how he'd defend his family against this siege, the child began to cry, a shrill, angry wail that strangled when the woman stuck a finger in its mouth.

Rufus relaxed. This wasn't war; troops didn't bring babies to the battle. This was a peace brigade, white-flagged and weary, gathering to learn what price a treaty would extract. If Negroes moved to their side of the avenue, would quiet be shattered with blues songs and laughter? Would weekends bring parties with big-butt women and gold-toothed copulating men who carried razors on their hips? Would yards fill with old cars and watermelon rinds; would white children begin to speak jive?

The people on the sidewalk (some of whom *were* thinking this) had no way of knowing that while Rufus still loved the blues, the fire had burned the laughter from him. Nor could they know that Meridian was all the woman he'd needed since 1915, or that he'd long ago abandoned straight razors for the range and good sense of a shotgun. Rufus didn't think that things would come again to shotguns. But he didn't want people loitering in the street to look at him; it was bad for property values.

"I'll build a higher fence," he said, and ran his tongue across the smoke taste, wishing he could brush his teeth.

The agent, who'd been holding her breath, smiled, relieved at the separatist, nonviolent solution. *So smart*, she thought, *so good-looking*. She'd meant the smile to be approving. It came out warm and inviting, activated a trembling in her thighs, and made Meridian's back arch.

They trooped through the other side of the house, a mirror image of the first, except that the kitchen, though serviceable, wasn't new, the attic was empty, the basement a damp gathering of dark. Back in the first living room, Rufus gazed at the ceiling, then turned to his wife. Ceremoniously, he put a hand on each of her shoulders.

"We'll take it."

"Don't you want to see more?" Meridian said. "We going to take the first house we look at?"

"Why not?" Rufus said. "If it fits."

"I don't need two kitchens," Meridian said. "Two attics, neither. Who's going to clean all this house? Who'll cook in the other kitchen?"

"Now, baby. That'll take care of itself."

Meridian stiffened. *Baby* was their code word. You ceased debate when it was spoken. *Baby* asked for slack, to let the other own the moment and he'd owe. It said, *We disagree, but remember that I love you.*

And he'd used it in the presence of this bitch.

Meridian blinked. To ignore the signal meant to make a hard time harder, meant there'd be hell to pay. Well, then, she'd pay it. But it would be in currency other than her self-respect.

"Rufus, we're talking about our home. *Our*. If you got reasons, I want to know."

Rufus shook his head, looking for all the world like a man on his way to cash a sweepstakes ticket, called back to take his hat. "I can't believe you, Meridian. You're good at arithmetic, why can't you figure it out?"

"Arithmetic?"

"For Max and the boys. For Carla and the baby. So they'll have room enough to stay—"

"Rufus."

"—They can bring their wives when they're ready—"

"Rufus."

"—They can have privacy—"

"Rufus! The boys is dead. Max is gone."

"And for the kids that's coming. We're starting over. We'll need the room."

"Rufus, please!"

At this he said, with a matter-of-factness that made her falter, "I'm the man here, Meridian."

"Rufus. . . . "

"Sh!"

Inside Meridian a voice began. *Girl,* it said, *if you cry, I'll kill you.*

Rufus studied the ceiling, Meridian the floor. Carla was struck by the stillness. The agent was dizzy. The fact that at the advanced and respectable age of forty-one she'd felt a sharp physical attraction for a colored man had shifted her balance. Now she was confused by the conversation and guilty that she'd apparently accomplished a sale with a minimum of effort. Like a politician avoiding a reporter's question, the truthful answer to which would sink the campaign, she turned her attention to the baby.

"What a beautiful child. What's her name?"

"*His,*" Carla said. "His name is Phoenix."

"Phoenix? That's from the Greek. Mythology. Where . . . ?"

"In school," Carla said. "They taught us."

"School?" Then, to her own amazement, the agent laughed, a high whinny that stopped in mid-note. "You like having a brother?"

"He ain't my brother. He's my son."

"Son?"

Rufus said, "You won't guess who his daddy is."

"*Stop it*," Meridian hissed.

The agent said, "Excuse me?"

"You won't guess who his daddy is."

"*Rufus!*" Meridian said.

"His daddy," Rufus said, "named Max."

Meridian turned her back, eyes closed. Her husband was smiling at the agent, poised for her reply. Carla stared at her father. So. She had one less secret than she thought. Since no one had challenged her, she'd begun to accept that no one knew. Even when she knew better. There was something to be learned from that, but she didn't know what. What she did know was that she felt a searing anger. Her parents were cowards. They'd failed to confront her. Then she was afraid.

"You've heard of Max?" her father asked the agent.

"Max?"

"Max," Rufus said, and held his arms up, as if, in that unlikely time and place, he was rejoicing. He turned completely in a circle, dance that made the loose change jingle in his pocket.

"Oh," the agent said. "*That* Max."

When the church doors opened in the middle of "Nearer My God to Thee," nobody turned to look at the late arrivals, not because they weren't curious, but because they'd been taught that to do so was in poor taste. Instructions had not, however, included how to act if the doors stayed open, creating a drop in temperature, and when chilled heads turned on that Sunday morning, it was to witness the March family framed in the entrance, lit by a sun whose strength, though uncommon for December, brought no warming.

Chins fell, and the singing stopped. By then Rufus had dismissed the usher who'd moved uncertainly to greet them. The usher recovered, closed the door, and the family that hadn't been to Christ the Savior in ten years filed smartly down the aisle.

It was quite an entrance: Rufus tall and menacing in his great brown coat, Meridian in mourning black, and if their heads were any higher, they'd have lost their balance and fallen over backward. Some were thinking that folks who'd not been to church for so long might have been less conspicuous and taken seats in the back. But the Marches, including the girl in the too-long navy blue dress, carrying the child she'd named, only God knew why, after a city in Arizona, sat in the second row.

And if that wasn't enough for a Sunday morning, no sooner had the door been shut on that rare December sunlight than that no-talking Junkman Douglas ducked into the church. He was wearing a black suit that might have belonged to his grandfather, and instead of the soft-brimmed fedora all the men were wild about that year, a red handkerchief covered his head in the style of a pirate. The usher sat Junkman by himself behind a woman in a green felt hat, who turned, smiled nervously, and whispered, "Praise the Lord." Because she was nervous, she sounded insincere. Junkman looked at her out of a long, dark face that featured eyes so black they were depthless. It was a face kept from being handsome only by its lack of expression, and it was this that made the woman feel accused of something overlooked in a life she'd thought was blameless.

As if to punctuate that discordant notion, a mangled melody came bleating from the front of the church, and everyone swiveled to see the Reverend at the lectern, his loud, off-key voice forcing people back into singing if only to relieve him of a tune he couldn't carry.

The Reverend wasn't thinking of the song's weight. He was thinking of Rufus March and what his presence meant. Rufus had caused him a lot of trouble, and while the minister was saddened by what had happened to the Marches, he wasn't unhappy that Max had disappeared. He didn't pray that the disappearance be forever, but he managed to let the Lord know that if that happened it would be all right with him.

Reverend Sweeny had the oldest black church in Kingston. Ten years ago it had been the only one. Despite his monopoly, the Reverend wasn't secure. This was a function of his background, one defined by disadvantages so deep their roots found water. In 1965, he'd come across the expression "poverty sucks," and he'd say that he'd spent a lifetime avoiding its lips. To warn him of those who might seek to take the comfortable life to which he'd grown accustomed, he'd perfected what he thought of as an "ambition detector." Over the years, the detector had gone off from time to time, alerting him with a series of low, short buzzes that he was in the presence of someone who had more than an average aptitude for enterprise. When Rufus joined the church twenty years ago, the device had screeched so loudly that the Reverend suffered a blinding headache until he adjusted the volume.

Back then, Rufus was working in the lumberyard, loading railroad ties, but that labor had done nothing to dull the brilliance of his dream. This was to one day run a business. It didn't matter what kind, as long as it was his. All he needed, Rufus said, was capital, a reference that confused those folks who thought he meant a city. But most people, including the Reverend, knew exactly what Rufus meant. The pastor also knew that one of the few ways a black man could have something in 1920 was by setting up a church. It was the Reverend's opinion that Rufus had as much chance of starting a business as a hog had of going on a holiday, and when Rufus realized this he'd change direction. Given the young man's carriage, good looks, singing voice, and drive, Reverend Sweeny prepared for the day when Rufus would be conveniently called to the ministry. From there it would be a short step to going after his church.

None of that had happened. Instead Rufus had left Christ the Savior to start his own church, with Max as the headliner. He called it the Temple of Love. The church was little more than a base to which Max returned after being in the field, during which time parishioners were left to worship on their own. They didn't even have a building; they met in parks, by the side of the river, a seasonal worship, until Rufus could afford to rent, on a once-a-week basis, the auditorium in the YMCA. Still, in less than a year, thanks to Max's revolutionary message that the Lord meant for his people to be rich as well as righteous, Rufus siphoned off half the Reverend's congregation. When the message began to insist that folks should be celibate outside of wedlock, and sexually circumspect within it, another third of the Reverend's flock defected. The irony was that the Reverend had stood up for Rufus when the county tried to take Max, said the Lord had revealed that Max's father was black, which would explain not only why the boy had been abandoned, but why his eyes didn't match.

Anyway, Max had stopped preaching, and a couple of months later, the Temple of Love began to slide. Over the last year and a half the Reverend's members had started to trickle back, and today Christ the Savior was nearly at full strength. The Marches hadn't returned until this morning, followed by Junkman Douglas, who, the Reverend had been told, had danced like an African at the fire. Junkman hadn't come to church since his father's funeral sixteen years ago, which he'd disrupted with screams for revenge. So why was he here this morning?

The Reverend, looking out over the congregation, knew that if he didn't clear up the mystery, the service would be marked by distraction, not least of which would be his own. He held up his hands to stop the singing. When he had everyone's attention, he welcomed the March family, making a veiled reference to the Prodigal Son. He said he knew that Rufus's heart was overflowing, and all of them were waiting to hear what he had to say.

The church was so still somebody later claimed she heard sunlight coming through the window. Rufus looked left and right, found the darting eyes of men who'd been his comrades before his success, men who'd come together to destroy the orchard. They'd been young together, strong, and now they sat with mouths slack. Some had gray hair, wives thickening next to them; they looked defeated, the last muscle withered in their manhood. If white men were to violate their homes, they'd barely have the energy to turn the other cheek.

Rufus was sad that his former friends had lost it all so quickly. He was about to mourn properly when he remembered where he was and why. He took a deep breath, unfolded to his feet. In a voice that shook with feeling, but which steadied as he spoke, he put his daughter's business in the street.

Carla, he said, had soiled the Lord's anointed. She, like Eve at the beginning of the world, had tempted Max, the result of which was the child now sleeping in her arms. And the Lord had caused His face to frown on them and had punished them with fire, into whose burning Max had vanished, translated, like Ezekiel before him, back to his father's throne, taking with him two earthly children whose only sin was Adam's. If any of them were to know peace and salvation, if Max and their sons were to return, and the prophecy to be fulfilled, that done beneath the cloak of darkness must be brought to light. And that's what he was doing, bringing it to light. For as the scripture said, the truth *is* the light.

And everybody knew truth's shining promise: The truth would set you free.

Two things happened. First, Lucinda Hancock, hair reaching halfway down her back, left her seat beside her mother and went to sit next to Carla. "Keep your head up," she whispered.

The second thing was that Junkman Douglas stalked, disgusted, from the sanctuary. Before he did that, he yanked off the pirate's handkerchief, revealing the stinging insult of his uncombed head.

Rufus sagged in his pew, spent, waiting for the power of confession to kick in and make him feel better. Meridian was staring at her knees, shaken by the desire to drive a knife into her husband's heart, in the process making her children fatherless. Carla sat ramrod straight with her baby on her lap. She was trying to focus on the weight of Lucinda's hand on hers, the way sunlight came through the window and made the Reverend's blue suit shine. So now everyone knew what she'd done, and that she'd done it for reasons no more compelling than Eve's. Somehow that wasn't the worst of it. The worst was having everyone hear what she'd known as long as she could remember: Her father didn't love her. Heat threatened to take her breath, and when she'd fought to the other side of that, she ached with the urge to scream and break things. This she stuffed inside. There was nothing to do with the shame except bear it.

Of a sudden, a woman's voice burst upon the stillness, and without pause, the congregation joined her. The song was "'Tis the Old Ship of Zion," and they sang it hard and loud, as if Rufus's betrayal had corrupted the air and music could beat it back into his throat.

Had Carla known what was in the minds of people in church, had they, after service or during the weeks that followed, shared their thoughts, she'd have found some comfort. Beyond forbidding their teenagers to have anything to do with her, lest they, through association, come to similar disgrace, grown-ups didn't harshly judge. Nobody present that morning had bought the story about Phoenix's father being an encyclopedia salesman, and once Max disappeared, they wouldn't have taken it for free. Their immediate response was that two babies had died, and a family was in trouble. They'd all pitched in, sat at Carla's bedside, brought food to Meridian, collected pots and pans, furniture and money to help the Marches start again. For weeks, the men combed the river's edge, and in the evenings gathered to support Rufus and keep his hope alive. The tragedy was that it had happened, not that Max had done it, not that he'd turned out to be one more holy man who hadn't practiced what he preached. There was no shame in Max's falling; the shame was in his inability to get past that which was divine to that which was human. If he had, he'd never have gotten caught up in something that resulted in the death of children.

In the weeks that followed, as black people talked of what had happened that day in church and recalled the events that led to it, the truth of their feelings surfaced. They were disappointed. Max had been taken in when his own folks didn't want him, been loved and cared for and finally exalted. There'd been a sense of joy during his heyday; all you had to do was turn your face to the sky to feel it. That boy had been a stone cold preacher. Maybe, toward the end, he had spent too much time hammering away at the ungodliness of sex, but it was kind of entertaining. Nobody was too quick to admit it, but he'd made folks reconsider sex, treat it as important, which meant, inevitably, that performance standards rose. Women who'd lain staring at the ceiling rediscovered ball joints in their hips, and the sweet pleasure of gentle rock-and-rolling. Men accustomed to going as hard as they could for as long as they could experimented with fuel-conserving speeds. True, nobody made any money except Rufus, but it was also true that Max had been a source of heat and light in that cold, dark corridor of the Depression. So they were disappointed when he stopped preaching, and more disappointed when they understood why he disappeared. The sad part was that he didn't have to; the sad part was that some of the fault was their own. They'd allowed him to be caught up in their long-lived hoping, encouraged him to believe he was the fulfillment of the prophecy, when all he was was another white boy with a gift. It was so unnecessary. Max could have confessed, stayed and worked it out; they'd have helped him. Two babies would be alive today.

As for Carla, she was not the first black girl this had happened to. Nor was it the first time someone had gotten his hat once what he'd left between a young girl's thighs had made her pregnant. Preachers and white men had been doing it longer than anybody could remember, and if the truth be told, black men had done it too. None of the women believed it was all Carla's fault; that was another habit men couldn't seem to break: blaming everything on females.

Those men who expressed themselves publicly had a different reaction. After they tightened restrictions on their daughters, they slapped each other on the back. "Old Max," they chuckled. "Should've known all that preaching about sex had something to it."

In one thing, however, male and female were in agreement. What Rufus did, making public his daughter's disgrace, was not right, and a wife who couldn't talk her husband out of such meanness didn't deserve the name. The disapproval Carla felt was directed not at her, but at her parents, and while no one expressed it to their faces, they avoided them. They justified their avoidance by saying that enough effort had been spent on the Marches, that the good will and support of a community had its limits. Besides, now that the worst of hard times was over, they had a lot of catching up to do, and they turned their energy to reclaiming what they'd given up for the Depression. In the middle of buying shoes and painting the kitchen, the war came, demanding not only their attention, but the bodies of their sons. With all that going on, one still had to find time to fish, laugh, go to church, and make love, all of which were possible despite the disappointment that nobody spoke out loud about, the one that walked into their homes and pulled chairs up to their tables. Good hosts all, they treated disappointment with the respect they'd have shown to any guest, allowed it to stay long past its welcome. Eventually, they were marked by it and started spinning in the streets.

The Reverend didn't spend a lot of time thinking about Carla. Had anyone asked, he'd have said that what her father had done was unfortunate. But she was young, would forget and heal and get on with her life. Sensing the need for consolation, he raised his hands, stopped the singing, invited the church to pray. He was in charge now, almost relaxed, almost convinced he'd nothing to fear ever again from Rufus. But what about Junkman? What had brought him to Christ the Savior?

Junkman was nine years old when they hung his deaf-mute daddy. His mother had died five years before, worn away, women said, by life with a man who couldn't hear her. The county placed the boy with the Josephs, a childless couple in their forties who owned a junkyard in the neighboring town of Tillson, and it was in school there that classmates coined his name.

For the next six years, in a room whose window looked out on rusting metal, Junkman fantasized revenge. One rainy day in 1930 he wandered into a moment whose impact lingered forever. He was not doing anything unusual, just standing at the window pressed against the belly of a soothing vision: A straight razor, silver in his own dark hand, etched a blooming across a pleading white man's throat. He pressed harder; a geyser mushroomed, lined his head with the scent of copper, and he waited for the warmth the image always brought him.

This time there was no warmth. This time he broke out in a cold sweat, his chest ballooned, and he buckled with the urge to vomit. Pursing his lips, Junkman fought the feeling, swallowed. Then his heart spoke, and he discovered the paralyzing properties of grown-up fear.

"Don't bring no more that shit in here," his heart said. *"That's it. I'm full. I've had it."*

Stunned, Junkman slow-motioned to his knees. It was as if the carnage of his dreaming—slit throats, crushed skulls, and gutted bellies, assholes stuffed with steel—all of it had crowded in his heart, distending chambers, pressure impossible to contain without explosion. Then, from a distance beyond terror, he heard his heart rip from his chest, plunge to his stomach floor, splatter fluid into space that shouted, *"Not here. This here's reserved for wonder."*

It was over. He was a dead man at fifteen.

"I don't want to die," he hollered. "Please don't let me die."

"Bradley, you all right?" Mrs. Joseph called from the hallway, using his given name.

He moaned, vomited all over the window.

"Yes," he said, and struggled to his feet, staggered across the room to lock his door.

"What's all that moaning?"

"I had a dream."

"Poor baby," she said, thinking he'd had another nightmare about his father. "I'm here if you need me. You hear? Call if you need me."

The event left him with a mess to clean, and the understanding that he had an inner life, a heart with standards, a space he couldn't, if he wished for peace, do violence to. Because of some personal flaw or quirk of nature, he was, apparently, doomed if he took a life, and sentenced to vomit if he thought it. He didn't want to accept it. The burning of trees didn't compensate for the death of a father. Murder was the only suitable revenge, and he'd find a way to reconcile it with his heart. Others had done it. Otherwise his father would be alive.

Though this reasoning didn't bring peace, he did experience the calm of a settled stomach, within which he discovered the possibilities of patience. Life was long; all he had to do was wait, and the secret of murder without consequence would come to him.

While he waited, he finished high school, and moved, in 1933, to Kingston, where he went to work for a Negro who owned two garbage trucks. He rented a kitchenette in a mixed-use building in the black community down by the river, and it was there, in a room above a hardware store, that he learned how hard it was to wait, how much it felt like doing nothing. That's when he devised what he thought would be a temporary answer: He refused to speak to white people, all of whom he held responsible for his father's death. He began, on his days off and in the evenings, to show up wherever whites assembled: in general stores and fish markets, at baseball games. At first he frightened them, but after they saw that his only agenda was to watch without comment, he became invisible in the way of a spouse or a servant to whom one has grown indifferent. Only once did he indicate to whites a motive, and this was four years after he stopped talking to them, and three and a half years after he'd grown so comfortable with silence that he didn't speak to anyone at all.

The decision to cease speaking altogether was not without obstacles. First, he had a job. Second, although he didn't care what whites thought of his silence, he didn't want to insult his own. He knew Negroes didn't take kindly to having their greetings left unanswered. In their eyes, the minimum standard for civilized behavior was to say good morning.

He dealt with his boss and co-workers by calling a meeting, at which his colleagues looked at him with squinched-up faces. But his boss said he didn't pay Junkman to talk; he paid him to pick up garbage, and as long as he did that he could stand on his head or speak in sign language, it made no never-mind to him.

For black people, Junkman had printed up five-hundred business cards, on which was the message that his decision was based on respect for his father, who, dead and unavenged, couldn't speak for himself. Some black people understood. Others said his father couldn't speak in the first place. Besides, his father *had* been avenged: There was an open field where an apple orchard used to be. But they didn't say this to Junkman because they didn't want to accuse him of being ungrateful.

The one time Junkman attempted to explain his speechlessness to white people was at a May Day celebration in Van Saun Park. The park was alive with families, blacks on one side, whites on the other, and the air was festive with flags and song and laughter. As he watched the revelers sprawled across the meadow, something turned over in him just behind the space reserved for wonder. When he closed his eyes he saw it was a small parallelogram the shade of wet tree bark. Inside this burned a fingertip of steady bright-blue flame.

Years later he'd understand the parallelogram was loneliness, the flame his longing to connect, be understood. Years later, he'd nurture the flame. But on that day he was bewildered by his need, and in the throes of this confusion, he wrote on a slip of paper, "I am your conscious," and gave it to a woman with wheat-colored hair. She, scarcely twenty, smelled of green peas and desire, and although she recognized Junkman from years of gatherings in public places, she didn't know his name or history.

" 'I am your conscious'?" she read. "This doesn't make any sense."

Heady with draft beer and a young man's promise to take her walking that evening, she balled up the paper, threw it away. Junkman wasn't aware that he'd misspelled the important word, and the exchange saddened him until he found a place to put it. It was as he suspected. Not only did white people have no conscience; they didn't even know what it was.

He spent the better part of thirty minutes brooding, and then his spirits lifted as he discovered that something wonderful had happened to his nose. The world had exploded, and he could smell it, young woman-flesh, sunshine, bird flight, and meadow. He stood trembling, wrapped in odor, and then he took off across the park. He spent the rest of the day exploring, smelling passersby, the variety of garbage, car exhausts, music, recreation so rich, so absorbing, he wondered if he'd ever need to bowl again.

In that same year, he went to hear Max preach at the fairground, which is how he saw Carla for the first time. She was eleven, wearing around her shoulders what he immediately knew was sadness, and he fell, with the velocity of a plummeting stone, head over heels in love. Being in love felt wonderful, soft weights in his palms, swift spells of tenderness. For years he hung out in the trees that ringed the March house, keeping a distance just within the range of a slightly raised voice. But it was not until Max was gone and the Marches had moved that he revealed his feelings, and this was by leaving on Carla's back porch a bottle of wild lilacs. Rolled and stuffed in the bottle neck was a note that said, "*I love you. Junkman.*"

The words *I love you* are powerful, producing in the recipient pride or gratitude, guilt or anger, all irrespective of intentions to respond. It was some measure of her condition that the words had no effect on Carla, were less interesting than the circumstance of wild lilacs in an unclean bottle. It was this that touched her: The glass was not clean. She brought the gift inside, removed the flowers, scrubbed the bottle until, when she held it up to sunlight, she was blinded.

After what Rufus did in church, Meridian refused to talk to him and moved into another bedroom. Rufus seemed dazed by her decision, took to walking around the house with his hat on, mumbling. He'd developed a taste for raw broccoli and collard greens, which he shoved into his mouth in handfuls. After he'd gorged himself, he'd disappear into the afternoon, where he continued to search for his boys.

Despite her own pregnancy, Meridian insisted on taking care of Phoenix most of the time, a task that left her without energy to continue conversations with her daughter. Not even the holidays brought quickening to that house. Christmas was solemn, without snow. Last-minute gifts sulked beneath a tree that sagged with too much tinsel, and the new year passed without remark.

Carla's days for the rest of that winter were marked by idleness broken by efforts to remember. She'd yet to discover the escape of reading, television was still in the research lab, and she had no interest in the radio. Sometimes she considered going back to school, which she'd quit after becoming pregnant, but this thought had no focus. Because she missed the diversion of talk, of ordinary human contact, she began to think of Lucinda Hancock, remembered how the girl had come to sit beside her, how she'd held her hand and said to keep her head up. For a while Carla allowed herself to believe that she and Lucinda were destined to be soul mates, that she'd one day come around a sunlit corner and find Lucinda there. Lucinda would hold her hand, and help her to remember.

But all the corners Carla turned that winter were marked by

gray, by frozen streets and a would-be girlfriend's absence, and in a while she reined in her fantasy of having an ally for recalling. Not knowing Kingston had granted her pardon, she dumped her memory on her bedroom floor, sifted through it for what she believed she'd forgotten, details that would make everyone understand why she'd done what she had.

All that year after the birthday talk, Max's sermons had been inspired, but Carla could tell he was troubled. An inevitable result of his preaching about sex was that females began to speculate that in him was a fire they wanted to be warmed by. One couldn't, they reasoned, preach that way unless one were an expert. They carried this speculation in their eyes, and found ways to let Max know that if he chose, as he put it, to be weak, they were willing; all he had to do was come and get it.

All of this frightened Max half to death. He was fifteen, and in the throes of his own temptation. He couldn't read his Bible or smell a flower without becoming aroused; the caress of clothing against his flesh was the hands of a woman who whispered that here and here were the solutions to his torment, the doors he'd been looking for to enter. Hot-breathed and writhing, the women crawled into his dreams, and when he awoke whimpering into the four o'clock hour, his sheets were stained with his spontaneous, unrighteous passion. Then, shaken, he'd fall to his knees where, until a rising sun lit the corners of his room, he called on the name of Jesus. He was holy, the Lord's anointed, and he begged God, "Please don't let me fall."

And Carla was subject to it also; she was seventeen, and inside her, full of breast and thigh, a rising woman. Sex was in the movement of tree limbs, the rocking of the car she took to church; sex stalked school corridors where her eyes feasted on the loveliness of butt curve, shoulder slant, and lip curl, boy-sweat like jewels in the hollows of their throats.

That was 1939, the war building up in Europe, a dry spring, hot, the year that mid-June lay in the air like August. Her mother had said it was the best stretch, financially, that they'd had, that

every time Max and Rufus returned from the road they were
swimming in money, although Max was complaining of headaches and kept mostly to the room his father had built for him
off the kitchen so he wouldn't be disturbed. And Carla, who'd
replaced the colors of emptiness with visions of men, moved
through the world dreaming of interludes with two lean strangers
who held her hands above her head while they licked her breasts
until she glistened and chanted *yes* with the intensity of prayer.

On this Saturday she'd been lying in the back yard, too sum-
mer-drunk to move even after the pressure told her she had to go
to the bathroom. The sun fell like a hammer; hot breezes wandered through the pines. Far above, almost invisible against the
blue, a black dot of a hawk was drifting, and she told herself that
when it disappeared, she'd go. When she couldn't wait any longer,
she jumped up, swept into the house, hurrying along the hallway,
dodged fire trucks and blocks, nearly running now, and burst into
the bathroom.

"Oh," she said.

Neither moved. Max, wide-legged in the dark, mouth open,
Max in a red bathing suit pulled to his thighs, one hand on his
hip; the other clutched his penis. The suit was dripping. She
looked from his hand to his eyes to his hand again and felt a
riveting excitement. It was large and sweeping, deeper than her
fantasy of breast-starved lovers. And there was the fear, the understanding that the door was open, that her mother, who'd taken
the boys shopping, might return at any moment, that her father
might come in from wherever it was he'd gone. Wordlessly, she
stepped inside the bathroom, shut the door, switched on the light.

"What are you doing?" he said.

His voice was a rasp, a whisper. She didn't answer, looked
straight into his eyes, the hazel one deepening to amber even as
she watched. The fear was gone now, replaced by something she
only later recognized as power, and as it filled her, she thought,
If I were a singer, I'd sing. The thought was unexpected and funny,
and she smiled that it had come to her. Still smiling, still looking
directly into his eyes, she reached a hand out, touched his flesh.
It was hot, and soft and hard.

"Carla!"

She waited, testing the limits of her power. Apparently they lay beyond where she'd gone. He'd whispered her name, but hadn't moved, hadn't insisted she open the door, release him. She felt as if she stood on the edge of a high place, about to leap toward an unseen bottom. She didn't care what was at the bottom; she was certain she'd survive. Quivering with that certainty, she peeled his fingers, replaced them with her own, held him lightly, as if testing for weight and balance, then closed her fist. In the instant before he groaned and shut them, his eyes went dark. She grunted. He looked so beautiful she could have wept.

"Don't, Carla."

"Why?"

"Because it's wrong."

"What's wrong about it?"

"You'll go to hell."

"For what?"

"You know."

She said, "Pray for me."

"Carla. You're my *sister*."

"No I'm not."

She began to move her hand, and he, eyes glazed, reached to push it away, but ended up enclosing her fingers with his own. He held her hand for a hard moment, then thrust it from him, pulled his suit up, fled. She swayed in his absence, dazed with what had happened, fired with knowing this was only the beginning. Then her neglected bladder called, and as she peed, she thought of her father and felt the warmth of satisfaction so deep she didn't even try to understand it.

That's how it began, that's how she discovered her power. How sweet it was, how lucky to have come upon her woman time and be living in the same house with beautiful boy-flesh. With a purpose whose concentration rivaled the density of diamonds, she stalked him. Whenever she caught his eye at the dinner table, she made a promise, whether with a faint, beguiling smile or the brilliance of her staring. Every time he was near enough and couldn't move without giving himself away, she found an excuse to touch or rub against him, licked her lips, fingered her breasts, her thighs, her belly. At dinner, she slipped her shoe off, inflamed him with her foot beneath the table.

Through it all, Max fought the good fight, avoided her when he could, pretended to ignore her when he couldn't. But most of all he prayed; in the gray light of dawn, in the midnight hour, in the heat of the afternoon, he'd fall to his knees and beg for deliverance.

Then the road called, and he and his father set out again. But as Max moved from town to steamy town, what he saw in the eyes of women everywhere reminded him of Carla. When they got back from the road, Rufus was exhausted, and decided to take off the month of August. He was aided in this decision by Max, whose hair had begun to lose its sheen, his eyes their light. Meridian complained that he only picked at his food; he was losing weight, was more moody than usual. When pressed by his wife, Rufus took Max off by himself and asked what was wrong, and Max responded, in an artful interpretation of the truth, that the Lord was testing him. Both Rufus and Meridian respected this and didn't pry.

Carla, on the other hand, was blossoming, whistling around the house, eagerly doing her chores, willing handmaiden for her holy brother. Transformed by the discovery of power, she was gathering courage to carry out her plan.

All during the day of August 6, 1939, she'd moved as in a dream, taut, so focused that details of that day, the weather, what she'd done at this hour or that one, were left outside her consciousness. All she could think was that tonight was the night, that what she'd waited for was finally to be hers. There was a moment in the early afternoon, when, lying in the back yard, she'd opened her eyes to sun shining at an angle, and in that instant of heat and not seeing, she'd once more considered being caught, the punishment her father would devise, the shocked eyes of her mother.

She turned her head. She wouldn't be caught; she'd planned too carefully. Max wouldn't make a sound. Even if he did cry out, or go crawling to her parents, she'd blame it on him, say the cause of his moodiness was in his pursuit of her, in her refusal to submit, refusal she'd clung to until he'd insisted that to lie with him was ordained and consecrated, for she'd be nourishing the Lord's anointed, relieving his burden, providing the harbor his stranded ship could dock in. And if he denied this, as he surely would, it would be her word against his, and she would weep at the tale of how, with his gift for preaching, he'd relentlessly persuaded, and how impossible resisting was.

It was knowing how she'd respond if caught that carried her through the day; it was this she took to bed, the solid thing she clung to when she began to shake an hour after her parents had retired. Then, with a steadiness that made her heart sink, a full moon rose to threaten her cover of darkness, filled the room's window like a white, reproachful eye. But she'd made her plans, and nothing would prevent her, not moonlight, not sinking heart. She whispered, "*I'm going to do it*," swung from bed wearing a gown the color of moonlight, one that scooped at the neck so the beginning swells of breasts showed, one that ended midway down her thighs. She'd chosen it so she'd be accessible, could simply lift the hem, baring her body without effort. Steeling herself, she walked through the doorway, stood at the top of stairs that descended into darkness. She went down, avoiding the places where the case creaked, the middle of the fourth step from the top, the ninth step in its entirety. At the bottom she could see into the darkened living room, the looming furniture, and she could witness, half washed with moonlight, the kitchen, on the other side of which lay Max. His room had the same exposure as the kitchen, so it, too, would be lit. In the tens of times she'd played out this adventure, it had always been in the dark, and the thought of seeing threatened her. She knew instinctively that light would make a difference; what she didn't know was how. Before not knowing could persuade her to postpone, she moved across the kitchen, carefully opened the door.

The light wasn't as bright as she'd expected; it was muted by curtains, by trees outside the window. Still it was enough to see Max lying on his back, sheet pulled to his throat. She took a last look behind, then stepped inside, closed the door, feeling, as the latch clicked, that she'd blocked her only exit to escape. She still had time to back out, could turn, sneak to her own bed. She decided she'd wait a moment; if Max moved, if she heard a noise outside the window or in the rooms above, she'd leave. She stood, listening to the silence, then tiptoed across the floor, stood above him. Now she trembled, not so much with fear as expectation. She'd known all along that she'd have to arouse him while he slept, so that when he awoke he'd be beyond ability to stop her. Stealthily, she pulled the sheet from his body; she smirked—the Lord's anointed slept in the nude. There, curved between his thighs, lay what she'd come to claim. Now her heart was in her ears, her breath caught, and she had to force herself to keep from whimpering. Before that could happen, she lowered her face, gently lifted his penis to her lips. Tentatively, she licked it. It was smooth, slightly salty, and his odor drove itself into her throat. She opened her mouth, began, as if his flesh were fragile, to suck him. Max groaned, shifted. She sucked harder, was rewarded by his cock's thickening on her tongue. She felt the heat between her own thighs, and at that moment nothing could have stopped her, not blinding light, or the earth opening up, or her father in the doorway. Max was pulsing in her mouth, and then he came awake, catapulted into sitting.

"Carla!"

His head fell back against the pillow. "God," he said; then he was trying to sit again, pushing at her head, and when she felt his hand, she sucked hard, and his push became caress. There was something inside her that was humming, and she labored until he held her head with both hands, until she knew that to continue was to end it. She released him; he groaned, cock waving above his thighs, and in a move so quick she couldn't, later, recall it, she was astride him, one hand guiding him to the place so wet it seemed as if a circle of liquid had burst there, and when she'd found its center, she violently sat. There was pain, but much less than she'd expected, and hard on its heels came the pleasure she'd woefully misjudged. It was so overwhelming that she sat, stunned, mouth opened, not simply feeling, but listening to the feeling. Max throbbed inside her; his face was twisted. It was then she recognized the chief property of light; she could witness the consequences of her power. She freed her breasts, lowered toward him, and when the nipples touched his chest, it was like a jolt of electricity. She heard the sound in her throat, "Uhhh," long and drawn as she began to come, a clutching inside her, a pulling until he grunted and exploded. Blown away, she collapsed against him, lay until her breathing started to subside.

"Carla," he said, and when she didn't answer, he began, astoundingly, to pray. She put a hand over his mouth, silencing him, and felt him surge inside her. She'd not expected that, didn't know it could happen again so soon, and she found his face with her own, captured his mouth, and began to kiss him, licked the insides of his lips.

When she came that second time, it was in the middle of thinking that if her father was right, and sex was the main competition for religion, religion didn't have a chance.

Later, she discovered the blood. Stealthily, she left the room. When she returned with clean sheets and two wet washcloths, Max sat on the bed, his back to her, head cupped in his hands. She made him move, made him help her with the changing, scrubbed his thighs.

The bloody sheets and washcloths she hid beneath her bed. She'd wash them in the morning.

After that, Max was hers whenever she wanted, although he could never bring himself to be joyful about it. He tried to talk to her about the sin, but when he did, she'd stop his mouth with kisses, and touch him in a way that instantly made him hard.

"What if you get pregnant?"

"I won't."

"How do you know?"

"I just know."

"This is wrong, Carla."

"What's wrong about it?"

"You're my sister."

"Max, I'm not your sister."

The rest of that month they made love in the woods, in the car, in the basement while the rabbits watched, and once, in a risk that nearly paralyzed her with excitement, in her parents' bed. After that was one of the times she chose to think about what they were doing, as she opened the windows to air the room, began to make the bed, Max nearly helpless in his shaking. That's when she felt it for the first time: Something bad would happen. She stopped, the edge of a bedsheet in her hand, eyes closed, but not even imagination could give the feeling features. She was so still that Max, despite the self-obsession with his own panic, was moved to question.

"What's wrong?"

"Nothing," she said and bent again to make the bed, quickly, in case, in that moment, her father approached the house, and would, in a little while, climb the stairs toward his room.

Max said he needed more time before he went back into the pulpit. Rufus relented, concerned and hurt that his son wouldn't confide in him. Now that Max was around, Carla took the opportunity to learn about this boy she'd grown up with. What was his life like on the inside; what did he think about being left on a stranger's doorstep? He was a white boy in a black world, one who loved to swim but played no basketball. Nor did he know the company of boys who wore hats at recently invented angles, youth built for speed, but stunned by immobility. These boys gathered in pool halls, ball fields, on corners; Max stalked pulpits above congregations who called him their bright and shining promise.

"Do you like being a preacher?"

They were up the river, in the clearing ringed by trees. Max wore green shorts, a white T-shirt, and sneakers. He was sitting against a tree, legs stretched, crossed at the ankles; her head lay in his lap. If she squinted, his face was high above her, on a mountain.

"I like," he said, "doing the Lord's will."

"What do you feel when you're preaching?"

"Filled with the Lord."

"But what does it feel like? Is it scary? Powerful?"

"It's . . . You wouldn't understand. You haven't been saved."

"Can you save me?"

"Do you want to be?"

"I want to know how it feels."

"You have to open yourself."

"Like I open to you?"

"You know I don't mean that. Don't blaspheme, Carla. God isn't mocked."

He'd start to shake; she'd rub his shoulders, soothe him. She felt so much older, a woman to his boy, he her man-child charge, her private pleasure. She'd take his hand, pull it under her skirt, beneath which she wore nothing.

They'd gone swimming, or he did; she waded out to her knees, then returned to squat beside the river. In the water he was tireless. Sometimes he jackknifed and dove toward the bottom, where he'd stay so long she'd come to her feet, gazing anxiously, and he'd pop up, yards from where he'd vanished, snort and shake himself.

Later they lay on a blanket. There were beads of water on his thighs. She burst one with a finger.

"Do you ever think about your parents?"

"My parents are Rufus and Meridian."

"I mean your real parents."

"They're my real parents."

"Max," she said, exasperated. She took his hand, held it against her own: vanilla white, sun-deepened nutshell. "Don't you see the difference?"

"Why do you bring this up?"

"I just wondered, that's all."

"The Lord brought me here. Rufus and Meridian are my parents."

At other times, she asked him about the places he'd been up and down the eastern seaboard. He'd preached in Rhode Island and Massachusetts, as far south as Virginia, on the way back from which they'd stopped in Washington, D.C. But Max could tell her nothing of these places; it was as if there'd been no monuments or White House, no countrysides, no seaports of Providence and Boston. He did say that Harlem had frightened him with its size, its crush, its people. What he remembered everywhere was sin; a great falling away from God, women made sick by wantonness, men driven by lust into everlasting darkness. He would start to speak of it in that singsong voice he used when preaching, mismatched eyes dazed by the magnitude of wickedness, and depending on her mood, she would let him continue or reach a hand between his thighs until he stopped.

"So what do you call what we do?"

She'd open his shorts, take the length out, move her fingers.

"Tell me, Max," she'd say, lowering her head, breathing on it, tongue snaking, and then, just before she went all the way, thrilled by the timbre of his groaning, "What do you call what we do?"

"Please, Carla. This is wrong."

"Don't close your eyes, Max. *Look* at me."

Six weeks after they'd started, she discovered she was pregnant. When she told Max, his eyes grew crazed, and he began to pace in widening circles.

"Are you sure?"

"I'm sure."

He was trembling. "You said you wouldn't."

"I didn't mean for it to happen. But it did. Now we've got to deal with it. What are we going to do?"

She was frightened, but not nearly as much as he, who met the question with a dumbness that infuriated her and a decision to lock his bedroom door. When she persisted, he said he was praying on it and to leave him be.

"You heal the sick," she said. "Can't you lay hands on me and get rid of it?"

He shrank from her in horror. "Are you crazy?"

In bed at night, hands as curious as a blind girl's, Carla explored her belly. There was a life inside her, growing. She'd be disgraced, her parents mortified. People would say she was a girl who'd "done it," and now her baby didn't have a name. But there *was* a father; his name was Max, and he was holy. When it was known what he'd done, he wouldn't be able to preach anymore, and her family wouldn't have any money. All this because she'd "done it," and had a life inside her, growing.

What would the baby be, what would it look like? Would it have Max's eyes? It would be hers, she'd raise and care for it. It would be hers, she thought, and turned on her side, staring into the dark.

Still, in the meantime, she had a problem.

Finally she devised her own solution, and Max agreed to go along with the story about the traveling salesman who'd come through Kingston at the beginning of the month, selling encyclopedias bound in imitation leather. Rufus and Meridian had bought a set; they were on a bookshelf in the living room, unopened but imposing. As the price for this invention, Carla made Max promise that he wouldn't lock his door, that if he continued, she'd tell her parents the truth. He kept his promise until Carla began to show. Then she'd find his bed empty in the night, and in the morning, he'd say he'd slept in the woods where he'd gone to seek the Lord. But the only way he could avoid Carla was to go back on the road, which he and his father did, Max on fire with his guilt, Rufus cursing the fiction that his daughter had stooped to fuck a white man, Meridian so disappointed she began to chew her fingernails.

It was during that fall of 1939 that Max enhanced his reputation with sermons so driven that sinners came to the altar in droves and filled to overflowing the offering baskets. But in Carla's presence he could barely speak. In her presence, all his power drained; he could only stare and stutter and go down with her.

He was in trouble. If it was found out what he'd done, black people would spit when they said his name. He'd be abandoned again, by God, his family, by the world, shame his sole companion.

Despondent, he'd go off by himself, sometimes to the river, in whose embrace he stayed until his flesh grayed. Or he'd sit in the woods, or bring the rabbit cage outside, kneel in the back yard where they'd buried the dog, staring at the wounds of rabbit eyes. He began to gather matches from the kitchen, always had a pocketful, would strike them, gaze into the miniature flaring until heat made him drop the stem and plunge fingers in his mouth. Meridian scolded him when she found him at the kitchen table, pondering a wilderness of scorched sticks.

And always the question: Why? He was the Lord's anointed, the fulfillment of the prophecy; where was his deliverance? He remembered the faces of those he'd caused to come to Christ; they were grateful and adoring, sweat glistening on their brows. Where were they now; why didn't they come to help? Where was his God? Was this what his father meant when he'd said the heart of the human condition was alone? What was the song his father had given him—could it help him now?

He began to sing, in the clearing deep in the woods, in the river, on his knees at bedside. On the streets he sang, whispered in the straight and narrow aisles of Kingston's stores, hummed when he paused, held and condemned on the corner by a traffic light.

His fame had grown. A newspaper reporter drove over from Montgomery, a hard-faced white man who didn't hide his skepticism. When Rufus left the room to break up a fight between the boys, the reporter asked Max what he knew about the legend of Joseph Drake.

"What everybody else knows," Max said.

"Do you believe it?"

"It's history. It's been recorded."

"And you claim to be the fulfillment of the prophecy?"

"I claim to be doing the Lord's will."

"The Lord speaks to you. Personally."

"Yes."

"Is anybody around when this happens? Has anybody else heard it?"

"The proof is in the work," Max said. "The proof is in souls brought to Christ."

The reporter, a short, thin man with stooped shoulders, rubbed his bald spot. "The prophecy said you'd cause Negroes to flourish."

"The prophecy made no mention of material things," Max said. "Negroes' *spiritual* lives are flourishing. And I believe that in time they will be blessed materially as well."

The reporter looked around him: the couch, the lamps, the thick rug, the bookshelves. Rufus had expanded the living room, put in skylights and a curved bay window so that in the afternoons, like this one, the room was washed with light. In the evenings you could lie on the couch or on the floor and watch the heavens. A wealth of silk flowers soared from a purple vase, beyond that a waist-high radio.

"You've got a nice place here."

"The Lord has blessed us."

"Your . . . father worked in a lumberyard. He doesn't have to anymore. Doesn't work at all."

"The Lord has blessed us."

The reporter looked up. Carla had come in, carrying a bag of groceries. She went through the living room, said good afternoon.

"Who's that?"

"My sister."

"You mean your foster sister?"

Max shrugged.

"She lives here?"

"Where else would she live?"

"With her husband."

"She's not married."

"But she's pregnant."

"Yes."

"Do you know how that happened? I mean do you know who the father is?"

"No," Max said. "All I know is that he was somebody passing through. A salesman."

"Now how did something like that happen in the home of the Lord's anointed?"

Rufus came back into the room. "How's it going?" he asked.

"Oh, fine," the reporter said. "We're just finishing up. One more question, actually. Tell me," he said to Max, "who's your favorite baseball player?"

"He don't pay no mind to baseball," Rufus said.

"A red-blooded American boy who doesn't like baseball? What do you like? You like your sister?"

"Get out of here," Rufus said.

"Come on, boy, tell me. You like your sister?"

Rufus led him to the door, stood there a long time after the reporter had driven away. Then he sighed and went outside.

Max sat, everything frozen except his heart. Did his father know? Would the reporter tell it?

But when the story came out, it didn't even mention that Carla was pregnant. It said that Max was reserved, and didn't like baseball, and that his foster father seemed overly protective. It reported that most of Kingston's whites, although they knew about Max and the prophecy, wrote the former off to the peculiar religious habits of Negroes, and the latter to the tendency all people had to create a history that made them feel important.

After his father left, Max went out the back way and slipped into the woods. There, he began to pray, to insist, for the first time, that he be provided a way out of his predicament. He had served the Lord, and he refused to be abandoned once again.

But in the weeks that followed, although Rufus didn't speak about it, neither was there an answer from the Lord. That last absence thoroughly confused Max. All his life he'd preached the certainty of deliverance, and now, when it was him, the Lord was silent. Maybe He was angry with him, maybe he should leave, pack a bag and disappear. But where would he go, how would he live? He struck a match, wondering who his birth parents were. Would they accept him if he showed up at their door, would they weep and beg forgiveness? Or would they turn, dismiss him, say, "That's why we left you on a doorstep, we knew you'd end up worthless."

No, he had no parents other than Rufus and Meridian, wouldn't go to them if he knew who and where they were. He bent again to patience, waited through the painted leaves of autumn, through winter and April's resurrection. And while he waited, the child was born that June of 1940, the midwife and Meridian with Carla in her room. The screams had chilled Max, blood-curdling cries as if pain had driven Carla to death's doorstep; his father held him while he wept. Rufus and Meridian swallowed their distress, began to love and care for the baby. But Max couldn't look at it. The child was an abomination; the infant sealed his deep, despicable sin: He, holiest of all, had lain with his sister. It didn't make one bit of difference that Carla said they weren't related by blood; they were related by life, by shared experience, they were the only family that he'd known. There was no way to get around it. He couldn't stay and daily look upon proof of his transgression; he had to go away. But where would he go, and how would he live when he got there?

Now he grew increasingly rude and irritable, jumped at the smallest unexpected sound: a pot dropped in the kitchen, a door slammed. He consecrated himself to his Father in heaven, prayed mightily for forgiveness, burned up a year's supply of matches.

Sometimes he turned his hopelessness on Carla. "You did this," he'd say. "You got us in this mess," and she'd remind him that she'd done none of it alone.

"You tempted me. You came into my room. I ought to tell it."

"You want to blame it all on me," she'd say. "You're the one supposed to be so holy. This is *your* baby, whether you want to look at him or not. You tell your story if you want, but don't think I won't tell mine."

At this he'd grow silent, and sometimes he'd say he was sorry and beg her not to shut him out. He couldn't make sense of it. She was the source of all his agony, but all the peace he knew was in her arms. Something terrible would happen; he could feel it.

They were up the river a ways, on the shore of a part of the land that thrust into the river. You could only see them if you were sailing on the water. He was holding himself; the day was sunlit, mild, but he was shivering.

"Max," she said. "You're making yourself sick."

"Hold me, Carla."

"It's not the end of the world. What's that smell?"

"The Lord's turned His face from me."

"No, he hasn't. You'll see. Where'd you get liquor?"

"Daddy keeps it in the cellar."

"Max, don't drink. It's no good for you."

"I might have to go away."

"What do you mean? Go where? Take me with you."

"I can't."

He'd be alone in the world, no one to love him.

"Carla, do you love me?"

There was this feeling in her, so much of it, rage, revenge, self-blame, and longing; this and connection. "Always," she said, and began to weep.

"Don't cry. Please don't cry."

"Max, don't leave me. Come back to the house. Look at the baby."

Her tears touched him, widened his own despair. He said, "If I go, I'll come back for you. Will you wait?"

"Yes, Max."

"Promise me. On your life."

"I promise."

"Will you pray with me?"

She even fasted with him once, went a whole day only drinking water.

Now, seeking consecration, Max fasted daily, and the fasting thawed flesh from his bones, and at night brought dreams with details as sharp as waking. In the middle of the last dream, a fire burned. A magnificent fire, flames and heat, consuming flesh, trees, stones, laying waste the city.

When he woke he understood the Lord had spoken, that what *would* be, for so long yet to come, was *now*. He rose, snuck down to the cellar to raid his father's whiskey, then returned, head reeling, to stare through his bedroom window. The lean, dark shape that paced the near horizon was his leaving. The wind was sin demanding sacrifice. For it was certain: Only great sacrifice would absolve the Lord's anointed.

In the spring of 1941, Rufus drew one hundred and fifty dollars out of the bank, all in one-dollar bills. He came home to the unlived-in side of his house and spilled the money on the floor. Then he sat wondering whose eye glowed above the pyramids, and why the former president wore a Mona Lisa smile. Irked by that ambivalent expression, he scooped handfuls of money and showered himself, rubbed cash against his arms. The scratching made his skin crawl. Fresh out of alternatives, he tried to pray, but couldn't.

Numb and disbelieving, Rufus sat cataloging his losses, most recent of which was that money wouldn't console him. He gathered the bills, walked back to the bank. Then, keeping one eye out for his missing boys, he went to see a lawyer, spent an hour across a desk from a man who talked of life after Rufus as if Rufus's absence wouldn't matter. Rufus had hoped the lawyer would speak of *his* anxiety about not being, so Rufus could talk about his own, but the lawyer, once the will was drawn, lit a pipe and told a joke about a probate hearing. Then he escorted his client to the door and insisted he enjoy the lovely day.

Dark and stolid, mouth bitter with the taste of smoke, Rufus headed home, eyeing building fronts, alleyways, trying to will his sons into his vision. Failure boxed his ears, promised to torture him forever. Rufus sneered at it. Failure wasn't simply rude; it was mistaken. Life didn't last forever; failure couldn't reach into the grave.

He stopped on the corner of his street, letting the idea own him, then looked to see what effect such thinking had on the afternoon. The lawyer was right; it *was* a lovely day, warm and bright, but nothing in it so much as blinked at his decision. Depressed by the world's refusal to mourn with him, Rufus slumped toward his house. In the kitchen, he made himself a plate of raw broccoli, drenched it in catsup, and told Meridian he'd decided to die. Death, he said, was his only answer. Death would blot out the grief of his missing boys, relieve the suffering his confession hadn't eased. He'd thought that by telling what Carla had done he'd preserve Max's reputation, and in the process rid his mouth of smoke. Neither had happened. Nor had he been able to act upon his belief that Max's child deserved special treatment as the son of the anointed. The truth was that he'd begun to avoid Phoenix, because to be in his presence was to be reminded of all he'd lost. It was mixed up; nothing made sense anymore except the need to stop suffering, and so he'd decided to die.

Meridian, turned off by the catsup on his chin, shrugged. "Okay, Rufus," she said. "Do what you have to. I'll be sure to tell this unborn baby why his daddy ain't around."

Accepting Meridian's cue, Carla didn't take her father seriously. But as the weeks stretched and he refused to rise from his bed, even to go to the bathroom, she began to worry.

One afternoon in May 1941, Carla sat in the unused living room. Phoenix was with her mother, the two of them napping. Carla thought of the height at which Meridian carried the unborn child, how that meant it would be a boy, how Phoenix so seldom cried, would lie for hours and not stir unless he was wet or hungry, how lucky that he was so good. Still, sometimes she wished he'd cry; his goodness added to the household's silence.

Now her mind wandered to the attic where her father lay, having had his bed moved there so he could welcome death in private. Soon it would be time to go to him. She was frightened by his wooing of death; if he died, she'd never be forgiven. She didn't hope anymore that he'd love her, just forgive; she clung to this, even though he wouldn't look at her when she brought his meals or came to fetch the stinking bedpan. This last she suffered with gratitude, for it seemed the last available act to prove her desire to be forgiven. It was why she wouldn't allow the fumes to distort her face, why she held the silver vessel as if it were a chalice while she asked how he felt, babbled of what she'd done that day: the price of meat, the small, unappetizing mound of grapefruit at the grocer's. She'd stand across the room at the open window so he wouldn't have to smell his shit, and he'd meet her chatter with indifference, eyes closed, and sometimes he raved into his pillow. "Listen," he'd say, and tell of a house reduced to rubble, flesh charred beyond identity. Sometimes he sang blues songs, some made up, some traditional, sometimes incoherently mixed, and though they spoke of pain, of struggle, the ability to laugh in spite of this, he sang them all in a voice defined by its thick, slow beat of anger. "I have had my fun if I don't get well no more," he sang, but he never identified the fun or how its memory sustained him. He sang, "If I had wings like Noah's dove, I'd fly up the river to the boy I love," and she wondered what he'd say to Max if he took that trip and found him.

While he sang, she stood, suffering his wrath-rich singing, wishing she could lend her voice to comfort, to console him. She'd have done anything for him, but it was impossible to do for someone if he refused to let you touch.

She sighed, went into the lived-in side of the house, into the kitchen, but when she got there she couldn't remember what she'd come for. She turned, climbed to the second floor, up the attic stairs. When she stepped into the room, the smell struck, and she remembered the disinfectant. Her father lay in a sore of a bed across from the room's one window, his view a corner of an undistinguished sky. A glass pitcher half full of water sat on a table near his head. When she cleared her throat to alert him to her presence, he stiffened and began to hum.

Max had been like that. He'd gone through a period when, if he didn't want to hear what you were saying, he turned his face and started humming. The louder you talked, the louder he hummed. She looked for the bedpan, didn't see it, then realized why her father hummed: He was ashamed. The bedpan was wedged beneath him. She took the pitcher downstairs, emptied and rinsed it, added ice, fresh water, squatted beneath the sink for disinfectant. When she got back upstairs, the bedpan was on the floor, covered by a red-striped towel.

She coughed; her father sang. She bent, then went to lean against the wall next to the window, the bedpan cradled in her arms, foul, and she a stoic, listening to his song. The words were garbled; she strained to make them out, but then, as though he sensed her effort to understand and would deny her even this, he abandoned the song, lay in spiteful silence. He was staring at the low, peaked ceiling, as if willing its destruction, as if he wished weight would find its weakness, rupture roof, bury him in nails and two-by-fours, tar paper, vacant sky. And she watched and felt beneath her yearning not her aching to be looked at, but her rage, sharp, unwelcome. She pushed at it to go away, thinking, *What can I do, will it be this way forever?*

And then memory was on her like a wave.

She leaned against it, fought to keep her balance, remembering what she'd struggled to forget. She'd been ignored, as she still was, hadn't existed, as she didn't now. She, her father's flesh and blood, his firstborn, banished for the foundling. She'd forget because remembering made her hard, locked the door against the small hope of forgiveness. But she couldn't forget. And there was reason why she couldn't; there was pleasure in remembering her power, deep strength and satisfaction despite the consequences. She'd done it. She, female and ordinary, had milked the blond boy's strength, left him speechless, at first out of her thirsting for revenge, but then because she *could.* It was *she* who'd had the power. And her father loved not her, but *him,* though she was stronger, smarter; it was to Max he turned his love-light, to Max he gave a song.

Once he'd made a song for her, so long ago she hadn't remembered, so long ago a verse was lost. Did he remember? What would he do if she sang it? Would it remind him how she'd been the apple of his eye? Would it jar him, make him look at her and weep, say he was sorry, would it smash his stupid heart?

Got a new baby girl, as sweet as a ripe cher-ry.
Got a new baby girl, sweet as a ripe cher-ry.
Want to know why I'm smiling, now you know what
   the reason be.

Build me a castle, finest you ever seen.
Build me a castle, finest you ever seen.
Don't worry 'bout money, just make it fit for a queen.

He lay, not moving, absolutely unresponsive, and she swallowed, remembering the night she'd slipped from bed, crouched on the stairs watching Max and her father in the flamelight. Max's head was in the angle of her father's thighs; the pine cones burned like jewels. "Who loves you?" her father said, and Max said, "You do," and her father said, "You got that right," and then he laughed and kissed him. To her he gave turned shoulders, grunts, blank stares, indifference.

She held her father's shit, poised to care for him, and he wouldn't even look at her, wouldn't even admit he'd once given her a song. She wanted to kill him, knew she could, easily, a discovery so startling that she replaced it immediately with one that merely hurt enough to get attention.

Then, furiously, she was singing.

I'm all alone, and all by myself too.
I'm all alone, and all by myself, too.
Got my song in my pocket...

And her father, eyes exploding, searching the room, and her own heart struck by its extraordinary leaping. He was *looking* for her, wanted to *see* her, face lit with impossible believing. *Oh, sweet Jesus,* she thought, singing, *oh, sweet*... and sagged; it wasn't her. It was his son returning, there, in the shadows, there, bare-headed, coming up the stairs. *"Maaaaax,"* he cried, great head swiveling, *"Maaaaax,"* and then he understood. His face, one instant beautiful and open, now gathered, eyebrows and stubbled jaw, nose cave, teeth snarl, and pearls of spittle. He tried to draw a breath, but outrage wouldn't let him. His lips moved, but words didn't come, and he moaned, lurched crazily to his elbows, mouth a black line, eyes pools of disbelief.

Carla, out there by herself, was wondering why she'd done it, knowing it was done, nothing else to do but finish, though it wasn't singing now, but whisper:

. . . I know just what to do.

And her father, wail of pain and hopelessness and rage, voice found way down in the hollow of his throat: "Harlot! That's my boy's song. I hate you. Harlot," and swung his ash-gray feet from the bed, preparing to cross the room and smash her, reach a hawk hand down her throat and claw the song back. But he was too weak for that, had given up his body, promised it to death, who was taking his own sweet time arriving. He could never make it out of bed, much less across the room.

Or could he?

Carrying the bedpan, she fled, went past her mother, who was lumbering, full-bellied, up the stairs. Meridian held her green skirt hiked, her shoe untied. "What happened?" And Rufus screaming, "Harlot . . ."

"What happened?" Meridian shouted, and Carla, not stopping, cried, "He'll never change. He's crazy."

So it was over; she'd made him reveal in words what he'd previously done only in action. You couldn't ignore words, couldn't call them back or reinvent their meaning like you could an action. She'd crossed a line, the other side of which she couldn't return from. She couldn't even go into the attic; he forbade it. She wouldn't see his face again until he died.

Meanwhile, in that spring of 1941, the city went about its business. Although everybody had made a big deal about avoiding the Marches, good manners and convention sent occasional callers to their door. That's how Kingston found out Rufus was sleeping in the attic, threatening to die. Nobody thought to talk him out of it. The best way to deal with a grown man's foolishness was to ignore it, or make a joke. In that spirit, somebody said Rufus might be on to something; you didn't have control over when you were born, why not determine your dying?

The joke wasn't funny, and it barely survived the week. The truth was that black people were contemptuous of suicide, believing it a weakness of character indulged in by white folks who'd lost their money. By December of that year, for another set of reasons, they'd include the Japanese. Two decades later, when they heard how their ancestors had leaped into the Atlantic rather than be slaves, and how, once here, others chose self-inflicted death before endurance, they were forced to reconsider their opinions. But in the spring of 1941, they didn't know this, and so they made a joke that wasn't funny. Someone did think to tell Reverend Sweeny. The Reverend said he'd look into it, and Kingston turned to other things.

Lord knows there were other things to turn to. First had been the winter of 1940-1941, the one that showed up draped in sunlight, without snow until January, when it proceeded to drop record accumulations well into May. On Mother's Day, eight inches shocked the rhododendrons. The snow vanished by the following afternoon, dissolved by blinding sun and heat that would have been at home in Cuba.

But the peculiar weather wasn't finished. A later, week, a colony of clouds moved in from Buffalo, took up residence above the city, and, once unpacked and recovered from their journey, began to rain. The rain fell steadily all morning, paused to catch its breath, and fell for five more days. Not content with that portion of earth it was allotted, water rioted everywhere, threatened to send the river up the hill, backed up sewers, left in streets and yards and parks pools that kids sailed boats on. Finally the rain stopped; the sun returned, the water grudgingly receded. On the same morning, Luther Birdsong skidded on a wet road in his Chevrolet and broke a utility pole.

It was not until Luther's body lay in state that folks realized that until him, all the blacks who'd died that spring were women. Nobody had noticed this except Lucinda Hancock, who'd been poking around her father's cellar. Lucinda hadn't said anything because she didn't want to explain what she was looking for among the dead. Her father, who'd prepared the bodies, had flat out missed the strangeness. Before anybody could figure out what had made Death so specific, Junkman began to come out in the evenings, strolling from one end of Broadway to the other. He was dressed in the black suit he'd worn to church that past December, and he swung from his right hand a lamp whose wick curled foul smoke into the air. On his feet were some of the fanciest shoes anybody had ever seen on a black man, blue suedes with four eyelets, black alligator pumps, and as the city stared, the mute began to sing.

He was twenty-five years old in 1940. For sixteen years, like clockwork on each Thursday, his father had visited in a dream that never varied. A grown man in the dream, Junkman was on the hill beneath the oak tree, standing helplessly as his father pointed to his neck. Junkman searched for something to stand on, something to make him tall enough to reach the rope's knot. But the hill was barren. He leaped, but couldn't reach. When the hanged man gagged, Junkman would bolt awake.

In 1941, he still worked as a garbageman; by then, his nose, honed by practice, was as delicate as a chef's palate. In the same way a chef could taste a dish and recite the ingredients, Junkman could stand before a garbage can, sniff, and know the contents. Carrots, he'd smell. Potato peel, stewed chicken. Fatback and pinto beans.

On warm days he'd identify all the life forms in the river—fish and turtle, insect and river weed—could know, without looking, which flesh behind him on a crowded street belonged to young girls, which to menopausal widows, and he could find in both men and women the increment that lived between desire and despair. With an ease that would have been the envy of physicians, he detected sickness: common colds, the thin, metallic scent of high blood pressure, and he could sniff, hours before it happened, when the wind would change.

Nobody knew that Junkman had this gift, or that its diversion was more absolute than bowling. Nor did they know that while his clothes were nondescript—overalls and work shirts, and in winter a black coat that swirled at his ankles—he'd developed a passion for fine shoes, footwear he ordered from an outfit in Detroit, only one pair of which he wore in public before 1941. Those were his cowboy boots, black, with silver stitching.

He modeled the boots in July of 1939, after a shower that littered the earth with puddles and made the pavement dark. As he walked up Broadway, head high, shoulders back, folks looked on amazed that boots so fine existed. Junkman wouldn't learn until later that Lucinda Hancock, who was out with her mother, had walked past him, gaping, finding in his toes two points that made her shiver. He hadn't seen Lucinda, but he'd smelled her: fish roe and lilacs, distilled water, diamond dust, scent so dazzling he'd have searched for its source had he not been so distracted.

The boots were elegant, but after six blocks, it was clear they weren't for walking. The high heels tipped him forward, made him feel as if he were on an angle, off the edge of which he'd fall should something as insubstantial as a thought come up and push him. By the time he'd adjusted to that feeling, the boots had put a serious headlock on his toes. On top of that, a car came flying past while he waited for a red light, sent brown water all over his pants and gleaming leather. So he left the boots at home to preserve their beauty and his feet, and he'd occasionally take them out, sit smiling at their splendor. Sometimes he'd try on his entire collection, twelve pairs he kept lined up in his closet.

He had no friends, no recreation other than bowling and smelling things and the movies, whose darkened rooms he felt at home in. He loved his father's memory and Carla, although the latter hadn't been expressed since his gift of lilacs. He did walk by the Marches' new house before Rufus took to his deathbed, but he didn't hang around because there weren't enough trees to hide behind, and Rufus, still smelling of smoke, had been abusive the couple of times he'd seen him. In his present condition, Junkman couldn't take much abuse.

Besides, he was annoyed with Rufus. He'd felt a kinship with the man, had been moved by Rufus's grief the night of the fire. Junkman didn't know what it felt like to lose your children, but he understood what it meant to be in mourning. It was this understanding that had inspired him to dance. Under other circumstances, he'd have gone immediately to Carla, knelt to comfort, whispered that he loved her. But there was a more important task: sharing in the ritual of Rufus's grief. The firemen were busy, the neighbors mesmerized by flame. Meridian was there, but she was female. Only a man could dance to another's grieving. Junkman didn't know how he knew this, but he did.

He'd gone to church that Sunday in December 1940 to find relief from suffering. Instead he'd been treated to Rufus's betrayal. In the months after he stalked out of church, he ordered two more pairs of shoes, rearranged his furniture, wrote a note so eloquent his landlord grudgingly painted his room. It was while standing unmoved by the redolence of newly painted walls that Junkman admitted none of this was working. That's when he decided to forgive himself by public mourning. Once he'd found comfort, he'd redirect himself and live a normal life. Perhaps he'd begin to speak.

Fired with hope, he cleaned and filled the kerosene lamp, replaced the wick. Then he took the black suit from the closet, dropped to his knees, and considered which shoes he'd wear. As he reached for a tasseled loafer, he thought how, long ago, in a room whose rain-streaked window looked out on hills of junk, he'd learned what would happen should he violate his center. For a quick, hot moment, he felt he had no being, just this thundering pulse beat in the air. He dropped the loafer, winced at his terror, wishing, for the second time since he'd given up his voice, that he could talk to someone. He waited for the terror to pass, and when it did, he went back to deciding which shoes he'd wear.

But the memory of what he'd done wouldn't leave him.

His love was suffering; he'd watched her belly swell. Sometimes he followed her and Max into the woods, saw what happened beneath the trees, his heart gathering first to sink, then bounding, a twist so singular he thought of pirouettes. Once he trailed silently after the preaching boy (his scent was slightly sour milk and apples, hers, cinnamon, and earth just after tilling), Max begging the Lord to light his darkness. Oh, how Max had prayed, voice rising to silence birds, to bead the eyes of chipmunks. Even though the prayers seemed heartfelt, the reference to the unborn child had a current of arrogance beneath it, and Junkman wondered if Max was really saying that given his status the Lord had no choice but to provide escape. He wished the preaching boy would go away, leave him to raise the baby. He'd take Carla and live with her, protect them both. Never again would she be sad and frightened.

Sometimes, when Max and Carla were together, there'd be anger, threats and counterthreats, but no matter how intense these episodes, they'd end with that coupling on the ground. And he, who'd never known a woman, would watch until they finished, and then he'd sneak away, later to lie across his bed, the flame in his loins unbearable until an egg-white seed gushed into his freshly painted room. He'd rise to clean himself, feeling disgusted, feeling he'd wandered into a condition that had no exit, walked a tread-mill driven by an engine whose brake he couldn't find. He told himself he needed more wholesome activity in his life, went bowl-ing twice a week, began to do push-ups and knee bends in the morning, to run in place at night until he collapsed into bed, where waiting was Carla's face in the time-still moment when her love came down. He'd groan; hands would fly like iron to the magnet at his thighs.

It was hopeless, the fire came, he did what he did; he agonized, commenced his public mourning. In the middle of it, drawn by the mystery of his speechless tongue, still weak for cowboy boots, Lucinda Hancock began to follow him through Kingston's streets.

Lucinda was the girl who'd come to comfort Carla that day in church when Rufus put his daughter's business in the street. The only child of Anna and Ulysses Hancock, she'd been born with a defective heart. Ulysses was an undertaker, a vocation whose stillness led him to discover the seductiveness of thought. By teaching himself to ask questions, he became a student of life. Some of his questions, like "Who invented deodorant?" were hardly consequential. But some, like "Why do so many black people have gaps between their front teeth?" were startling and profound.

The question that eventually consumed Ulysses had been lying in his path for years, and when he finally stumbled over it, he stood straight up from the body he was draining. Tall, thin, a frame that seemed constructed entirely of elbows, he took the cellar steps two at a time, burst into the kitchen where his wife, washing dishes, talked over her shoulder to the baby sleeping in a stroller.

"Anna," he shouted, waking the toddler, who immediately began to cry. "Why do people die so soon?"

"Fool," Anna said, "you scared the baby."

"I'm sorry. But why do you think?"

"I declare . . ." She'd claimed Lucinda from the stroller, rocked her. " 'Cause they get old. They get old and sick or have an accident. So you can make a living."

He said, "It's not fair that humans die so soon."

"Fair?" Her voice was like her body, not an ounce of soft. "You want to talk about fair? You know what the price of groceries is? You know what they want for a quart of milk?"

It was on his way back to the body that Ulysses started feeling sorry for his clients. He knew it was appointed to everyone to die, and he'd known, even before his wife's inelegant observation, that this assured him a decent living. When he thought about not dying, he realized living forever held no attraction. It wasn't about dying; it was about living such a little while, about investing flesh with life and snatching it away so quickly. Why not take six or seven hundred years per lifetime? That made more sense than seventy. Time could take it. Time didn't do anything but move along.

Needing to counteract the senselessness, Ulysses resolved to honor his clients' loss by refusing to cheat their survivors and by doing his best on the bodies. He forgave himself for the times he'd done a less than perfect job or padded the bill. Now his incisions from groin to breastbone were made with a tenderness resembling love. He enrolled in classes at the beauty school so he could do his corpses' hair and makeup. If you placed your dead with him, you knew there'd be a couple of days before the wake; the new Ulysses took his time. But you also knew the body would be done right, that whatever its condition, he'd render some aspect the person had shown in life. His skill led consistently to the mortician's ultimate praise: that the dead appeared to be sleeping.

Anna, his wife, was a talker. Before Lucinda, she talked incessantly to her husband, often perched on a stool while he worked. After he fell in love with thought, he asked her not to disturb him during office hours. The rest of the time she could chat to her heart's content. And no, he wasn't messing around. He loved her. He just did his best work in private.

Anna's response was to reexperience a childhood feeling which she'd expressed back then by pulling wings off flies, by stoning dogs, and surreptitiously pinching the thighs of infants from whose screaming she'd leaned back, innocent. A couple of times she'd been caught and punished, but the truth was that though her parents frowned on her behavior, they blamed it on her being high-strung, and far too athletic for a girl.

As a child Anna had loved to climb trees. She could power a softball with the most talented male peers, and knew only a handful who could stay with her in a foot race. But her family insisted that none of this was proper, and they dressed her in starched dresses, and braided her hair so tightly she was afraid to close her eyes. They insisted she learn to walk with her back straight, and sit so her thighs were hidden. The result was the pent-up feeling that resulted in mutilating flies. Anna never forgot that feeling. It was why she promised that any child she had would grow up to be free.

Marriage to Ulysses was wonderful. For their first anniversary he surprised her by installing a chin-up bar in the kitchen doorway. He encouraged her to take exercise classes at the YWCA, and played catch with her in the yard. The pent-up thing softened as her muscles firmed, and she said she wanted a baby. She was eight weeks pregnant when the test showed positive. Immediately upon paying the obstetrician and staggering into an afternoon made brand new in her absence, she began a conversation with the fertilized egg. When doctors said that Lucinda had a heart problem, Ulysses didn't say what he suspected: The child had been *talked* into a faulty valve. He kept quiet because he was assured Lucinda would grow out of her condition, and because he was relieved she wasn't deaf.

Not only did Anna talk too much to the child but, guided by the misbelief that food would make her daughter's heart strong, she overfed her, so that Lucinda by the age of fifteen weighed 180 pounds. More tellingly, Anna confused freedom with safety. That's why Lucinda couldn't share a sandbox with kids whose physical abilities might create a lack of confidence or whose runny noses exposed her to disease.

So Lucinda, her playmates screened and channeled to other houses, played alone, gave tea parties only her dolls and her father came to. Then, when she became fat, the distance between her and other children widened.

She was saved from despair by the frequency with which her father held her, by his patience in teaching her to play catch and to jump rope, by her imagination, and by an intelligence that resulted in her skipping third grade and going, at sixteen, to the university at New Paltz. There she discovered that the sensation she'd had for as long as she remembered hadn't come to college with her. The left-at-home feeling was a weak place in her head, like a bone, once broken, that had never properly knit.

Her mother celebrated her intelligence, showered her with books, pasted the straight-A report cards from high school on the refrigerator. She also raised her in the church, being one who refused to follow Max to worship at the sides of rivers or in the totally inappropriate YMCA. She did, however, take Ulysses and Lucinda to hear Max preach in Van Saun Park, and she made it an outing, packed a lunch and spread it on a snow-white cloth.

That was how, in the summer of her eleventh year, Lucinda came to be alone with Max. Her mother was chattering with two women; her father had his eyes closed, wondering why men's beards turned gray before hair on their heads did. Lucinda slipped away, walked to where the platform had been raised.

There, off to the side, was the March family, the strange and distant Carla, who, at school, always walked close to the corridor walls and didn't smile. There were the two little boys, one the color of caramel, the other chocolate. Past them, standing at an angle that made Lucinda imagine he was lonely, was Max.

Curious, she approached him. She could see the perspiration on his collar from the strain of preaching; he was thin, wore the baggy pants to a jet-black suit, and as she looked into his mismatched eyes, she was startled by their beauty.

"How are you?" she asked.

"I'm fine."

"I enjoyed your preaching."

"Thank you."

She had with her the small red ball she used for jacks; she reached a hand into her dress and squeezed it. The sun was swimming across the park, the grass was painter's green, voices murmuring behind her.

Lucinda asked, "Want to play catch?"

"Catch?"

She pulled the ball out, tossed and caught it.

"Oh," he said. "Okay."

"Move away a little. You're too close."

He backed up, rapidly.

"That's too far," she said. "A little closer. That's good. You ready?"

She tossed the ball, and he reached for it the way an old man reached for a threatening mosquito. The ball sailed past him, bounced and rolled under the platform, and Max watched it, turned to her.

"Go get it," she said.

Obediently, he retrieved the ball, stood, a half smile on his face.

"Throw it."

And he wound up and threw it with all the elegance of someone with polio.

The boy doesn't even know how to play catch, she thought, not meanly, interested.

"Max," Rufus called. "Come over here and rest yourself. Max."

"I've got to go," Max said.

"Okay. See you again," Lucinda said, although she never did, alone. But she'd never forget his parting comment, direct, like a child's, the tone a grown-up's, severe, but yet a compliment, messages she stood decoding when he'd left.

"Your hair's pretty," he said. "You ought to lose some weight."

At college, Lucinda majored in speech. At seventeen she was five feet five, clear of complexion, fawn-colored with a lovely smile. Hair cascaded halfway down her back. She weighed one hundred eighty-seven pounds and suffered in hot weather. It had been six years since the examination that decreed her heart recovered, and subsequent annual tests were negative. But Anna said being careful didn't hurt, and she continued to prescribe a life of restricted movement and avoidance of excitement. Yet neither mother nor daughter followed the doctor's urging that the patient lose some weight.

Predictably, Lucinda knew nothing about boys. She'd not had a date by the time she got to college, wasn't asked out there. Until the second semester of her freshman year all she knew about sex was what she'd picked up from her classmates' whispers and her mother's lecture at the onset of her period. That monologue stressed facts: Bleeding flushed the body of impurities, caused vicious cramps and headaches, a heaviness that made you snap at those you loved. She could look forward to this for the next forty years, interrupted only at such time as she was with child by her husband. How this last would happen wasn't explained; there wasn't even reference to a stork.

In the second semester of her freshman year, Lucinda signed up for a health course. While others giggled at diagrams of the reproductive systems, she sat enthralled at the mystery that hung between male thighs. Halfway through the term she began to glance at her classmates, wondering about length and thickness, the degree to which the norm was rivaled, which ones were circumcised. It was then she set a goal for herself: to witness, before she was a sophomore, a penis in the flesh.

She worked hard, but soon understood she wouldn't reach her goal on campus. In 1941, dorms were strictly segregated by gender. Because she was fat, no one made the effort to lure her to a secluded place where they could take the advantage she'd have gladly given. Despite her heart's recovery, she didn't have enough of it to walk up to a boy and say, "Excuse me, I'm doing a project for health class. Can I see your penis?" She took to pausing in the hallways outside men's rooms on the chance that a widely swinging door would provide a glimpse; on weekends she tried barging in on her father in the bathroom. But the bathroom was Ulysses's favorite place for thinking, and he always kept the door locked.

The weekend before Easter, a solution came to her. She got through dinner, dutifully discussed life on campus, courses, teachers, her roommate's passion for tea, the flavors of which—chamomile and jasmine—lived in her roommate's hair. When the rest of evening fell, she complained of tiredness and asked to be excused from church. The request granted, she went upstairs and listened until her parents left. Then she tiptoed down the stairway, opened the door to the basement where her father worked, switched on the light. When she reached the cellar floor, she ran smack into a dizziness that made her draw deep breaths, made her reach and brace against the cool, rough cellar wall.

There on the table were three bodies, side by side, covered by two sheets stitched together. Before she could give herself time to think, she grabbed the cloth and pulled it. First the fear again, like heat. This time she dismissed it; the dead couldn't hurt you. Then, like a fist, the disappointment.

All the dead were women. Two were old, sunken-faced; the third not yet thirty, stunning, firm-breasted, splendid thighs, rich and curved mahogany. She must have loved perfume, it was on her belly slope like lilacs; Lucinda leaned and gulped it, felt her head spin, straightened to stare at the fingers on the woman's limp left hand. Two bands lighter than the rest of her skin; rings had lived there, rings had swallowed sun before flesh could. Were they gifts, a mother's heirlooms reclaimed to pass on to the living? No other marks, no sign that death had come by accident or illness, no imperfection. Who was she? How'd she get to be so lovely? And how'd she die?

For the first time since she'd gone to college, Lucinda felt the weakness in her head. Gently, she covered the nakedness, first the old ones, the corrugated ribs, the withered breasts, then the young one with whom she felt a shattering alliance.

I want to look like you, she thought, *I want to be beautiful.* She lifted her skirt, regarded her own thighs. "Thunder thighs," the boys said. She pulled her blouse to her armpits; were it not for the bra her breasts would sleep against her stomach.

There in the presence of women who would have consoled her if they could, would have hidden her nakedness, crooned "Hush, now, it's all right," Lucinda wept. When she finished, she rearranged herself and went to raid the refrigerator. In the days that followed, she stuffed herself with food, gaining twenty-eight pounds by the morning of the storm that buried Mother's Day. But the grief wouldn't go away. None of it was at the absence of a penis to witness; all of it was for the women: two elderly, the third with *oh-my-Jesus* thighs. It was a good grief, opulent, ornate, and she might have held on to it forever except that Junkman, wearing shoes whose elegance made her throat dry, began to come out in the evening. As she looked on, astonished, the mute began to sing.

In the spring of 1941, once the shocked rhododendrons had recovered, and the smell of rain had been replaced by sunshine,
Reverend Sweeny asked Ulysses and Anna to call on the Marches
and report back to him the status of Rufus's decision to die. He'd
chosen the Hancocks because they'd been loyal during the mass
defection caused by Max, and because he trusted the undertaker's
judgment.

"I ain't visiting no one," Ulysses said to his wife. He was
incensed with Rufus for trying to throw away what any of his
clients would have killed for. You shouldn't be allowed to waste
your life, Ulysses fumed. If you didn't want it, there ought to be
provision made to pass it to someone else.

Startled by her husband's uncharacteristic fury, Anna chose
not to argue, and said she'd do it by herself. But she was nervous
about the visit, and relieved when Lucinda offered to go with her.

For a while after that day in church, Lucinda had kept one
eye out for the girl she'd gone to sit beside. At times, she'd
thought about just knocking on Carla's door, but she, like the
rest of Kingston, had been diverted by the weather, and later there
was the distressing fact that only women died. The weather meant
the indignity of wearing boots in May; the dead women triggered
a tired she thought might be connected to her heart. That worry,
that she wasn't healed despite what doctors said, didn't go away
until Luther Birdsong was delivered to her father. After that she
shimmered with energy, lusted for ice water and fresh fruit, a diet
that dissolved flesh and inspired daydreams of lying beneath silk
sheets thin enough to see her knees through, surrounded by the

radiance of shoes. Junkman sat across the room, hands behind his head, drinking her presence until classtime.

"Hold your mouth like this," she'd say, for in these dreams she taught the mute to speak; she'd opened a clinic where anyone who'd lost his voice could find it. She was famous, lectured all over the States and Europe, things, in 1941, folks would have said were impossible for a plain black girl to do.

The fruit made Anna suspicious, since it was known that pregnant women craved peculiar diets: Argo cornstarch, chocolate syrup and tuna, ice sprinkled with garlic, and had she witnessed Lucinda eating these, it would have been a sure sign that yet another Kingston family was disgraced by one of its daughters. But Lucinda had taste only for fruit and water, the consuming of which knit the bone in her head and melted the abundance of her flesh. Finally her body called for vegetables, lean meat, a soft-boiled egg or two, and she ate these sparingly.

On the day of the visit she and her mother took the long way to the March house, up Broadway four blocks to Albany Avenue, where they turned right into a neighborhood of huge Victorian houses, white like the people, with deep porches wrapped around them. In front stretched flawless lawns, dogwoods disorderly with blooming, tulips so perfect they didn't seem real.

When they got to Jefferson, they walked three more blocks to Manor. On the southeast corner was the green, two-family house the Marches lived in. The women went up the sidewalk, hesitated before the east door. Anna raised her fist, rapped lightly, then stood listening for footsteps. When none came, she knocked again. Carla, wearing coveralls and T-shirt, opened the walnut door.

"Good afternoon," Anna said. "Is your mother home?"

Carla, staring at Lucinda, nodded.

"Would you tell her Sister Hancock here to visit?"

"*Mama.*"

From the bowels of the house came a muffled response.

"You got visitors," Carla called. She turned to Anna and Lucinda. "Please. Come in."

They walked through the vestibule, into a room hushed by varieties of brown. The couch was chocolate-colored, the piano a walnut that matched the room's wood trim, the beige walls a shade lighter than the carpet.

Meridian came into the room drying hands above her belly; she'd been in the cellar washing clothes. "Sister Hancock," she said, sounding genuinely pleased. "And how are you, Lucinda, how's college?" Without waiting for a reply, she asked Anna, "How's Brother Hancock doing?"

"Just fine. Is that baby ever going to get here?"

"Don't seem so, do it? Come on to the kitchen, I'll make coffee. Carla, why don't you take Lucinda on the porch? There's lemonade in the icebox."

"Would you like some lemonade?" Carla asked.

Lucinda said, "How about some water?"

On the back porch the girls sat on the steps, the porch roof's shadow at their feet. A car passed with two middle-aged black women, and their eyes latched on to it as if it were the most engaging thing they'd seen all day. Then, in a voice that was small and careful, Lucinda stepped into the silence.

"I'm glad to be here," she said. "I've been wanting to talk to you."

Carla watched her. Lucinda was looking across the yard, at the tree, at the clothes in the sunlight stiffening on the line.

"About what?" Carla said.

"Being your friend."

"My friend? Why?"

"You need one. I used to watch you in school, how you kept to yourself. I wanted to come over to you then, but there was something in your face that said not to." She paused. "I'd like to have a friend, too."

There were creases in Lucinda's neck. She'd dusted them with powder.

"You go to college," Carla said. "You don't have any friends there?"

"I have people I know. My roommate, some others. But not a real friend. No one to tell things to." Lucinda shifted her bulk, turned to look Carla in the face.

Carla raised the glass to her mouth, sipped the sour lemonade. "I waited for you. After you sat next to me in church that day? I waited, kept expecting to see you walking up the sidewalk. I guess I could have come to you, but. . . . "

"Why didn't you?"

"Afraid. You might not like me. Your parents might make you stay away."

"I felt the same," Lucinda said. "Afraid you might not like me."

"That's not all of it. It's about being hurt. About getting close and that someone goes away."

Lucinda squinted. "Why would I go away?"

"People are always leaving."

"Not always."

Carla shrugged. "I never had a lot of friends. Part of it had to do with being Max's sister. Part, I guess, is just who I am. But I did have one. You remember the Morrisons? Cindy, the oldest? She was my friend. Her family moved; I was eight, I think, maybe nine. After that, I never got close to no one. Then, with me having Phoenix, even those I'd talked to didn't talk to me. When I think about Cindy I can't remember what she looked like."

"It's been a long time."

"I was thinking about going back and finishing high school. I've only got one more year. But I couldn't stand being up there with everybody looking at me, whispering behind my back. 'That's Carla March. She had a baby.' "

"You ought to go back. You ought to finish and go to college."

"I don't feel like doing anything right now."

Lucinda picked up her glass, swiveled it, stared at the swirling ice cubes. "I know that feeling," she said. "Listen. You want to be friends?"

"I guess so."

"Why only guess so?"

Carla studied her bare feet, knowing this was what she'd

wished for, this the hope that lit her when she held her breath
before turning Kingston's corners, imagining Lucinda there, her
would-be friend's surprise, her own heart rejoicing at its blessing.
She wanted a friend, Lord how she longed for one, had promised
that if Lucinda so much as leaned in her direction, she'd reach
and take her in.

And now this moment, defined not by leaning, or chance encounter on the street, but by close enough that shoulders almost
touched, and simple words: "You want to be?" Exactly what
she'd wished for, and what Carla felt was fear. Fear that made
her mouth dry and said she couldn't move a hand, a foot or
shoulder, fear that claimed her for itself, pulled her away from
where something that might cause great pain had asked, "You
want to be?"

It was a fear so strong she couldn't say from where she got
the strength to break from all its pulling. But she found the
strength, and did it. She'd thought to say, "Yes, oh, yes;" instead,
she whispered, still staring at her feet, "Okay."

It was hardly a hallelujah that her longing would be met, but
it was a beginning; even this smallest of affirmations began to
work its magic. Something eased in Carla; she sipped her lemonade, felt her fear subside enough to speak of it.

"I'm scared."

"Of what?"

"That you'll stop liking me. That I'll start to need you and
you'll leave."

"I won't stop liking you. Even if I went away someday, we'd
still be friends, still stay in touch. But I'm not going anywhere.
Let's not talk about leaving. We're at the start."

Lucinda reached her hand out; Carla took it. The hand was
warm—substantial.

"Friends?" Lucinda asked.

"Friends."

They squeezed hands, experimentally, then stiffened as a howl
seeped from the housetop.

"What's that?"

Carla looked away. "My father."

"Lord. Is he really trying to die?"

"I think so." She took her hand back. "That's what he said."

"Why?"

"I don't want to talk about it."

Lucinda touched her arm. "It must be hard for you."

For a moment, for reasons she couldn't explain, Carla wanted to deny it. "It is," she said.

Anna stuck her head through the back-porch door. Visibly shaken, she said it was time to go.

"Already?" Lucinda asked.

"I'm in no mood," her mother said, and drew back into the foyer.

"I gotta go."

Carla nodded.

"I'll be back," Lucinda said. "I promise." She leaned forward, kissed Carla on the cheek, then stood. "I'll see you later."

"Lucinda?"

"What?"

"Thank you. For what you did in church."

"You're welcome," her new friend said. "I bet you'd have done the same for me."

On the sidewalk, Lucinda asked her mother why she looked so stricken.

"I went upstairs to pay respects," Anna said, "and the man took one look at me and started carrying on like I'm some kind of evil. And the *smell*." She stopped walking, turned to face her daughter. "Do I look like anybody's evil?"

Lucinda assured her that she didn't.

Two weeks later, the girls sat on Carla's porch.

"Are you sick?" Carla asked.

"I'm fine. Why?"

"You're losing weight so fast."

"No, I'm not sick." Lucinda laughed, and for no reason except that laughing seemed to be contagious, Carla did it, too. She liked the sound of her laughter. She realized that when Lucinda was around she laughed a lot, allowed herself, even, to be silly. It was a little hard to get used to, like discovering another person in a room where you'd moved alone. But she liked the person.

"So why you losing weight so fast?"

"You wouldn't believe it," Lucinda said.

"Try me."

"Okay. How many penises have you seen?"

Carla laughed again. "What's that got to do with losing weight?"

"Come on, how many?"

"Phoenix's. . . . ."

"Not a baby's."

"Just Max's."

"What did it look like?"

"Like a penis."

"Come on, Carla."

"It was a penis. About yea long, this thick." She held her hand out, extending the thumb and first finger, then formed a circle about the circumference of a quarter. "The head always made me think of a mushroom. But that's the only one I seen, except my brothers', when they were . . . little."

"No others?"

"Well . . . " The memory moved in her.

"What?"

"One time, my father's."

"Your *father's*? How'd that happen?"

"He was coming out of the bathroom, and his robe came open."

"Was it big?"

"Gigantic."

"What'd you feel?"

"I don't remember. I think I was embarrassed. And . . . *interested*. But I don't remember."

"My Lord. I've always wondered what my father's looks like."

"Why don't you ask him? Say, 'Daddy, can I see?' "

Lucinda leaned all the way to one side, whooping so hard her hair bounced. "Can you imagine?"

"And what if he said, 'Certainly, dear. Soon as I finish the paper'?"

Lucinda shrieked. "You are *something*."

"You started it. Why'd you ask?"

" 'Cause I finally saw one. I even touched it. And ever since, I've stopped craving cornbread and mashed potatoes, and I'm losing weight." She smiled, triumphant. "What do you think?"

"I think you're making this up."

"You do? Then we'll forget it."

"Whose was it?"

"I don't know why you want to hear some made-up story," Lucinda said.

"Okay, I'm sorry."

"You don't sound sorry."

"Cross my heart and hope to die sorry. Whose was it?"

"Luther Birdsong's."

"Luther *Bird*song? The man just *died*?"

Lucinda nodded.

"How in the world . . . ?"

"In my basement. My daddy was working on him. I'd never seen one and I wanted to, and I didn't know how else to do it. The first time I snuck down there, all the dead were women. Three of them. One had beautiful thighs. It made me cry. After that, every time I asked my father who he worked on, he'd say a woman, tell her name, who her family was. He didn't seem to notice only women dying; no one did.

"When Luther Birdsong passed, I didn't have to ask my father. Everybody talked about it; it wasn't till a man died that they looked back at all the women. I'd come home that weekend. When my father stopped for lunch, I slipped down to the basement. The body was covered, a white sheet with a brown stain. His feet stuck out, big feet, they made a V. I picked the sheet up, and there it was. It was long, curled across his thigh. When I held it, it felt light, no heavier than a finger. You know the way a turtle's head comes out its neck hole, flesh wrapped around it? That's what it looked like.

"So I did what I set out to do, I saw one. Now I want to have one inside me, to know what *that* feels like."

"You better be careful," Carla said. "You see what that got me."

"Oh, I'll be careful. I'll make sure he uses a rubber." Lucinda's face changed. "Tell me, what *is* making love like?"

Carla shook her head. "I can't describe it."

"Can't? Or won't?"

"Can't. Come on. Let's take a walk."

"Where?"

"The river."

They walked arm in arm through tree-lined neighborhoods quiet in the sun. Along Broadway, stores had doors flung open, inviting spring inside. In the street, few cars, a city bus that was all but empty. From the top of the hill that reared above the black community, they could see the sagging structures leading to the river: apartment buildings, empty storefronts. Past the drugstore slept a vacant lot.

The girls went down the incline, nodding at people on the

street. Most were old and black; children were in school. In front of the pool hall young men wore beautiful hats and dazed expressions until longing rearranged their eyes. "Hey, sweetmeat," they called. "You need a boyfriend?" "Can I just touch the back of your neck? Your elbow?" then moaned when the girls pretended they didn't exist.

"Ain't neither of 'em eighteen," one boy said. "They'll put you *under* the jail for messing with them." Another said, "They'll *be* eighteen," and all of them laughed, and a few swaggered back into the pool hall.

When they were out of earshot, Lucinda said, "I am *too* over eighteen." Then she sighed. "Did you see the one in the green hat? The one smoking a cigarette? Is he gorgeous or am I blind?"

"He's all right," Carla said.

"All right?" Lucinda squealed. "Are you kidding?"

"He's not doing anything with his life but hanging on a corner. He needs to get a job."

"A job? For what? He can get what I got for free."

"You ought to stop," Carla said, laughing, and Lucinda giggled, squeezed her arm.

When they reached the river's edge, they sat on the grass beneath a tree that spread above them. A hundred yards to their left was the spot where, in the summer, the river was roped off for swimming, and to their right, up the river a ways, were the Parks Department rowboats available to residents for three quarters of the year. Past these, about the distance a city block would claim, beyond a shore littered with rocks the size of softballs, was the foundation of the house Carla had lived in.

"What's that?" Lucinda said.

Carla pulled at her dress, hid her thigh. "Scars. From the fire."

"Can I see?"

"No. They're ugly."

"I don't care."

"Not now."

"That must have been awful."

"It was," Carla said. She looked behind her; a breeze ruffled the water's edge. "You know where we are? This is where Deadstreet's dog tracked Max to."

"Really?" Lucinda gazed at the spot, then turned her vision to the middle of the river. "You think Max is out there on the bottom?"

"I don't know."

Lucinda shook her head. "He's not. He took that boat to freedom."

"Or got translated back to heaven with my brothers."

"I prefer," Lucinda said, "the boat. Less bitter."

"I been re*buked.*"

"*And* scorned."

Carla sighed, leaned back, and looked above her. Through the tree limbs the sky was covered with clouds so thin they looked like gauze. "I'm so tired of being sad, Lucinda. Max gone, my brothers dead. My father threatening to die. I can't even talk to my mother like we used to."

"It'll get better. Here, let me hold you." She put her arm around her girlfriend's shoulder, pulled her head into her chest.

Carla whispered, "That feels good."

"Don't it? My daddy do this to me all the time."

"Your father *holds* you?" She could smell Lucinda, a clean clear smell; she thought of miniature soap in flowered paper.

"Yup. Ever since I was little. He doesn't talk a lot, but my mama makes up for that."

"She sure can beat her gums."

"Now don't you be talking about my mama," Lucinda said. "You know what I used to do when I was little?"

"What?"

"Get up early in the morning and listen at their door. That's when they used to talk. The strangest things."

"Like what?"

"Why people had fingernails, why a nose had two holes instead of one or three. I'd sit there. It felt so safe."

"I can't remember feeling safe. You know what scares me most?"

"What?"

"That my father will die, and I won't be able to grieve. I can't grieve for my brothers. It's there, but it won't come out."

"Maybe it's too big to come out," Lucinda offered. "Grief is like that sometimes, so big you can't even cry it."

"My mother said that. That I'm grieving but just don't know it. You think so?"

"It'll get better for you. And stop worrying. Your father won't die."

Carla didn't answer.

"I got this feeling," Lucinda said. "He won't. And Max will come back for you."

Pulling from Lucinda's embrace, Carla stared out at the river, knees drawn to her chest. *If I go*, Max said, *I'll come back for you.* Across the water, a white boat sat motionless against the shore.

"I feel it," Lucinda said. "He'll come back for you and the baby."

"He can't come back. He'd be arrested. He set a fire that killed my brothers."

"Do you think he meant to? You know I talked to him once. He seemed so . . . harmless. I can't imagine he set that fire on purpose."

"I can't, either. He fooled around with matches all the time. Mama was always after him about it. But if it was an accident, why'd he run away? Why'd he tell me he might be leaving?"

"He said that?"

"Said if he had to go to wait for him."

"So you think he planned it?"

"What it sounds like."

"I don't know. Maybe he left because he was ashamed. And scared. I'd have been scared."

"Maybe."

"Do you want him to come back? Could you forgive him? Could your parents?"

Carla clutched her legs, chin against her knees. "My father

would. I guess my mother would. Me, I don't know. I don't think about forgiving, except for him leaving me with a baby, *his* baby, not facing it with me. I ought to be thinking about my brothers, and what's happened to my family, but I end up thinking about myself. And when I do I get a hole in my stomach that I think, sometimes, is wanting him. But I don't know what I want him for. To explain, maybe, even though I think I know why he did it, if it wasn't an accident. I couldn't make him understand that I wasn't his sister, not by blood." She shook her head. "I don't know what I want. Except for my father not to die. Something awful will happen to me if he dies. I know it. I shouldn't have done it. Everything that's happened is my fault. I shouldn't have done it."

"Don't say that. It's not your fault."

She didn't answer.

"It's not your fault," Lucinda said. "And your father won't die. Max didn't mean it. It was an accident."

Carla didn't answer.

"And Max is alive. He'll get in touch, explain it all. Here, hold my hand. You feel it?"

"I feel your hand."

"Let yourself go. You have to let go to feel it," Lucinda smiled. "Believe me. I can tell the future."

"Sure. And I'm the queen of England."

"You could be. You've got a royal way about you."

Carla laughed, swallowed the good taste of it, allowed for a moment the farfetched notion to move at center stage. Max would come back, explain, reverse the leaving.

Sure. And she'd be queen of England.

"We'll be happy," Lucinda said. "You and me and Phoenix and Max. Our kids will grow up together. You'll start a business."

The boat was not motionless; it had turned at another angle.

"A shoe store," Lucinda said. "A bakery. Sweet rolls every morning. Or you'll go to college, teach school, or be a scientist. I'll open a speech clinic. I'll marry someone rich."

"Ain't you the storyteller."

"You have to be able to dream," Lucinda said. "Go on, add your part."

She'd never sailed on anything larger than a rowboat. She'd never been farther than the state capital at Albany, a class trip an hour's drive away.

"Come on," Lucinda said. "Add your part."

"What?"

"What will your house be like?"

"What house?"

"You're not even trying," Lucinda accused. "The house you'll live in."

"Oh." She thought about it. "It'll have a big window in the kitchen. . . . "

"Why the window?"

"I like light. So I can watch the birds feed."

"Good. What else?"

"I'll have someone to do the housework. We'll meet for lunch."

"Tell it, girl! We'll go to New York on the weekends. Sail to Paris."

"Can we go someplace warm in the winter?"

"Sure. Where do you want?"

"Cuba."

"Si, señorita. I'll have seven kids."

"Seven!"

"My husband will be rich, remember?"

"Not me. I might be rich, but I ain't having no more babies."

"Why?"

"'Cause it hurts."

"Having a baby?"

"It makes you want to *die*."

"It can't be all that bad," Lucinda said, "otherwise women wouldn't keep doing it."

"Let's talk about it when you have one."

"Won't be anything to talk about. I'm not going to have a midwife. I'm going to sleep, like they did my mama. She said she woke up wondering what in the world she was doing in a hospital. She wasn't sick."

They laughed, then sat a while in silence.

"You know what?" Carla asked.

"What?"

"I want your hair."

"My hair?" Lucinda lifted the wealth of it from her neck. "It's my best feature. If I could, I'd give you some. But there's nothing wrong with yours. Besides, you're beautiful."

"You think so?"

"I'm looking at you."

Carla felt she'd been given an unexpected gift. There was a white boat on the water that only turned when she wasn't looking. "We'd better get back," she said.

As they walked up the hill, Lucinda peered into the pool hall, searching for the young men who'd called out to them, sighed when they stayed inside. The girls leaned forward, climbing.

"At least something's happened in your life," Lucinda said. "Not all of it's so wonderful, but nothing's happened in mine. I want to make something happen."

"It's hard for girls to make things happen."

"You know what I want?"

"What?"

"To talk to Junkman."

"It would be a one-sided conversation."

"I'm serious."

"Me, too. You better stay away from him. Ain't you heard how he's walking around with a lamp, singing songs without any words?"

"That's what's so fascinating. That he's making sounds. I think I understand why he doesn't talk. I came across it when I was doing a paper. It's not that he can't, or at least I don't think so. What he has, well, you don't really *have* it, but it's called 'voluntary mutism.'"

A car horn blew; they looked. A green car, a driver whose hat obscured his forehead.

"Voluntary what?"

"Mutism. When a person stops talking because of something that's happened to him. When he chooses to stop."

"You mean he can talk but he won't?"

"My mama said he used to talk, then stopped in respect for his daddy. Talking is like anything else. If you don't use it, you lose it. If he worked, maybe he could get it back. Wouldn't it be great if I could teach him?"

"Maybe," Carla said, "but why would you want to?"

"So he would say, 'Oooh, baby, baby, you so fine.' "

"And you call *me* crazy," Carla said.

Lucinda said, "Because it's something to do. Because nothing ever happens to me, and I'm bored. I want to be smart and beautiful—well, I am smart—but I want to be beautiful, and rich, and make love, and I want to feel like I took some chances in my life."

"That's all?"

"For starters."

"Where do you get these ideas?"

"From Cuba," Lucinda laughed.

"You're dangerous."

"You think so? I think I'm interesting. And I love his shoes. Did you ever in your life see anything so fine? I've always liked men with pretty shoes. Once I saw him in a pair of cowboy boots. Gorgeous. Made me feel things my mama would have slapped me for. Don't fine shoes get next to you?"

"No. But I do wonder why he's singing."

"I'm out of school now. I'll find out and let you know."

"When you do," Carla said, "find out why he used to hang around my house."

"He did?"

"He was there the night of the fire."

"I heard that. They said he was dancing."

"He was."

"Like jitterbugging?"

"Uh-uh. My mama said like grieving."

"You think *he* set the fire?"

"Not really. I just wonder why he was there. Why he'd been

there, never doing anything but watching. What was he watching *for*?"

"Hm," Lucinda said. "You got no idea at all?"

"Not really. Except once he left a note. After we moved to Manor. Said he loved me."

"He did?"

"Yup."

"What'd you do?"

"Nothing. What was I supposed to?"

"So maybe that's why he was there. Maybe all that time he loved you."

Carla shook her head. "I don't think so. I think I would have felt it." She smiled. "That's a lot of love."

"Did he say anything since then?"

"He doesn't talk."

"You know what I mean."

"Not a word."

"Well, *that's* a mystery," Lucinda said. "Maybe I'll solve that one, too."

When they reached the corner, they kissed. Carla stood watching Lucinda move away, felt the surge of loving. It was good to have a friend.

"Lucinda."

She turned. "Yeah?"

"You want to know what it feels like?"

"It?"

"You know. What you asked."

"Oh. Hell, yeah. Speak on it."

"It's warm. Connected. Stretched out on the edge of pleasure. But mostly power."

"Power?"

"You're in control."

"It's like that for everybody?"

"I don't know. It was for me."

"Well, then, more power to you," Lucinda laughed, and did a little bump and grind before she waved good-bye.

Carla watched her swing along the sidewalk. She was trying

to put together what she felt. First there was no longing, no sense that Lucinda's leaving was forever. Her friend would be there for her, always. They *would* go to Cuba, and she, she'd have a kitchen filled with light.

I'm going to be all right, she thought. *I'm going to be all right.*

So Lucinda began to follow Junkman through Kingston's streets keeping a suitable distance between them, so that neither he nor anyone else would know what she was doing. She'd found employment as a receptionist in a dentist's office, a job that allowed her time to ponder the mute's condition. She went to the library to see what additional information she could gather, but nothing there was very helpful. Finally, referred by one of her teachers, she contacted the American Psychiatric Association, which sent a number of articles and wrote to tell her that the condition's name had been changed from *voluntary* to *elective* mutism. Generally, it was caused by childhood trauma. Some of its symptoms were persistent refusal to talk in one or more social situations, isolation, phobia, and disordered sleep. Extreme cases sometimes resulted in mental retardation, but violent conduct was virtually unknown. What intrigued her most, Lucinda told Carla, was *how* Junkman had chosen to break his silence, behavior that none of the literature reported, and she wondered what had unlocked that part of his voice that revealed itself in song. Evenings of shadowing him provided no answer, and she'd decided to make contact.

"That's crazy," Carla said.

"Why? He's not dangerous. And I'll be out in the open. What's crazy about it?"

"Leave it alone. Let it be."

But Lucinda insisted, and the next day, a Friday, she went up to Junkman where he'd paused, as he did most evenings, in the park across the street from the Governor Clinton Hotel. The park was the northern extremity of his daily journey, and when he reached it, he'd change the volume and intonation of his singing. Then he'd squat, or kneel, or sit on one of the benches, and in a little while he'd rise, retrace his steps. Sometimes he drifted to the river, stood looking at the water; sometimes he strode directly to the building where he lived. She'd watch him climb the stairs, wait for a light to flash in a window. None ever did, so she knew he lived at the back.

Of course he'd noticed her, knew she was Ulysses Hancock's daughter, but since she'd never gotten close enough to smell, he didn't link her with that day two years ago, when, after a rain that darkened pavement, he'd gone walking in his boots. Today, as he'd done before, he admired the loveliness of her hair, which she'd taken to piling on top of her head, noted the intelligence in her face, saw how the fat she'd lived in all her life was melting. But he didn't know why she followed him, or why, this afternoon, she stood almost close enough to smell. Her presence made him anxious, but he wouldn't allow it to divert him. He turned, stared across the street toward the hotel, where roses and a deep-green awning marked the shadowed entrance. Lifting his hand as if in blessing, he knelt, began to sing.

Lucinda waited, patient, calmed by the beauty of the scene, charmed by the strange, atonal music—mixture of chords both blue and spiritual, grunt/groans of dissonance, whose meaning, if meaning they had, were in their pitch and rhythm. At one point, distracted despite his resolve, he looked at her, held the gaze, and she found herself considering the quality of his eyes. They were large, fastidiously empty, irises obsidian against a porcelain white. He finished his song, still staring, on his face nothing she could call expression. She realized she didn't know what to say, and, more interestingly, wasn't nervous, even though she stood face to face with a man whose silence had caused some folks to consider him insane.

Now Junkman's eyes veered from the hotel to a sky streaked with eggplant, to the clots of pedestrians who passed, pretending not to see. She still hadn't spoken when he bent, fumbled with the lantern, lit it. There was a puff of black smoke, a ragged flame, and when the burning steadied, he stood and walked away. He was wearing his brown-and-white two-tones. They looked good enough to eat.

"Wait," she called. "Junkman."

He stopped; she came to face him. "Can I walk with you?"

He stiffened; questions filled his eyes, spilled, clung to lash and lid, the precipice of cheekbone. Then she did something she didn't understand. In motion that pulled blouse from skirt waist, she reached, found pins, let down her hair. She shook her head, looked all the way into his eyes, trying to read the questions. But there were so many, and they were wrapped around each other like vines or snakes. How could she answer questions she couldn't identify? If she were him, what would *she* want to know?

"I won't hurt you," she said. "I'll be your friend."

It was as if her words had struck him. He flinched, looked above him, and there it was again, the small dark thing inside, the solitary flame that hadn't visited in so long he'd forgotten. Its glow relit anxiety, made him weak with something very much like hunger. He dropped his gaze, touched his heart, his belly.

She said, "You're grieving."

He nodded.

"For what?"

He shook his head.

"Tell me what you want," she whispered. "Show me."

He raised his right hand, palm up, slowly, as if the movement caused him pain, then made a fist against his mouth. In the street a car horn sounded, the roar of an accelerating engine. Lucinda looked at him and knew.

"Yes," she said. "I'll comfort you."

And that was why, on that June evening in 1941, the spring before the bombs fell on Pearl Harbor (it was how the event would be remembered, placed in time), those folks who happened to be on Broadway witnessed Junkman and Lucinda, he in his two-tone shoes, not singing, but carrying the swinging lamp, she in a blue skirt, white blouse disheveled, hair falling down her back. Since everyone who saw them had a life to lead, they took a look or two, noticed this additional unlikelihood in a year defined by strangeness, and went about their business. All except Melvina Turner, who came out of the fried fish joint on the corner of Jones and Broadway, gasped, and flew to the Hancocks' house. Melvina was denied the pleasure of witnessing the panic; neither of the Hancocks was home. Anna was at the Catholic hospital visiting the sick, activity that provided her with captive listeners. Ulysses was presenting at an undertakers' competition in Brooklyn where he took third prize in the category *Keeping the Casket Open: Minimizing the Effects of Facial Trauma.* On the way, he'd found food for thought at the Lincoln Tunnel tollbooth. There, in red letters, in the blue light of approaching evening and the exhaust of a truck with Florida license plates, was a sign that read: *Depart Slowly.* So completely did the words rivet Ulysses's attention that the attendant had to shout at him to take his change.

So Lucinda went home with Junkman, through streets of a dusk-ripe city, trailed silently upstairs to the third floor, waited in a hallway sharp with disinfectant while he fumbled for his key. When he opened the door, she stepped into a spacious single room with white walls newly painted. He switched on the light and revealed the bareness. At one end was a kitchen, a saucepan on the stove. To the left of the refrigerator was the open door to a bathroom, followed by the closed door of what must have been a closet; after that a wall as empty as his eyes. Against this, a table with three chairs and, close enough to fall into it from the chairs, the bed.

She was aware that he'd closed the door, stood watching. Slowly, she moved to a window. The view was the back of a building similar to this; at its feet a fenced plot sprouted litter.

"So," she said, and turned to face him. "This is where you live," and he nodded, lifted and let his free hand fall, motion that said, apologetically, *This is where I live.*

Gesturing again, he invited her to sit at the table, set the extinguished lantern on the stove, crossed the room, knelt, reached beneath his bed. He pulled out a shoebox, took from it a pencil and pad, sat across from her. The pad was white, with blue lines. The tablecloth was made of yellow plastic. Like the hallway outside, the room smelled of disinfectant. He wrote with the concentration of a child, pushed the pad toward her. She read: *You have beautiful hair.*

"Thank you."

He wrote: *I'm glad you're here.*

"Why," she asked, "are you grieving? Is it still for your father?"

No. I grieve for me.

"Why?"

I can't tell you.

"How can I comfort you?"

He looked at her, embarrassed that despite his need, he didn't know. Confused, he consulted the memories of funerals attended, the witnessing of accidents in the street, the times Max had healed the sick. He thought of what stirred in him when he came upon the bodies of dead things, a dog by the side of the road, a sparrow stiff beneath a wire it so recently had sung on. He'd wanted to touch the dead things, pick them up.

Please touch my hand.

She reached and held his hand. It was big. She traced his veins, the hard places where the bone lived. She felt tender, certain.

"Is this enough?"

He nodded.

"Has anybody ever comforted you before?"

His head said no.

"The best comfort is in holding. Can I hold you?"

He hesitated, and she stood, indicating that he rise also, and when he did, she stepped against him, closed her arms around his back. She lay her head on his chest, and he stood, uncertain, smelling of Lifebouy. His black suit was soft against her face. She felt his heartbeat, felt the blood like freight trains boring through her veins, passage so real she could've accepted the long, high wailing of a whistle.

It wasn't comfortable standing like this. She moved, and before his eyes could finish recording disappointment, she took his hand, led him the short step to the bed. They lay on their sides; he kept a distance. She touched his face. Here it was smooth, there the pricking of a day-long growth. She fingered lips, cheekbones, explored earlobe and cavity. When he stirred, she slid her leg between his, skirt riding up her thigh, bare flesh against the fabric of his pants. She felt safe, the kind of warmth and connection she found when her father held her; she felt blessed, and she made up her mind to do it. As if the thought were in the air, magnetic, Junkman shivered, hardened at her thigh. She moved away, his eyes came open in alarm; she touched his face, then reached, undid his belt and found the zipper, pulled. She pried past the tightness of his shorts, breathed deep, and held a living penis in her hand. She took it out so she could see, the head like a plum above the circle of her fist. The blood pulsed in his shaft; it was like holding some small and frightened animal that all the time was swelling. She thought *whoa!* and he, groaning in the way of singing, came, ropes of white liquid gushing once, twice, three times, a pause, and then one last magnificent spurt. She held him until his body lost its stiffness, understanding perfectly what Carla had said about the power. Then she swung from bed, removed her blouse and skirt, her underwear.

"Take off your clothes," she whispered, and he, dazed by the miracle of what had happened, sat up to do her bidding, realizing it was only now he'd allowed himself to register conviction that she was here. He took a deep breath, part air, but mostly odor. He remembered. She smelled of young girl-flesh: fish roe and lilacs, distilled water, diamond dust.

Later, after they'd stripped the blood-stained sheets, she asked that he do her a favor. He collected all the beautiful shoes, arranged them in a circle on the bed. She sat in their center, explored the loveliness of pigskin, cowhide, alligator, suede, held the shoes against her cheek, touch that quelled her anxiety when she remembered Junkman hadn't used a rubber. While she mar-

veled that fine shoes could quiet the soul's misgiving, he, lit with
the desire to speak out loud, wrote to tell her why he grieved.

Outside, she leaned against a lamppost, trying to still her racing
mind. There was a stench in the air like fruit on its way to rotten.
She sniffed; it wafted from the river.

She had to tell Carla. Junkman had wanted to walk her home,
but she'd said no. She couldn't let him know she was telling Carla.
She'd tell nobody else, but Carla had to know. And oh, this feeling!

Two old women passed in the street, set down shopping bags
to stare with disapproval. Lucinda took a deep breath, waited,
and there came the heat of guilt. She instantly dismissed it. She
hadn't betrayed anyone. Carla didn't love *him*. She headed up the
hill, went past the pool hall; the young men promised to worship
her forever. What was in their voices touched her; she began to
relive what had happened in that room, the way Junkman had
swollen in her fist, the feel inside her, the loveliness of shoes, the
glory of the rocking and the power.

Carla wasn't home, had gone walking, Meridian said, and
blinked, wiped a weary hand across her face.

"Tell her to call me," Lucinda said. "Please. As soon as she
gets back. It's important."

When Lucinda approached her house, haunted by what Junkman
had told her, and trying to figure out if what she felt was love, her
mother came rushing up the sidewalk, waving the note left by Melvina Turner. She looked at her daughter and knew, dragged her
into the house, for the first time in her grown-up life slammed backward into silence. She pushed the frightened girl up the stairs to her
room, demanded that she undress and spread across the bed. All
the signs were there, the pubic hair matted with sweat, the mute's
still-glistening seed, the blood trace on her thigh.

Anna stared at the evidence, and then she stormed to the kitchen, steeped bitter herbs in water. When she returned, Lucinda hadn't moved.

"Drink this," Anna commanded, forced her to sit up.

Lucinda drank it. She felt the corruption at the bottom of her stomach, the liquid like a knife, and when her eyes glazed, she vomited. Unfazed, Anna pushed her to the bathroom, washed her, then retrieved the remainder of the brew, filled the douche bag, cooled it with cold water. She set her daughter on the toilet, shoved the nozzle in. She went back into the room, changed the linen, returned to lead Lucinda to the bed, shoved her to the cool, taut sheets. Lucinda's eyes bulged; she vomited again.

Dazed by the filth, Anna considered fresh sheets ironed to perfection, corners turned. She remembered how she'd hovered over Lucinda when her heart was sick, celebrated her success in school, labored to give her the chance to be somebody, and it had come to this, her daughter mating with a common nigger. The pent-up feeling, the one that had softened through the years, was there again, had moved to knot her throat, made it impossible to swallow. There were no flies to pull wings from, no dogs to stone, no infants whose thighs she might, in secret, punish. It was this absence that fired her rage, and she began, with a deliberation made more terrible by silence, to beat the flesh she'd given birth to. Not like a woman chastising her child, but like a man beating another who'd had the insolence to sleep with his wife, or to lean against his car. Lucinda didn't move or cry out, lay, eyes closed, absorbing the blows until her mother quit, brought to her senses by exhaustion.

"Jesus," Anna said. She put a palm to her mouth, stumbled to the kitchen, turned in a circle, sat. "God, what have I done?"

She sat, waiting, and when God didn't answer, she rose to go to Lucinda, to tell her she was sorry. On her feet, she swayed. How could she even look her daughter in the eye? How could she do anything? There was something way back in a corner of her mind insisting something must be done, that in not-doing lurked her punishment, wide and deep and terrible, and so she began to clean her kitchen, polished already spotless counters, attacked the four eyes of the stove, dropped to her knees, where she savagely scrubbed the floor.

When she went upstairs, Lucinda, cross-legged in the soiled bed, sucked at the blade points of scissors, in her lap the black lake of her hair.

"Oh, no," Anna said. "Lord, lord, lord." She allowed for one more moment of self-blame, nearly fainted from it, pushed it away forever. It wasn't her fault. It was the times they lived in, the erosion of values, the great falling away from God. It wasn't her fault. It was Junkman's. As she stood, confronted with the horror of her puke-stained, head-shorn daughter, she began to create a solution, and when it was whole she rushed to the phone, first to call the police, then her relatives in North Carolina.

When she'd said good-bye, she spun at the whimpering at her back. Lucinda stood in the kitchen doorway, naked, hunched, clots of hair sticking to the vomit.

"I'm not going to North Carolina," she rasped.

"You'll go where I tell you."

"I'm not going," Lucinda said. The soft thing was giving way in her head. She had to do it before it broke. She held a hand to her skull top, holding it together, staggered across the room, reaching for the phone.

"I've got to call Carla."

"Go back upstairs."

Lucinda screamed, *"I've got to call Carla. I've got to tell her what I know."*

The phone rang. Anna held her off; Lucinda flailed. They were going in a circle, fused to one another, the naked child, the frantic mother, and Anna reached and ripped the instrument from the wall. As if she'd been held by its wire, Lucinda crumpled, her screams drilling into the room until Anna clamped a hand across her puke-smeared mouth.

"Hold still," Anna hissed. "Hold still, and hush that screaming."

*   *   *

"Something must be wrong with the phone," Carla said. "She didn't say what it was?"

"Just to call her."

"I'll try later."

Later, when the phone still wasn't working, it was too late to walk to Lucinda's house. She'd go by in the morning.

Junkman didn't want to wash away the odor, but he needed to be warm and wet. He took the stained sheets, held them to his face, then folded and put them in the closet with his shoes, so he could smell Lucinda when he wanted.

When the police broke down his door, they found Junkman in the shower, face dripping as he tried to talk. The sound of his speaking voice had given him a headache, but he'd persisted, finding in spoken language what he didn't understand were identity and power; he only knew that talking made him feel good. He hadn't started with language, but with grunts and groans he utilized when singing, and then he said "a" and "cat" and "tree." He was going to say "Dad," but that word brought tears to his eyes, and he instinctively understood this was a time for celebration. He tried more small words, "floor," "window," and when he'd developed an expertise that made these less than challenging, he felt he was ready for the articulation of a sentence. He decided to make one about his feelings, but they were so complex he couldn't. He began to form one about being in the shower. The ability to record a part of his life in speech ignited him, and the words came tumbling out. But they were grating, guttural, without music, or magic, or force.

He paused, disappointed, trying to figure out the source of speaking's power. Was it in the mere ability to do so, in the sound, or was it in the message? He remembered what Lucinda had said, the most beautiful words he'd ever heard, and he steeled himself, vibrating with expectancy, said the words out loud, the sound painful but exhilarating:

"Yes. I'll comfort you."

When the policemen barged into the bathroom, Junkman, behind the curtain, didn't know who they were. Why were strange men violating the privacy of his home without the courtesy of knocking? Why had they come upon him in his nakedness, shouting in two sets of voices that they were cops, and he shouldn't move, but still come out of the shower with his hands up?

So Junkman did what any reasonable person would have done; he panicked. He expressed his panic by slipping on the tub's slick surface, by throwing up his hands to break his fall and thrashing so violently that he ripped the shower curtain from its rings. Blinded by wet plastic, he struggled mightily. Water drenched the floor; the heavier policeman, frightened, but bound to do his duty, reached to restrain the bleating suspect while the other hand sought his gun. The wet, tiled floor was treacherous. The hand that would restrain was cautious; the holster snap wouldn't come undone. All of it conspired to make him lose his balance. Feet in ugly shoes took off from under him; he fell, hit his elbow against the sink, cracked the back of his head on the toilet. The sound was sickening. His partner heard it and expressed his fear by stepping on the chest and legs of his fallen partner and by hitting Junkman with a billy club until the naked man was as still as the policeman on the floor.

When he was well enough, Junkman stood trial for the manslaughter of a policeman, for assault, resisting arrest, and for the rape of Lucinda Hancock. The jury sent him to prison. There, impressed by his size, his silence, and the mane of hair that grew eventually to his shoulders, inmates decided he wasn't suitable for fucking, and let him be.

Once his head cleared and the shock subsided, Junkman accepted his punishment. He'd simply been sentenced for the wrong crime. His relief at being in prison reminded him that a large part of his grief was that he'd violated that space in him that was reserved for wonder.

As he adjusted to prison's inelegant shoes, and to the fumes that spewed from an adjacent factory and clogged his nose, he reexamined the moment in the bathroom before the police had come, and practice-talked into his pillow. Finally, just for the pleasure of it, he began conversing with himself. He chatted with Lucinda, told her how grateful he was for what she'd given him, and though he was at first upset that she'd not come to visit (only the Josephs did, weeping when he explained what had happened), he understood when told Lucinda had been sent away. And he talked to Carla, telling her how much he loved her, that when his term was over, he was coming to make her his bride.

One morning, five years after they shut the prison doors behind him, Junkman realized it was Lucinda to whom he mostly talked. All day the revelation hung above him, then fell on his head in the mess hall at a quarter after five. He was on his way from the food line to the table, carrying a tray of pork chops, mashed potatoes, lima beans, and orange juice, and he stopped, mouth open, so abrupt a stop that the juice spilled into potatoes, ran off the tray, and dripped onto his foot. He experienced a moment of blinding light, a vacuumlike stillness, a chorus of voices wailing in the distance. Everybody made a wide berth around him, and he stood thinking: *Well, I'll be damned. It's not Carla I love. It's Lucinda.*

With this discovery came another light that reminded him of a sunset he'd once communed with: half the sky fading into yellow a painter would have sold his soul for. The light had filled the heavens so magnificently he'd fallen to his knees.

"Well, I'll be damned," Junkman repeated, and began to laugh and cry at the same time. Jesus, he felt good, so good he had to tell somebody. He shook himself; still carrying his ruined supper, he began to tour the hall, a trail of footprints left by his juice-stained shoe.

"It's Lucinda I love," he announced to every table, where inmates hardened by prison blessed him with smiles, wished him early parole, long life and peace, a house of bouncing babies.

"Thank you," Junkman answered, full of joy and wonder.

So Lucinda was gone, shipped off to North Carolina, and Junkman was in prison. He'd been begged by his lawyer to testify, if only to deny the prosecutor's insistence that Junkman was untouched by the civilizing effects of speech and human contact, a beast who'd risen from his isolation to kill a cop, and rape and drive insane a harmless black girl. If, by some lapse of judgment, the jury freed him, he would again be at liberty to kill those who protected decent folk from darkness. This, if you were human, was a thought to freeze the heart, and if by some small chance it didn't, consider that it was altogether possible (nay, it was certain) that were Junkman freed, his beastly lust would carry him into white neighborhoods, and none of their daughters would walk again in safety.

The prosecutor called Anna Hancock to the stand where, with a hand that limped from her lap to her forehead, she told how Lucinda had arrived home dazed and noncommunicative, and how, in that stupor, had cut off the hair everyone knew was a woman's glory. In the middle of his testimony of how Junkman had leaped at them in rage, the surviving policeman shocked the courtroom by bursting into tears, causing the judge to call a thirty-minute recess.

Junkman's public defender was not gifted, but he understood the impact of these witnesses. He invited the jury to imagine themselves in Junkman's position, how they'd respond if two men violated the sanctity of their homes and surprised them in the shower. He noted the absence of witnesses other than the policeman, argued that the psychiatrist who testified to Lucinda's insanity, as well as the doctor who confirmed sexual relations, were paid by the prosecution. And it was Junkman who yet bore the marks of his beating; the policeman was without blemish.

Still Junkman's lawyer couldn't effectively refute the portrait of his client as an animal unless he placed him on the stand. This he couldn't do, since Junkman refused. So the lawyer was reduced to arguing that if speech were defining, then the defendant *was* human, for he *could* speak, though not with the eloquence the rest of them possessed. He managed to convince Junkman that it wouldn't hurt matters to say good morning to the reporters. Beyond that, however, the accused man wouldn't go.

There was little hope of creating reasonable doubt about the charges of manslaughter, resisting arrest, or assault, but the defense managed to win the concession from Melvina Turner that nothing in Lucinda's demeanor that evening suggested that Junkman either lured or forced her to his room. After Melvina's testimony, several others corroborated her impression, and had it not been for the liberal judge, Junkman might not have gotten as much time as he did. The jury was concerned by the policeman's death, and was inclined to ignore the fact that a Negro was accused of raping one of his kind. But the judge believed that justice should be color-blind, and that if Negroes were to be treated equally (as he believed they should), such treatment must extend into the courts. All that mattered here, he instructed, was whether the crimes had been committed. Race was not a factor.

That eloquence, along with Melvina's testimony, kept the jury deliberating for two days while they argued the merits of the judge's philosophy. When they came back with their verdict, the judge sentenced Junkman to eighteen years for the policeman, one for resisting arrest, two for assault and four for the rape of Lucinda, to be served consecutively.

On the Tuesday after Junkman's trial began, Rufus screamed and lashed out at the attic shadows moving menacingly toward him, in the process smashing the lamp and keeping his promise to die. Three weeks later, Meridian gave birth to a baby boy. Battered by grief and anger, and the complications from a difficult delivery, she came home, lay batting her eyes in a room whose drapes she allowed no one to close. She was weary, visited by bones that ground in their sockets when she moved, causing her to moan and chew the collar of her nightgown, by issues of blood that spotted sheets with scarlet, by swollen breasts that leaked even in the hour after feeding.

Six months after Willis had battled into the world, Meridian, on her way to the bathroom, made faint by the enthusiasm of her hole for bleeding, collapsed on the hallway floor. Two hours later, in a hospital room that had no windows, breasts spurting, lids and lashes worn from beating, she called for her husband and found her eyes wouldn't close.

What Carla feared most had happened: She was not yet twenty, and everyone had left her. Then came the next stage of her punishment: She discovered Phoenix was retarded. This rocked her, left her light-headed. Marshaling strength, from where she didn't know, she labored to reclaim her child from idiocy. She forced him to sit up, which he wouldn't do until he was two, insisted that he crawl, which he managed at four, and wept when, at seven, he took his first steps. Speech he never mastered, despite the hours she read to him, despite the constant talking. And she ached with knowing that if Max knew the condition of his child, he could have reached a hand and healed him.

But Max didn't know. He'd vanished. *He'd* left her, too.

Now, as if someone had turned a page or begun to sing in a different key, Kingston's blacks were changing. The first stage was that they stopped telling stories. If you'd asked why, they'd have said they were tired of the same tales; they'd begin again when they met with something new.

But new had nothing to do with it. Negroes were silent because for the first time in their history, they couldn't bounce back from misfortune. Accepting that Max wasn't the fulfillment of the prophecy had rekindled deep suspicions that in spite of legends to the contrary, they weren't special. They still mourned for the charred bodies of the March children. The way the police beat Junkman exhausted them, made them remember what had happened to his father, but some were also furious with Junkman for putting himself in a position to be accused of committing a crime whites said blacks had probably invented.

Then the war came grinding to a halt, and when the smoke cleared, blacks found the world still wasn't safe for *them*, much less democracy. In 1952, United Business Machines moved to town and refused to hire them except as custodians and security guards. Flush with the discovery that an inexpensive poison quadrupled the yield of corn, a group from Memphis built a chemical plant down by the river, and soon fishermen as far south as Staten Island complained that their catch tasted funny. In 1956, the school board backed away from the promise it had made the year before, when, in the heat following *Brown* v. *Board of Education*, trustees of a system already integrated voted to include black history in the curriculum. That decision drew the wrath of the day's leading academics, who charged that "inclusion" was nothing but a code for lowering standards.

Now this might seem like a lot, but to a people used to hardships, it was spit in a bright, blue ocean. At another time, Kingston's blacks would have created something splendid from the setbacks: another soul food dish, a new way to wear hats, a home-run record. But this time they responded with self-pity.

What triggered this were the receptions to the discovery of blood plasma and the invention of the traffic light. Black genius was responsible for these. But even when Negroes jumped on the world stage with science that saved lives and stopped Buicks in their tracks, neither was celebrated as their triumph. Weakened by events, insulted, but mostly disappointed, blacks resolved to conserve the energy it took to keep alive a past nobody else thought worth recording. They didn't give up telling stories all at once; it's hard to break a people's habits, but eventually, they stopped.

The results were alarming. First came an emptiness at their

backs, a feeling so pervasive that for a while Kingston was known up and down the Hudson Valley as a city where blacks spun suddenly in the street, looking for landscapes some sixth sense said had vanished. All that spinning left them dizzy and led to fainting spells. Then the emptiness moved inside, took up residence in the heart, and in an effort to fill the void left by the absence of telling, blacks fell back on strategy as old as slave shacks: They began to imitate the white majority. The outcome this time was neither cakewalk nor cotillion, but that they became modern.

As black people understood it, there were two notions at the heart of being modern. One was that God was dead. The other was that beneath ordinary things seethed a complexity defined by contradiction. Experts on blues songs and white folks' behavior, they were already on a first-name basis with contradiction, and there was some ironic head-shaking when they found that what they took for granted had become a metaphor. Made bold by the familiar, they leaped feet first into the modern movement. Because they were blessed with a sense of timing, they were immediately in step, although their refusal to accept God's death until they'd seen the body required a small adjustment. In no time they were claiming to be like everybody else: anxious, buffeted by a world whose events were beyond the understanding and control of common folk. Much of it looked like the *same old same old*—war, famine, greed, and general nastiness—but being modern meant knowing it wasn't. It also meant being mobile. A few folks sold their homes and moved to California. Those who could afford them bought automobiles and went on day trips. One woman hung white sheets on her clothesline at which she tossed buckets of paint in motion that made passersby weep.

Then, in the late nineteen fifties, Kingston's black kids began to echo Lucinda's complaint that they lived in a place where nothing happened. Girls married too soon; black boys who'd never had a fistfight went off to join the army. In the early sixties, however, young people began to do more than grumble. They grew irreverent, fed up with history books that didn't offer a clue that they existed. When they asked old folks, they discovered none would talk about the past. By then, some of the kids had gone to college; it was these who said if you didn't repeat your history, you'd forget it. If the kids were so smart, grown-ups said, why didn't they have the sense to get a haircut? Smart people didn't risk their lives with nappy hair and climbing into bed across the color line (most of the time without washing). Smart people respected their elders.

The grown-ups were pissed and talked openly about going upside young people's heads, but after a while they let it be. The kids were, after all, only doing what they'd been put on earth to do, which was to act the fool and test their elders' patience. One day they'd fall back, dazed by the fist of a world that took shit from no one. This depended, of course, on kids lasting long enough, which wasn't certain, given their contempt for people over thirty. But if they lived, they'd learn. They'd learn that not only was it hard to change the world; it was a bitch to change the self. They'd learn that love was an impermanent miracle, a discovery that would be more devastating because it would arrive hard on the heels of the doomed effort to find an honest mechanic. If they survived this, and the dismay that *their* children now voted Republican, they'd be led kicking to that room in the soul, the one they'd been avoiding, the one where heartbreak lived. Grown-ups waited for time to smash young people's dreams, after which they could hold a decent conversation.

But this generation was different; these kids weren't easily dismissed. By 1964 they were marching in Kingston's streets, scaring the daylights out of white folks and black. Some went south; when they returned, they talked about a place called Mississippi as if it were another country, or a patient they'd one day pull the plug on. It was clear that something had happened to them; their eyes had deepened, grown old, and their mouths were stamped in fierce determination. They stayed a while in the city; they marched and rallied and littered the streets with leaflets. Some of it was for peace and justice, and some of it for justice even if there were no peace, but then they stopped, began to trickle out of Kingston, alone, in groups of two or three, and once an entire busload headed back to Mississippi. Others left for college or the Peace

Corps, some for New York City, all vexed that people who'd birthed and raised them refused to tell them who they were. They wanted to know where they'd come from, the source of conventions that marked their lives, why they were scorned in spite of their breathtaking beauty.

And Carla was there through it all, but when she witnessed, she didn't see, when she heard, she didn't listen. Although she'd developed a passion for reading, she never made the connection between what she read and what was happening around her. Everyone else was "other," living, she assumed, ordinary lives, an accomplishment beyond her reach. She lived with her brother and her son, a recluse, waiting for the boy with mismatched eyes, a fantasy inspired by the friend she loved, but who, despite her promise, left her. After her brother was gone, she had nothing to give her life meaning except Phoenix, and reading, and the inventions she crafted from alone.

One thing about the change was constant: People all the time were leaving. That's why she didn't even have the consolation of surprise when, in 1966, the man who could have been a dancer cut out for Arizona while the sirens wailed. She'd known from the beginning that he'd go; it was why she'd sent him. Not that it would have mattered, but he hadn't even said good-bye.

III

All through that fall of 1966, small things reminded Carla of his leaving. Somewhere someone surrendered to a laugh, or she'd glimpse in a child a movement so elegant only Miles's hands could match it. Once a fishing pole on an old man's shoulder made her breath catch, and in October, baseball's sleepy roar was on everybody's radio.

But she didn't weep or rage. By the afternoon that winter arrived, she'd gathered herself to her self. Patient as a blind man at a window, she settled in to wait, to see if this most recent leaving would be one she'd recover from or if it would be added, like lead around her heart, to all the others.

Winter was slow, whispered of uselessness, of waste. She thought of cleaning closets, organizing clutter. She'd take a night class at the high school, tune the piano, learn to play. Each activity had merit; each spoke of life defined by choice, direction. She did none of them.

Time inched, the city ice-bound; there was a wind in whose velocity Kingston bowed its head and leaned and moved with purpose, and now, inside of her, a story needing to be told. She whispered, "Come, story," in the kitchen; "Come," she called, sorting laundry in the basement, in the attic, where she closed her eyes to see her father in his bed.

When nothing came, rather than fret, she held to what she'd learned about invention; if she waited, it would come. She dressed and harnessed Phoenix, in the evenings walked with him through frozen streets, past the jaundiced eyes of houses to the river, edges icebound, back again. She read, and took no lovers; she sat and listened, and when the story still refused to come, she retold what she'd been for so long telling. Max coming up the porch steps, knocking at her door; Max in a handmade suit, a shining car, a driver. Nothing was changed except the details: the suit, forever blue, she changed to gray; the crystal candle holders now were silver. Minor alterations; still, it was exhausting. Maybe, she thought, telling was so hard because *she'd* changed, crossed bridges, gone all the way to New York City, considered living with a man who could have danced. Or maybe she'd told the story once too often, and it had lost its power to quicken.

Unsettled by this absence, wondering if telling was hard because its space was fallow, she broke up new ground in her heart. And in a little while, though it was an ordinary, snowbound winter when nothing else would grow, the old story bloomed again and flourished. She shaped and embellished it, left the porch light on, carried home foods Max would enjoy: tinned fish, dried figs, a jar of currant jelly. She bought a yellow smoking jacket, indigo silk pajamas she'd one night dress him in. These she hung in her closet, left the door open so she could lie in bed and watch them. The jacket was lamplight and marigolds, the pajamas were a blues song's melody.

Time moved, but had no rhythm: a minute whose second hand refused to sweep, an hour that whiled away the evening. Then a handful of days devoured, Tuesday's morning merged with Sunday's afternoon, and abruptly, on a Monday, winter up and left. Robins strutted, insects crawled and flew and slithered, and her back began to itch. How curious: all these years, and now this itch as if burn scars were newly healing. If the palm of your hand itched, that meant you were coming into money. But what did an itching back mean? She strained to reach it, and when she couldn't, scratched with broom handles, wooden spoons, writhed against walls and tables.

Maybe it was the stroking against hard things that did it; maybe all that rubbing redirected the flight of molecules, reversed some polarity in the universe whose field had for her lifetime pulled loved ones away.

Whatever the reason, the phone rang in April 1967. It was Willis.

"Hello?"

"Carla?"

"Sweetie, how are you?"

"Fine . . . Listen, Sis, I'm coming home."

"Home? When?"

"Shipping out in three days. I'll be in the states on the fifteenth. Stopping for a couple of days in L.A., and heading east."

"You bringing the family?"

"Yup."

"Great. How long you staying?"

He hesitated. "The other side of the house still empty?"

"Sure."

"We'll be staying for a while. I'm not re-upping."

"You leaving the navy?"

"Yes."

"Is everything all right?"

" . . . Yeah. We'll talk when I get there. It's no problem for us to stay?"

"It's your house, too, Willis."

"Thanks, Sis. I'll see you on the eighteenth or nineteenth. I'll call again to let you know."

When she hung up, she wandered into the kitchen, stood, thought-bound, at the sink. When Willis had stopped by with his new wife on his way to Okinawa, he'd planned to spend his career in the navy. He'd never lost his love of boats, and the precision of military life, he'd said, was made for him. In the navy he was rewarded for his ability, promoted when his time came. He'd stay, put in his thirty years.

And now he was leaving, and for reasons too complex, apparently, to go into on the phone. What time was it in Okinawa, and why was he coming home?

She looked up; night gathered at the window. She turned away, trying to focus only on her joy that she'd see her brother and her niece, began preparing. There wasn't all that much to do. Since she seldom went into the second side of the house, it wasn't cluttered. She'd only to dust, make sure there was enough linen and add to the food she'd bought for Max. She remembered that both Willis and Elizabeth, his wife, were coffee drinkers, although Elizabeth only drank it during breakfast.

They arrived at two o'clock on a morning that would end in rainfall. The taxicab was yellow, a headlight out. Willis, tall, lean as always, wore a close-cut beard. Elizabeth had dyed her hair red. The niece Carla had only seen in photographs was sleeping.

They put the child to bed, and Carla made tea and sandwiches. Elizabeth was tired, strained. Once Willis touched her wrist and she flinched, and from then on held her tea with both hands. They talked of turbulence and leg room, lights as the plane dropped above the city. Then Elizabeth excused herself.

When she'd left, it was as if she'd taken dark with her. Carla said, "She looks worn out."

"Well, we crossed a lot of time zones."

"You want more tea?"

"Please." Willis studied her. "You look good, Sis. Not a day older than the last time I saw you."

"Maybe not to you. I do to me."

"No way. Not a minute over thirty-five."

"I look *that* old?"

He laughed, and she said, "It's good to see you, too, Willis." She got up, kissed the top of his head. She could smell his hair oil, coconut. He had their father's mouth and cheekbones; the beard didn't hide that. She moved to the stove, fired the kettle. "I've got some herbal tea, no caffeine. It'll let you sleep. You want?"

He stretched, movement that threw the shadow of his arms across the table. "Give me the one with the drug in it. Sleep's the last thing I need. Slept most of the way from Okinawa. Fell asleep flying here from California. Slept on the bus. And that was after sleeping most of two days in L.A."

"Why you sleeping so much?"

She came back to the table, sat, and he shrugged and rubbed a hand across his face, tentatively, as if he weren't accustomed to his beard. "Tired."

"You don't have to talk about it," she said.

He leaned elbows on the table, wedged fists beneath his chin. She found herself remembering him as a child; this was how he'd sat and listened while she read to him, before he'd fallen in love with boats.

"I know," he sighed. "But if I don't talk to you, who do I?"

She said, innocently, "Your wife?"

"Me and Elizabeth are in trouble. And you know it."

"Okay," she admitted. "I just don't know what kind."

"The *bad* kind." He paused, took a deep breath. "I've sure been sighing a lot." He dropped his fists to the table; his hands were huge, like their father's.

"I don't want to lose my family, Sis. I want my marriage. I quit the navy in order to save it. Or at least to try."

"What's going on?"

"Elizabeth said she didn't want to spend the rest of her life as a military wife. Said the military was a violation of her political beliefs. I told her she knew my plans when she married me. She said she'd thought she could compromise because she loved me, but found she couldn't. I could respect that.

"But I don't think it has anything to do with politics, or who I work for, or where. I think it's her father."

"Her father?"

"I didn't tell you at the time. I didn't want to worry you, or maybe I was embarrassed. Maybe both. But Elizabeth's father disowned her when we got married."

"*Disowned* her? Because you're black?"

"Sometimes I think that's it, sometimes I don't. When we were going out, I thought he *liked* me. I *expected* him to. She'd told me how she grew up, all kinds of people in and out of the house, an 'everybody's equal' childhood. The family had black friends, people they associated with, went to dinner with, stuff like that. Her father loves black music. I didn't *imagine* I was welcome there. I *was*. Until we announced we were getting married."

"Did he know she was pregnant?"

"No. We were going to tell them, but after what went down. . . ." He leaned forward. The ceiling light made his face look younger than he was.

"Elizabeth made the announcement at her parents' house at dinner. Talk about silence. Her words just *loomed* in it. Then her mother made a kind of cooing sound, and when I look she's got her hands against her heart, like this, surprised, but happy. She's a nice-looking woman, and I remember smiling kind of stupidly at her, and then I looked at her husband. I thought he was sick. His face was dead white, his eyes closed. 'Lincoln,' I said. 'You all right?'

"He opened one eye, but it was like he didn't see me. He excused himself, got up, and left the table. His wife went after him.

"I'm thinking, 'Ain't *this* a trip?' Elizabeth's shaking like she's about to come apart, her mouth open. Neither of us moved. Her mother came back. Lincoln wasn't feeling well, she said, and would we please excuse her.

"So there we were." Willis leaned back from the table, laced hands behind his head. "Elizabeth and me not looking at each other, and I'm feeling bad for her, and feeling bad for *me*, and the only thing I could think to say, maybe because that's what we'd been talking about, was: 'What a country.'

"What did I say *that* for?

" 'This is *not* about anybody's country,' Elizabeth says, in this absolutely icy voice. 'This is about *family*,' and she stands up and says she's going to get to the bottom of it. 'Strangeness,' she called it. She said she was going to get to the bottom of this 'strangeness.'

"So there I am, right? Not knowing whether to leave, follow Elizabeth, or sit there, and just when I figured the best thing was to *go*, Elizabeth came back. 'He's swimming,' she said. 'He's out back in the pool, *swimming.*'

"I hear the swimming, but it doesn't make sense. 'He feels better?'

"She didn't know, he wasn't talking.

"Well, I got out of there. Elizabeth called me in the morning. After I left she'd tried to talk to her father again. That's when he forbade her to marry me. If she defied him, not only would he cut her off without a penny, he'd never speak to her or let her in the house."

"Anyway, we got married, little ceremony with a J.P., a few friends, her mother, who had to sneak to come. I was already on orders for overseas. Elizabeth kept in touch with her mother, but her father wouldn't answer her letters.

"Cassie was born, and Elizabeth began to change. She said it was about the military, but the truth is she's all messed up about her father and can't find anyone to blame but me. I don't have any proof except the way she is. Polite, just this side of indifferent. Moves away when I touch her. Real quick in bed, the female version of 'slam, bam, thank you ma'am.' And not a lot of that."

"It was her decision. How can she blame you?"

"I didn't say it made any sense."

"It doesn't. It's too quick the way her father changed."

"I said the same thing to myself," Willis said. "And sometimes I think maybe it *wasn't* so quick. I didn't give it a lot of thought at the time, but her father went through a little *funny* time with me, cool, nothing obvious, the kind of thing that, if you call somebody on it, can make you back off if they deny it. It lasted a couple of weeks. I thought maybe he knew I'd seen him, and was afraid I'd make a comment."

"Seen him?"

"I was downtown one day. I saw him come out of a store with this stunning black woman on his arm and a bunch of packages. I didn't think anything of it, like I said, the family had black friends, the woman could have been a secretary or a client, he owns a ladies' undergarment factory, or his wife does, and I was going to call him when he turned to look behind him like he didn't want to be seen. The sun was directly in back of me, so I don't know if he saw me or not. But I think he did. Anyway, he was acting so odd I didn't speak.

"So when he got cool with me, I thought that was why, that he was messing around, he *had* seen me, and was afraid I might say something. Later I figured maybe that had nothing to do with it. What triggered it was once he knew Elizabeth and I were serious about each other. I think some kind of reality hit him. You know, it was one thing for her to be going out with a black man, even sleeping with one. But marrying me was another story. But then I remember the conversation we had, and I just get confused again."

"Conversation?"

"He'd invited me into his study. I think he got a kick out of turning me on to black stuff I'd never heard of. He was playing a record, Robert somebody was the singer, and he was lecturing me, not in a pushy way, saying this style of blues came from the Delta, while this came from further south. It was a nice afternoon, you'd have liked where they live, it's up in the hills in Santa Monica, you face out over the tops of these pastel-colored houses and you can look all the way to the sea. We were drinking wine, and he started, in a clumsy kind of way, to talk about his family. He said it was wonderful to have a family, that family was the most important thing a person had.

"He sounded sad, got quiet, sat looking out the window. This Robert somebody was singing: 'Accuse me of forgery, can't even write my name,' a hell of a line, I thought, and then he said, 'I suppose Elizabeth's told you about me?'

"When I said I didn't understand, he told me he was an orphan, that his parents had been killed in a train accident, and he'd grown up in foster homes.

" 'I didn't know that,' I said. 'I'm sorry.' He said I could understand why he placed such a premium on family, and I said, 'Yes, sir, I do.'

"Then he wants to know about *my* family and I tell him my parents were dead, and how you'd raised me and Phoenix, and I told him about Max. He was fascinated. 'Really,' he kept saying,

'Really? What an extraordinary story. Really?' and poured another glass of wine.

"We sat there for a while, and then he got up, I thought to turn the record over, but instead he shut it off. He said it had been a pleasure to spend the time with me, but he had to go out for a while. He looked a little shaken, but I didn't know what to make of it. I thought maybe his reaction came from opening up. I had a friend used to say never let a white man tell you his business, 'cause once he's done it, he'll start to feel ashamed of being vulnerable and look for ways to prove he's still more powerful than you. But when I told Elizabeth, she said her father only talked about his past to people that he liked.

" 'Did he say anything about his heart?' Elizabeth asked.

" 'No,' I said. 'What about his heart?'

"She said he had a heart condition, that this was something else he only told to people that he cared about. So what was I to think? He told me half. 'That means he halfway likes me,' I said.

"Anyway, we got married, came to see you, and shipped out to Okinawa. Cassie was born, Elizabeth began to change, we decided to come home. We flew into L.A., Elizabeth rented a car and drove over to Santa Monica with Cassie. She had this idea that if her father saw his grandchild, he'd relent. No one, she said, could disown Cassie. So she showed up, unannounced."

He paused. His hands were palms down on the table, and he balled them into fists.

"Her father shut the door in her face. Didn't slam it, just firmly shut it. She said it was how calm he was, 'unmoved,' she said, that made her finally understand she'd live the rest of her life without a father."

He shrugged. "And here we are."

Outside, the light of a predawn thick with rain collected at the window.

Carla said, "She was all right about coming here?"

"She said we're all the family she's got left."

"Then that's what we'll have to be for her."

"If she lets us."

"We're here for one another," Carla said. "She'll let us."

Willis stared at her. She saw the hurt and confusion in his eyes, the child's helpless question, *Why me? What did I do to deserve this?* She knew the answer: *very little, if anything at all.* She also knew the answer didn't suffice.

"It's late," she said. "Why don't we go to bed? We'll talk some more in the morning."

"Okay. You know, I haven't even asked what's been going on with you. How *you've* been."

"There'll be time for that. Let's go to bed."

"Carla?"

"What, baby?"

"You think Daddy would have liked me? If he lived?"

"*Liked* you? He'd have *loved* you. He loved you before you were born. I was there. I saw it."

"Really?"

"Really."

"Then why'd he will himself to die?"

"He was hurting, baby. Sometimes pain can make you crazy. His mind wasn't right, that's all."

"That was it?"

"That was it."

"God," Willis said, and shook his head. "I feel like I could use him now. Mama, too."

"I know."

They stood together; she reached and pulled him to her, held him, her own sorrow alive and deepened, quickened by his grief. She rocked him, whispered the only words of comfort that she knew.

"It'll be all right," she said. "I promise."

In the morning, Carla got up before the rest of the house, brought Phoenix down for breakfast. Outside, a soft, persistent rain fell. Phoenix hovered over his bowl of Rice Krispies. As she watched him, Carla was thinking of what had kept her from sleeping well: how families, meant to nourish, could smash you, leave you empty. No one who'd slept in this house last night was free from family's damage.

Her spirits plummeting with the rain, she looked up as Elizabeth came into the kitchen, purple bathrobe clashing with her hair. Phoenix stiffened, but didn't raise his head. "Good morning," Carla said. "You sleep okay?"

"Like a rock."

"I remembered you're a coffee drinker. It's ready."

"That was sweet of you."

"I'll get it. Milk and sugar, right?"

"Uh-huh."

As Carla turned her back, moving from stove to refrigerator, she considered telling Elizabeth what she knew of her suffering. But to do so would reveal that Willis had talked to her, and might cause more strife between them. As she opened the refrigerator and reached for milk, she wondered if, instead of words, a touch was called for, the curve of a womanly embrace. Except that Elizabeth didn't invite that. Her physical greetings were tentative, the cheek cautiously turned, and when you reached to hug her, she swiveled sideways, gave nothing but a hip. She needed, Carla had decided when they'd first met, to learn it was all right to give yourself fully to embracing. And the lesson needed to be abrupt;

somebody ought to grab and hold her. She was imagining Elizabeth's reaction if she did this—eyes luminous with alarm, rigid—when she spun around to find out what had frightened Phoenix. The sound punctured the kitchen, high and sibilant. Elizabeth was rising from her chair, backing away from the table, and Carla thought instantly that it was the hair, that Phoenix had confused its red with fire, whose flame still panicked him. But when she looked at her son, the hissing halted now, it was to find him smiling. He was staring at Elizabeth, not in fear, but with devotion.

"It's okay," she said to her sister-in-law, who'd retreated until the counter stopped her. "It's okay," she said to Phoenix. She went to him, touched his hand, and he laid his head against her stomach, made that hissing sound.

"What's wrong with him?"

"I don't know. I think he's trying to talk."

Elizabeth blinked. "Has he tried before?"

"Don't you remember? He did it when you were here the first time. When he was sick. We thought it was the fever."

Her sister-in-law leaned against the counter, dubiously staring.

"He's smiling," Carla said. "I think he likes you. Say something to him."

"Like what?"

"Anything."

"Good morning, Phoenix," Elizabeth said. "The rain's stopped."

He looked at her, hissed in pleasure.

"Come touch him."

"I'd rather not."

"It's okay. He won't hurt you."

Elizabeth approached, cautiously, reached and touched Phoenix's shoulder. He shivered, beamed. Carla was wide-eyed. Her son had tried to speak. Something had triggered his desire to communicate. What was it, and what was he trying to say?

Willis came into the kitchen, carrying Cassie in one arm. "Good morning, family," he said. "Boy, that coffee smells good."

He bent to lower his daughter to the floor. Carla smiled at the child. Miles was right. Her niece *did* look like Phoenix. The same golden skin, the same unruly hair a shade darker than blond. Both noses turned up at similar angles. Cassie went to her mother, kissed her, ran to her aunt for a hug.

"What a darling," Carla said. "Like she's known me all her life."

Phoenix was nodding his head up and down hard enough to break it, and Cassie, as if she'd known *him* all her life, climbed into his lap, stuck a finger in her mouth.

"Well, ain't this something?" Willis said. "What we have here is a mutual admiration society."

"Is she safe?" Elizabeth said.

"She's fine."

Phoenix was wearing that grotesque grin, looking like the world's proudest cousin.

Carla said to Willis, "Phoenix tried to talk."

In the days that followed she watched the change in her son, saw the new alertness. While he continued to hiss in Elizabeth's presence, it was Cassie he was drawn to. The child loved him also, played house and blocks with him, and Carla would tether Phoenix in the back yard, where he would sit with his cousin and dig holes in the earth. Aunt and mother, she watched, heart filling with the wonder. They were a family. Family was a miracle.

Then Elizabeth left, taking Cassie with her. Not for long, she said, just a couple of weeks, to a girlfriend's house in Maine, a woman with whom she'd gone to high school.

"She says she needs some time to herself," Willis said, and raised a limp hand, let it fall. "She says she needs to sort things out."

Not smiling, he put them on a bus on a Tuesday morning before he left for work. He'd gotten a job down at the marina as a mechanic, worked the noon to 7:30 shift. Phoenix spent two days searching the house, looked under beds, in closets, behind furniture.

"They'll be back," Carla said, and held him.

There was the dream. In it, a hissing she couldn't locate or understand the source of. She searched from cellar to attic, checked front porch and back. When she went outside, Max prowled the clearing, made his eternal promise. Miles listed against a tree, white shirt open at his throat, arms folded.

"Well?" he said.

She had to make her mind up *now*.

She couldn't.

"Give me a minute," she called, and above and behind the dream, that hissing, and while she listened and kept one eye on each man, lest he leave before she decided, she was trying to understand what the hissing meant, and why the clearing had moved into her yard. It was too many things to be doing in a dream, and she came, mercifully, awake, lay thinking not about her lovers, but her child.

Phoenix hadn't responded to Willis, whom he'd lived with, yet Elizabeth inspired him to speak. What was it about her sister-in-law, and what was he trying to say?

The clock read 4:13 in the morning. She swung from bed, padded down the hallway to her son's room, stood in the dim glow of the night light, watched him sleeping. He was on his back, legs and arms spread. Something moved across his face; was he dreaming? Would he remember when he woke?

One of his pillows lay on the floor; she retrieved it, went to her own bed. Elizabeth was in Maine. Her father was an orphan who'd disowned her. He loved black music. He'd been all right with Willis until he found out who he was.

She turned, looked over her shoulder. It was 4:16, three hours earlier in California. When he'd gotten upset, he'd gone swimming. He'd closed the door in his daughter's face. Phoenix hissed when he saw her. What did hissing sound like?

She shifted onto her side, thinking of the dream again, Miles leaning sardonically against a tree, Max's broken record of a promise, and she in the middle, torn. Her son had tried to speak. The same sounds every time, two syllables, a hissing followed by a "ter." She was frowning, tense, and when she felt the pulse beat at her temple, she relaxed and tried to drift toward discovery. She waited until her mind took to spinning aimlessly, then focused and spoke the sounds, " *Hiss-ter.*" They startled her; she'd not meant to say them so loudly, and then her heart was racing and she sat straight up in bed. *Jesus.* What if the hissing was "sister"?

Amazed at herself, she fell back against her pillows. "Hold up, girl, you're losing it. Don't get carried away."

It was startling, wonderfully invented, but nothing but a storyteller's wild conjecture. Once she'd admitted this, she dismissed the speculation, only to find that admission freed her to make of it an exercise, a way to fill the bleak time before dawn. So she allowed herself, for no reason other than the pleasure, to imagine it was true. Max was alive, was Elizabeth's father, a man now called Lincoln, who lived in Santa Monica in a house above the sea. Now his reaction to Willis made sense. Now she could explain why Phoenix responded to Elizabeth the way he did; he had some mechanism (triggered by scent? vibration?) that allowed him to recognize his closest kin. And that was why he looked so much like Cassie. What wasn't explained was why Max hadn't called or written.

Why hadn't he? Not caring? Thoughtlessness? A head injury, some rare disease that stuck memory until Willis showed up to dislodge it? She turned, alert; a car passed in the street. Who was up this time of morning? But Max had no way of knowing how she felt; maybe he feared she'd go to the police, and so he couldn't let her know. Or maybe he thought she'd died in the fire.

She reached for one of the pillows, curled around it. How had he gotten to California? What was he like now? He'd touch Phoenix, heal him. They'd be a family.

There'd be difficulties, hard moments. They'd have to talk about her brothers, her father crazed with loss, a mother driven into silence; she'd have to forgive all of it, death and the years of waiting. Could she? Not if his failure to get in touch was thoughtlessness. If that were so, she'd haunt him. Send cryptic notes hinting at what she knew, fly to California to confront him. Except she'd never flown—what was it like to fly? She'd get there somehow. She'd tell all his neighbors, send his wife a letter, show up in her living room, say, before the police came, *My name is Carla, and I'm your husband's lover. The one he's thinking of when he's with you.* She'd hire someone to cut his brake lines, murder him in his sleep. No, not in sleep, she wanted him to suffer. *This is for Carla,* the murderer would say, and pull the trigger.

Or maybe he'd explain and she'd forgive him.

What had happened that night her house burned down, the night her brothers died, and her father sang, and the mute was moved to dancing? Something gathered in her belly; it was concentrated, sweet. She turned on her stomach, deep in that quickened place that only storytellers know, where she was wonderfully alone, smart and fascinating, the world in all its majesty forgotten for the one she was constructing. In this world answers called before the questions finished forming; its air was fluid, its light more riveting than flame. This was the story she'd been waiting for, and Lord, how it was coming. . . .

It was August, but Max needed fire's consolation, soothing fire, lovely in its leaping, and he built one in the hearth, poked until it roared. The stick was flaming.

She paused. Here was the turning point, here the defining moment. Had it been deliberate? Or was it accident?

She closed her eyes, saw Max kneeling, white shorts and naked back; above him, through the skylight, night held on a festival of stars. She couldn't conceive of his doing it on purpose, no, he'd probably waved the stick, luminescence slashing darkness; it slipped from his hand, went tumbling toward the curtains. It would have been so quick, one moment the glow of stick's end, the lovely patterns, and then the whole side of a room in flames.

Fear mesmerized; he stood for precious moments staring, turned in going-nowhere circles, bumped against the couch that felt so human he screamed a tiny scream. He needed water, something to haul it in; he started for the kitchen, turned that last time to find the fire a roar beyond control. And in that instant of understanding that he couldn't put it out, not without rain or diversion of the river, he raced to his room, dressed, grabbed the knapsack that had been for weeks now waiting in the closet. He'd gone back to the kitchen, taken a pot from below the sink, banged it against the stove to wake the others, then fled the house, out past the evergreens, ran smack into something sad and strong and mocking. . . .

"Something white," her mother had said, "something white was moving in the trees . . . "

What stopped him? (something sad): *Where are you going, how can you leave the family that loves you, how will you make it in the world?* He'd stopped for one more sight of them, all except that *it,* sin's consequence, golden unbearable he couldn't look at. Just one more sight of them, and then he'd leave.

The trees were sweet-smelling, strung with glitter, the house an outline drawn by flame. As his family streamed into the yard, the fire sucked, the roof caved in with the sound of a rushing river. Meridian turned to look and Rufus shoved her, and Carla, her back on fire, the child held to her chest.

Still Max stared, not moving, and why didn't it register, why couldn't he feel? Trucks came, the people gathered, lines shifting in the moonlight, and his mind, as if it had only now discovered such diversion, posed questions: What drew humans to disaster; what kept them there? Had anyone saved the rabbits? Where were his brothers?

It was time to leave, to shake free from questions. He slung the knapsack to his shoulder, bent to look that last time, tried to move but found he was rooted, feet the sharp points of his body stuck into the ground. First there was fear, and then he gave in to acceptance. So be it. He wouldn't run. He was the Lord's anointed. He'd fall to the earth, he'd rest, lie there until they found him. He'd explain and all would be forgiven. He lay his knapsack down, sat down beside it. Such *peace* came with surrender, such consolation.

And then, astounding in a night designed for weeping, sounding as if it came from all directions—the river, the burning house, the heavens—someone, or some*thing,* began to sing. Deep and rich, beautiful, so wonderful with wrath that it instantly made Max watchful, for he knew that what seemed full-blown from an angel's throat could as easily be a devil's imitation. He stood—if it were devil, he must fight—he clenched his fist, scanned the gathered crowd, brought his vision back toward burning, and there, arms lifted toward the sky, huge, defiant, lurched the singer. It was his father, Rufus; the song, grief-struck and terrible, roiled the night. Rufus carried it across the clearing, raging at circumstance, saying that all collected here would be his witness: This crime would never be forgiven.

This crime would never be forgiven.

That promise became the thing that freed Max. He turned to sprint, headlong and sick with guilt and terrified. And all he had was this: a knapsack with a change of clothing, his toothbrush, and a Bible, a blanket, the fifty dollars stolen from Meridian's hiding place. No skills other than a gift for preaching, not an inkling of how the world worked, in his head a song, not his father's but the one sung once he'd whipped the church to frenzy, and he above them, spent and watching, waiting to see if the Lord would move tonight and a sinner come to Christ:

> *Take me to the wa . . . a . . . ter,*
> *take me to the wa . . . a . . . ter,*
> *take me to the wa . . . a . . . ter*
> *to be baptized.*

What a beautiful song, chords of skin-tight harmony, lifting the church, binding. Yes, he was headed to the water, like a slave who flees from bondage, heart conflicted, leaving those who loved him, knowing nothing of where he headed, just needing to be free.

Carla slowed her breathing, turned onto her back. *Now Max could see the river.*

There was a moon, her mother had said, a full moon, sumptuous, and in its light Max went to where the boats were tied, dragged one to the water, heaved inside. Was he afraid still, or had his heart grown hard? Had he steeled himself now that he was leaving? Or was he again in that place between the doing and the grasp of consequence, that still place where feeling couldn't live? She put him there a while; lay him in the boat's rough bottom where he gasped, a blank wall before his eyes. He sat up, grabbed the oars, rowed to the river's center.

There he rested, allowed the boat to drift downstream. He could see, way to his right, the fire scene, smoke curling in a searchlight, could see dark trees and darker people. He gripped the oars, began to row again. The river was long and wide, and he was pulling with it, concentrating on the rhythm of his strokes and breathing. He rowed until clouds washed across the moon's face; then he turned toward the river's other side. It was wild there, trees and brush and thicket. He beached the boat, stripped to his shorts, swam the vessel back into the river; he tipped it, treaded water while it filled and sank. Then he stroked powerfully to the shore. Shivering, he pulled the blanket from his knapsack. In this place unvisited by humans, he covered himself, closed his eyes, thinking not of what he'd done, but of his glory. That was him stalking above adoring faces of a host of congregations, that was him filled with that wide and shining power. Even when the beast had risen in him, even then he had the power, even as he preached, and the fire came not from God, but from the memory of Carla when she pulled him down, and, oh! the pleasure! That it might have lasted forever, side by side with power, the miracle of her mouth. *Don't close your eyes, Max, look at me.*

Thunder grumbled in the heavens. Rain began to fall.

*   *   *

When Carla looked again, light had tiptoed to her window; the sun was rising. If she didn't get some sleep she'd be irritable all day. She considered what she had. The story wasn't bad; it needed work, and an ending, but she could make it happen. Yawning, she curled up on her side. Invention was diverting, but it also made you tired.

Back on the riverbank, beneath a rock whose ledge deflected rain, Max slept. Full, spent with the effort to create, so did Carla.

In the bright light of that Wednesday, as she'd known it would, it all seemed less compelling. Still, later, on the back porch watching Phoenix dig at the foot of the oak tree, an activity that distracted him from whining, she called experimentally, "Sister?"

Instantly alert, Phoenix hissed at her.

She studied him across the yard. Interesting, but hardly airtight proof. At the same time, it didn't *dis*prove. Suppose for the moment he *was* saying sister. Given all the words in the language, why that one?

"Phoenix."

His head came up.

"*Blister.*"

He watched, unmoved. She looked above her, searched for simple rhyming. A jet left a plume against a washed-out sky.

"*Mister . . . kissed her . . . dissder.*"

He watched.

"*Sister.*"

"Hisss," he said.

Across the street, a neighbor in a blue dress waved to Carla. She waved back, nodded. She could be reasonably sure about that, she could make it seem a certainty. Phoenix was saying sister. Phoenix thought or knew that Elizabeth was his sister.

She leaned forward, face cupped in hands, elbows on her knees. How did he know? What had told him? She'd read about idiot savants, who could recite the dates of long-ago events, or solve complex problems in arithmetic when they couldn't count to ten. Was Phoenix one of those; was his gift a rare ability to recognize his blood?

Breathing deeply, she considered what she had so far, and liked it. She fetched her son from the yard, took him upstairs, washed him, locked him in his room. She brought her story to the bedroom, where she changed her linen, to the kitchen where she lingered over tea. How would she end it?

In the days ahead the question pleasantly consumed her, even after she discovered that beneath it was a rage that for all these years Max was alive and hadn't kept his promise. Despite his fears that she might give him away, he'd made a promise, and hadn't kept it. She began to lean toward his dying.

And all during this time, her refusal to acknowledge that she was one short step from believing that she'd been sucked toward invention's vortex, courted it. She carried this refusal like a handkerchief between her breasts, inside of which was wrapped a coin so rare it couldn't be purchased. And while she wondered what to do with it, knowing the best thing would be to bury it in her yard or throw it in the river, her back began to itch. For the second time that spring she writhed against hard surfaces, danced with brooms. The last time that had happened, Willis had come home, and so she now knew what the itching meant; someone who'd left would be returning. Even when she heard who'd died, it never crossed her mind that this someone would be anyone but Max.

When he was released from prison, Junkman returned to live in Tillson and to manage the junkyard the Josephs had bequeathed him. By then, his hair, which he wore in a gray-streaked ponytail, had grown halfway down his back. All the labor on his speech had paid off; his voice was deep, mellifluous. But his feet, abused by years of jailhouse leather, cursed fine Italian shoes.

One day in June 1966, after tiptoeing eighteen holes with a golf bag on his shoulder, Junkman sat under a tree next to the putting green. Way above the gentle slope of fairways, a red sun eased into the trap door of a narrow, sky-blue stage. Junkman studied the crimson globe, considering how, as far away as it was, it still managed to warm an entire planet. And it was dependable; each day, discounting cloud cover, one could watch it rise and fall like clockwork.

He grunted, took off his brown-and-white two-tones, removed his socks, exposing the irregularity of his feet. Irregularity was a kind word, he decided; these bad boys were *ugly*. Gnarled, corn-studded toes, nails thick as bird beaks; bad leather had done them in. Even before he'd gone to prison his feet weren't much to look at; they'd just had the decency not to hurt if he avoided cowboy boots. He rubbed his toes and thought how funny life was, how there was always something going on you wouldn't understand till later. Maybe that's why he'd fallen for beautiful shoes in the first place—he was compensating. If he'd had nice-looking feet, he might have been content with the kinds of shoes most men owned: wing tips and penny loafers, white bucks, footwear so uninspired someone should apologize to cows.

He dug his feet into the grass, nestling corns and calluses against the cool. The calluses he could live with; it was the corns on his little toes that were the killers. Neither was larger than a dime; each made you say nasty things about people's mothers.

As he wiggled his toes, Junkman looked out over the empty golf course and experienced a sense of isolation. It was as if the world had fallen away, leaving him stranded with nothing but the company of bad feet and introspection. He recognized the feeling, so he wasn't worried. It was the one he'd run into twenty years ago in the prison mess hall when the light was yellow, and he'd learned it was Lucinda whom he loved.

"Hm," Junkman said, and settled back against the tree, wondering what he'd find out this time, and how long before it came. Part of him hoped for a miracle, that his gift of smell would come back, or that he'd wake in the morning with an erection.

This time discovery was prompt, showed up just before the sun's crown disappeared beneath the sky's stage.

"*Listen,*" discovery said. "*There's no way to live a full life if your feet hurt.*"

Junkman looked at the proposition from sixteen angles; each vantage point revealed the same. After twenty-five years of prison schedules, this additional immutability shook him, and he put on his shoes, drove home, and reached for his razor. He held it, mother-of-pearl, steel glistening weight and balance. Then he looked through the bathroom window at mounds of junk, contemplating the fate of porcelain toilets, automobiles, bed frames that had all once been essential. He thought about what he'd lost, the gift of smelling, the long-time lack of sexual desire. But mostly he thought about how it was sometimes necessary to desecrate what one loved. Then he wiped his eyes and marched into his bedroom, where he did what he had to do.

Junkman returned to Tillson in May 1966. Eleven months later, driving a rented, smoke-gray Plymouth, Lucinda Hancock careened around an April corner, slammed on her brakes, and looked up and down the length of Lake Street. When she saw there wasn't a parking space, she backed up to the corner and drove across somebody's lawn onto the sidewalk in front of Christ the Savior. Then, considerately leaving keys in the ignition, she dashed up the church steps to catch what was left of the funeral.

Inside, the congregation was queueing up to view Ulysses Hancock's body, sobered by Reverend Sweeny's eulogy, which had featured the deceased's long and honorable relationship with death. When Lucinda trotted down the aisle wearing a short tight Afro, no stockings, and a backless dress so yellow it made folks blink, they respectfully backed away. They did this despite her haircut, despite remembering she hadn't bothered to show up when her mother died, despite noting her outfit was inappropriate for a funeral and belonged on a woman half her age. Those adept with numbers did a quick computation, and decided that if age were a hill, Lucinda was well down the other side of forty. The bottom line, however, was that they were glad she'd made it, and had apparently put behind her what had happened. They saw how healthy she looked, how she didn't cry as she stared into the casket, how she reached and touched her father's thoughtful face.

That was why, later, in her parents' living room, they were so astonished at her reaction to being told about Junkman's shoes. How could she weep for the shoes of a man who'd done to her what he had? This was so unsettling no one thought to tell her that Junkman was talking.

"Where's he living?"

"At the junkyard over in Tillson. But this time on a Monday afternoon, when the weather's nice, you'll probably find him at the golf course."

They sat, dismayed and disapproving, while she washed her face, applied fresh makeup, and left to look for Junkman at the club.

When he saw her loping across the parking lot, Junkman was sitting on the storage room steps, cleaning a set of irons. He stood, aware of how long it had been since the small thing had stirred at the back of his heart, wondering if the color yellow had aroused it. Then he noticed that Lucinda's face was a fist of worry. When she reached him, the fist opened; she smiled, and he looked down to see what caused it. She was smiling at his black suede loafers, at the holes he'd cut in the leather to relieve the pressure on his corns.

"They don't look so bad," she said. She stood until the smile faded, and then she said, "I didn't expect to see you again."

He was too overwhelmed to do anything but nod.

"I didn't expect to come back to Kingston. But I couldn't let my father go to his grave without being here. And when I heard you were free, I had to see you."

He nodded.

"For a long time I was in this hole, dark and stinking. I didn't know anything. Then, when I did, I didn't want to. There was nothing I could do. I got you in there, but I couldn't get you out. Will you forgive me?"

He held his hands out. "Not just forgive. I'll comfort you."

Her mouth flew open; she shrieked, surprise and pleasure, not because she was forgiven, not even because she was forty-six and had just been promised comfort.

"You're *talking*."

"Yes," he said. "It took a while, I had to practice, but now ain't nothing to it." Tall, heavy, dark, he smiled a smile that made her want to climb inside it. "You like?"

"It's beautiful."

"You cut your hair," he said.

"It doesn't grow."

"Well, it's the style nowadays, now ain't it?"

"It sure is good to see you."

"You, too."

They stood, wearing matching silly grins. In full view of the country club members, backdropped by trees flagrant with spring, Lucinda pulled him into her arms. She held him long enough to make her thighs weak, then led him to the Plymouth and drove above the speed limit to her parents' house. The mourners had gone home, and in the space left by their departure the two ate funeral food, grinned, and drank red wine. Then she sat across from him and made him talk. When she asked, he said that Rufus and Meridian had died within eight months of each other. Carla had lived all these years by herself, alone with her son in that two-family house. For a while, there was a man who'd come around, a month or so, but that had ended. Now her brother lived with her, had showed up with a white wife and a baby. Sometimes he saw Carla on the street, a kerchief around her head in the manner of an Indian, bright-colored dress so long it touched her ankles. Sometimes alone, sometimes holding the leash, at the end of which was Phoenix.

"Phoenix is on a leash? Like a dog leash? He's grown by now."

Junkman grunted. "Grown in size. But his mind didn't grow. I guess the leash keeps him from wandering off and hurting himself."

"My father told me something was wrong with him. And that her mother had the baby. Carla's brother."

"Meridian died of childbirth complications. Carla raised Willis. He was a navy man."

"How is she?"

"Carla? She looks the same."

"I mean how does she seem?"

"Seem?" He thought about it. "Sad."

"Sad?"

"What it looks like."

"She still doesn't know about Max."

"I didn't tell her."

"I didn't either. I would have. . . . " Lucinda looked above the chair where a photograph of her father hung, face composed and thoughtful. "I've got to go see her. I can't tell the whole truth, but I can tell her some of it. I was wrong to never get in touch. I should have written to tell her."

"Ain't she going to want to know?"

"Know what?"

"How *you* know."

"Jesus," Lucinda said. She fell back against the couch, deflated. "I can't tell her."

"Well," Junkman said, "she might not ask."

"*I* would."

He nodded. "Me, too."

"If she does, I'll just have to figure something out . . . I don't know. Maybe I'll just leave it alone. If it gets brought up . . . I won't have you ending up in jail again."

"I ain't going to nobody's jail."

"She was my friend," Lucinda said. "I let her down. I should have written."

"Don't blame yourself," Junkman said. "You don't know the situation. It was a long time ago. Might make her no nevermind at all."

He moved closer, touched Lucinda's hair. She smiled at him. "You still use Lifebuoy soap."

"Wouldn't use no other."

She bent, quickly kissed him, then leaned back against the sofa, sighed.

"You tired?"

She said, "A little."

"Why don't you go lie down?"

Her face changed, gathered. "You know what I want to do? I want to walk through the house. Come with me?"

"Sure."

·They got up, walked arm in arm down to the cellar. The tables were still there, the bottles of chemicals, on their shoulders epaulets of dust. She touched the wall, remembering the women, the two old ones, the one with gorgeous thighs she'd yearned to look like, the slight weight of Birdsong's penis in her hand. Junkman was right. It was a long time ago.

They went upstairs, through the living room, into the kitchen. This was the floor she'd slumped to, puke-stained and disfigured. She turned on the porch light; they stepped outside. The back yard was small and fenced, the swing her father built for her still standing. In the garden flowers held their heads up; someone had pulled the weeds and watered. She led Junkman upstairs, gazed at the neatly made twin beds in the guest room. She opened her parents' door; the stolid, somber furniture filled the dark space like a threat. There was the bathroom, the door open, and next to it a room she wouldn't enter.

"Why?" Junkman said.

"Just no now. Later."

Downstairs, they talked and drank red wine. They huddled, sat at opposite ends of the couch.

"You still love Carla?"

"No," he said. He took a deep breath, swallowed. "I love you."

She looked away. He sat for what seemed an hour, not daring to speak or move. When she faced him, she was solemn.

"I'd planned to come bury my daddy and leave," she said. "But I think I'll stay a while."

"That's outstanding," Junkman said. He wanted to shout, thrust his fist in the air. He wanted to dance, but he was afraid to tamper with the moment. Instead, he pretended an ordinariness he didn't feel, said, "You can just do that? Leave where you been living? Your job? Friends?"

She laughed. "The answer is yes, I can do what I want. The job I can do anywhere. And friends . . . well, most of them are gone. Those left will be my friends wherever."

"What kind of job you do?"

"I work in the movement. Or what's left of it."

"Movement?"

"I help people register to vote. In Mississippi."

"I heard about that," Junkman said. "I saw it on TV."

"You know what? I'm going to call you Bradley when we're alone."

"Okay," he smiled. "But I might not answer. The lady who raised me is the only one who called me that. What do I call you?"

"Sugar, sweetmeat, honey pot."

He said each name, gravely. In the wake of their laughter, she took his hand, traced the lines in his palm. "When we made love that day," she said, "on my way home, in between trying to make sense of what you told me, I kept wondering if what I felt was love. Whatever it was, it's still there. I'd like to know. I don't want . . . I can't make any promises. Only that I'll try. Is that all right?"

He said it was and held her. She snuggled against him, spoke into his chest.

"What happened with that policeman? The one they accused you of killing?"

"It was an accident, '' he said. "I never touched him. The floor was wet and he slipped."

She put her arms around him. "I knew you didn't. . . . What was it like for you in prison?"

"Hard. I know you have to be punished for breaking the law, and Lord knows there's some bad folks out there. But prison don't do nothing but make them worse."

"They never gave you parole."

"The sentences were consecutive. When I finally went before the board, one of the women had a brother who was a cop. The next time someone thought my hair was too long. Then they wanted me to admit to the crimes I hadn't committed. I wouldn't do that. So they let me stew."

"Did they hurt you?"

"No. Mostly I was left alone."

"I'm glad they didn't hurt you."

He paused. "It was in prison I found out that I loved you. I'd always thought I loved Carla. Then I knew that ever since you'd let your hair down in the park, I'd loved *you*. It was five years before I knew that. It made me wonder how you could love somebody so long and not know. But once I knew, I loved you hard. In the morning and at night I made a prayer of it. The thought of loving you kept me going. Even though I never expected to see you again. It was just knowing I could love, that what I'd done hadn't taken that from me."

"Oh, Bradley." She moved away, looked down into her lap. "I'm not the same girl who went to your room that night."

"People change," he said. "I know that."

"Oh, *do* they change." She shook her head, then leaned back, looked unflinchingly into his face. "This might not be the time to talk about it, and it may or may not be important to you. But I've had other men."

He didn't answer.

"I never loved nobody, but I've been . . . *with* them. Lots. I won't lie and give you a story about I was lonely, although sometimes I was. And sometimes I was afraid. But mostly I reached because that's what I wanted, because it made me feel okay."

"It's all right."

"I don't know if it's all right, but it happened."

"It ain't like that for me," Junkman said. "You're the last woman I made love to. And the first."

She stared. "You're kidding."

"I'm not," he said and poured another glass of wine. "I think prison shut the door on my desire. I think about it knocking, then giving up and going off to someone who'd let it in. Sometimes I study on it, but it don't cause no discomfort."

She said, carefully, a voice that made him think of wading into water, "It's very important to me. I mean I'd still care about you, but . . . well, I won't lie to you, you know?"

"I understand."

She glanced across the room. Darkness pressed against the windows. "You think you're all right?"

"You mean like a disease or something?"

"Not a disease . . . a condition. Something in your diet, maybe. Or up here." She pointed to her head.

"The God's honest truth is I don't know."

"You want to find out?"

"Now?"

"Uh-huh."

"Jesus," Junkman wondered, "why do I feel the need for prayer?"

"Me, too. Come on. Wait, let me have another glass of wine. No, you can't have any."

She poured and gulped, took his hand; they rose, climbed the stairs, entered the room she'd recently avoided. There, fully clothed, on the bed where her mother had defiled her, they lay in each other's arms, each thinking of the moment, all that had happened, all that they'd lost. Lucinda tightened her grip around his waist. Had he lost more than his share? Would that be taken, too?

She took a deep breath and sent a hand between his thighs. Junkman shuddered. His eyes closed, and he made a sound, wet, inarticulate. The sound belonged to the small thing he'd felt at the country club, and its movement had nothing to do with color. He tried to figure out *what* it had to do with, but Lucinda was making it difficult to think.

"Bradley. My goodness. I don't remember all of this."

"Me, neither. Maybe it grew. You know how sitting around puts weight on you."

"It ain't the weight I'm talking about. Uh-uh. Control yourself."

"I'm doing," he gasped, "the best I can."

"Ain't nothing wrong with you, baby."

"We just started. Might be too soon to tell."

"Trust me." She sat up, turned on the light.

"Why you do that?"

"So I can *see*."

"What do you want me to do?"

"Do? Absolutely nothing."

She undressed him. She hiked her yellow dress to her waist, scooted out of her panties, tossed them to the floor. She kneeled astride him, bent to kiss his mouth, holding him against the hot wet place between her thighs.

"I ought to wait a while," she said. "I ought to take my time, get so ready I can't stand it. But I can't. I'm al*ready* ready.

"Here I come," she warned, and sat, grunted, began a slow, deliberate moving.

"My goodness, Bradley. Jesus. What made you think something's wrong with you?"

He tried to tell her, but once he'd given up the breath he'd been holding, he couldn't handle the complexity. More astonishing than the fact that he was making love to a woman who wore nothing but a yellow dress was that while he thrust toward her, his nose, which factory fumes had clogged, was coming open. He smelled: fish roe and lilacs, distilled water, diamond dust. Tenderness embraced him; tears streamed across his cheekbones, found his lips.

While he cried, Lucinda sweetly rode him.

They slept till eleven, made love, and slept again. At two in the afternoon, starving, they ransacked the refrigerator.

"Oh, Lordy," Junkman said around a mouthful of scrambled eggs.

"What?"

"I completely forgot about my car. I left it at the golf course."

"No problem. I'll take you. They won't tow it away, will they?"

"I don't think so."

They planned the day. She'd take him to pick up his car. He'd go home, shower and change, meet her back here at 5:30. They'd eat and go to Carla's. In between she'd spend some time driving around the city.

"You want another cup of coffee?"

"Actually . . . ," Junkman said, and raised his eyebrows.

"What?"

"How about going back to bed?"

"Back to bed? You tired?"

"No."

"Then *what*?"

Neither could stop grinning.

"It'll have to be a quickie," Lucinda said, but later, she changed her mind.

All that day, Carla felt a stirring in the air, a temptation to look over her shoulder, to go to the window and peer into the street.

By noon her back was itching, and after contorting against the edge of a kitchen counter, she stepped onto the front porch, examined the sky, as if Max, when he arrived, would come smiling out of heaven. The day had dawned cool and cloudy; a medallion of sun, visible behind the cover, struggled to burn away the gray. By two o'clock the sun had conquered. Hungry for signs, she took this as an omen, curled up on the couch to read. But Phoenix, still in the grip of the mood he'd been in since Elizabeth and Cassie had left, consumed the afternoon with whining at her shoulder. Finally, a little before seven, exasperated, she fed him, made him undress for bed, and locked him in his room.

Despite the feeling she carried through the day, she wasn't prepared when, at a quarter after seven, someone came knocking at her door. Her first response was fear, a hole in her stomach, a weakness that left her limp. What would she say when she and Max at last faced one another? Then she dragged herself to the door, snatched it open, stood full of joy and contradiction, and what was Junkman doing here, and Oh, my God, a miracle of red silk dress and matching shoes, *Lucinda*. Joy leaped over disappointment, shouted, and she wept.

And Lucinda, saying, "Oh, Carla, don't you weep," she, too, crying, each falling toward the other's open arms, laughing, and all Carla could say, after all those years, in the middle of a coming back to her, was, "What happened to your hair?"

"I cut it off," Lucinda said. "It doesn't grow," and they swung around the porch until Carla, breathless, stopped and said, "I'm sorry, Junkman, good evening." He nodded, smiling, and Carla cried, "Lucinda, *look* at you."

Later, Junkman would say their happiness had touched him so much he'd thought he was going to cry for the second time in two days, but he got hold of himself, trailed behind them, Carla pulling Lucinda to the kitchen, "Don't take my arm off," Lucinda said. Carla whirling, gathering pots and pans, peering into the refrigerator, Lucinda giggling, "What on earth are you doing?"

"What's it look like I'm doing? I've got to feed you."

"Sit down, we went out. No need for fixing us food."

Hands on her hips, Carla stared. "You mean you're on your

way to *my* house and you stop in some *restaurant*? I can't believe you."

"If you've got to do something," Lucinda said, looking like her face would break from smiling, "make some tea."

"Tea? Junkman, you care for tea?"

"No, thank you. I'm going to sit out back a while if you don't mind. Got me a cigar to celebrate."

"You can smoke it here."

"It's a pleasant evening," he said, and winked, and went on out the door.

Carla, eyebrows raised, turned. "Well, now. What's this with you and Junkman?"

"We're going to try to make it."

"Get out of here."

"I ain't doing no such thing."

"He *didn't* rape you."

"No, he didn't."

"Somebody told me something about you and Junkman once, I didn't believe—" She stopped. "*Look* at you. You and Junkman." The thought had come so swiftly: *He loved me first. He wrote to tell me.* At the time she hadn't cared.

Lucinda said, "I thought you were making me some tea. And while you're doing that tell me what you've been up to for twenty-five years."

"It won't take that long to tell it." Carla laughed, then put a hand to her cheek. "It's been that long?"

"Give or take a couple of hours. Where's your son?"

"He was in a state today. I put him to bed early. Girl, it sure is good to see you."

"It's good to see you too," Lucinda said. "Look at you. Not a spot of gray anywhere, and you haven't gained a *pound*."

"Lucky, that's all. Weight ain't nothing I've *ever* had to fret about."

"Well, you look terrific. How *are* you? On the inside?"

The asking unsettled Carla. She had to slow down. "Fine," she said. "Fine. Willis—you never met him, he's my brother—he lives here too, but his wife and baby, they're in Maine. A visit, someone she went to school with. Where'd you get that dress? Like you stepped out of a magazine or something. Red looks good on you. I . . . I heard your daddy died, I'm sorry. . . . I had this feeling, this itching, you know? not my hand, that would of meant money, and I knew someone was coming back. I thought . . . I never dreamed . . . Where've you been? How come I never heard from you?"

"You mad?"

"No, I'm not mad. Just so good to see you. You don't know."

"I know," Lucinda said.

Carla paused. "*You* all right?"

"I think so." Lucinda pulled a chair from the table, sat. "I mean, I'm here, I'm walking, I'm alive. And I just might be in love." Her smile faded. "But there is the question. Maybe always be."

"Question?"

Lucinda shrugged. "I was sick. Then, when I was better, I headed in the opposite direction from here. Didn't feel like anything to come back to in Kingston. I certainly didn't want anything to do with my mother, and I figured you'd gotten on with your life. And I guess I was a little ashamed for all that happened, how I'd caused everybody so much grief. Coming back would just make people remember and relive it, including me, and I work real hard nowadays at looking forward." She rubbed fingers against her mouth. "All that felt like a reason at the time, important."

She did something with her face that made lines gather in her forehead. "I tried to call you, Carla. That day, before everything blacked out, I tried to call you. I didn't want to go off like that, without a word. I remembered what I'd promised, that even if I went away, I'd never leave you. But they made me. Later I figured getting in touch would raise more pain than it was worth. I'd learned I didn't have much tolerance for pain."

Carla said, "I went by your house. Your mother said you were sick and wouldn't let me in. The next day she said you were gone. What happened to you? Where've you been?"

"For fifteen years, I was in and out of a hospital in North Carolina. Turns out I was never wrapped too tight in the first place, and when I slept with Junkman, and my mother doing what she did, I just went . . . *off.*" She had a quizzical expression on her face, as if she were wondering still why it had happened.

"What did your mother do?"

"That never got out, huh?"

"The word was you were sent to live with relatives. So you wouldn't have to deal with people talking. Nobody said anything about a hospital."

"*My mother* . . . seems like my being with Junkman violated her. Like she was some god who couldn't stand that her child wasn't in her image. So she beat me. She beat me until she got tired. By the time she stopped, whatever it was that made me whole and sane and *me* was broken. It took," she said simply, "a long, long time to fix."

The kettle began to sing. Carla moved to take it from the stove, opened the cabinet above the sink, found cups, filled and brought them to the table. Lucinda picked hers up, blew on it. "I was in this hospital," she said, "getting better. . . ."

Things were clearing up, the darkness she'd lived in giving way to light. Twice a year her father visited, brought slippers, a robe, a slew of numbered paint books; her mother never came. Ulysses had wanted to transfer Lucinda to a hospital closer to home, and when his wife refused, he pleaded with Anna to move with him to North Carolina. People died everywhere, he said, he'd always make a living. But Anna wouldn't go.

"It was late May," Lucinda said; "everything was blooming. . . ."

. . . Roses and marigold, dogwood white and pink, and she in the pale blue robe her father had brought her, the one with ugly matching slippers that had the fur inside. They'd gone walking on the grounds, sat in a quiet place, deep green trees and benches. In the center was a broken fountain. . . .

"I asked my father about Junkman. That's when I learned he'd gone to prison. . . . "

" . . . For what?" she'd asked. Her father turned away; she could see the nick on his chin where he'd cut himself shaving. "For what?" she'd asked, and then he told her. . . .

"You know that expression: 'Could have knocked me over with a feather'?" Lucinda said. "Girl, talk about somebody in *shock*. I just sat there until I could manage to say, in a reasonably controlled voice, inside of me I'm in pieces, that Junkman didn't rape me. To the contrary, to the *sweet* contrary. 'We made love,' I said, 'willingly, and it wouldn't have happened at all if I hadn't led the way.' "

. . . Her father threw his head back, away from her. His eyes were shut. . . .
　　"Do you understand me? Do you hear what I'm saying?"
　　If he'd opened his eyes, sun would have blinded him. . . .
　　"Daddy," she said, "we've got to do something."
　　"There's nothing we can do."
　　"We got to tell the judge or the prosecutor, or somebody. Junkman didn't do *nothing*."
　　"You were my child," her father said, in this funny, wounded voice, and she knew it wasn't just his head, something in his *heart* had turned away as well. . . .

" . . . And I hadn't done anything but make love and like it," Lucinda said, "you know? Hadn't killed, or robbed, hadn't even gotten pregnant, but still the one person in my life who'd always been there for me *wasn't*, at least not in the way he used to be.

And that's when I decided if fucking was such a big deal, if folks could make that much fuss over it, I'd spend the rest of my life doing it as often as I could. At the same time I'm thinking this, this feeling's coming on, the dark one that left me not remembering. I fought against it. Junkman's life was on the line. . . . "

" . . . He didn't rape me," she'd said. "We have to do something. Tell somebody."

Her father said, "There's nothing to be done."

"There has to be. What if I write a letter to the judge . . . ?"

" . . . I thought he was troubled by the idea of Junkman's innocence, but he was trying to hang on to something, to the way things were, to the conviction that his only child, his daughter, had been forced, to his *image*. . . . "

. . . He said he didn't know. . . .

"Daddy, tell me who to write to."

"It won't do any good."

"Why?"

He looked at her.

"It won't do any good," he said. "He killed a cop."

"What?"

"When they came to arrest him, he killed a cop."

She held to the bench with both hands so her body wouldn't fly away. She wanted to scream, but she couldn't. She wanted to break things, but if she moved her hands, her body would fly away. She was listening to her voice, understanding that her tone was even, wondering why.

"They came to arrest him for something he didn't *do*."

Her father didn't answer.

She held to the bench. Her body wanted to fly, but her voice was even.

"If they know he didn't rape me, won't they reduce his time?"

"I don't know," her father said, "but if you want, you can write to the district attorney." His eyes closed. "But I'm telling you, I doubt it'll do any good."

So that's what she did. Wrote the letter, sealed it, and gave it to her father, and he took it home, where, for reasons he'd never explained, he showed it to his wife. Anna stared at him in utter disbelief. What made him think anybody's district attorney was going to pay attention to a letter written by a woman in a crazy house? Why didn't Ulysses have the sense God gave him? Hadn't they been shamed enough? Now he wanted to make public their daughter's raving that she'd opened her legs to a raggedy-assed nigger who didn't have sense to say good morning? What on earth possessed him . . . ?

" . . . And she took the letter, all the time, my father said, staring at him with this absolute loathing on her face, and she tore it in little pieces and burned them in the sink. . . . "

Lucinda glanced at the window. Gray light hovered, a center tinged with blue.

"My father was so guilty that he told me, but he wasn't guilty enough, or strong enough, to go against my mother. When I heard, I had one wish in life, one thing I wanted to do, and then I could die in peace. I wanted to kill her. And I'd have done it, stepped over her body and gone down to the sheriff and had them put me in jail next to Junkman. But I couldn't get out. Even though I was better, my father wouldn't sign.

"Girl, you talk about *enraged*. I wanted to tear up anything, any*body*, and I tried. They locked me up and gave me drugs that made my head sing. I lost the will to do, gave up on life, falling deeper into this hole, like the way you fall in dreams, you know?, but never getting to the bottom. Years passed. *Years*. It makes me cry to say it now, because even though I knew I was sick, still part of me understood that if I fought back I'd get better, and there was a part of me that just refused to fight, as if that would punish everybody, including, I guess, me. So all those years, that chunk of my life . . . wasted. I know I'm not supposed to think that way. My shrink told me I couldn't help it, that who I was then did all that I could do, but I knew I had responsibility."

She sighed. "It's a long story, Carla. Like I told Junkman, I can't tell it all at once. But I got better, my father finally signed me out. It was weird being free, like turning in circles trying to figure out which way the wind was blowing. All I knew was I wasn't going home. The country was changing, I figured I'd be part of it. I went South in 1958, to Mississippi. I've been there since. I kept in touch with some of my people in North Carolina, although I wouldn't tell them where I was. I kept up with my father. We'd meet a couple of times a year when he went away to a conference, or he'd say he was going to a conference and fly to see me. I never asked him anything about Kingston, except if you were all right. He said you were, that there was something wrong with Phoenix, but you were fine. When my mother passed, I didn't come home. Then my father died. I planned to slip in for the funeral, slip out. When I heard Junkman was free, something moved in me I didn't know was there. I went to see him. And here I am."

"I didn't know," Carla said.

"How could you?"

"I'm glad you're home. I'm glad you're staying."

"Me, too. Hold on a minute. Let me see about Junkman."

She got up, full hips swaying in the red dress, went out onto the porch, came smiling back.

"He's fine. Reared back smoking that old nasty cigar. You should see how long it is. Take him half the night to smoke it.

"Now," she said, and sat back at the table. "Tell me about you."

"Me?" Carla shook her head. "Ain't much to tell. I stayed right here. I raised Willis and Phoenix. I read a lot." Her answer seemed shopworn, inconsequential after Lucinda's telling. Her whole life did.

"You got anybody special?"

"No."

"And I guess you never heard from Max."

"Not yet."

"You still waiting?"

Carla said, "I guess so."

"You *guess* so?"

"I mean . . . sometimes I think of him." She couldn't admit it, couldn't look Lucinda in the eye and say she'd been waiting all those years, had forced herself to wait, even when the desire hadn't been there.

"Carla."

"I'm all right," Carla said.

Lucinda said, "I used to imagine how it was for you. I remembered you telling me you didn't want any more children. But I always saw you happy, *with* someone. Making a life for yourself. Whenever I thought of you, that's what I saw."

Lucinda didn't understand. She did have a life. Even if it wasn't as interesting as other people's, still it was hers, not what anyone imagined. "Miles couldn't understand me either."

"Miles?"

"A man who came and stayed a while. And left."

"Did you want him to?"

"No," Carla said. "I wanted him to stay."

"Why'd he go?"

"He couldn't make up his mind."

"And?"

"So I helped him."

"You drove him away?"

Carla shook her head. "I helped him make up his mind. I'd have stopped waiting for Max if he could have made up his mind. But he couldn't. And I couldn't," she said, "or I *wouldn't*, stand another waiting."

Carla's shoulders were hunched. One other time, with Miles, she'd tried to explain her life. She hadn't liked the feeling then. She didn't like it now.

Lucinda said, "Remember that day we walked down to the river?"

"Sure. I told you what making love was like."

Lucinda was in college, but hadn't known. Lucinda had only just then seen a penis, didn't know what it was like to have a baby.

"Remember I had the hots for that boy outside the pool hall?"

"The beautiful one with the green hat," Carla said. "You planned our lives for us. You said we'd sail to Paris."

"You wanted to go to Cuba in the winter."

"'Cause it was warm. I remember you saying how your father used to hold you."

"And I held *you*," Lucinda said. "For as long as you would let me."

There was a white boat on the water. "I remember."

"And I said your father wouldn't die. Your father wouldn't die, and Max was coming back. You believed me."

Carla frowned. It sounded like an accusation. She didn't answer.

Lucinda whispered, "I was wrong."

"I know. My father died."

"I was wrong about Max, too."

"It's not over," Carla said. "Just like it wasn't for you and Junkman. All that time, all these years and you found each other. If you'd told someone ten years ago that this would happen—" She stopped, then said it anyway. "They'd have called you crazy."

"I was crazy."

Something behind Carla's eyes was tilting, and she shook her head to right it, struggled to contain her feelings: jealousy, rekindled rage, and everybody leaving. It wasn't Lucinda's fault, God knew it wasn't, but you'd think that she, of all people, would at least have the compassion not to judge. Lucinda had found what she'd been looking for. That's why she could judge so easily; Lucinda had what she craved.

But she wouldn't say this; she'd control it. That meant sitting absolutely still, focusing on breathing and commonplace details:

the sharp red of Lucinda's dress, fingernails the same bright color. *Her* nails were plain, her long dress gray and shapeless. She wished she were wearing something different, the black number Miles had loved her in.

Lucinda blinked, watched the woman across from her lean back as if pushed into a corner, face stiff and distant. They'd only had each other for half a summer, but in that brief time Lucinda had felt as if their flesh were one. She'd brought it up too soon. She should have waited, a day or two, a week; why'd she leap into it before reconnecting had proper time to set? That's what she'd planned. But it hadn't worked out that way; she'd trusted her instincts, she'd trust them still.

She said slowly, clearly, as if she were explaining to a child, "I said what I did to make you feel better. I was trying to be a friend. Max isn't coming back."

"Is that another promise?"

"Yes."

"Does this one get kept?"

"Yes."

"How'd you get so sure? A crystal ball?"

"Carla."

"Where'd you get your story?"

If you had a story, the pieces had to fit, you had to tell it in a way that made folks push aside their doubts, embrace it. You had to have answers to their questions. That was something else Lucinda didn't know.

"You come walking in here telling me this," Carla said, "you got to give me proof."

Lucinda said, "Max isn't coming back."

"Max is alive and well. He lives in California."

Something widened in Carla; it took a moment to recognize the panic. Later she'd understand how all the feelings had come together and made her reach for her invention. It was the desire to have something to point to beyond Phoenix and a succession of lovers and her abiding rage and say, *I have a life; and my waiting has a purpose.* Saying what she had was stupid, but she needed to feel that she, like everyone, had something to call her own, even if that something was only incomplete invention. All of this she sensed in an instant, not in words, but a quick hot feeling, one that, when she inhaled, threatened to engulf her. *I'm only telling a story*, she thought, *I made it up*.

"Speaking of proof," Lucinda said, "How do *you* know?"

It wasn't too late; Carla could stop it. She could say it was a story made up to entertain, to comfort, to justify her life. Lucinda would understand. Then it would be over; panic would go away, the room stop tilting.

"I put two and two together."

"What two and two?"

"Max is alive. He lives in California. His daughter's married to my brother."

"What on *earth* are you talking about?"

"About putting two and two together." And she told Lucinda about Elizabeth's father, the orphan who loved black music, who took to the water when upset and disowned his daughter when he found out who Willis was. All during her telling the room was tilting, all during her telling her disbelief that she was doing this, her certainty that disaster waited at the end. She told her story well, leaned back against her chair, tried, unsuccessfully, to smile.

"That's crazy," Lucinda said. "How can you believe that?"

Because if it was well conceived and told . . . "I believed *you*."

"We were kids. It was—"

"I believed you," Carla said. "I ain't *blaming* you for nothing, but I believed you."

"So because you believed me then, I should believe you now? Does that make any sense? You never even loved Max. You were furious with him."

"What's that got to do with him being alive?"

Carla felt quick, smart, and powerful. Lucinda was furious with her. Well, it wasn't Lucinda's life. It was hers, and she a woman grown, one who'd taken care of herself despite everybody leaving. Even now she could hold her own with someone who'd been out in the world. She said, in the deadliest voice she could find, "And while we're on the subject, don't tell me who I love. Don't *ever* tell me who I love."

"Somebody's got to tell you. *You* obviously don't know."

"And there ain't no need for shouting," Carla said.

"I'll stop shouting when you listen."

"I'll listen when you give me proof."

Lucinda stared past Carla's shoulder. Junkman, drawn by the commotion, stood in the vestibule, peering through the kitchen doorway's window. The women sat poised as if about to leap at each other, both rigid, trembling; Lucinda's hands were fists. Then, in what seemed like perfectly synchronized motion, they turned. The front door had opened. Someone was coming in.

"Hello," Willis called. "I'm home."

Lean, good-looking, he came into the kitchen. "Oh," he said, "I didn't know you had company."

"Willis, this is Lucinda."

"Good evening," Lucinda said. "Nice to meet you."

"Good evening." His face a puzzle, Willis pointed. "Who's that?"

"Junkman," Lucinda said.

"What's he doing?"

"Come inside, Junkman," Carla said. "Don't stand there like you're not welcome."

Junkman stepped inside, spoke to Willis, who looked skeptically at Junkman's mahogany-colored loafers. Red socks blinked through holes cut in the sides.

Willis said, "Is everything all right?"

Lucinda smiled at him. He wore a mechanic's blue uniform, black grease in patches on his hands, eyes of confusion. Should she leave it alone? She tried to catch Junkman's attention, but he'd found something interesting in the floor. Carla, without moving, was steadily building walls. Already, they reached her shoulders. Willis waited for an answer.

Lucinda said, "I don't know who this man in California is, Carla, but I know he isn't Max. And you know, too. Otherwise you'd have asked your brother what he looks like."

"What do you mean, what he looks like?"

"Pardon me," Willis said. "But—"

"*What does he look like?*" Lucinda said.

The question stunned Carla, carved a stillness in her head that rang with fear and its silly echo. She'd put together all the pieces, artfully, and she hadn't asked the one question that would have made it certain. And she knew why she hadn't, for that would have meant abandoning the tale, giving up the pleasure. It would have meant acknowledging the wasted years, confronting rage without hope's consolation. Her mouth was dry, her infant heart alive and pounding, and she sat, stricken at the self's capacity to delude the self, amazed that invention could blind as well as make you see. She put hands over her ears, started humming. Lucinda reached, grip wiry and strong, tore the hands away and held them. Carla stared, eyes twin points whose fury ought to have frightened, but Lucinda, not blinking, looked straight into their depths.

"Willis," she said. "What does Elizabeth's father look like?"

"Look like?"

"Stop it," Carla said.

"Willis?"

"A little taller than me. About six feet, thin. Blond hair. Why?"

She held to Carla's hands. "What color are his eyes?"

"Blue."

"Both of them?"

"What do you mean, both of them?"

"Are both his eyes the same color?"

"Yes," Willis frowned.

Carla said, "Why are you doing this to me?"

"I'm not doing anything to you," Lucinda answered. "I'm doing *for* you. Max is dead."

"He isn't."

"Believe me."

"I *won't. How'd* he die? Where's the body?"

"Why would I lie, Carla?"

"Where's the body? How'd he die?"

Lucinda blinked; her grip, as if triggered by her eyes, relinquished power.

"You don't know," Carla said, and pulled her hands away. "You made it up."

"She didn't," Junkman said.

"*Junkman*," Lucinda wailed.

"No," he said, "it's not fair. She's got to know." He closed his eyes. "I killed him, Carla. I'm sorry, but I killed him."

"You *killed* him?"

"He burned your house down," Lucinda said. "Killed your brothers. Drove your father mad."

Willis said, "What's going on here?"

"I used to love you," Junkman said.

Carla said, "You used to *what*?"

"I used to love you."

"I loved *him*."

"You didn't," Lucinda said.

"Bastards." Carla stood, swaying, tilting with the room. She took a step toward Junkman, stopped. "I *hate* you. I hate all of you." She'd tried to spit the words, but they came out limp and ineffective. The room closed in on her. Then she was still, head angled as if listening. Her face changed, all the rage departed, left it blank. She spun, stalked from the kitchen, climbed the stairs to her bedroom. There, she took off all her clothes, left them on the floor, climbed into bed.

"Will somebody tell me what's going on?" Willis said.

"It's a mess," Junkman said.

Lucinda sighed. "Indeed it is."

"Okay," Willis said. "But . . . "

"Sit down," Lucinda said, "I'll tell you. . . . Junkman?"

"Please," he said, "excuse me."

Junkman slumped outside, fumbled for his half-smoked celebration, lit it. Across the yard, night was busy falling. Woodenly, he sat on the top porch step.

Yes, it was a mess, and it was his fault, but what else could he have done? He couldn't let Carla go on not knowing, waiting for a dead man. Had he known she'd spend her life that way he'd have told her long ago. But it had never occurred to him that she would do this. Should he have known, or, at the very least, suspected?

He crossed his legs, leaned forward. Now that she knew Max was dead, that he, Junkman, had killed him, what would happen? Would she go to the police? Would Willis? The prospect of jail wasn't pleasant, but that was out of his control. Prison had taught him if there was nothing you could do about a thing, you held your peace. He drew on the cigar; the tip glowed red. As he blew smoke into the yard, Junkman remembered. . . .

He was tired. For the last couple of days a nasty cold had clogged his nose, which still managed to drip with the regularity of rain. Today, a co-worker had stayed out with a bellyache, and he'd worked for him, put in a sixteen-hour shift. On top of that, it was Thursday; tonight he'd dream of his father, come hurtling awake, sleepless until the final image faded. He could deal with the dream; he was used to the self-loathing it inspired. But tonight he needed sleep, needed to rest and fight this mother of a cold.

He was coming down the hill toward his room, resisting the devilish incline that made him walk faster than he wanted. To compensate, he shifted weight onto his heels, leaned his head back, and saw, staining sky above the stair-stepped rooftops, smoke billowing black toward an abundant milk-fed moon. He grunted. Whatever was burning was down by the river, and if the smoke was any indication, it was raging. Maybe refuse, maybe someone was getting rid of something worthless. Perhaps a barge out on the water. Anything, he hoped, but someone's house.

Above and behind him sirens commenced their deep, monotonous warning. Suddenly the buildings he passed had people in their windows, heads turning left and right, and some came through the darkened doorways, and some, tightening belts as they reached the sidewalk, went running down the hill. In a minute, red trucks hurtled past, in their shrieking wake a snow-white ambulance. Junkman quickened his pace. Despite his tired, and his plan to rub himself down with Vicks the minute he got home, he knew what his duty was. Whatever was burning had gotten out of control. Somebody was in trouble, and he went to lend a hand.

Now he was part of a stream of people that flowed onto a street of abandoned tenements lit only by the moon. This street angled toward the road that paralleled the river, and when he went past the last forsaken building, he could see the water, a pool of moonlight in its lap. Some of the people were silent, some talked in hushed voices, and some were laughing. He rolled with them around the road's curve; the crowd slowed and surged, and at his side a woman's moaning. He looked where she did and stepped into a fear that took his heart. It was Carla's house, wrapped in a fiery blossom, flames so consuming that the firemen fell back, hosed it from the road, on the other side of which the neighbors gathered. Junkman looked for Carla in the crowd, in the trees that ringed the house; he didn't see her. Meridian, in a shin-length robe, a sheet covering something at her feet, was calling out for Rufus. On the ambulance a red light swung.

Junkman shook. Like a thief at the scene of disaster, fear was claiming anything not nailed down, the ability to breathe and think and move; he fought it, bolted through the crowd, stepped on feet, elbowed women old enough to be his mother. They saw his face and swallowed protest, and he was through them, into a yard lit by red light, moon and fire. There, on the ground, was Carla; her back was smoking. A huge man dressed in white fell to his knees, he put his face to hers, he called: "Jesus. Bring a stretcher. *Move*, goddammit, move."

Junkman breathed again. *You move*, he thought, *let me, I love her*, and stumbled forward, then stopped, hot/cold, arrested. Something white had moved among the trees. He stood, focused on the spot. The evergreens were tall, lit fitfully with flames' illumination. In their midst, now gone again, now there, was Max, more still than statue before he disappeared.

And in that instant Junkman knew who'd set this house on fire. He knew because the blond boy was hiding in the trees; he knew because all during the period when Max refused to preach,

Junkman had been a witness to his woe. And when Phoenix was born, the mute watched as Max embraced the mystery of fire, saw him worship it in pyramids of brush and newsprint, heard him cry there'd be no mercy until flame had purified. Back then, it hadn't occurred to Junkman that Max would actually start a fire, only that he was waiting for one from heaven. That's why he hadn't feared for Carla. Fire from heaven wasn't coming no time soon, and when it did it wouldn't single out a household. When *that* fire came, the whole world was in for hell.

But he'd been wrong; he should have feared.

"Oh, Goddamn Jesus. Oh, Goddamn Jesus."

Transfixed by Max's presence, stunned by deduction, Junkman sneezed above the orderly who was methodically taking his savior's name in vain. It was all so overwhelming: Max in the trees, the huge man's blasphemy, Carla smoking; beyond this, diminished flames, exhausted by consuming, licked halfheartedly, from habit, at what was once a house.

Junkman felt whipped, and sleepy; the sneeze had unleashed a river in his head. He took out his handkerchief, wiped his nose, tried to blow, then looked above him. The moon was heavy, ripe enough to fall, the constellations drawn in delicate perfection. He was confounded, body-blowed by fear, stifled by a nose he couldn't breathe through. That's why, though he looked, he didn't see the beauty. Still he gazed, because it was something to do, and what was on the ground too horrible to look at, and because with his head thrown back his nose didn't leak so bad.

And he didn't even think it strange when stars spoke: *Read, boy, what's written here.*

He looked behind him: a man wearing a gray fedora, a woman with glasses sliding down her nose. Then he raised eyes back to the sky.

What did you say?

Read, boy, what's written here.

Okay, he thought, *I'm reading.*

He searched from point to blinking star point, studied dark and shining, but if there was a message there, it was in African or Greek. Bewildered, but anxious to believe, Junkman closed his eyes. The inside of his skull expanded—colored lights, miniature eruptions—and in a rush of warmth, the message filled his head. It was the season for revenge, stars said; it was iron hot and strike time, and he a mute, avenging angel.

I read you, Junkman thought, even though there were no words. *I read you.*

He opened his eyes. On the ground a shovel, blade smeared with ash, steel blade, a weapon, and as he bent, nose dripping, the orderly peeled the dress from Carla's back. The crisp, quiet rasping stopped the mute, made him reel in the smoked-wreathed, unfamiliar moment. Then he heard what he thought was a second utterance from heaven, but it wasn't. This voice was deep and rich and mighty; it was soaring. *My Lord.* Who filled the night so achingly with song?

There, backdropped by ruin, framed against destruction, was Rufus; he was broad and tall and singing. A spotlight prowled the yard, and when it trapped him, Rufus raised and shook his fist.

"Oh, Goddamn Jesus," the orderly wept, and Rufus sang.

Junkman bit his lip, unable to taste his disbelief that it had come to this. What manner of night descended, foul deed and messages in constellations, moonlight, defiant song? Smoke drifted, stung his eyes, he closed them, thinking: No, Rufus must not grieve alone.

Who'd join, who'd take part in this ritual?

I will.

Who?

Me. Junkman. I will.

Lit with the rightness of his mission, Junkman shuffled in circles toward the singing, held out his hands, the shovel in his left. He hopped on his right foot, shimmied hips and shoulders; then, with a grace that snatched the crowd's breath, leaped toward the moon. He hung there long enough to challenge gravity, came slowly down; his feet touched earth, he sneezed. "God bless you," someone called, and Junkman danced.

Oh, hadn't he danced, wasn't he a dancer! Everything he knew of sorrow: the splintered bone marking the spirit's fracture, all he'd learned of loss so deep in flesh no palm press or fingers' search could reach it, all this he put to dance. He was sweating and his nose ran, his arm ached, but he persisted, jumped and whirled and twisted until the neighbors gathered on the road began to hum in three-part harmony, until humming erupted into song, and instinct said responsibility was finished. Then, the shovel lofted like a spear, he aimed himself and charged into the woods.

He didn't get very far. Trees swallowed moonlight. Here and there was scattered illumination, but most was shadow that didn't let him see enough to track Max with his eyes. And his nose just wasn't working. He knew Max's scent had to be there, only devils had no smell, but he couldn't detect it. His spirit sank, but he pushed on, the river on his right, swinging spade at brush and undergrowth, cursing summer colds, the need for time-consuming ritual. He was hot, sweat soaked his clothing; he was cold.

When he stopped after some fifteen minutes, he understood he'd been going in a circle. He could hear in front of him the sounds of the fire site's activity: the faint shout of a man's voice, a bell ringing like a call to supper. He remembered he hadn't eaten, then looked around him in the darkness, tried to sniff. He blew hard, an instant of scents too quick to identify, and then the closing. His nose was worthless; he'd have to wait. There'd be no tracking Max tonight.

Junkman slumped, depressed, felt his tired come settling down. Lowering to the ground, he leaned against the broad chest of a tree, stared at the stars that showed above him. He thought of his love, smoke spiraling from her back, the sound skin made when pulled from flesh. He thought of his own body's failure, the refusal of his nose to answer when he called. Was this what being old was like? The mind willing, the spirit ready, but the body weak?

Physically drained, emotionally exhausted, he closed his eyes. He needed to rest. He'd sit here for a while. Not long . . .

Come on, Junkman, he thought. *Get yourself together. Be a man.*

He drew air into his lungs, reclaimed determination. As long as Max had scent, he'd find him. If it were days or weeks before his nose cleared, still, he'd find him.

Weak and feverish, but his will restored, Junkman struggled to his feet, turned homeward, took the shortcut that would bring him to the bank where the town rowboats were kept. Twice he pulled out his handkerchief and wiped his dripping nose. That second time he'd stuffed the soggy cotton in his pocket when he stopped, alert and galvanized. There, to the left of the path, in a small clearing, curled the dim shape of a sleeping figure. Junkman crouched, moved forward. *Max?* The figure slept on its side, curved like an infant, blond head nestled on an arm.

The mute reached for his sodden handkerchief, blew hard; a passage opened for a moment, closed again. But this time the moment was long enough to recognize the stink: whiskey and vomit, apples, sour milk, another scent too quickly gone to label. At the end of an outstretched hand, a bottle, black in the clearing's dark.

Junkman smiled bitterly. Had the Lord's anointed practiced anything he'd preached? He stood, considering the question Max would never wake to answer. Never again would he rise to strut and rage of sin, never set another fire.

Yet, ambivalent in a moment that demanded to be seized, the avenger swayed, immobilized by his heartbeat, remembering that organ's warning long ago in a room whose window framed rain-soaked hills of junk. *Killing would cost his life.* For all these years he'd listened to that warning. In dreams he brandished sticks at killing's image, roared and drove it away with such commotion that he'd fly awake, only to face the sinking realization that without killing, his father would never be avenged. Then he'd hurl stinging curses at his circumstance, and berate himself for being a coward. He was ashamed of being afraid to die.

Had any of it changed? Had his faint heart reconsidered? Here in the middle of a half-lit wood, he strained to listen.

But his heart, though it was beating, didn't speak.

He didn't want to die, God knew he didn't. But weren't there consequences worse than death? How long could you walk the earth convinced you weren't a man?

Junkman looked above him. What did he heed, starlight or pumping organ?

Speak, heart, he thought.

But his heart, though full, was silent.

He stood, nose dripping, trembling, telling himself to act, not think about it, and just before he accepted never acting, he thought (it was such a *quiet* thought, so flat and unassuming), *If I die, I die*, raised the shovel high with both hands, brought it, singing, down. The steel said *thwuck* when it struck the head; it bounced; he thought he heard a whimper. *Do it.* Again he raised the shovel, brought it whistling down. *Whoomp! Whoomp!* He kept swinging until he couldn't anymore, until the muscles in his arms wept, and then he turned away, depleted, loath to witness what he'd done.

When he did look, he buckled. In the dimness, the blond boy's face was pulp. A sliver of bone showed through a mutilated cheek. Dragging air to the locked door of his nostrils, Junkman caught something sharp and copper. That was the blood, he knew, but something else. No matter.

Like a man checking his moving parts in the wake of an accident, Junkman carried out a self-examination. He could see, he was breathing. He could feel the damp shirt against his chest. His heart had yet to speak, or burst as it had promised. Was the heart subject to the stars? He'd think on that later; what was important now was that his heart wasn't *going* to speak, he wouldn't die. And if he were going to live, he had to protect himself, to hide what he'd just done.

He closed his eyes. All his thoughts were independent, refused to be connected, star messages and subject heart, what men called justice and its consequence. He had to hide what he'd just done. He left the body, the shovel next to it, trotted along the path, cut to the railing that separated street from riverbank, cleared the knee-high barrier in a leap so weary one foot caught and nearly sent him sprawling. He recovered, crossed the street. He took the stairs to his room two struggling steps at a time, fumbled for the key, closed the door behind him, leaned against it, feeling, for the moment, safe. Then he walked into the bathroom, rolled toilet paper into fingers, dipped them in Vicks, stuffed the paper up his nostrils. The menthol burned his membranes, but didn't unlock his nose. He took sheets from the closet, thread and needle from the box beneath his bed. He was sweating. His hand shook as he sought the dancing needle's eye. He sat on the floor sewing sheets to make a shroud.

In time the task consumed him. In the stitching a certain peace, a mourning for human life, twisted, deserving of death, but human still. Outside his window, thunder rolled.

He looked up, electric with anxiety, remembering that he'd left the shovel. Everyone had seen him take it. What if someone came across the body, sent cries into the night; what if they were already on their way to seize him?

He steadied himself, resumed his stitching.

While he sewed, a thin cloud moved across the moon, cut in half that planet's brightness.

When Junkman returned, all was as he'd left it—the shovel, the mutilated body. No one stood there, face accusing. He got the body into the sack, careful to keep the blood and gore from him, not looking at where the dead boy's face had been. He dug up the ground, shoveling dirt into the sheets with bits of flesh and bone, smoothed the earth with a tree branch, then shoved the bottle between the blond boy's legs, along with his makeshift broom. He hoisted the sack onto his shoulder, headed for the river.

It was true what he'd heard; the dead *were* heavy. At the water's edge, he lay down the body, gathered rocks the size of softballs, then walked the bank to where the rowboats slept. A lance of lightning split the sky, thunder growled, clouds nearly closed the moon's eye. He dragged a boat back, lifted the body into it, gently slid rocks into the bag, paused to rest. Then he climbed into the boat, rowed to the center of the dark and glistening water. He sat a moment, knowing here was yet another ritual, wondering if he should observe it with stillness or with prayer. When he couldn't decide, he threw the shovel into the water. He lifted the body, held it a moment, feeling its weight, its soft, smashed configuration, dropped it. A splash like a huge fish leaping; water rippled, rowboat rocked. White bulk slid toward the bottom.

Numb, empty, Junkman sat, raised his face to heaven. Clouds had pulled the plug on moonlight, lowered sky, blocked the perfect constellations. In the distance, thunder rolled.

Father. I did it. I took revenge. Now rest.

As he leaned forward, gripping the oars, pulling toward the shore, he was waiting for something to happen: the sky to open, a beast to rise snarling from the water, his heart to burst, but there was only deep exhilaration, and the rain began to fall. He'd done it, avenged his father, freed Carla to be his.

It was not until he thudded against the bank that mourning hit him, choosing not his heart, but stomach, driving belly flesh to backbone. He groaned, doubled in agony, fought for breath, staggered onto land, where he fell, rolling, gouging at his skin, beating fists against his thighs. He lay on his back, drummed heels into the shore.

In a little while he sat up and rubbed a hand across his face. This was no place for a man with a cold to be, on the edge of a nighttime river in the rain. He found his snot-soaked handkerchief, wiped his nose. Neither was it a time for self-pity. He'd done what he had to; whatever it cost, he'd pay. He stood, gathered himself. Then he stared at the raining sky, and knew.

It will come again. Be ready, it will come.

It did come again, not as body blows or writhing, but in a feeling that there *was* no him, just sinking heart shipwrecked by violation, a troubled pulse-beat in the air. But mercifully, as if there were a balance in the scheme of things, he no longer dreamed of his father. Still, he knew he'd sinned and must seek absolution. He thought how best to do this all through the winter that knew no snow until January, and in the spring of 1941 he pulled his black suit from the closet and took to Kingston's streets to grieve.

Carla kept to her bed, in a dreamlike state, dimly aware she was never unattended. When she moaned or cried out, or moved fitfully, Lucinda's hand would stroke her; Lucinda washed and fed her, supported her weight to the bathroom. Sometimes, when Carla opened her eyes, her friend was at the window or reading at bedside, and once, when she'd been sleeping on her stomach, she woke to a feathery finger traveling her scars. At times Junkman relieved Lucinda's watch, or Willis, and twice the small, sparrow-faced Mrs. Sharp sat quietly at knitting.

None of them knew that all during that time the woman they sat beside was working. Carla worked at two things: first, to think of nothing; second, not to look at the white weight poised above her head. If the light was right she could see its shadow at the border of her vision; it was larger than a mountain, patient and alive. She knew she couldn't refuse to look forever, knew *it* knew. And when she did turn finally, drawn by its pulling and her terrible need to know, the weight would fall to crush her. So she did what only those who've tried can appreciate how difficult: She didn't look, and tried to think of nothing.

And in the middle of this labor, (yes, it was labor, exhausting; it was why she couldn't rise), there grew in the middle of her forehead a chilled coin, which, when she rubbed it, had no features, and never warmed to touch. It was days before she understood the purpose of the coin: It was there to purchase healing. But if she would be healed, then she must spend it, which meant surrendering, accepting all: ill-founded hope, the useless waiting;

she must turn to face the white weight though looking meant her death.

She'd face it, but later, in a little while. And not simply because she was afraid of dying (wasn't death a kind of healing?) but because there was something left to do. If she looked now and the weight came down, she'd have left her half-told story. There was a knowing in her that said you no more left a tale unfinished than you allowed your child to die. What you did with your own life was your business; it was, after all, your own, but mothers and storytellers, if no one else, were bound by a certain duty. So she set about the task of completing, not for pleasure (there was none), only purpose, a one-track-mindededness as singular as rage. At the end she'd look and face the weight. But not before she'd told her story, not before its ending.

"Take care of Phoenix," she whispered, and slipped into a place that had no walls or doors or colors, only her conviction that it was no accident. Max had *meant* to set that fire.

For all those years, though he thought often of Carla beneath him in the bed, above him in the clearing ringed by trees, Max refused to reconstruct those details not so pleasant. All he'd accept was that he'd obeyed the Lord and made the sacrifice. He didn't dwell on incidentals: that he'd set his family's house on fire, that this fire had claimed two lives. He'd simply done the Lord's will, and later, when it was clear that debt remained, he'd made the final payment. He was certain of this: The Lord blessed those who obeyed Him. Look at his life. Who could deny he'd been blessed?

And then all of it falling apart; out of the blue Willis come to tell him he'd not accomplished what he'd sought. All he'd done was kill two innocent children; the child of his own perverted flesh still lived. Had he needed further proof that to lie with his sister was the blackest sin, proof had arrived: The child of that union was an idiot. God had simply been stringing him along, biding the punishing time. This punishment was great; not only did the child still live, but his daughter was delivered into the very arms of what he'd fled. Had it been someone else's story he'd have laughed, but it was his, and there was nothing in the least bit funny. Neither was there a solution. If he told Elizabeth why she couldn't marry Willis, he'd have to reveal his identity, acknowledge what he'd done. Killing Phoenix would have been a holy sacrifice; killing Alton and David was murder. There was no statute of limitations on murder; he'd be pulled from his home, humiliated, thrown into prison, even though he'd paid for what he'd done with half his vision.

He rubbed a hand over his right eye; the smooth glass felt like stone. He'd been working for the plumber, had gone into the house in Palo Alto, probing for the source of a leak that, in an hour's time, had flooded the cluttered basement. And he scurrying under and over scarred heaps of furniture, paint cans half full in the dimness, wondering if these people had ever thrown *anything* away, and his boss calling, "*Over here,*" and Max, ducking one beam, spun to answer.

The nail was driven through the two by four, an inch and a half of rusted metal, his head abruptly turning, and his eye, the hazel one, impaled. The pain was so impossible it took his breath, sent its searing current to split the angle where his thighs met, froze him, and he thinking stupidly, *There's a nail in my eye*, wanting to jerk his head back, to free himself. But he was terrified that the slightest movement would intensify the burning and cause the further splitting of his flesh. He moaned, thinking, *Don't move, stay absolutely still, don't move*, and understanding struck him. His reckoning time had come, payment was finally exacted. *This was his punishment.* He stood, awaiting confirmation, and when he had it, in a single savage moment, he paid the full price, drove his head against the timber, nail point assaulting deeper flesh, capillaries, iris, on its way to socket wall. Then he screamed and ripped away his head, felt the raw split widen between his thighs, felt the blood spurt, the inside of his eye, bits like egg white, bird brain, clinging to his cheek.

They'd taken him to the hospital. Days later, the bandages unwrapped, the hole stared back at him. He'd worn a patch until he married, then got an artificial eye.

Blue, to match the one remaining.

It was over. He'd paid for what he'd done.

But it wasn't over; he was still paying. This was what infuriated him, not that he'd murdered, not that he'd decimated the family that had loved him, but that he was expected to continue paying, had incurred debt defined by refusal to be satisfied. It didn't occur to him that the loss of an eye was hardly compensation for a house burned to the ground, for a man driven into madness, for a woman who couldn't look at the world without blinking, for children who'd known what it felt like for blood to boil.

She'd placed him in the room Willis had told her of, the one whose windows looked out at the sea; he poured a drink, drew on a dark cigar. Of course he knew why punishment persisted; the Lord's will wasn't done: The idiot still lived. If he were to know peace, he must finish what hadn't been completed. But how? Hire someone? Send him to Kingston to set another house on fire? That was crazy; he couldn't take the chance on an accomplice, the deed being traced to him, someone official knocking at his door saying that something small and overlooked had caught him. And he didn't want to harm his daughter. It was his daughter's husband's sister's house, and Elizabeth was there. What he needed to do was be still and listen for the Lord's instruction.

He sat, studying a glass-smooth, shining ocean, mountains half a ring around it, houses pink and white, and it was from that loveliness (she made it come to him in sunlight rising off the water) that the revelation dawned. His punishment was loss of his only daughter, the destruction of his family, burdens he'd carry to his grave. His punishment wouldn't end until *he* did.

Now his rage returned; its weight was in his groin. He twisted, grunting, and Carla turned rage in a heartbeat to desire. He thought of the young black woman he'd been with yesterday; she knelt before him. "Deeper," he'd said. "Take it deeper." His cock hardened, and he was remembering, not the woman, but waking in the night, a moon-illuminated room his father built, and there, above him, Carla, his penis in her mouth. The feel of it so wonderful he'd never stopped comparing every woman he was with to her. It was so clear, the memory so real; if he reached he could touch the lovely angle of her cheekbone, if he listened he could hear her lilting voice, *"What do you call what we do, Max?"* and he opened his pants, held himself, thick with wanting, with anger and confusion, licking at the fist around his length, couldn't reach it, groaned.

Carla sees the end now, clearly, rushes to tell it, must have all of it told.

He's sitting up, Max is, listening, stuffing himself into his pants. A car's pulled up in the driveway. A door slams, he goes to greet his wife. She's tall, turns away when he leans to kiss her.

"What's wrong?" he says, and she, "I'm leaving you."

"Why?"

"Because you have the gall to ask. Because I have a daughter, and she has a child."

"I'll make it up to you."

"Oh, no you won't."

"Alice!"

He trails her to the bedroom, pleads while she packs.

"Good-bye, Lincoln."

Her car fades into distance. He looks above him at the mighty, endless sky. There's a God up there, and he's that Lord's anointed. He's done his best, and still he's been forsaken. He staggers to the garage, furious with God, with life, carries the can of gasoline inside. Sets it down, goes into the bathroom, finds the sleeping pills. Retrieves the can, lurches to the room whose walls are windows, pours another drink, washes down the pills. Goes to the record player, selects an album, turns the volume high.

Then, in every room, deliberately, he sows the gasoline. Lies on his back, hands behind his head; he's waiting. Blues song fills the house with complex contradictions: *"Accuse me of forgery, can't even sign my name."* Sleep is coming on. He lights a cigar, draws deeply, exhales, draws again. Holds the smoke, the stinging in his throat, tosses the cigar across the room.

Instantly, flames leap. In their heat and beauty he'll be purified. His eyes close, he's seeking peace, but Carla won't let him find it. She brings sleep closer, and just before it comes, strikes him with final understanding. *Max. Max. What are you doing? This is hardly necessary. You're the Lord's anointed, what you went through was just a test, wait it out, you don't have to die. You're forty-five, in the prime of life; you can replace wives and daughters. You're the Lord's anointed; there's no sin that can't be forgiven.*

In control again, he sits up, discovering his body wrapped in fire. He waves at it to go away, beats palms against it. Then the agony, and he screams, long and hard, drowning out the singing.

There, it was finished, not as well told as it could be, but done, and she could go now. She touched the cool place on her forehead, felt the fear settling like a net, strangling breath and movement. "Oh, Lord," she said. What was dying like? Would it hurt? Would she panic?

"Take care of Phoenix," she whispered.

"You awake?" Lucinda asked.

Carla looked above her. Only a wall, a ceiling cracked, a shadow like a bird's wing. The white weight, the one larger than a mountain, wasn't there.

"Hm," she said, then slept to gather strength for the one task still remaining.

When Carla awoke that next time, hands rubbed her shoulders; cool lips kissed her brow. She pretended to be asleep until Lucinda

left the room. When the door closed, she began to make herself
ready. She took a deep breath, steadied, and went to meet her
grief.

Max was dead, had been for all her years of waiting. But that
wasn't the heart of her sorrow. Sorrow was in understanding
what she'd done to herself. As she began to work through this,
she thought of Miles, how that, too, was part of it: driving away
a man she'd known could make her happy. That's why she'd been
so stupidly afraid of him—he threatened the continuation of her
self-inflicted pain, pain so familiar she'd thought she needed it to
live.

Oh, this was hard; she rubbed her eyes, then stopped and let
the tears come. Max was dead. There in the closet hung the smoking jacket, the silk pajamas, blues song and marigold, and who
would wear them? All these years she'd made herself believe he'd
come leaping up her porch steps, wearing a smile borrowed from
a sunrise, a fist of flowers, and he'd been dead. She mourned the
waste, the absence of joy longer than fleeting, the deep, abiding
loneliness, her constant rage. She mourned all the simple, ordinary
things it meant to have a life: the warmth and safety of the marriage bed, a family, a place in the church, women friends to laugh
with. To be, simply, *normal*. All this she'd missed, not because
she'd been kept from it, but because she'd refused to reach and
claim it as her own. This refusal called for a separate rite. So she
curled up on her side, held herself, and mourned what might have
been.

Lucinda came into the room, started to say something joyful;
Carla waved at her to go.

The door closed; she resumed her mourning. It was beautiful
and sweet, and frightening. She'd never wept this way in her life;
she'd never have imagined so much feeling for herself. Now it
was as if some wall had smashed inside her, and when its last
brick crumbled, she stepped into a green, well-lighted place, held
out her arms, stood weeping for her brothers. Wept for their fat
legs and open faces, their stolen childhoods. For their waking in

a burning room, and no one in the doorway to save them. She wept for being deprived of their company, for the women they'd have lain with, for the children they'd have had. When she'd done with Alton and David, she wept for her parents, for Willis, for Junkman's secret, for the trouble so thick above Lucinda's head that her hair refused to grow. Because her grief was big enough, she wept for everyone who'd suffered longer than they'd needed to, those who'd had their families smashed, their confidence eroded, those who feared to move freely in the world. Then she slept, deeply, through the night, well into morning. When she woke that time, Lucinda, like a well-kept promise, was reading at her side.

"Hey."

"Hey. Welcome back."

"What time is it?"

Lucinda glanced at her watch. "Eleven-thirty."

"What day?"

"Thursday."

"How long I been this way?"

"Eight days," Lucinda said. "You want some tea?"

"Please. Is Phoenix all right? Where's Willis?"

"Phoenix is fine. Willis is getting ready for work."

"Tell him I need to talk to him."

"Okay. How you feel?"

Carla lay back against the pillow, did the inventory. "I don't know yet. Could you let some light in?"

Lucinda rose, went to the windows, pulled the drapes. Sunlight poured into the room. Someone had cleaned while Carla slept away the week; light lit the neatness.

"You hungry?" Lucinda asked

She nodded.

"I'll be right back."

Carla lay, watching the sunlight, wishing it could bend its beaming, turn to warm her bed. She'd lost things, things had been given. She was connected, had a family, a past. The past didn't govern, only said you must remember. Past made the present possible; no *now* without *had been*.

Lucinda returned with a tray of tea and orange juice, a slice of whole wheat toast.

Carla said, "I think I'm starving."

"You ought to be."

"Where's Willis?"

"Right here, Sis." He stepped into the room. "How you feeling?"

"Fine. How you feeling?"

"I was worried about you."

"We all were," Lucinda said.

"Willis, we can't say nothing about Junkman. You understand?"

"We've already settled that," Willis said. "Whatever Junkman did he already paid for. Nobody will know."

"Where's Elizabeth? She back yet?"

"Tomorrow."

"You can't tell her either. None of it."

"We already figured that out, too," Willis said. "Elizabeth won't be told."

Carla said to Lucinda, "You been coming over here every day?"

"Hell, no. Not with all *these* empty rooms. I moved in. Temporarily."

"Why don't you make it permanent?"

"You forget, honey, I got a man."

"Bring him, too."

Lucinda laughed. "I'll talk to him about it. See what he says."

"I'm going to work now," Willis said, and bent to kiss his sister. "I'll see you later."

When he'd left, Carla said, "Thank you."

Lucinda smiled. "What are friends for?"

"Come here."

"What?"

"Lie down. I want to hold you."

"Um," Lucinda said. "A treat."

There was a body in her arms, warm and solid. It seemed a long time since she'd held someone this way. She lay her cheek against Lucinda's hair.

"Lucinda?"

"What?"

"I love you."

"I love you, too."

"Remember that day down by the river?"

"Uh-huh."

"Remember how you held *me*?"

"But not for long," Lucinda said. "You wouldn't let me."

"I'll always let you. From now on, I'll always."

"It feels good," Lucinda said. "I love to be held. Being held's the best comfort." She snuggled deeper into Carla's arms. "I saw your scars. They're not so bad."

"Nothing's so bad. Not anymore."

Sunlight painted bright shapes on her walls. Her life had been in pieces; she'd make it whole again. She had the power to do this. She'd surround herself with loved ones, with her family.

"Lucinda."

"Sh. I'm falling asleep."

"Sleep later. I need your help."

"For what?"

"I need to get my hands on a copy machine."

"No problem. They're all over the place. What you need it for?"

"To make some copies."

"Yeah," Lucinda laughed, "you're better."

"I'm going to try to find Miles. The man I told you about. The one I drove away."

"How's a copy machine going to help?"

"I don't know where he is."

Lucinda shook her head. "And a copy machine will find him?"

"I mean I don't know exactly where he is."

"Didn't you say he was Melvina Turner's nephew? Why don't you ask her if she knows?"

"How come I didn't think of that?"

"'Cause I'm the brains in this relationship."

"Call her for me?"

"I have to get up?"

"You can come back."

"It won't be the same position."

"I won't move."

Lucinda groaned. "Okay, I'll make the damned call."

She left the room, came back, sat on the edge of the bed. "Melvina doesn't know. She got a couple of postcards from Arizona. No return address."

"Well, I know he was going to the Grand Canyon," Carla said.

"That doesn't help much. There's no address for the Grand Canyon."

"But he's got to be staying somewhere around it. So I'll send letters to all the post offices. General Delivery."

"That's why you need the copy machine."

Carla grinned at her. "You *are* smart."

"But how's he going to know? A man doesn't put a return address isn't looking for any mail. It's a long shot, Carla."

"It's the only shot I've got."

"I guess you're right. You need anything else?"

"Yes. An atlas. And I need you to help me address the envelopes."

"An adventure," Lucinda said. "Boy, I love an adventure. Now tell me about this Miles character. Is he fine? Does he have any money? Is he any good in bed?"

"The answer to the first question is yes. The second is I don't know. The third ain't none of your business."

"Well, excuse me." Lucinda laughed. "When do we start this project?"

"Today." Carla rolled from bed, reached for her robe. "But first I've got to go see Phoenix."

"When you come back, remember what you promised. To hold me some more."

Carla said, "I will."

When she reached the doorway, she felt a sudden dizziness, and she buckled.

"You all right?" Lucinda asked.

Max was dead. Had been for all these years. Now that she knew, it was over. She took a deep breath, straightened.

"I'm all right," she said, and went to see her son.

"Junkman likes the idea," Lucinda said two weeks later. "Both of us are moving in. He's trying to figure out what to do with the junkyard."

"What needs to be done with it?"

"Well, somebody's got to be there to look after it. He's not really interested in running it anymore. I told him to think about selling it. You know," Lucinda said, "I've got this money. Insurance policy, savings my father left. I'm thinking about putting the house up for sale, selling my father's equipment and starting some kind of business. If Junkman sold the junkyard, we could pool the money."

"What kind of business?"

"I don't know. A child-care center, maybe. Something that would benefit somebody. I can't spend the rest of my life doing nothing."

"I know what you mean," Carla said. "I went up to the library yesterday, got my job back. It's not a lot of money, but it's something to do. I talked to Mrs. Sharp. She's happy to be taking care of Phoenix again." She paused. "What you said about pooling money? Willis has some. I do, too. Maybe we should put it *all* together."

"If we had something like a child-care center, Elizabeth could work there, too." Lucinda shook her head. "Is that child ever going to stop moping?"

"She'll get better."

"I hope so. Nothing yet from Arizona?"

"No."

"You all right with that?"

Carla said, "I made myself all right. Had a good talk with *me*. I spent all that time waiting—I'm not doing that anymore. I'm sending one more batch of letters, then I'm leaving it alone. Either Miles will come back or he won't. Either way, I've got a life to live."

"I hear you," Lucinda said. She folded arms across her chest. "What would the men do at a child-care center?"

"Care for the children," Carla said.

So many names of places ended with the letter O.

Miles had headed northwest that early autumn of 1966, figuring that on his way to Arizona he might as well look in on cities he'd never seen. He spent a night in Syracuse, a week in Rochester on the shore of Lake Ontario. He went through Buffalo, crossed Pennsylvania's tip into Ohio, stopped in Youngstown, bypassed Cleveland for Toledo and South Bend. The balance of that fall passed in Chicago, a town that made him think of rolled-up sleeves and bulging forearms, and he stayed until the wind whipped off the lake in gusts that would have snatched his hat if he had worn one, and the weather grew too cold for golf. The first snow fell November 3 in Iowa, on the road between Dubuque and Waterloo, and for reasons he'd never know, he did a U-turn, headed north, drove until Lake Michigan rose in familiar, leaden view, this time behind Milwaukee, a small, clean city wrapped in a bitter cold. There he stayed for the winter, in a rented house on a street named Dumont, lived off his savings, did nothing except cook and clean and make love to a small brown woman he came to think of as "My Silent."

The house was hers. He'd met her on a Tuesday afternoon in a bar that was all but empty. She sipped cream sherry, the only alcohol she cared for; she had long hands and a gold tooth that startled when she smiled. Thirty-five, she drove public buses for a living.

He was drawn to her for three reasons: her privacy, the way she leaned toward him when he talked, and because his heart was rearranged, and he was lonely. They went out twice, and he moved in with her. It took him a while to identify what was missing in her house: There wasn't a book, not even a magazine. He grew used to this, found comfort in cleaning and cooking, a little disappointed that she seemed to need nothing else besides his company and warmth at night. Depending on her shift, she watched sitcoms in the evening, game shows in the afternoon. He'd sit beside her, arm around her shoulder, or her head held in his lap. Sometimes her body shook at something funny, but she never laughed out loud.

In March, when he was ready to go, he agonized for a couple of days wondering how to leave, then returned from a walk one afternoon to find she'd packed for him. Their good-bye was in a rain, not talking, holding one another. It was she who'd broken away first, her smile so thin the gold didn't show, and he, feeling incomplete, who'd tried to kiss her right. But she'd moved, and he'd left the last kiss on her cheek. He stared; for a moment he thought she'd speak; she didn't. He wiped the rain from his face and headed south/southwest, fighting his sense of desolation that he knew nothing about her but her name and birthplace. Bessie. Bessie Monroe, born in Montezuma, Georgia. That crazy part of him wanted to go back, stay long enough to penetrate her silence, teach her talk and expectation, how to laugh and make the last kiss right. He carried the feeling through Iowa, across Nebraska's corner, drove the speechless plains of Kansas to Colorado's line, rolled like a storm cloud into New Mexico. There, in that unending sunlight, he swallowed hard, and buried the feeling at the side of a two-lane highway. He spent four days in Santa Fe, which he would always associate with leathery skin and cowboy boots, then headed for Phoenix, a city famous for the quality of its golf.

There he'd stay until the spirit moved him.

When Miles finally looked into the Grand Canyon he did get dizzy, but not with vertigo. All that stone and space and sky, the ribbon of water below, the hugeness of it, spun him into a feeling of insignificance. As he gaped, watching the largest hole in the universe unveiling in the light, he wished he could have known it as nothing but a riverbed, been witness to centuries of nature's carving. Nothing, he figured, would ever move him quite like this; for the rest of his life, anything of magnificence would pale when compared to this.

He'd driven to the canyon in the dark, had to turn the heat on in the car; he headed back to Phoenix in a brutal morning sun. He put the air on, marveling at the desert. It stretched on both sides of the highway, vast and glorious, conspired, as if it took personally his raving about magnificence, to blow his mind. Gray-brown expanse, the myriad shapes of cacti, and why hadn't he known that in springtime, in the desert, flowers bloomed? Flowers furious and delicate at once, exploding, spoor left by giants gone to live in mountains red against the sky.

He'd found a room in a Phoenix boarding house, worked as a caddy at a course in Scottsdale. By midday the heat was oven dry; members played early in the morning. In the evenings he worked on his golf game, or went to the movies, or explored what little of the city there was. After six weeks, he rented an apartment. He thought about going back to work as a chef, felt the stirring of a need for permanence. When he thought of Carla it always ended with his admonition to forget her, to understand that what she'd done was unforgivable and, most important, had nothing to do with him. It was her problem, and it would have happened to whoever had come along. She hadn't been waiting just for him.

On Mondays, as usual, the course was closed to members, and Miles played with the caddies and a few guys they'd invited. One was a postal worker, who, in June of 1967, mentioned to Miles how some woman back east had flooded most of the post offices up around the Grand Canyon with letters to one man. Miles, deciding whether he should hit a seven or an eight iron to the green, idly asked where the mail had come from.

"New York. Kingston. You ever hear of it?"

A seven iron was too much club. "Who they written to?"

"Somebody named Oliver Henry Jackson."

"That's me," Miles said.

"You? Your name is Miles."

"Miles is just what people call me." He bent, picked up his bag.

"Where you going?"

"The Grand Canyon. I'll catch you later."

There was a sack of letters in the post office in the village of Grand Canyon, another in North Rim, a third across the Colorado River in Tuweep. Then he headed south, drove all the way to Flagstaff, where he stopped to buy a six-pack and a sandwich. There, in the parking lot of a general store, the motor running as evening fell, he ate, trying to still his apprehension that there were other letters in other towns, and that those might be the ones that told the crucial story. He ought to go back, scour every place north of here that had a post office; why was he headed back to Phoenix?

He took a deep swallow of beer and began opening the plain white envelopes. He stopped after a dozen. All the letters were identical. "Dear Miles," they read. "I love you. I lied about the bank vice-president. Please come back."

By the fall of 1967, after a quarter century's silence, black people in Kingston were telling stories once again. This was due to Carla, who, when she emerged from isolation, went public with the past everyone had ceased to talk of. She'd gone to work again, and in a trunk way back in a corner of the library cellar, discovered the nineteenth-century journals of Harriet Dusenmeer. Before historians came to take the melancholy record from her, Carla read through five volumes written in a tight, neat hand.

"It rained all day," one entry said. "I spent the morning trying to recall when last the sun has shone."

"Mother is ailing. I think she's soon to die."

Toward the end of the fifth volume: "Such a curious thing. Today, a day drowned in an unforgiving gray, a group of Negroes came from Canada. Father says their leader was already three days dead. One of the women's time had come; she gave birth to a baby in the street."

The last entry read: "Today Joshua smiled at me. I do believe it's as Amelia says, he's interested. More on this later."

Carla went to speak to the head librarian. "We ought to have a storytelling hour," she said. "For the children."

She made up signs and placed them in store windows. The signs were on white typing paper, hand lettered in blue ink. "A Story," they said.

On that first Saturday, only two people showed up, an elderly white couple on public assistance who'd long been interested in colored people, and who counted as their most prized possession a collection of every issue of *Jet* magazine. The story that Carla told that day was about Joseph Drake, and when she'd finished, the white couple hung around to talk. They said their grandparents were in that circle the day that Drake arrived, had used to tell that story to them.

The next Saturday, the couple brought a few friends, and while Carla told about Max, three black kids doing term papers on Red China stopped at the door of the room, then came in to sit, spellbound. When they got home, Red China forgotten, they asked their parents about what they'd heard, wanted to know if there really was a preaching boy named Max, and if what Carla told had happened. A couple of the parents mentioned it to somebody else, who, in turn, brought it up in an otherwise uninteresting conversation, and several, because, they insisted, they'd nothing better to do, said they'd stop by to hear for themselves what a woman who for all these years had barely had the decency to speak was telling to their children. That was why, on the following Saturday, the room was packed with black folks of all sizes and descriptions, leaving the storyteller hardly space enough to turn in.

When she'd finished the tale of Joseph Drake, Carla invited everybody so inclined to get up and tell what they remembered. They could tell about the morning Max arrived, or that winter that knew no snow until January, or how they'd survived that rainy spring when all the dead were women. It didn't matter what, or how well the others knew it; what was important was that you told it.

And so it was that in the room of a library whose books they hadn't read, black people began to resurrect their stories. As they told, their eyes filled with tears despite the smiling. The tears came from understanding how much they'd missed the activity, and from recalling that it was disappointment that had shut their mouths. For all these years they'd suffered the feeling that something vital in their lives was missing, and not one had guessed that it had to do with a past they'd left to die.

Nothing that was told or heard was new. All the surprise was in remembering what had been forgotten. Sure, there was embellishment, and because each was storyteller, not historian, each openly invented. But the essence of what they told was true and known, and each piece was connected to another, part belonging to the whole. This startled those who'd said it was a waste of time to continue telling the same tale, and that they'd begin to tell again when something new had happened. Now, here they were, moved to tears by the familiar, liberated by the discovery that there is always for a people, or an individual, only one story, and if either is to live life to its fullest, that tale must be repeated, for it is in the telling that consolation and instruction lie.

One last thing for the record: On a day that was shimmering, one of those mornings when cicadas rasped of heat to come, in the middle of Elizabeth's weeping flight to California for her father's funeral (a sudden, massive heart attack), a colony of birds swooped down on Carla's yard. They perched on trees and wire, fence, and once assembled, began to sing so beautifully that Phoenix wept. Carla looked on, rapt, as Cassie sat on the porch step where, given crayons and paper that she asked for, she drew large and startling figures: a man with an oversized head, birds dark on his blue-green shoulders, a woman whose three red eyes stared from a coal-black knee. Sometimes the child paused, stared up above the yard at the singing birds, the trees, her face serene and lit and focused, head tilted as if she sat for an artist fluent in all the languages of light.

So we've come to a place made suitable for stopping. Of course, you don't know everything you'd like to. You don't know that Lucinda sent Junkman to a podiatrist who fixed his feet and scolded Junkman about his choice of shoes. You don't know that Carla and the rest bought a building down by the housing development where Melvina lived and opened a child-care center Willis was chief engineer and custodian, Lucinda did the books; Elizabeth and Junkman and Carla taught the children. Miles, still moving like a choreographer's dream, took care of the cooking, and found time for some catering on the side. Healed by the presence of so much love, Elizabeth rediscovered passion for her husband. She went to night school and studied anthropology, and all of Cassie's teachers agreed she had a gift for art.

But you don't know everything. You don't, for instance, know why the birds came back, or what happened to Ezra Van Etten, the mayor's son, or who took the rowboat that was never found. You know how Carla finished her story of Max, but you don't know she never shared that conclusion with anyone but her heart.

The hope is you're not bothered by the questions, that you're diverted by the ending, which, though happy, isn't perfect. If this smacks of judgment, trust that it's nothing more than observation. Nor is it copping out to say that it's the nature of most extended telling to be a little ragged at the end. And if you've felt, been moved, you tend to be forgiving.

So while you draw conclusions from this story, hold fast to what you know. Above all, don't ever hesitate to tell your own tale. If you need a reason, know that you carve light in the darkness when you do.

ABOUT THE AUTHOR

Richard Perry was born in the Bronx and raised in Monticello, New York. He graduated from the City College of New York and holds an MFA from Columbia University. *No Other Tale to Tell* is his third novel. His second novel, *Montgomery's Children*, won the Quality Paperback Books' "New Voices" Award in 1985. He is the recipient of a fellowship from the National Endowment for the Arts and is a three-time winner of the New Jersey State Council on the Arts Award for Fiction. He teaches at Pratt Institute in Brooklyn, New York, and lives in Englewood, New Jersey.